THE HERETIC'S WIFE

ALSO BY BRENDA RICKMAN
VANTREASE

The Mercy Seller
The Illuminator

THE
HERETIC'S WIFE

BRENDA RICKMAN
VANTREASE

ST. MARTIN'S PRESS
NEW YORK

This is a work of fiction. All of the characters, organiza-
tions, and events portrayed in this novel are either products
of the author's imagination or are used fictitiously.

www.stmartins.com

LIBRARY OF CONGRESS CATALOGING-IN-PUBLICATION DATA

Vantrease, Brenda Rickman.
    The heretic's wife / Brenda Rickman Vantrease. — 1st ed.
        p. cm.
    ISBN 978-0-312-38699-3
    1. Great Britain—History—16th century—Fiction.   2. Illumination of books
and manuscripts—Fiction.   3. Bible—Translating—Great Britain—Fiction.
4. Heretics—Fiction.   5. Wives—Fiction.   I. Title.
    PS3622.A675H37 2010
    813'.6—dc22

                                                                    2009045299

First Edition: April 2010

10 9 8 7 6 5 4 3 2 1

*For Julie with memories of London
and the search for Sir Thomas*

ACKNOWLEDGMENTS

I am grateful for the scholarship of several historians upon whose work I relied in finding my story. Their understanding, erudition, and insight into the religious strife of pre-Reformation and Reformation England proved invaluable to me. They are as follows: Peter Ackroyd in *The Life of Thomas More*, Benson Bobrick in *Wide as the Waters*, G. R. Elton in *England under the Tudors*, Carolly Erickson in her biography *Great Harry*, John Guy in *Tudor England*, and Brian Moynahan in *God's Bestseller*. Reading their works inspired and enabled my search for the individuals, both celebrated and uncelebrated, who participated in the struggle for religious freedom.

I wish to express my appreciation to my publisher, St. Martin's Press, and the fine people who work there. I am especially grateful to my editor, Hope Dellon, who acts as midwife to my books and holds my hand during their birthing. Like any good midwife, she knows when to say "push a little harder" and when to say "well done." Much appreciation is also due my agent, Harvey Klinger. His efforts on my behalf have far exceeded any reasonable expectations. And of course, I wish to thank my readers. What a joy it has been to hear from people near and far and know that together we have created a work of shared imagination.

I have been blessed with supportive family and friends, too many to name. I love them all and wish them to know their words of encouragement are like pearls to me. My ongoing friendship with my writing pal for more than a decade, Meg Waite Clayton, author of *The Wednesday Sisters,* remains a professional and personal resource even though she now lives a continent away. Most of all I wish to acknowledge publicly the tireless and enthusiastic support of my husband, Don, for this and all my efforts. Finally, I thank my God for putting all these people in my life.

THE
HERETIC'S WIFE

PROLOGUE

LONDON,
APRIL 1524

illiam Tyndale patted the breast pocket of his jerkin for the twentieth time since leaving St. Bart's Fair. Still there. But of course it was. Even the pettiest thief among this lot would not risk the stocks to steal a book worth no more than three shillings. It had probably cost no more than ten pence to print, but it was priceless to him.

He strode down the middle of the street to avoid the slime-filled ditches, ignoring the jeers and catcalls from the drunks and painted women who groped each other in the shadowy doorways of Cock's Lane. He kept his head down to avoid direct eye-to-eye contact, and wondered how many of them could read—not the book he carried in his pocket, of course, but in English, in their own language. If he could provide enough cheap copies of an English New Testament to scatter on the refuse-laden street, would some literate, hell-bound soul pick one up and read it? Just one soul!

But not today—and not ever if the Bishop of London who had refused him patronage had his way. William quickened his pace in anticipation of the moment he would be alone in his chamber to compare Erasmus's Greek edition to the Vulgate, the only translation allowed by Rome.

A light rain fell from a leaden sky as he passed Smithfield. Its damp smell carried an odor of butchered meats and fresh blood from London's slaughterhouse. The mist was always thicker here. Close. Smothering. Was it a fancy of overwrought imagination to think it carried the ghosts of long-dead Lollards, martyrs burned in this very field by Wolsey's predecessors simply because they challenged the iron dogma of Church doctrine?

Old wives and children claimed that the ghost of Sir John Oldcastle, a nobleman and a Lollard who disseminated contraband English Bibles, had hung about this place for the last one hundred years. But William knew Sir John had not died here. He had been hanged and then burned less than a mile west, where all traitors were hanged. And yet, the swirling miasma of this place bothered him much, for the memories it evoked—and the persecution it presaged. He'd heard it said that Wolfsee—that was the name William had given Cardinal Wolsey—was not a "man-burner," but he quaked in his soul at the very thought of it. Like a frightened child clinging to a favorite toy, he patted again his breast pocket. The promise of his mind's delight gave him courage as he hurried from that hateful place.

The clamor of bells chased him down Cheapside toward the Steelyard by the Thames where he was to meet his benefactor. He covered his ears—the bells of St. Mary le Bow, the loudest bells in a city of clanging bells, and he had the misfortune to live within earshot.

Damnable peals of vanity!

The same Bong! Bong!—that interrupted his preaching at St. Dunstan's—Bong!—and scattered the wagtails that roosted peaceably outside his chamber window—Bong!—scattered his thoughts, too, as he labored over his translating. He broke into a trot, as if by walking fast he could lessen their clamor.

As he turned into Cousin Lane, he recognized the brawny figure of Humphrey Monmouth, resplendent in the usual fur-trimmed doublet and silk hose that his wife Bessie made him wear, pacing impatiently before the large carved doors of the hall of the Hanseatic merchants. William had no idea why his patron wanted him to meet with a gaggle of wealthy German traders. Their talk of wool and profits was so much babble to him, but he was keenly aware that he owed Humphrey Monmouth the very roof over his head and every morsel of sodden meat and swallow of small beer that slid down his gullet.

The pressure of the Erasmus Greek Gospel stuffed into the too-small aperture of his jerkin pocket beckoned mightily. What good fortune to have found it at the fair. The Greek Gospel, like Erasmus's Latin translation, was not banned because only elite churchmen and scholars, men who embraced the new learning, could read the ancient Greek and Latin, but neither were they widely circulated. He longed to immerse himself in the text, but Monmouth had spotted him and was beckoning urgently.

As William entered the arched gates of the great stone hall with his benefactor, one glance showed him this was a company of wealthy men. Ample light filtered through large glazed windows at one end of the hall, but the torch lights had wastefully been lit in their sconces, their glow picking out the silver threads and jeweled rings and gilt chains of the merchants sitting on wooden benches around the hall's perimeter. Fresh herbs, scattered among the rushes on the floor, spiced the smell that powerful men gave off when engaged in negotiations. One of the merchants looked in their direction and with a thick German accent shouted, "Monmouth! Bring Master Tyndale here."

Startled that they knew his name, William suddenly remembered he was capless and smoothed his hair back with his hands, which, as he was acutely conscious, only accented the knobby expanse of his brow. Monmouth pushed him forward toward the table centered beneath the merchants' coat of arms.

A burly man with a red-gold beard and the assurance of a Viking lord leaned over the table and grasped him by the hand, addressing both him and, judging by the loudness of his voice, the entire gathering. "Monmouth has told us about you, Tyndale, and we are all anxious to hear what you have to say."

William's gaze darted about the hall. All eyes looked in his direction. As conversation muted to a faint murmur, he tried to remember when he had last trimmed his beard or changed his shirt. The bells of St. Mary le Bow ceased their clamoring, and the silence deepened. A pulpit jutted out from one wall—he'd heard the merchants held devotional services here. Were they expecting him to preach? Monmouth was a regular worshipper at St. Dunstan's, but he'd said nothing about William preaching to the merchants. He'd just said, "Come with me to the Hanseatic meeting."

William glanced uncertainly at Monmouth, who was grinning as if he were delighted to find his verbose protégé suddenly wordless, and swallowed hard. "I'm afraid . . . that is . . . I feel unprepared to . . ."

Monmouth laughed. "I didn't bring you here to preach to my brothers,

William, but to meet some like-minded souls. We are engaged in the same cause as you. We are a merchants' league, true, but we are also known as the Fellowship of the Christian Brethren and, along with certain Merchant Adventurers abroad, we plan to paper England with cheap printed copies of an English Bible. With your help, we can win England for Martin Luther's reformist cause—" He paused and waved his hand in a sweeping motion to gather in his comrades as he winked. "And we'll make a profit at the same time."

When the merchants' huzzahs and applause had died down, Monmouth continued. "We have a plan . . . and if you sit down and relax—Master of the Table, bring Master Tyndale a cup; he looks parched enough to drink a barrel—we will tell you your part."

William sank onto the velvet cushion of a high-backed chair and made a pretense of sipping his drink as he listened with growing incredulity. The merchants told him how they'd been long engaged in the importing of Martin Luther's writings, and now they had a plan to circumvent Cardinal Wolsey's prohibition on the printing and publishing of English Bibles. Under their proposal, Tyndale would simply do his translating and his printing on the Continent. And the importing and distribution, well, they could see to that: false manifests in legitimate cargo, single sheets of Scripture in a bolt of cloth, a barrel marked FLOUR and filled with Bibles—it was not William's concern.

William looked at Monmouth, whose grin had vanished, the seriousness of his demeanor, like his burly physique, at odds with his fashionable togs. When he spoke his voice was firm.

"This is not without risk to you, William. Wolsey's reach goes way beyond this little island. And there are others. The king's councillor, Thomas More, is dedicated to maintaining the pope's control at any cost. Should you cast your lot with us in this venture, you may incur the wrath of some powerful enemies." He put his hand on William's shoulder. "Do not give your answer in haste."

William merely nodded, trying to show considered thought. If he had heard aright, here was a whole company of patrons offering him what the Bishop of London had refused him—a chance to translate the New Testament into English. It was the commission that his heart profoundly desired. As to powerful enemies, he'd already had his mettle tested when he was tutoring Lord Walsh's children in Little Sodbury. The prelates there had not backed him down with their threats.

A burst of affirmation and encouragement broke out among the men, then settled to a polite murmur, giving him time to consider. Monmouth walked away and engaged the other officers in conversation, his voice low.

What was there to consider? William was hardly able to stifle his exultation. A pox upon the Bishop of London! An image of Cuthbert Tunstall happening upon a Tyndale translation of the New Testament flashed through William's mind. He imagined the bishop finding his translation at a bookshop in Paternoster Row, picking it up gingerly as though he were handling some noxious thing, opening it up with his ring-choked fingers—only to see Tyndale's imprint. What he would give to be there to witness such a moment! Finally, the Bishop of London would see that the scholar he had snubbed had succeeded without him. *Pride goeth before a fall*, he reminded himself. It was enough that God had provided the way. God and Humphrey Monmouth.

❧

Three days later, William Tyndale left for Germany. In his pocket he carried twenty pounds from the Hanseatic merchants of the London Steelyard, along with Erasmus's Greek New Testament. He would use it and Luther's German Bible to make his own English translation—not to further the humanist cause, not as an exercise in the classics for the "new learning" of the intellectual elite represented by Erasmus and Sir Thomas More, but to do for Englishmen what Luther had done for his countrymen. He'd allotted himself one year—six months to learn the German language and six months to make his English translations. In the land that did not burn Luther, he was sure to gain the freedom to print.

As he boarded ship in Bristol, he patted the pocket of his leather jerkin to feel the bulging outline of the Greek New Testament. When he returned he'd be carrying another in its place, and this one would be in English.

William had forgotten all about the Smithfield ghosts and their warnings.

ONE

MARCH 1528

Let it not make thee despair, neither yet discourage thee, O reader, that it is forbidden thee in pain of life and goods . . . to read the Word of thy soul's health; . . . for if God be on our side, what matter maketh it who be against us, be they bishops, cardinals, popes . . .
—FROM WILLIAM TYNDALE'S
THE OBEDIENCE OF A CHRISTIAN MAN, 1528

A scream reverberated against the walls of Gough's Book and Print Shop and echoed down Paternoster Row. An ugly, devil-eyed rat scrambled inside the baited jar, clawing to get out. When no manly presence asserted itself, Kate Gough closed her eyes, sucked in a deep breath, grabbed the fire poker and brought it down with such force she almost lost her balance. The jar shattered. A streak of gray scuttled behind a large codex on the bottom shelf of the book cupboard.

Damnation! All she'd got for her trouble and fright was a glob of grease and ashes and a pile of broken glass on her floor. Where was a man when you needed one—though Kate could boast no man in her life save her brother John, who had gone off to the Frankfurt Book Fair on some grand adventure. All two of her suitors, the miscreant son of a spice merchant and a journeyman thief, had slunk away when they learned she had no dowry and that the business belonged to her brother.

"Nasty, evil creatures," Kate murmured—under her breath since there was no one to hear.

Even had she not encountered the marauder eyeball to eyeball, there was evidence aplenty of another invasion: ragged corners of leather bindings, chewed pages, loathsome black pellets on the deal boards of the bookshelf. The poker thudded to the floor, masking the creak of the door, but as she bent to pick up the largest shards of greasy glass, a sweep of cold rushed in.

"Just look around," she called over her shoulder. "I'll be with you shortly."

She picked up the broom beside the hearth and swept the mess into a pile. "I've broken a bottle and wouldn't want someone to step on the bits," she called.

"Please, it's urgent." It was a woman's voice.

Kate felt her hackles rise. How could the purchase of a book be urgent? "Shut the door, please, you're letting in the cold. I'll just be a minute more," she repeated, trying to keep the edge out of her voice.

"Please. I can't wait. Just watch my baby. I'll be back. Soon. I promise." The woman's voice was low and breathless, as though she were being chased.

Baby? She said she was leaving a baby!

Kate whirled around in time to see another streak of gray—this one larger and in skirts—darting out her door. "Wait! I—" But the woman was as fast as the rat had been. "Wait—come back!" she shouted to the skirt and shawl disappearing around the corner that led into St. Paul's courtyard.

"By all the painted saints and the virgin too," she muttered to herself, forgetting all about the rat and the shattered glass, forgetting about the broom in her hand as she looked incredulously at the bundle on the floor. It moved slightly inside the swaddling. How dare the woman! How presumptuous and careless and stupid to leave her child with a stranger! Kate didn't know anything about caring for babies. The only person she'd ever taken care of was her dying mother and she'd not been very good at that.

What if the woman was lying? What if she didn't come back for hours? Her next thought made her breath catch in her throat. What if she didn't come back at all! She was probably one of the destitute women who loitered around the steps of St. Paul's, their eyes as hungry as the pigeons who pecked for food scraps left by the vendors on the dirty paving stones. The bundle writhed a bit and made a sucking noise. Why hadn't the silly woman taken it to the almshouse or to the nuns at Black Friars? Why did she have to leave it here, for God's sake? *Oh Holy Virgin, it is starting to cry.*

"Shh, shh, don't cry. Please, please don't cry," she begged. "It's not good to cry, crying never helps," as if the infant could be reasoned with.

Kate stood the broom beside the door and, kneeling on the floor, peered at the child. "You must not cry. It is not allowed," she said, pulling back a faded, but clean, blanket to reveal a doll-like face and a rosebud mouth working itself into a scrunch of rage. One tiny, perfect hand broke free and pumped the air. The creature let out a thin, high screech, and then another, until its tiny body writhed in rhythm to its squalling.

She picked up the child gingerly and, cradling it in the crook of her arm, bounced it gently. To Kate's surprise, the squalling dropped a pitch and paused intermittently. "There, there," Kate crooned as she bounced and rocked the baby.

That was not so hard.

The crying stopped and the baby opened its eyes. They were the color of the Madonna's robe in the old illuminated Bible she had inherited from her grandmother, a pure and perfect virgin blue. Kate paused in her bouncing. The blue eyes shut and the tiny mouth scrunched again. Kate resumed her bouncing and her crooning and the world righted itself. The infant—which Kate with her limited experience judged to be about two months—fastened a gaze on Kate's face and smiled. Both the gaze and the smile seemed wise with some primal knowledge, as if to say, I know who you are and I pronounce you worthy. A gurgle followed the smile. Then another.

In that moment Kate's heart grew about three sizes.

She was still holding the child, exchanging tentative endearments in some ancient language known only between women and babies, when the mother came back.

"So sorry. Thank you so much for watching my little Madeline." She paused to catch her breath. "She was slowing me down. A cutpurse snatched my day's wages, and I had to give chase." She grinned and held up the thin little bag. Coins clinked inside it. "My name is Winifred. I'm a seamstress at the shop one street over and my mistress was out. I couldn't leave the baby alone."

"Madeline? That's a beautiful name," Kate said. All her anger at the woman for abandoning the child on her floor had melted away. "She's a beautiful child."

"Her daddy is a Frenchy," she said, by way of explanation for the name, or perhaps the good looks, judging by how her face lit up when she spoke of him.

The baby was still gurgling and Kate was still bouncing the child in the crook of her arm. She was momentarily distracted by the apparent fearlessness of the young woman, who couldn't have been more than seventeen—Kate's own age when the apprenticed printer with whom she'd exchanged only a few fumbling kisses was found with his hand in the bookshop coin box and sent away in disgrace. This girl already had a husband and a child and was chasing down cutpurses as though it were all in a day's work.

The woman reached out her arms. "She likes you. She doesn't usually take to strangers."

"You are very brave—or very foolish," Kate said, unconsciously drawing the child closer to her.

"Oh, 'twas just a lad. I boxed his ears and sent him home to his mama a little wiser. He was probably hungry, but I can't afford to feed him. My man would be that unhappy if I came home empty-handed. He works as a waterman in Southwark. It takes every penny we can scrape together to feed the three of us. A lot of people on this side of the river won't use him 'cause he's a foreigner." Her arms still outstretched, the woman moved a step closer. "I'll take her now. I've imposed long enough."

Kate reluctantly surrendered the little girl. "No imposition," she murmured.

Winifred lifted the baby into her arms, buzzing her on the nose with her own. "You were Mama's good girl, but now we have to go. Your pa will want his supper," she said. She exited the shop in a rush and a swoop, almost as quickly as she had entered it, throwing a "much obliged, mistress" over her shoulder.

"Please, anytime," Kate called to her retreating back. "No trouble. Really."

She stood for a moment in the doorway, not feeling the rush of cold air, her arms remembering the weight of the child. The lamplighter was at work and the beadle had begun his watch. Soon it would be dark outside, the night stretching out before her. She would light her own lamp, read a bit from a recent translation of Dante that they had for sale, careful not to smudge the pages, of course. Then she would eat some stale bread and cheese, maybe a bit of dried fruit. She did not cook much since her brother had married, been glad to be relieved of the burden these two years. Then she would bank the fire in the shop and go up the winding stair to her small bed—just big enough for one.

First she had to sweep up the broken glass. She picked up the broom, but just leaned on it, wondering what had changed; whence came this sudden sense of loneliness and dissatisfaction? She thought of the poor women who slept in the shadow of St. Paul's in whatever doorway they could find shelter. You should thank God, Kate Gough, she scolded herself. You have a roof and hearth—and books. If you have an itch to hold a child, there's always little Pipkin—and you can give him back. When would you have time for books if you had a brood of squalling children and a husband? But she didn't feel thankful.

The girl—she said her name was Winifred. She would be home by now. She and her husband would eat their evening meal together and laugh about her catching the would-be thief. She might even tell her Frenchman about the bookseller who had watched her child.

Was she nice? he might ask. *Nice enough. But there was something sad about her. It was almost as if she wanted to keep little Madeline for herself. I felt kind of sorry for her.*

Little Madeline. Kate remembered the baby smell of her, the perfect little hand that clutched Kate's finger as though it were a lifeline.

Stop it, Kate!

She whisked the broom more roughly than she meant to. A piece of glass scuttled across the floor and startled her, causing her to wonder if the red-eyed vermin would peer at her tonight when she blew out her candle.

Blinking back tears of frustration, she couldn't help but wonder for the second time that day, *Where was a man when you needed one?*

⚬⚬⚬

The next morning Kate woke to the sound of pounding on the door. Maybe whoever it is will go away, she thought and rolled over to go back to sleep. The day was gray and overcast and spitting snow; she could tell from the small window on the wall set high in the eaves above her bed. Her bed was warm, and cold floors and a dead hearth waited for her downstairs in the empty bookshop. She pulled the covers up over her head.

The pounding persisted.

"Go away," she shouted, but she put her feet on the cold floor and pulled her skirt over her chemise. Another customer *urgently* in need of a book. But it might be the only customer she had all day. She twisted her braid into a bun and pinned it and started down the stairs. Then the thought occurred to her that it might be the woman with the baby again. She had invited her to bring her back anytime. "I'm coming," she shouted.

But when she lifted the latch, her brother John pushed into the room and shut the door quickly behind him. Kate threw her arms around him, forgetting all about the woman and the child, then stepped back to look at him. His nose was pinched with cold and snowflakes dusted his cap and mantle. He looked so wan and tired, he must have traveled all night. No wonder he pounded so impatiently on the door.

"Did you leave the books outside?" she asked, looking around for a satchel or a small crate. "They'll get wet. We should bring them in. Right away," she said, opening the door again.

He reached over her shoulder and gave the door a push. It slammed shut. "There are no books," he said, swatting his hat against his cloak to remove the snow, then hanging both on a peg by the door. "I didn't buy any."

"Didn't buy! Why on earth—" Then her thoughts caught up with her mouth. "You lost the money! Oh merciful saints, you were robbed! Are you all right?"

He sighed wearily. "I did not lose the money, dear sister. I bought books, but on the way home I learned this is not the time to be bringing more Lutheran sermons or English Bibles into England. Fortunately, I was able to recoup some of the money I'd spent. I sold what I'd bought at a discount to an Englishman who was going abroad to live."

"That sounds like a very good business decision," she mumbled. "Maybe we should get a bigger shop so we can sell more books below cost."

He did not answer her sarcasm with a witty barb of his own, as he usually did, but picked up the poker and stirred in the ashes, coaxing the coals to life, flinging on a piece of kindling from a basket beside the hearth. His movements, usually so deliberate, were hasty, almost frenzied. The flames leaped up, melting the snowflakes from his hat and cloak. A small puddle formed on Kate's beeswaxed floorboards as she fumed silently about the books. She had been looking forward to the new books, and their inventory was pitifully low—mostly what he'd been able to print in the back room, and that wasn't much since he couldn't get a license for any of the Lutheran materials that were their stock-in-trade. The fire was blazing now, banishing the morning chill.

"Have you seen Mary and the baby?" she asked, changing the subject in order not to ruin his homecoming with her scold's tongue.

"No. I came straight here," he said. He was rummaging in the book cupboards gathering up pamphlets. She recognized the Antwerp imprint on some of them. Those would be Tyndale's—all they had left.

"What are you looking for? John, really, I am glad to see you but you probably should have gone home to see your wife before coming here." Then she added under her breath, unable to resist, "Especially since you have returned empty-handed."

He strode across the room and examined the pamphlets before striding to the fire and feeding them, first one, then another, into the fire.

"John! What in heaven's name—"

The bright flames leaped higher, devouring the paper and ink that he'd smuggled in at great risk. He was already at another bookshelf, rifling its contents, discarding some, clutching others to consign to the hungry blaze. He picked up the last two of Tyndale's English New Testaments and leaned again toward the fire, shielding his face from the heat.

She grabbed for them too late. "John! Have you gone mad? That's the Holy Word you're burning! And the last of our inventory."

"I have to do this, Kate. They've arrested Thomas Garrett," he said.

Her hand froze in midair. Thomas Garrett was a bookseller to Oxford scholars and one of their chief suppliers. What smuggled shipments John did not meet, he bought from Garrett. The heat from the fire was sucking the air out of the room, but she found breath enough to ask, "What will they do to him? Does Cardinal Wolsey have him? Or the king's soldiers?"

"Same difference. Henry VIII, Defender of the Faith," John said with bitterness, "will do whatever the cardinal says. Fortunately, Garrett had his wits about him enough to escape. But others have been arrested. They tortured a parson from Honey Lane along with his servant."

He paused and looked hard at her, his gaze locking with her own; suddenly they were children again, and he, ever the cautious one, was warning her away from danger. "Kate, Garrett sent me a message. I may have been named."

His voice was calm, but she saw the fear in his eyes and suddenly his anxious, hurried movements made sense.

"But even if that's true and you have been named . . . you aren't in any real danger, right? The Church has never gone after the booksellers in a serious way. It would interfere with commerce. Pope's pony or not, the king would never allow it."

But even as she stammered out the words, she was remembering the new laws against printing unlicensed works and disseminating Lutheran materials in particular. They had considered the edicts hardly more than a conciliatory nod to the clerics since they seemed to have more to do with commerce than heresy. "Aren't you being overly cautious? It's not like you are a Lutheran preacher or something. Our customers come to us, asking for the books. Surely, you would get off with no more than a fine or a threat to shut down the shop. If that happens, I agree, then we burn the books."

"What is Thomas Garrett, Kate, but a bookseller? That's why he was at Oxford. And he found a ready enough market. Several of the students are being interrogated," he said, stuffing another gospel onto the fire. She stepped back, away from the searing heat.

"That was the Gospel of Saint Luke! You printed that one yourself." She had a sudden vision of him bent over his press, laboring secretly at night in violation of guild rules for printing after dark. She gathered what was left in her arms, hugging them to her as she spoke. "Why can't we just hide them until this passes?"

"It's not going to pass this time. They'll not stop until they've made examples of some of us—lit a few fires of their own." His voice was firm, determined. He held out his hands for the books she held.

She thought of the translators in self-imposed exile on the Continent and the smugglers who had risked so much to bring these books to England. She thought of their own expenses tied up in the books. "You're just going to give in to them, then? John, it's wrong to burn the books. It is a sacrilege and an insult to those who've suffered so much in this cause. Cardinal Wolsey and his crowd burn books. We do not burn books." She could hear her voice grow strident.

John answered her in measured tones. "Burning the books is exactly what Humphrey Monmouth did two years ago when they raided the Steelyard and dragged him in. When they searched his home, they found no evidence. He was let go. I've Mary and the boy to think about. And you," he said evenly, no temper in his voice, but his step was hurried, and the vein tracing the center of his forehead stood out like a blue cord. "If you are right and Wolsey and Cuthbert Tunstall find something else to chase, and forget about us, then we can print more."

And what will we sell in the meantime? How will we make a living without inventory? But she said nothing. He was the one they'd come after, not her, so she supposed it should be his decision.

He gave a bitter little laugh. "A lot of the books Bishop Tunstall burned at St. Paul's Cross he'd bought and paid for out of Church funds to make a greater show. Tyndale used that money to fund another and better edition. One with even stronger glosses against popery." He reached to the top shelf where the Wycliffe Bible lay, the Bible that had belonged to their great-grandmother.

She stayed his hand with a tight grip on his wrist. This time it was her tone that was firm. "Not that one, John. You shall not burn that one. It cannot be replaced."

For once, he gave in. Frowning, he handed it down to her. "Take it away from here, then. When they search this place, they need to find it clean of all contraband books—all, Kate, do you understand?"

As she took the heavy Bible, she dusted the cover with her hand, encountering the roughened edge where the rats had chewed the edge of the leather binding. Nothing was sacred from the vermin.

"That's the last of it, I'm sure," John said, looking around.

"What about the Bristol shipment?" Kate asked.

He shrugged. "I'll not meet it, of course. Too dangerous. If I should be caught with this suspicion already against me . . ."

All those Bibles dumped into the sea, she thought, all that labor wasted, all those dear-bought words turning into sea foam to feed the fish.

The fire was already dying. Kate put down the Bible and picked up the broom to sweep up a few fragments of broken glass that she had missed in last night's lamplight.

"What did you break?" he asked as he put on his cloak in preparation to leave.

"It was a jar I baited to catch a rat," she said.

He stood in the doorway with his hand on the latch, a little smile tweaking the corners of his mouth for the first time since he'd returned.

"Did the rat get away?"

"Damn vermin."

"You swear too much. You'll never find a husband."

"Then I'll spin at your hearth until I'm a gray crone."

It was an old joke between them. But lately she did not find it so funny.

"Humph," he grunted, as always. The smile stayed, as always.

"Give Mary my love and kiss little Pipkin for me," she said.

They were both startled by the sound of a blunt object pounding on the door. "Open in the name of the king!"

A glance and a nod and Kate grabbed the old Wycliffe Bible and fled up the back stairs of the print shop to her bedchamber. She heard a shout, and then muffled voices. She recognized John's well-modulated tones. Gathering her composure, she descended the stairs and entered the stationer's shop just in time to see the beadle and two soldiers leading her brother away.

TWO

More is a man of an angel's wit and singular learn-
ing . . . For where is the man of that gentleness, low-
liness, and affability? And, as time requireth, a man
of marvelous mirth and pastime, and sometimes of as
sad gravity. A man for all seasons.
—ROBERT WHITTINTON IN
PRAISE OF SIR THOMAS MORE, 1520

riday was Sir Thomas More's favorite day. On Fridays, after the
daily mass, after the Te Deum, after the last chanted psalm, he did not don
his striped robes and go to Lincoln's Inn to lecture in the law or even to
Black Friars where as Speaker of the Commons he would plead for parliamentary funding of the king's French enterprise. Dressed in the scarlet hood
and cloak of the powerful Mercer's Guild, he did not take the short walk
to the guildhall in Ironmonger Lane to report on his latest negotiations with
the Hanseatic League. Nor did he adorn himself with the golden Tudor livery chain and sail his private barge down the river to Westminster to attend
the king's council. He did not even go to Oxford, where he served as steward, to pass judgment on the miscreant scholars there.

Fridays belonged to him.

After Sir Thomas had dismissed his family from the obligatory mass to
their individual and sometimes raucous pursuits, he would remain alone in

the chapel, prostrated before the Holy Rood. Only after his limbs were stiff with fatigue, and his thoughts as tangled as the knots on the little corded whip, would he take out his flagellum and begin to lay on his stripes.

The first hit over his left shoulder was for his patron and sometime friend. Wolsey—Wolsey with his cardinal's hat. These first stripes, Sir Thomas laid on more in anger than in repentance, just to catch the rhythm, to crack open the doorway to the ecstasy of pain. Wolsey! A cardinal! With a secret marriage. A cardinal with both the power of the clergy and a wife.

Then three more stripes for his lawyer father, John More. His father who must be pleased. His father who must be praised. His father who must be obeyed.

Then a shift over the right shoulder, angrier still, his rage still hurling outward. Rage for Luther and his *furfuris,* the ape of a translator William Tyndale. *Merda, stercus, lutum.* Shit. Dung. Filth. Dangerous, villainous heretics! Breathing heavily now. One who took a whoring nun to wife and one who lived like a monk, even as he dared praise marriage for the clergy.

Then a deep inhalation and two more strokes. Left. Right. This time in penance for his own sin, payment for his own pleasure. One for his dead wife, his young and docile Jane. He had enjoyed her overmuch. Inhale. For his lust of her, he'd abandoned his little cell in the Charterhouse, his Carthusian monk's cell. Exhale. And another for his second wife. Dame Alice— her tongue, scourge enough for any man. Her will as powerful.

Left, right. One to pay for his son. Two. Three. To pay for Alice's daughter. Jane's daughters.

The burn began in his shoulder and spread between his shoulder blades, little tongues of flame licking at skin already raw from his hair shirt.

Two more stripes for Meg, the daughter he loved best. Once over the left shoulder. Once over the right.

Ten. Eleven. Twelve . . . one laid on for each of his grandchildren, until his flesh quivered with repentance, until he'd paid for all his pleasure, both innocent and carnal. Thirteen. Fourteen. Until his body and his mind were as exhausted as when he'd first lain with a woman. This traitor to his vocation. This sinner, too carnal to live celibate and too lawful to live a lie. As Wolsey did, Wolsey who wore a cardinal's robe.

Only when his flagellation was ended, his sinner's soul new-cleansed and the embers of his anger banked for a season, could Sir Thomas reenter his Friday domestic bliss. In summer, he would picnic with his family across the wide lawns of his new Chelsea palace. In winter he would practice the lute with Alice and their daughters in the winter solar or retire to his library to discuss Aristotle with his daughter Margaret.

But if one did not count the chapel where his spirit gained redemption, or the library, where he wrote his poetry, dreamed out his *Utopia,* held intelligent discourse with his Meg, the pearl of his heart, the rose garden was Sir Thomas More's favorite place. He had an aviary there with exotic birds for song and color, and a few ferrets and weasels—even a caged ape named Samson for entertainment. The roses, washed by the misting English rain, or bruised by the bright sunshine, were always fragrant in summer.

But it was not yet summer.

On this early spring morning the buds would be mere swellings on the bare and prickly vines. Yet, the garden beckoned. For in its forbidden heart, where his grandchildren and his daughters never ventured, a thorn tree of a different sort flourished, often blooming red and out of season. But that tree bloomed only at night, and it was yet day, and Meg would be waiting in the library.

After the day had ended, after Alice began to snore and the sounds of the great house stilled, Thomas left his slumbering wife and whispered to the servant who slept outside his chamber.

"It is time, Barnabas," he said, and handed the servant the coiled whip.

As he passed the library, he noticed the tapers were still lit, their yellow light spilling from the half-closed door—Meg, working late again, leaving her husband to a lonely bed. But he'd little sympathy for William Roper. Thomas feared he harbored a Lutheran heretic in his very bosom. Only this one favorite daughter would be allowed such forbearance.

He smiled, thinking of her working on her Greek translations late into the night, her face bent over the desk, her fine script flowing from her cramped fingers, the words from her nimble intellect. What did it matter that she was the homeliest of the lot? She was possessed of a fine mind; one might even say a beautiful mind. She was too good for William Roper, though the match, like all the marriages made in the More household, had brought its share of wealth and good connections.

Thomas carried the torchlight as he and the servant descended the darkened stairs and entered the slumbering rose garden. Past the songbirds who slept with their heads tucked under their clipped wings, past the ferrets and the weasels who foraged in the darkness for food, treading across the knot garden where the smitten rosemary released its chastened winter fragrance on the night air.

They reached a small clearing.

The cold light of a frosty quarter moon picked out the figure tied to the whipping post. More's "Tree of Troth," Bishop Cuthbert Tunstall called it. Thomas preferred to think of it as Jesu's Tree.

The man was stripped naked to the waist and bound at his wrists and ankles. His chin rested on his chest as though he slept too, like the winter garden. A knotted rope was wound tightly around his forehead. His blond hair fell forward, obscuring one side of his face. Sir Thomas lifted the torchlight to inspect his prisoner. His anger, so lately purged, rose inside him again. Even the man's posture was a sacrilege, as though his unconscious body conspired in the Christ-like pose.

"Wake up the Lollard," he said, "so that he may be made to see the error of his ways. The sting of the whip may clarify his mind so he can return to the true faith."

The servant lifted the whip and curled it around the naked chest of the prisoner, who opened his eyes and settled an unwavering blue gaze upon his questioner.

A woman's high, sweet voice called out, "Father, are you there?"

Startled, Thomas motioned for the servant to recede into the shadow as he recognized Meg's voice. He shouted, his tone unusually harsh. "Is that you, Margaret? You know this part of the garden is forbidden. Where are you?"

Her tone was chastened when she answered. "I'm by the fishpond, Father. There was a messenger for you from the king."

"Wait where you are. I'll come to you," he shouted. Then to the servant, he hissed, "Take him back to the porter's lodge," indicating with a toss of his head the circuitous direction the servant should lead the prisoner.

"Aye, milord. But the porter said to remind you that this is the tenth day and under the law—"

"The porter reminds the king's legal advisor of the law? How very *judicious* of him. Tell him I know the law as well as any man in England, and under the law a prisoner under suspicion of heresy may be interrogated. And so can a servant in sympathy with heretics." His gaze locked with the prisoner's. Thomas looked away. "Put him back in the stocks," he said as he stalked off toward the fishpond.

The moonlight reflected coldly off the pond, picking out a slight ripple in the water where the wind ruffled the surface, picking out, too, his daughter's pale face beneath her velvet caplet. She hugged herself and shivered in the moonlight. "I'm sorry, Father. It's just that I thought you—"

He immediately relented. "If I sounded curt to you, it's because I care only for your safety. At night the keepers let Samson roam free. And during the day, if he should see you, he might frighten you."

"But he doesn't frighten you."

"Ah yes, daughter. But you see, I am very familiar with the beast. Where is the king's messenger?"

"He is in your library. Actually, there were two messengers. The first was from Bishop Tunstall. He left his message after I assured him I would place it myself in your hands. But the king's messenger . . . I thought . . ."

"You were right to summon me," he said, "but next time, send one of the grooms."

Putting his arm around her shoulders, he led her up the front steps. The dark face of the red brick façade loomed over them, its black windows like all-knowing eyes. As they approached the library, Thomas could see the Tudor-liveried messenger pacing before the fire. Best not to keep him cooling his heels overlong. He bade his daughter good night at the door, watching her affectionately as she curtsied and then melted with a swish of satin skirts into the deepening shadows beyond the hall.

The messenger was a familiar face that Thomas had seen often at court. With a curt nod of recognition, he took the scroll and quickly broke the king's red wax seal. He scanned the words quickly, his heart sinking.

"This requires an answer," he said, without looking up. "It is late. I will consider it and give you my written response in the morning." He pulled a rope and a servant appeared almost immediately. "Sam here will provide you with a bed in the guesthouse and refreshment—or whatever else you require. You will not find the hospitality of Chelsea House lacking. Return to this chamber after prime; I will give you a message for His Majesty."

Sighing wearily, Thomas laid the court document on his desk and settled into the chair beside the fire. He rubbed his fingers back and forth across his furrowed brow as he studied the embers. *So. Finally it has come. You can no longer dance around it,* he told himself. There had been hints, both subtle and not, but he'd always been able to sidestep the implications. Now here it was. A direct request from Henry VIII, Defender of the Faith—a title Sir Thomas had helped his sovereign obtain by writing the refutation of the Lutheran doctrine that gained him that honor—to help the king with his "great matter."

There was a sudden chill in the room. He shivered, igniting the fire beneath his hair shirt. The shifting coals on the hearth sighed, as if in reminder that one refused a king, especially this king, at one's peril. Thomas was fifty-one years old, and he felt every birthday in his bones. He had served Henry well, but it appeared he was not to be allowed to retire. How could he answer "nay" and not provoke his king to wrath? But how could he answer "yea" and preserve his public honor? He got up wearily and poked at the fire, gathering the coals back together. His eye fell on a small bound packet.

Meg had mentioned another message. He recognized Cuthbert Tunstall's familiar seal. He tore this one open with more enthusiasm. It contained a small book and a few pamphlets. Although the two colleagues often exchanged books, Thomas examined this book with curiosity and some surprise. It was Tyndale's English New Testament! He'd heard about it, though he'd not seen one before because, like all works containing Lutheran doctrine and glosses, it was banned under the bishop's recent monition.

A scrap of vellum fell out and fluttered to the floor. Thomas bent to retrieve it. The letter, written in Latin, as was all correspondence among More, Bishop Tunstall, and Cardinal Wolsey, gave More specific dispensation to possess the book along with a request to help catch out the "sons of iniquity" who were spreading Luther's poison across England. The letter further suggested that Sir Thomas could best serve this cause by writing a refutation of Tyndale for publication and distribution, and offered monetary compensation.

Thomas opened the English New Testament with curiosity and, squinting in the candlelight, flipped through the pages. Tyndale was a capable translator and a cunning one. Each page fueled Thomas's anger more: the base Anglo-Saxon word choices, the plainness of the verbiage, the use of the word *congregation* and not *church*, the use of *elder* in place of *priest*, deliberately stripping the Church of its claim to being Christ's body on earth. Even the use of *repent* and not *do penance*, a blatant slap at the Church's penitential system of indulgences. He scanned the heretical Lutheran glosses that railed against the power of the Church, feeling his temper rise. *Coenum!* Excrement! A foul heretical document!

His fingers itched to begin.

Thomas would not help Henry make a legal wife of his whore, but this he could do. This he would do. And for free. He slammed the little pocket-sized book shut, the profane thing, cheaply bound, cheaply printed, and made to throw it in the fire. But no, not the book. The book was evidence. It was the book's author who should be consigned to the flames. He and all other foul and stinking heretics like him, who would sully England with this profane offal.

From somewhere deep in the heart of the garden, he heard an animal roar. Samson. The keeper had given the beast a brief furlough from his cage. The sap was rising in the earth, and Samson would be feeling the stirrings inside himself. He would be beating on his chest, lunging at the leash that kept him inside the walled garden, anger in his wild cry. Sir Thomas thumbed through the other heretical samples, feeling a great sympathy with Samson's rage. But he could not beat his chest and scream into the silence of slumbering Chelsea House. Sir Thomas More was a civilized man. A great scholar. A man of classical learning. An honorable man. And a Christian.

He slammed the New Testament down on the table and pounded it with his fist, then stood up and, gathering his ermine-fringed cloak, strode from the room. The door slammed behind him as he went in the direction of the porter's lodge.

THREE

By burning Luther's books you may rid your book-
shelves of him but you will not rid men's minds of him.
—ERASMUS OF ROTTERDAM

he daffodils were blooming in the window box outside Gough's
Book and Print Shop, but neither their brave yellow blossoms nor the thin
sunlight lifted Kate's spirits. Not one word from John since the day two
weeks ago when they had taken him away. He would have gotten a message
to his wife, or to her, unless he was dead—or in prison. Each day they
waited, thinking he would be home today or tomorrow. Today and tomorrow and more tomorrows came and went, and no John.

Her sister-in-law came to the shop every morning. When the door
opened sharply at nine bells, Kate didn't even have to look up.

"Tell me he's not dead, Kate. Last night I dreamed I saw his body in a
winding sheet. Tell me John is all right," she said, her large brown eyes
overflowing while the two-year-old squirmed in her arms.

"He's not dead, Mary. I would know if he were dead," she said, reaching
for the boy who held his arms out to be taken. "That's just your own fevered
brain conjuring demons from your fear."

What she did not say was that at this very minute he could be undergoing
the most grievous kind of torture or languishing in the Lollard prison, a

horror she had first heard whispered about as a child. The Lollards had been persecuted for two hundred years, since John Wycliffe first called the Roman Church to account for its abuses and dared to call for the Scriptures to be translated from Latin into English so that every man could discern the truth for himself. Her family had been engaged in that struggle for liberty for almost as long.

She buried her head in the boy's blond curls, feeling its softness as she brushed the bone of the skull underneath with her lips. So hard, and yet so fragile. The baby smell of him reminded her of the baby Madeline.

"If they had killed him, we would have heard about it," Kate said to reassure herself as much as Mary. "Why else do it, if not to noise it abroad to strike fear in the hearts of their enemies?"

"They say that Wolsey doesn't like the killing. That he gives them a chance to abjure . . . but I'm not sure that John would—"

"John would abjure for you, Mary. And for his son," she said flatly, remembering the resolute look on his face as he had burned the books. "He would for you."

"And you do not approve."

"I don't know what I would do in his place. But I know what our father did. He died in the Lollard prison because he stood fast for his beliefs. He would not deny that a man should have the right to read the Gospel in his own language, and he would not proclaim allegiance to a Church that taught false doctrines."

"And is that what you would have your brother do? Your father wasn't the only one to suffer. What about you and John? What about your mother? She didn't die of weak lungs. She died of grief. Whenever you speak of your father you have that same look of . . . worship on your face that John has."

At the word *face,* the boy put his hand on Kate's cheek and repeated the word as though they were playing the game they often played: nose, hand, face, ears. Her heart clutched with affection at the touch of his hand on her face.

Her sister-in-law persisted. "Would you do it, Kate? Would you recant?"

"I said I don't know what I would do, Mary," she said, feeling resentful that her sister-in-law was pressing her. "It would be as though our father died for nothing. And those before him. Our family has always been involved with reform. You know that. We grew up on stories of martyrdom and heroism. We inherited those stories along with that big old family Bible." She looked down at Pipkin squirming in her arms. "But I do not have as much to lose as John."

Kate liked to think she knew what she would do, but who could ever know? Many brave men had broken under torture. How could a woman hope to endure?

"Air," said the child, pulling on Kate's hair.

"Here, take your little wiggle worm back," she said as she disentangled his hands from her hair, then reached for her cloak on the peg by the door and struggled into it. "I'll be back in time for you to go home before dark. If anybody asks for a Lutheran text, just say—well, you know what to say."

"I'll say we no longer sell those. They are illegal," she said, her chin thrust out, her eyes snapping with fire.

Mary might be a gentle soul, Kate thought, but she had a streak of determination hard as iron.

When Kate did not correct her, Mary asked, the harshness of her tone softened, her eyes once again soft and moist, "Where will you look today?"

"Maybe down by the docks. The Hanseatic Merchants League. They might have heard something."

"Some ting." The boy nodded, his face grown suddenly as solemn as the two women he trusted.

But Kate turned her back. She could no longer bear to look at him. She opened the door and headed out to begin her search as she had each day for two weeks. The sharp March wind bit her neck, forcing her to pull up the squirrel-lined hood of her cloak. There was no such protection for the cold that squeezed at her heart.

❦

Kate learned nothing about her brother from the Merchant Adventurers at the Steelyard except how widespread the sweep had been.

"What about the shipment from Antwerp?" Kate asked the sergeant at arms.

"Ruined. It was off-loaded while the carrier was still out to sea, but don't worry, mistress. There's more where that came from. Print and paper are cheap. Lives are not."

"Will there be no other shipment, then?"

The merchant grinned. "There's already another on the way. By the time it gets here in late April, the king's men won't be watching the Bristol docks.

They've already caught Garrett. He's in a cell at Ilchester in Somerset, poor sod."

"But won't they want to know his source?"

"The king doesn't want any trouble with the German merchants." He grinned. "He wants good English wool on the backs of rich burghers on the Continent. He'll not be looking to break the trade agreement. Unless we rub his nose in it, he'll just go after the English smugglers and distributors."

"Who will meet the next shipment with Garrett arrested?"

"Some of the booksellers are meeting it directly. If you find your brother, and he's still got the stomach for it, tell him to check in with Sir John Walsh in Little Sodbury."

"If I find him."

"Don't worry, mistress. They've just cast a broad net. They'll let the small fry go—sooner or later. The jails are already full. I heard they've even got some of the Oxford students who bought from Garrett locked in the fish cellar beneath Cardinal College. They'll put the fear of the pope into them all and send them home."

"What about Master Garrett?"

"Well, now, they may be more reluctant to let him go. He's considered a major distributor—and somewhat of a preacher. And he's already been warned. Once you've been warned . . ." He finished his sentence with a shrug.

Now John will have been warned, Kate thought. But she couldn't think about what that might mean. First she had to find him.

✦

The fish cellar stank. And not just from its name, the aptness of which lent sufficient foul odor, but also from human excrement and mold clinging to the damp walls and something else he could not name. It might be fear, his good sense said, the collective fear oozing from the pores of himself and the five other fellows from Cardinal College who had been detained on suspicion of possessing Lutheran books. John Frith recited Homer in the original Greek—aloud—to keep from going crazy in the filth and the darkness. But this last week his able chorus had fallen off.

"My God, man, will you give it a rest. Clerke is sick," came a voice from the darkness.

"I know. I smelled it. I'm sorry. But we can't give in. They *will* let us out. Even Dean Higdon can't keep us in this stinking cellar without a trial! He's just trying to frighten us. Let us ripen a little."

"He's doing a damn fine job, then." Sumner's voice. It was Sumner he worried most about. He'd been sickly before they were locked up.

"We must keep faith," Frith said, trying to sound assured. "The steward will make his rounds soon, and then we'll be let out with a threat and probably a public scolding in chapel."

"Humph! I'd not pin my hopes on the steward. Thomas More is a heretic hunter. He'll be the last to let us out." Bayley's voice.

"How do you know that?" Frith asked.

"Garrett told me. When he was staying over Christmas in quarters with the choirmaster. He said he knew Bishop Tunstall and More were after him."

"Sort of 'buy my books and by the way they may get you killed.' Fine time to tell us," Frith said a little snippily.

"Would it have stopped you?" Bayley asked.

"You have a point," Frith said, brushing the gray salt from his cloak as he removed it and handed it to Sumner. "Put this around Clerke. A man shouldn't be sick *and* cold. We can't lose heart. The cardinal and the dean and even More will not want it known that the college is 'infected' with heresy. Why do you think they shut us up here instead of a public gaol?"

"May be that the gaols are full," Sumner said weakly. "Or may be they just intend to let us rot here, like this stinking fish." He pointed to the barrels in the corner.

"Ah no, Sumner. We'll not rot here. Don't worry. There's enough salt to preserve us," Frith said, trying to lighten the mood. "They'll let us out when they think our Lutheran fever is sufficiently chilled. Maybe tomorrow. I'll bet you my Herodotus *and* my Virgil that we'll all live to see old Thomas More and Wolsey laid out in their Roman funerary clothes. Now"—as if their incarceration were a mere inconvenience to be borne with equanimity—"this time you are Ulysses and I am Telemachus." And he started his recitation again.

"Firth, you're either a fool or you're a saint. I don't know which."

I don't know either, he thought. But whichever, he was already quite ripe and more than a little chilled. And it had only been three weeks. *Be still my heart, thou hast known worse than this.* But John Frith found scant comfort in Homer's words, for in truth when had he known worse?

The afternoon shadows were lengthening when Kate made what she thought was her last call of the day at the palace of the Bishop of London. The cleric who answered the door frowned in recognition.

"Bishop Tunstall is in conference today."

"But he was 'in conference' yesterday."

"As he will be tomorrow. Look, mistress, I do not mean to be unkind. I assure you I have given him your message, and he says he knows nothing of the matter. He says you should petition the sheriff or the Lord Mayor of London."

"I have already done so. Several times. I've bribed the wardens of Newgate and even the Old Compter. They know of no John Gough."

"The Fleet?"

"The Fleet too."

Kate tried to soften her tone. She knew the cleric would not respond to harshness. He was young and had a kind face. "Please. A man doesn't just disappear. My brother was a good citizen . . . is a good citizen." She would not speak of him in the past tense. "He is a bookseller and printer of some reputation."

A light seemed to go on in the clerk's face, "Ah, a printer." His expression hardened. "Check the Lollard Tower," he said, and before she could tell him she'd already been to Lambeth Palace with its infamous and dreaded square tower built to house and torture heretics, he shut the door in her face. She'd gone to the Lollard Tower the first week, her heart in her throat, almost faint with relief when the warden had said the prison was full and they had taken no new prisoners for weeks. That being the case, she thought, they might just frighten John and let him go. But that relief had vanished as the days crawled by and he did not appear.

She reached up to knock again at the door and then let her hand drop. What was the use? It was getting late. Mary would want to be by her own hearth when darkness fell. Kate should head home, though she dreaded facing her sister-in-law, hated seeing her banked tears at Kate's no-news report. So when Kate neared St. Paul's churchyard with its cacophony of familiar bells, she did not turn into Paternoster Row and homeward but went west, past Ludgate Hill.

There was still time to check Fleet Prison again.

The effluvium from the river Fleet was always worse with approaching dusk. All day the human waste and refuse from the city's gutters had bled into the river as it made its noisome way to the Thames. The smell of it made her heave, but nothing came up. She had not eaten since this morning and then only a bite of the heel from a stale loaf. There'd been no time for a proper breakfast. But when had John last eaten? she wondered as she approached the gates of the Fleet and entered its grim courtyard.

The same old grizzled watchman she'd seen before slouched against the door of the gatehouse.

"I told ye last week, and the week before, and the week before that, mistress, I don't know of a John Gough here," he said before she could even ask.

"He may be here under another name. He could have been . . . unconscious when they brought him in. They might not even know his last name. Just let me describe him to the warden." Kate fumbled in her purse.

"Ha! As if his greatness the warden is ever here! And the deputy warden will not see ye again so there beint no use fer ye to waste yer pennies trying to get to him." He leaned forward to whisper as he scratched his greasy beard. She steeled herself against the onslaught of his breath and tried to ignore the suggestive shouts directed their way from the knot of prisoners playing at dice in the center of the yard. "Ye'd be better served to save yer ha' pennies for the prisoners begging at the grill on the Common Side. They'll know more than the deputy warden. He scarcely ever dirties his boots in the galleries."

"The grill?"

The watchman jerked his head toward the right wing of cells with their barred windows opening onto Farringdon Street where the lowborn prisoners begged for money from passers-by to buy food and fresh straw for their lice-ridden cells. She'd always avoided that end of the street, after that first time when she'd walked past to the hoots and hollers and banging of tin bowls on the bars. But she saw the logic in the watchman's suggestion.

Stiffen your backbone, Kate. Just do it.

With a vision of Mary's disappointment prodding her courage—and the certainty in her soul that her brother was still alive—she walked to the first window and peered inside. The cell looked to be about twice as long as a man was tall and about as wide. It had no furniture, just a pile of rags on the floor in front of a fireplace wherein no coals glowed. Her presence at the window blocked out the only light.

The cell's lone occupant stood gazing out the window an arm's length from the bars, but Kate could see the prisoner clearly, like some caged animal, visible to all who passed by.

She appeared to be oblivious to Kate's scrutiny. The shadows under her eyes, the bruise above her cheek—or was it dirt?—all unsettled Kate. The woman was dressed in rags and painfully thin—except for the bulge of her belly. Yet she was not banging on the bars and shouting at passers-by, begging as the others did. Instead, she was just staring dumbly into space, her eyes half shut, her face vacant of any expression. This one would be no help,

Kate thought. She was obviously mad with grief or fear. Kate started to turn away, but pity pulled her back. She loosened the strings on her little leather purse again and withdrew two pennies.

"Here, mistress, I am sorry for your plight," she called, and held out the pence.

The woman looked frightened and withdrew farther from the window. She opened her eyes a little wider and stared at Kate, unblinking, but she did not move to take the money. Kate stepped a little closer. *Not too close,* she warned herself. The woman might turn on her. Even try to grab her.

Kate gripped the tuppence between her forefinger and middle finger and slid her arm through the narrow space between the bars.

"Come on. Take it. For the baby in your belly."

The woman did not move.

Kate let the pennies fall. They thudded against the grime-caked stone of the floor. As fast as a serpent's strike the woman swooped down and with long thin fingers clawed them from the dirty straw.

At least she does have some sensibility, Kate thought, encouraged. "Mistress, do you know of a prisoner named John? A tall, blond man with blue eyes . . . he has a vein that is prominent on his forehead. He is a gentle, quiet man."

The woman retreated from the window and shook her head violently. Kate could barely see her in the shadows.

"I suppose not," Kate said, and then added as she turned away, "God's blessings on you, mistress."

Kate thought she heard some whimpered response and perked her ears. But no. She could see the woman's silhouette in the corner of her vision. She had not moved.

"Here, over here." The clanging of a tin bowl against the iron bars accompanied the words. It was a male voice, coming from the next cell.

"I know a man named John," the prisoner shouted. "He may be the one you're looking for. If you have any more pennies in that bag."

Kate's heart gave a little thump. *Likely not,* she told herself. *He saw me give the woman money and figures me for an easy mark.*

"John's a proud man," the prisoner said. "Too proud to beg. Or too melancholy to care if he starves. He came in fairly beat-up." He paused, then snaked a hand from between the iron bars, motioning for her to come to his window. When she did not respond, he continued. "Raves in his sleep about a woman named Mary. Might you be Mary?"

That could be naught but a cunning guess. There were hundreds of men named John and more women named Mary. Still . . . *too proud to beg*! She looked hopefully at the gate to see if a gaoler or some sentry stood watch on the street.

None did.

Backbone, Kate. She moved over to the grilled window where the prisoner stood with his face pressed against the bars, but she kept a safe distance.

"Will you take a message to him for me, then? Will you bring me news of him, or bid him come in person to this window to meet his sister?"

"Sister! So I'll be guessin' you're not Mary. I might do it," he said, nodding purposefully.

He was not an old man, though it was hard to tell through the stringy black hair, hair as sooty as a raven's wing. He had a wide straight mouth with smooth lips that curved scythelike within a stubble of dark beard. She grew uncomfortable beneath his scrutiny. His eyes were jet-bright and bold, both searching and staring. The eyes of a man who is always on the hunt, she thought. A dangerous man—maybe even a Spaniard—her good sense said, a man who would always seek the advantage. His shirt was filthy with a ragged bit of lace at the throat and full sleeves. Not the usual dress of a beggar. Probably stolen from some wealthy merchant, maybe even the reason for his incarceration.

"I suppose you would not do it out of human kindness?" she said dryly. "I am courting poverty myself by always paying for information that is never forthcoming."

He laughed. "I'm not too proud to beg. Or to negotiate. I have to eat. And I have no loving sister to look out for me." His voice dripped sarcasm.

"Have you some offer of proof," she said, "that this man is the one I seek? John is a common name. So is Mary."

"This John speaks like a man with an education," he said. He had withdrawn his hand from the window, now that he had her attention. He leaned against the bars, picking nonchalantly at a ragged cuticle, his tone as light as though they were equals engaged in gossip. "There are ink stains beneath his nails. Maybe an artist—or a printer, I'd say."

He lifted his gaze and looked directly into her eyes, one eyebrow cocked like a crow's wing.

Her heart raced. *An artist or a printer!* The question tumbled out before she realized she was giving her adversary the advantage in negotiation. "Is he . . . is he well?"

The prisoner shrugged then, looked up at her and gave her the crooked smile of a survivor. Strong, white teeth flashed within a scythe of a smile. The teeth of a predator, she thought. She thought she saw a little gleam of triumph in his eyes, like a man who'd run his quarry to ground. "'Is he well?' I'd say that is a relative term. He is alive. And he's not in the cellars."

Kate didn't know what that meant, but she could guess. These last few days she'd learned more than she ever wanted to know about the prisons, such as the hierarchy of bought justice at the Fleet, ranging from the relative comfort of the dilapidated houses of the Liberties outside the prison walls to the rank, putrid condition of the cellars. At least John had access to this window on the street. Or so she surmised.

She reached into the bag and withdrew a penny. The sentry had left and another was standing guard at the gate. He had his back turned, but he would hear if she screamed. She held the coin just out of the prisoner's reach.

"Will you bring him to me here? Tomorrow?"

"Maybe, if you can spare a coin for poor Tom Lasser." He nodded, grinning, but it was not a grin that purchased trust. He thrust the shallow tin bowl through the bars. She dropped the coin in. He pulled it back through the window, then frowned when he saw its value. "Either you are truly impoverished or you don't value your brother very highly."

"I will return tomorrow. If my brother is at this window, I will give him money, money enough to see to his needs—and share with another. He will not be ungrateful."

Without waiting for a further rejoinder she turned away. "Tomorrow morning," she said. She walked away to the sound of his laughter.

As she left the odor of the Fleet River behind her, she reminded herself not to be too hopeful, for what faith could be placed in the words of a felon and a rogue who was even now laughing at how desperate she was, how easily duped? But at least she had something to offer Mary when she reached the little shop in Paternoster Row where the windows were already glowing faintly in the clabbering twilight.

FOUR

Of Merry Margaret
As midsummer flower
Gentle as a falcon
Or hawk of the tower.
—FROM A FIFTEENTH-CENTURY
POEM BY JOHN SKELTON

he next morning Kate returned to the Common Side of Fleet
Prison and walked the gauntlet of barred windows along Farringdon Street.
She was almost light-headed with anticipation and anxiety as she tried to
ignore the obscene hoots and lecherous shouts and pleas for money. This
is what I have to do, she thought, and steeled herself to do it. But when she
reached the remembered window, one quick glance showed it and the one
beside to be occupied by other prisoners. She counted back in her mind. Yes,
this was the right window. The woman had been in the first one, closest to
the courtyard entrance, and the man in the other.

The same old snaggle-toothed watchman leaned against the iron post
of the gate. His eyes watched her warily as she considered how best to approach him.

"Yesterday there was a woman in the first cell. What happened to her?"
she asked.

"We change them out regular. To give everybody a chance."

Her heart skipped a little beat. "Do you mean to say that everybody gets a turn, then? How often do you change them?"

"Nay. I don't mean to say 'everybody gets a turn,'" he mocked. "Just the ones that pay for the privilege."

"But the woman—surely she was too poor to pay and she showed no interest in begging at the window. She would hardly take the coin I gave her."

"The prisoner in the cell next paid for her. Tom Lasser, I recollect. I tried to tell him 'twere a waste."

The black-haired thief? Kate wondered. He hardly seemed the kind to give charity . . . more the kind to steal it. Still, he was in the next cell. "What happened to him? Is he still here? May I see him? I think he knew . . ."

"Nay, mistress. He beint here. Some fancy-dressed lord bailed him out, like always."

"Bailed him out?" she asked. "But . . . how . . . ?"

"Paid surety for him."

"Do you know the man's name who bailed him out?"

"I can't remember his name. Big hulk of a man in satin knee breeches and furred doublet."

That was it then, she thought, feeling suddenly very tired. The late March wind whipped at her skirt, tightening it against her body and blowing back the hood of her mantle. The sentry leered. Kate pulled her mantle in and her hood back up on her head. She stepped back, widening the space between them. Why hadn't the scoundrel Tom whatever his name was told her John would have to pay to get to the window? She would have given him the money. It was probably all a lie anyway. He probably didn't even know her brother. She turned to leave, but a voice in her head held her back.

Raves in his sleep about a woman named Mary. And there was more. Something behind these forbidding walls pulled at her. She fancied she could feel John's despair weighing on her own heart. Or perhaps it was just the weight of so much communal misery seeping through the walls. Whichever, she turned back for one last try.

"I have reason to believe that my brother is here. If you would just let me in to take a look."

He coughed and loosed a string of spittle over his shoulder. "This stinking place is a hotbed of disease. No fit place for the likes of ye." His brow furrowed and his eyes bulged with this pronouncement. "Like I done told ye afore. There beint nobody here by the name of John Goll."

"Gough. John Gough," Kate said quietly. "It would be spelled *gh* on a list, but it is pronounced like an *f*," doubting that he could read, but hoping her own measured tone would settle his temper. "I know he's here. The man in the cell next to the woman described him to me. You said his name was Tom something. This same Tom said my brother is here. He is a tall, blond man. His features are somewhat like mine. Except he has blond hair where mine is dark. Same high forehead." She threw back the hood and swept back her hair with her hands so the watchman could see her features clearly.

He peered at her intently for what seemed like an eternity. "May be." He nodded. "Just may be. I do recollect—a quiet sort. His back all bruised and bleeding when they brought him in. Spent a week in the infirmary. Didn't have much to say for hisself. Not even after he healed up. Tom told me to put him on the list—'course he didn't pay enough to get him on the list, so I didn't."

Kate dug in the little leather purse tied at her waist just inside her cloak. She handed him a shilling with a question in her eyes. He looked at it and raised an eyebrow. She dug out two more.

The watchman slid the coins into his pocket so swiftly she hardly saw his hand move. "Come back tomorrow," he said. "Be here early. I can't vouch for the whole day."

⁓ ⁓

At first Kate wasn't sure.

She'd gotten up before dawn, restless, pacing as she waited for day to break. Finally, she'd put on her cloak and gone out into the darkness of the silent street, carrying a tallow-dip lantern. A light dawn mist settled rather than fell, fogging the streets so that her smoky lantern looked like a ghost-light bobbing along—had any soul been abroad at that hour to notice.

The prison was eerily quiet as she approached at first light, no street traffic except a lone ragpicker with his cart creaking down the lane on his way to a more lucrative street. Even the pigeons roosting on the rooftop still had their heads tucked beneath their wings. All the cells looked empty. Then suddenly, as though the walls had ears enough to hear her light footsteps, one or two prisoners began banging their shallow tin bowls against the window grills. She approached the second window gingerly and looked in, careful not to get too close lest one of the prisoners poke a skinny arm through and seize her.

She held up her lantern and peered into the cell's dim interior. A man sat on a pile of rags on the floor, his back resting against the wall, his head slumped forward between his knees. Greasy strands of pale hair half covered his face. But she wasn't sure. The damp fog had penetrated the cell though the open window. The shoulders, the head, so slumped in defeat, that was not John's proud posture at all.

"John?" she said, pressing her face against the cold iron of the bars. She might as well have been talking to a statue. "John, it's me. It's Kate."

The man raised his head. A face as pale as the dead ashes in the cell's cold firebox peered at her from the deep gloom. It was John's face—and not John's face. He was so gaunt and haggard she had to fight back tears. "Come to the window," she coaxed, trying not to startle him.

He shielded his eyes with his hand against the light, peering at her for a long moment as a man would look at an apparition.

"Kate?" he said softly, not moving.

"Yes, John. It's me. Kate. Come to the window so we can talk."

He stood up slowly and took a couple of steps forward, then hesitated as if uncertain what to do next.

"Come on, John. Come to the window so we can talk," she repeated softly.

"Kate?" he whispered. Then took another step. "My God, it really is you."

It was raspier, more tentative, but it was John's voice. Her cheeks were wet with tears. She brushed them hastily away. She did not want him to see her cry. He moved to the window and stuck his hands through the bars to seize her cloak as though he feared she might run away. "Thank God, Kate. I thought I'd never see you—see any of you—Mary and . . . ?" His voice broke. "Are they—"

She put the lantern on the window ledge where it rested precariously and reached through the bars to touch his face. "Mary's fine, John. Don't you worry, we're all fine. Pipkin too. He asks about you constantly. We just tell him his da's on a trip and will return soon. Mary's going to be delirious with happiness to hear we've found you."

The flame in the lamp was sputtering, its wick smoking. Forever after, Kate was to associate the smell of a dying wick with this moment, but now she scarcely noticed. The creeping dawn provided enough light for her to see his face.

Her fingers caressed an angry scab that had formed across his forehead . . . time enough later to ask about that. She ran her fingers down the line of his jaw. It was like touching her own face. "You are so thin. Don't they feed you?" she asked, trying to keep the rasp from her voice. He was too near the edge to see her break down.

"Maggoty porridge twice a day. It comes from the almshouses for those who have no money to pay for food."

"Will they let me bring you food?"

"I probably wouldn't get it. If you give them money, I'll be fed better, but give the money directly to the deputy warden."

She unclasped his hand from her cloak. "Let me go, so I can see to it straightaway. Can I bring you clothes?"

Even the ragpicker would have scorned the filthy remains of a shirt and trousers he was wearing.

"There's slim chance I'll get them unless you give them to me directly. If you bribe the turnkey, they'll let you visit me." His voice was stronger now, as though he were drawing some strength from her. "If you hurry, I might even still be here." He paused. "But Kate, don't bring my wife and boy. I don't want them to see me like this."

"I understand," Kate said. "When you've cleaned up a bit." A milk cart rolled by on Farringdon Street. Kate used the clip-clop of the dray horse that pulled it to cover her sniffing. "But I can't put Mary off very long, John. It wouldn't be right to make her wait after what she's been through."

He nodded. "Not long. Just one more day. To give me a chance to prepare. I don't want to frighten them. And if there's enough money—a straw mattress. But only if there's enough money."

The tears welled in the back of her eyes threatened to spill. "There's enough money, John. You'll have your mattress."

"They didn't close the shop then? I've been so worried about how the three of you would live. We spent so much on the inventory that we had to burn."

"They haven't been back since they arrested you. Mary has been tending the shop while I looked for you." Thank God, she thought, that the topic had turned to more mundane business matters. Maybe she could control her emotions now. "We sell enough to keep going, but there's much we need to talk about, John. We need some new way to distribute the books when we get new inventory. Do you think—"

His face turned hard, the blue vein standing out in protest, the scabbed welt crossing it in the shape of a cruciform. "New inventory? If you mean of the Lutheran sort, there can be no new inventory."

"But how can—"

"Gough's Book and Print Shop will no longer sell contraband books, Kate. Promise me." His hands started to shake violently.

"John, be calm. We are safe and we are careful. Don't worry. All will be well." How foolish of her to talk about such unimportant matters. "Let me go home and get some money—and tell Mary I've found you. You'll have a good meal and get some fresh clothes. Time enough to talk about the future later. Our first job is to get you out. At least they didn't lock you up in the Lollard Prison or execute you. That means you are just in here for a little while, right? There may be some fine we can pay. What is the charge?"

"There is no official charge."

"But surely . . . the law . . . surely they cannot keep you without due process."

He laughed bitterly, more a grunt than a laugh. "Thomas More and Cardinal Wolsey are the law of England now. They can do as they please."

"But—"

He dropped his gaze as he interrupted her. "I abjured, Kate."

"You confessed to heresy and recanted?" she said, not wanting to think about what they must have done to him.

"I confessed to nothing. But it's the same thing. I denied that I had any knowledge of the English Bibles or any sympathies with Luther, and promised that I would not print his or Tyndale's or any other Lutheran works." He looked up at her then, and she could read the shame in his eyes. "It's not just about me," he said.

It was a plea for understanding. And Kate wanted to understand. Who was she to judge him? Yet she felt a strange sense of loss, as though he'd somehow brought dishonor to their father's memory, as though his denial had been the act of a coward. Then she thought of Mary and the baby. John was right. It wasn't just about him.

"You did what you thought was best," she said.

"It's what we all have to do. There can be no turning back. Do you understand, Kate?" He squeezed her hand hard. "It'll be the fire next time."

She could not argue with him. Not after all he'd been through. "I understand, John." She reached up and touched the long horizontal scab running along his forehead, the forehead that was so much like her own. Her own flesh shuddered with the pain of it. "No contraband books will ever again be sold at Gough's Book and Print Shop," she said. "I promise. Now, let me go, so I can get you some food."

❦

By mid-May, John Gough's circumstances had improved. Kate had not only found money for a mattress, but she had scraped together enough—by selling everything they had that was portable—to get him released to the Liberty of the Fleet. It cost her dearly: the rent on one room in an old dilapidated mansion plus eight pence a day plus another twelve pence for a keeper who supposedly kept watch but never did. It wasn't necessary. She had put up the deed to their shop as surety that John would remain within the environs of the Liberty. It was what the old gaoler had meant by bail.

Once or twice in her comings and goings, she thought she glimpsed Tom Lasser going into one of the many taverns and stew houses that had grown up like mushrooms in the environs of the Liberty. But no, this man was well dressed and much too jolly to be in gaol. Yet on one occasion, he had turned his dark-eyed, mocking gaze toward her and she had thought she saw a flash of recognition. She had looked hastily away and blushed at the sound of his familiar laughter.

Though John's movements were restricted to the taverns and houses within the Liberty, he had a small but decently appointed room where he enjoyed what basic comforts Kate could afford. Every day Mary and the boy came to visit him, bringing him fresh food and clean linen. Sometimes Mary even stayed with him there. But without the print shop running and because of the prohibition against dealing in Lutheran materials, Kate faced a daily challenge to keep him in Liberty quarters. The rent was high—even for the ramshackle old great houses gone to seed. Mostly only wealthy merchants and nobility, who had had the ill fortune to fall into the Crown's disfavor, could afford it. More than one nobleman had found himself incarcerated in the Fleet after a visit to the Star Chamber.

John slowly gained his strength back but not his old spirit. Though he had always been a quiet sort, introspective and thoughtful, there was about him now a pensive melancholy. Oddly, she noticed it most in the presence of his wife and child. Like now. Mary, as she always did when she visited John, babbled on about nothing, as if her cheerfulness could somehow bring her husband back. John just sat beside her on the cot and stared out the door, which was open to the spring sunshine. The little boy sat on a blanket that Mary spread on the floor and played with the woodcut blocks that Kate had brought, thinking to spur her brother's interest. If she could spark him back to life, they might set up a makeshift press in one corner of the room—at least print some broadsheets they could sell.

John sat idly watching—without seeing—as the little boy banged the print blocks together like cymbals, squealing with delight at the dull thudding noise they made. Kate thought to take them away from him, lest such constant banging chip the woodcut. Such blocks, especially the finely detailed ones—and these two were finely detailed enough to pique any printer's interest—were expensive and these were the last ones John had ordered. He'd never even had a chance to use them. Kate stuck out her hand to take them away from the child and then withdrew it.

What did it matter? John had just stared listlessly when she showed them to him.

"See, John," she had said, "look at this one. It's an excellent piece of workmanship. You can see the wheat grains in the sheaf. And this one—each rosemary sprig. See—this one would make a fine frontispiece for an almanac and this one could illustrate a garden calendar. We could set up a simple press, and if you could print up a few broadsheets we could bind them and sell them in the shop. Or perhaps even sell them in the market, singly. A farthing for a sheet."

John had run his thumb along the finely carved wheat sheaf, then pushed them aside.

"There's not enough room here for a press," he said.

Kate bit back her observation that they'd better find room if he was going to continue to enjoy his quarters in the Liberty. Mary was pleading with her with eyes that seemed to say *Give him time, Kate. Don't bedevil him about this.*

But Kate didn't know how much time they had. They'd nothing left to sell except the presses and punches. Then without the tools of the trade how would he ever make a living for his family?

⁓≫≪⁓

By the time summer came, Kate was desperate. They'd sold all their remaining stock, and there were no funds to buy more. John continued to languish in the Liberty and had fallen into such a depression that he no longer even seemed aware of their struggle to keep him there. It was still early in the day, plenty of light streaming through the windows, when she decided to set up the press herself in the back of the print shop. How hard could it be? She'd watched John do it often enough, even helped him set the forms once or twice when the work was backed up.

The trick was to start with something simple. She cast around for something short and chose one page from a book of poetry, one of the three or four volumes of inventory they had left. She picked out four lines of a love poem to a woman named Margaret by John Skelton—four short lines. Margaret was a common enough name, and surely any love-smitten swain with a yen for a woman named Margaret could vouchsafe a farthing for a pretty page to impress his love.

Then she sat down at the type case and went to work, picking out the letters, arranging lines of text on a handheld composing stick, and wedging the composed text into a metal frame along with a random border of twining ivy. She stood back and admired her finished work, a perfect mirror image of the pretty little poem. That wasn't so hard.

The next part would be trickier, but she remembered John instructing her journeyman suitor, and if that lazy, fickle, no-account ne'er-do-well could do it, surely she could. It might take a couple of practice runs, and it looked to be a messy job that she did not relish. John never splattered a drop, but maybe she should put on the printer's apron.

She picked up the composed form and carried it over to the hulking wooden press in the corner. "Here, feed on this dainty little morsel, you big, wooden monster," she said, as with some difficulty and much heavy breathing she wedged the form onto the press bed. The next step she knew was to ink it with the big leather-padded daubs from a large jar of ink sitting at the base of the press. But how much ink? She stirred the ink, which had glopped during John's absence. How much turpentine to add? She poured in a bit, stirred, poured a bit more, then began to mop the leather pad. A few drops splashed, then a few more, then a glob. She should have folded the paper over the form before she'd started with the ink—next time she would know—she thought as she wiped her forehead with the crook of one arm and struggled to clamp the sheet of damp paper into the holder; it always looked so easy when John did it. She slid the entire apparatus under the plate—the "platen" John called it—and shutting her eyes lowered the plate to press it against the inked form.

The result was a blotched and smeared waste of paper.

She crumpled it in a ball with a hearty "Damnation!" and began the whole process again. A couple of hours later, and after a few attempts, one thing was becoming clear: she was not nor would ever be a printer. There was only one thing left to do. She had to somehow secure his release if they were going to hold on to the shop.

She was still fighting back tears, still cleaning up ink splatters, when the bell tinkled in the bookshop. It should have been a welcome sound, but who needed custom without inventory? She sighed heavily and, wiping the sweat from her forehead, went to answer the bell.

FIVE

*I have borne a long time with thy husband . . . and
given to him my poor fatherly counsel, but I perceive
none of all this able to call him home; and therefore,
Meggie, I will no longer argue nor dispute with him.*
——Sir Thomas More to
his daughter Margaret concerning
William Roper's Heresy

y the time Kate entered the bookshop in the front room, the bell
jingled for the second time. She drew her stained apron over her head, flung
it toward the peg by the door, and lifted the latch just enough to peek at the
woman standing there. She was a young woman of about Kate's own age.
Clearly nobility from the looks of her—richly dressed, her face framed by
a heart-shaped cap edged with seed pearls—but not a beautiful woman, not
even a very pretty one. Her nose was too big and her brows a trifle ragged,
and her eyes were too wide set in her face for perfect symmetry. But those
wide-set eyes carried an intelligent gleam, and she bore herself with the
grace and self-confidence that only a plain woman of the upper class could
master. She was perfectly groomed. Kate's hand went self-consciously to pat
at her own disheveled mop.

"I'm sorry, my lady, the bookshop is temporarily closed for restocking.
Our inventory is pitifully low," Kate said as she made to shut the door in her
customer's face.

The woman put a gloved hand on the door and shoved gently. "Then I've come at an opportune time," she said. "For it is not the bookseller I seek, but the printer."

"As I told you, we are closed. My brother is the printer. And he's not here."

"Oh, I thought—" She glanced meaningfully at Kate's ink-stained clothing.

"I was just cleaning up the press."

"Well, when will your brother return?"

"I can't say."

"Then I think I shall wait for him a while," the woman said, maintaining her regal position. She crossed the room and settled herself onto the lone chair. "Don't let me keep you from your work," she said and gave an imperious wave of her hand.

It was accompanied by a smile and an "if it suits," but the gesture irritated Kate. How could she say, *No, it does not suit,* without being unforgivably churlish to her betters? So what she said was, "Then it may be a long wait, my lady. The printer is in gaol."

A look of shock at such a blunt declaration was quickly replaced by genuine distress. "Oh my dear. I am verily sorry." The honest sympathy in this strange woman's face, together with Kate's disastrous afternoon's adventure with the printing press, undid her, and before she knew it, tears were spilling down her cheeks and ill-considered words out of her mouth.

"It's not right," she declared, swiping at a tear. "The legal system is a travesty—Wolsey, More, the whole lot of them, the Church and the king's lawyers all acting as though they are the law of England. They talk of righteousness and virtue while they destroy the lives of those with whom they disagree."

She would have been wise to notice the hardening aspect of her would-be customer's face, but she was too upset.

"And the king's chief councillor, Sir Thomas More—I have but to mention the man's name in my brother's presence, and he starts to tremble. He's the worst of the lot. A pious hypocrite, who delights in the pain of others."

Kate was surprised at the vehemence of her diatribe. Her brother had never mentioned Sir Thomas by name—or any of his interrogators. But once, when she'd suggested that they try to appeal to the powerful Thomas More for intervention, John had grown pale and agitated and would not settle down until he'd extracted a promise from her that she would not seek him out.

"I understand your distress," the woman said with somewhat less sympathy in her voice, "but you are wrong. If your brother is truly innocent he will be released. It is only a matter of time. Once they hear—"

"Time, you say. We have no time! And how can they hear, if they won't listen! I've been to them all—turned away too many times to count by the bishop and the lord mayor. I'd even approach Sir Thomas More myself if I could afford the bribe. You don't understand, Lady—"

"Margaret." Her visitor's voice had chilled, her earlier compassion frozen. "Margaret Roper. Mistress William Roper—daughter of Sir Thomas More."

Kate wanted the floor to open up and swallow her. Now she'd done it. Gone and made everything worse. John would never get out of prison. That remark about the bribe. Dear God, if she could only call it back.

"I'm sorry, my lady. I should not have spoken so bluntly," Kate stammered. "I did not mean to offer insult. I should have kept my opinions to myself."

"So then you are merely sorry for the words and not the sentiment."

"I would be less than honest to proclaim other than what my heart and reason teach. That would be equally an insult to my lady."

Mistress Roper's mouth twitched at the corner, an almost smile. "Well said. I admire honesty. And I shall repay the compliment by being likewise honest with you. You know that it is a sin to repeat idle gossip offered up by those jealous of another's good fortune. All of England knows of my father's greatness."

"I do not deny he is a 'great' man, if greatness is defined by power. He hath the king's and the cardinal's private ear. But if as our Lord teaches, true greatness is to be found in compassion, then his reputation suffers in some quarters."

Mistress Roper got up from her chair and moved with a swish of her finely woven skirts to the window. Kate's gaze followed hers out to the street to where a liveried servant waited, holding a gray palfrey by the reins. Kate felt relief that the woman was leaving, but then she turned back toward Kate, apparently unwilling to let it lie.

"It might inform your opinion to know of the many good works for which my father is known. I have just now come from the poorhouse Sir Thomas keeps. Twice weekly, I make the trip down the Thames from Chelsea in a boat laden with food and healthful potions for the inhabitants there. Foodstuffs from my father's own storehouse. Physics from his own apothecary."

It occurred to Kate that Thomas More must be a man of some vestige of goodness, to inspire such love in his daughter that she was bent on securing the good opinion of one who mattered so little. Kate was about to apologize for speaking so bluntly when her memory conjured John's hollow face and haunted look, and she could not stop her tongue.

"Charity is a necessary thing in a great man. Sir Thomas is a man of public virtue."

She could tell by the flash of irritation on Mistress Roper's face that she caught the implication of those words, but she recovered quickly.

"I was returning from a *private* errand to this almshouse, when I decided to stop in Paternoster Row. I am a great lover of books. My father sees that all his daughters receive a classical education, even his wards. As a bookseller, surely you appreciate the value of that." She paused to see if this had any softening effect. Kate remained silent. "I saw your printer's sign, and as I am in need of a printer's services, I thought I should stop in."

A likely story, Kate thought. She knew Sir Thomas's works were printed by his brother-in-law Rastell. The woman was probably spying for her father.

When she said nothing Margaret Roper continued. "You may be wondering why I did not go to our usual printer. But this is mine own translation, and I wanted to surprise my father with it. Your shop would have been very convenient, since I pass so close by . . . twice weekly."

Her voice rose slightly on the *twice weekly*. As if to remind again of Sir Thomas's charity.

"I'm sorry we cannot claim the custom of so noble a house, Lady Margaret, but as you see we are practically out of business." She made a sweeping gesture with her hands to indicate the empty shelves. "There is a printer on the other side of St. Paul's. He can probably help you."

"I'm sorry too," Mistress Roper said, moving to the door. "But perhaps I can help you in another way."

Why would you want to help us? Kate wondered. *What are we to you?* But she had the good sense to stay silent. She thought she knew why. Kate had challenged the perception of her father's greatness. Mistress William Roper *née* More could not let that go unanswered—both for love and argument's sake.

She was standing at the door, her back to Kate, fingering the door latch. "What are the charges against your brother?" She turned around to face Kate.

"There are no charges. He was arrested under suspicion of disseminating Lutheran materials."

"Does he disseminate Lutheran materials?"

"They found no evidence either on his person or in this shop to support such a charge. None gave witness against him. He made no confession even under torture. He is being held without due process in the Liberty of the Fleet where his wife and I battle poverty to ensure he has a minimum of creature comforts."

"Does he have Lutheran sympathies?"

Mistress Roper was not a lawyer's daughter for naught. Kate paused, weighing her answers carefully.

"My lady, no person can know another's heart. His testimony is a matter of public record."

"I see. And what of you? Do you have Lutheran sympathies?"

Kate hesitated and looked her interrogator directly in the eyes, so there could be no mistaking her answer. "I have promised my brother we will never sell Lutheran materials in this shop. Whatever my opinions are regarding reform or any other matter are mine alone, and I choose to keep them to myself."

Lady Margaret smiled faintly. "A politic answer and one my own father would admire. I do understand the lure of such sentiments. They have infected our own household. My own dear husband has been seduced by the Lutheran zeal for reform."

"And yet he remains a free man."

Lady Margaret nodded as if to say, I take your point. "I will speak to my father and see what benefit to you and your brother may be gleaned. What is your brother's name again?"

"Gough. John."

"And your name?"

Kate hesitated just a fraction of a second, a hesitation that she was sure did not go unmarked by Lady Margaret. But what choice did she have? And there was compassion in the woman's demeanor. She could hardly be faulted for loving her father. Perhaps she could use her influence to make her point whilst at the same time doing "a good work."

"Kate Gough," she said, curtsying lightly. "My lady, we will be forever grateful for your kindness."

"I will do that which I can do, Kate Gough," she said, "and I shall pray that both you and your brother find your way back to the bosom of the one, true Church."

The next day Kate returned from visiting her brother to find the latch bent, the front door to the bookshop open, and the printing press smashed.

Three days later John came home.

❧ ❦ ❧

Kate was disappointed when John did not come back to the shop immediately but stayed at home with his wife and child. He just needs a few days to rest, she told herself. But when she told him about the destruction of the press, his reaction was not what she'd expected. He'd seemed numb to any emotion, even anger.

"It is a warning," he said. "We shall heed it."

"But how shall we print without a press? And since you burned all our inventory, what shall we sell?"

"Nothing for a while, I think. It is not a good time to be a printer in England. We can print nothing that is not licensed by the king, and he will never grant a license to the kind of books that have been our stock-in-trade."

They were sitting in John and Mary's daub-and-wattle cottage, sparsely furnished now, with little more than a bed and a table. They had sold the cupboard and most of the plate, even sold the wall hanging that had been a wedding gift from Mary's parents—sold it all to keep John in the Liberty. The rent on the roof over their heads was due and they could not pay.

"How shall we live, John, without the press? Shall we sell Pipkin's cradle next? Are the four of us to live crammed into my tiny room above the shop? Of course, without a press, I suppose we could set up a bed in the print shop," she said wryly. "But we still have to buy food."

She regretted almost instantly the remark about the cradle, but at least it brought some fleeting expression to his face. Pain was after all better than feeling nothing, wasn't it?

He did not look at his wife or at her when he answered, just stared at the floor in that habit he'd acquired in prison. "Mary's father has offered to let us come and live with them in Gloucestershire."

He did not even say *until the trouble passes*, or *for the time being*. His voice was weighed down with resignation. Kate felt a sudden surge of fear, as though she were watching some fast-flowing stream carry him away from her, and he wasn't even struggling. "You mean close our father's shop?" she whispered in disbelief. "Permanently? Move to Gloucestershire and . . . do what?"

Mary, who had been bouncing her restless son on her knees, set him on the floor and put her arm across her husband's shoulders in a protective fashion. "It will only be for a little while, Kate. Gloucestershire is really pretty country. And there's not all the fighting over religion there. Not a bishop within a hundred miles. It smells better than London too. Lots of fresh air for Pipkin. You are to come with us. My parents have plenty of room. They bade me tell you to come. John is going to help my father. His back's been poorly."

Before Kate could stop herself, she blurted out, "John? Herding sheep!" The look of pleading in Mary's face made her instantly regret the words. "I suppose the fresh air will be good for him," she added lamely.

"Good. It's settled then." Mary gave them her bravest smile. "You're coming with us?"

Kate shook her head, unable to quite believe what she'd just heard. "That is very dear of your parents, Mary. But I think I'll stay right here for a while and watch the shop. I have a bit of money still and one or two things left I can sell. I can at least make it through the summer. Who knows what may happen by then?"

"But you will come for a visit? Tell her she must come for a visit, John."

John raised his head and looked at her. The deadness in his eyes frightened her. "You must come for a visit," he said.

❧

It turned out that the only thing Kate had left to sell was the Wycliffe Bible that had been passed down to her from her great-grandmother Rebecca. She had never known her grandmother Becky, but even as a child she'd loved the big Bible, loved the way the words with their funny spellings crawled across the crowded pages, loved the little pictures in the margins. It was not like the books the printing presses turned out. This one was all written out by hand, supposedly by some long-ago relative, an illuminator who lived in Bohemia over a hundred years ago.

On the July morning that John and Mary and little Pipkin, who held on to her and could only be pried away with the promise of a lamb, departed, Kate took the Bible out from its special hiding place beneath a loose stone in the hearth. Who would buy such a thing? she thought as she removed the linen wrappings and rubbed her hand over its tooled leather binding. Few could afford it. Who would dare take the risk of owning it in such perilous times?

She opened it carefully, remembering how her father used to show it to her with such pride before he was arrested, how her mother could no longer bear to see it after he died. It opened to a brightly illustrated picture of the baby Moses floating down a blue Nile River in his little basket. Everything was in miniature—his perfect baby's face, each rib of the basket so perfectly executed she could almost feel the texture of the reed—and all within the intricate capital that swirled and swooped in brilliant reds and blues and a tracing of gold down the margin of the page. The face of Miriam, his sister, peered into the basket at the child. That long-ago artist had captured in her expression the love she must have felt for her baby brother. It was a beautiful face. Kate wondered about the model. She looked so different from the women Kate knew—exotic somehow, with a fall of dark hair and almond-shaped eyes and tawny skin that glowed.

How could she could bring herself to sell such a book?

She sat for a long time on the cool stones of the hearth, tears pooling in the wells of her eyes. She thought of Pipkin and his little lamb and how she should have gone with them but knowing that she could not for she would surely wither like a flower in winter without her books or literate companions, with only Pipkin and his little lamb for company—and the worst part: she would be existing on the charity of others. She was turning the pages absently, no longer absorbed in the parade of colors but mired in her own gray loneliness, when she came to a folded piece of parchment interleaved and stuck so tightly that she thought at first it might have been bound with the text. She tugged gently and it came away.

She wiped her eyes, her little wallow in the slough of self-pity momentarily banished by her curiosity. She unfolded the yellowed parchment and squinted to make out the faded ink. No brilliant pigments here but just a few words written in the familiar hand of the rest of the Bible and centered like a poem in the middle of the page.

My dearest Anna, please hold these words in your heart until you believe them: "All shall be well and all manner of thing shall be well. For this is the great deed that our Lord shall do, in which He shall save His Word in all things—He shall make well all that is not well." These are the words of a holy woman I once knew. Now that I am an old man I understand them better—though not completely. I spent so many years grieving that I sometimes overlooked the treasure that I had been given in you. I hope one day you will understand these words too. I hope you know that I have always loved you. You were the fulfillment of this promise in my life.—Your loving grandfather, Finn.

Anna squinted at the date: *14 June 1412*—over one hundred years ago. She had a sudden curiosity about this Anna. Had she found all things well? Had she even found the note? They had certainly never found it in all the years they'd had the Bible. Had it lain, hidden for over a century, perhaps a message to her and not to the Anna for whom it was intended?

In which He shall save His Word in all things, the note had said. What would John make of it? Would he see the reference to the "Word" as affirmation, or would he read it as condemnation? He had certainly been carrying out the family tradition of helping save the Word—at least until recently. Or did the "Word" refer to some promise that had more to do with the hope that was carried in the Word than the actual preserving of the Scriptures? It was a cryptic message—hard to decipher without knowing the writer and his Anna, this ancestor who might have been bone of her bone, flesh of her flesh.

She wrapped the great Bible back up and hid it beneath the hearth, then placed a big iron pot over the loose stone. She placed the note there, too, but separate from the Bible; even if she sold the Bible, she would keep the note. It was like a gift from the past to give her courage. "All will be well," she repeated, and then, "He will make all things well." But Kate needed hope now, not when she was old. She needed money and she needed somebody to love and be loved by. If He was going to make all things well now would be a good time to start.

The only place she knew to make discreet inquiries about selling the Bible was down on the docks. John had often had dealings with a man named Humphrey Monmouth of the Merchant Adventurers League. He would know where she could sell the Bible. There was still light enough to go there and be back before dusk.

At least it wouldn't hurt to ask.

SIX

A purgatory! There is no one only, there are two. The first is the Word of God, the second is the Cross of Christ: I do not mean the cross of wood, but the cross of tribulation. But the lives of papists are so wicked that they have invented a third.
—JOHN FRITH IN RESPONSE TO THOMAS MORE'S WRITINGS ON THE DOCTRINE OF PURGATORY

on't stir, Alice," Sir Thomas More said to his sleeping wife. "Cook will give me a cold biscuit and a cup of tepid milk."

Dame Alice didn't stir. He slapped the bulky mound of his wife's hip underneath the linen coverlet.

"What's it? Thomas—"

Her scowl was not something every man would want to wake up to.

It was Tuesday—one of the four days that the king's council met each week. Thomas More had risen early, before his household was astir, and gone outside to summon a waterman to convey him downriver to Westminster. The cool morning air caressed his face. The summer had been an unusually hot one, and he was not looking forward to leaving his Chelsea paradise for sickness-infested London—not even for the grandeur that was Westminster Hall. Reluctantly, he'd gone back inside to collect his papers and bid his wife good-bye.

"I said, Alice, no need to make a fuss that your lord and master is going off to labor for your bread."

She opened one eye only. "The only thing laboring will be your stomach at His Majesty's board, I'll wager."

Thomas sighed. Tongue like an adder and not even fully awakened. One had to admire such a supple if biting wit, he supposed. In a great beauty one might even tolerate it amiably. But Alice was no beauty by any stretch of a man's imagination and hardly young, older than he by some years and not overly inclined to intellectual pursuit. Yet in spite of those shortcomings, she was a suitable enough wife. Laying her scolding tongue aside, she supported him in his ambition, and she knew how to run the house of a great man. The servants held her in greater respect than they did him. In matters at Chelsea her word was law.

Besides, if she had been a winsome maid with soft thighs and milk-white skin and shining hair—he squeezed his shoulder blades beneath the hair shirt—how could he ever do enough penance for his carnal thoughts, let alone his pleasure?

His wife raised her head from the pillow, her nightcap as askew as the drunken judge's cap whose case was on today's docket. He suppressed a laugh. One ridiculed Dame Alice at one's peril. She opened both eyes and locked her cloudy blue gaze onto his as he bent to plant a dutiful kiss on her forehead.

"You'd best tell me now if you'll be bringing anybody back like that Dutchman you're so fond of or that portrait painter."

"Would that I could bring Erasmus back. Or even Holbein. They would offer intellectual diversion. Everybody who can walk has fled London because of the sweating sickness. I'm afraid, dear wife, you'll have to be content with my poor company."

She sat bolt upright in the bed, eyes wide with outrage. "You're a fool, Thomas More. Did you just hear what words came out of your mouth? All of London is fleeing, and here you go tearing hell-for-leather right into the heart of pestilence so that you can bring it back like some proud gift to your family."

"Take care, Mistress More, that you do not o'erstep your bounds," he said, shrugging into his surcoat. His tolerance of her harping mood wore thin whenever she questioned his familial devotion. He did everything for his family. "A man must do his duty whether it is convenient or not," he said. "Besides, what pestilence could thrive on that acid tongue of yours?"

She lay back down and pulled the sheet up to her chin. "You're a great one for duty. I'll give you that," but it did not sound like a compliment. "Go off with you, then. Have it your own stubborn way. When have you not? Your duty and your legal reckonings and ciphers may be important, but I'd not put too much faith in them. In the end it's people that count."

"My legal reckonings and ciphers have served you well enough, my lady. I'll not put my faith in people." He reached for his favorite hat. "The king whose favor we currently enjoy would not hesitate to put my head on the block if he thought one castle could be gained by it. No. I'll put my faith in the law. It is not fickle. You should do likewise."

He sighed, wearying of this verbal sparring that had become their language.

"I'll try to return before bedtime," he said.

"Ever the dutiful husband," she muttered, as turning on her side, she pulled the sheet over her head.

❦

Thomas noticed, as he entered the first of the eight rooms that must be navigated on the way to Westminster Hall's Star Chamber, that the usual traffic was absent. He had grown accustomed now to the rich furnishings, the tapestries, gold candlesticks and sconces, the gilded ceilings, even the star-studded ceiling of the aptly named Star Chamber where the council met, but they looked grander emptied of their human detritus. When he opened the door to that great legal chamber, he was somewhat taken aback. This room, more sumptuous than the others in its rich tapestries and gilded ornaments, was empty.

Except for Wolsey. He sat alone in the center, ensconced upon the chancellor's woolsack, his scarlet cardinal's robes spread out like a courtesan's skirts. The scowl on his face gave him the look of a giant red toad, a giant red toad who held an orange pomander ball to his nose to ward off the sickness that he was sure was about to enter the room. When he saw it was only Thomas, the scowl gave way to a half-smile, and he put down the clove-studded orange. Its spiced fragrance competed with the herbs scattered on the floor, weighting the stale air of the closed chamber with a cloying odor.

"Thomas," the cardinal said in the tone that he used when especially gratified by some fortuitous turn of event. "It appears others are not as conscientious as you and I. We have no quorum so I've cleared the dockets. The sergeant at arms has sent all the supplicants and prosecutors back to their respective dunghills. They will not spread their infection here. I did not send a messenger because I knew you would be already in route, and besides, I wanted to see you."

He heaved himself up from the woolsack and went over to the table where the writs were usually processed. "Take a seat, Thomas," he said affably—he could be jovial when his temper was not raised, or when it suited his purpose—"there is a small matter I would discuss with you."

Thomas steeled himself against what he knew was coming: a request for his intervention in the king's "great matter." The cardinal sat down heavily across the table from him.

"Concerning the king's divorce from Queen Katherine, Thomas, His Majesty is bothered that you do not join your voice to his cause. And I would like your opinion as well." He said it lightly, as though the subject had never been broached between them and they were only engaged in an afternoon's gossip. Thomas knew a trap when he saw one. If he said he thought the king should have his divorce, then his recruitment to that cause would be taken for granted. If he said he thought it a sin to put aside a wife of twenty years in favor of—well, that way certainly was perilous.

"I have no opinion, Eminence, other than a legal opinion." Thomas sighed. "And that you already know."

"A careful answer. But so there can be no misunderstanding between us," Wolsey snapped, all joviality gone, "give me your legal opinion once again, now that we are alone, just the two of us."

"The fact that you and I are discussing this in seeming privacy does not change my answer. It is not lawful for King Henry to divorce the queen and marry Anne Boleyn unless the pope grants dispensation."

Wolsey considered quietly, forming his full lips into a pout. "That is not helpful, Thomas," he muttered almost as to himself. "There are many forces against this king. I have heard even of a holy nun from Kent who prophesied that if the king divorces the queen, he will die and his kingdom will come to ruin. Have you heard this, Thomas?"

"I have heard somewhat of that. It is women's gossip. I take no stock in such ravings."

"Wise, Thomas. That is wise."

Sweat beads adorned the cardinal's upper lip. It was a warm day to be clothed in cardinal's robes and a sable scarf, but Thomas figured Wolsey would sweat on a mid-winter's day clad only in his shirt—if the question of the king's great matter came up. All Wolsey's attempts to petition the pope had been in vain. Henry's Spanish queen was very well connected—better connected than the great English cardinal and chancellor, apparently.

The cardinal wiped his brow with a silk handkerchief. "You are not quite off the hook yet, Thomas. I have another matter that requires your legal opinion. And as you are steward of Cardinal College at Oxford this matter imputes to you a professional interest."

Well, at least this was safer ground, Thomas thought.

"A bit of a problem has arisen with some of the students, some of the scholars who have fallen under the Lutheran influence. Have you been informed of that?"

"I've heard somewhat about it," Thomas said. "But I thought all that was put to rest back in the spring with the bookseller Garrett's arrest. I assumed the students were disciplined and made to see the error of their ways."

Wolsey heaved himself up and began a slow pacing, his full robes swishing on the floor. "They were disciplined. Therein lies the conundrum. As to seeing the error of their ways, that's an entirely different matter altogether. Do you know a student by name of John Frith?"

Thomas shook his head. He really didn't have much to do with the day-to-day affairs of Oxford, though his title carried a good stipend.

Wolsey sank down onto the woolsack and stared into the middle distance, past Thomas. "He's a brilliant young scholar. Ironic, isn't it, Thomas, that some of the brightest Cambridge students that I recruited to seed my new college at Oxford, now repay me with these little intellectual excursions into heresy? You will hear of young Frith, you may mark it, if he's still alive."

"What do you mean, 'if he's still alive'?"

"It seems in disciplining them Dean Higdon may have gone a bit further than was prudent."

"How so?"

"He locked Frith and four or five others in a cellar beneath the college."

"Well—I suppose that was within his powers of discretion. They are students—"

"For three months."

"Three months!" Thomas repeated the words to make sure he'd heard the chancellor aright. "Without due process? Without even a hearing? Eminence, I'm surprised you would allow—"

"I did not allow it, Master More. They were apparently forgotten about."

"What are the conditions in the cellar?"

"Not good. I'm told it is used for storing salted fish. Not a very pleasant place."

"Let them out immediately," Thomas said.

"It's not that simple, I'm afraid." The cardinal twisted the large seal ring on his fat sausage finger. "A couple of them have died. Probably of the sweating sickness, but . . ."

Thomas's mind began to whirl. This was stupidity on the part of both the college and the cardinal, but it was a stupidity that would accrue to his reputation since he was steward of the college.

"Tell Dean Higdon to notify their families immediately," he said. "Express sympathy that they have died. And say because of the contagion within the city, their bodies have already been buried and the college will pay for the families to visit the gravesites et cetera, et cetera. Say nothing about the conditions under which they died."

"What about the others?"

"Release them immediately."

"But surely they will shout it abroad that they were unlawfully imprisoned and ill-used."

"How many are still alive?"

"Two or three, I think."

"Two or three? Which is it?"

The cardinal lowered his head like a ram about to charge, warning Thomas that his tone was offensive. His lips barely moved as he said, "Frith and Betts and I can't remember the name of the other one."

Thomas looked away. One did not interrogate the chancellor of England in the same tone one took with a common criminal at the bar, he reminded himself. "Be reassured, Your Eminence. This is manageable," he said with soothing tones.

"I was sure we could count on you for this at least," Wolsey said, pursing his lips.

Thomas ignored the barb. "These students have not only broken the law of the school but they have broken the law of the land. For this latter they shall have their due process: official interrogation and then a charge of heresy. When the law is done with them, they'll be in no condition to shout anything abroad. I can virtually guarantee they will be begging to kiss the pope's jeweled slippers."

"All done within the law?"

"Always within the law, Eminence."

Wolsey smiled. "Your reassurance has given me an appetite," he said, the joviality returned. "The king has invited us to dine in his chamber."

Thomas hesitated, wondering if he dared offer an excuse.

"You do not need to look so uncomfortable, Sir Thomas. He will not broach the subject of the divorce with you—not in company. Sounding you out and persuading you to our side on that matter is my job."

"Your Eminence—"

"Say no more," Wolsey said, holding up his hand, "lest I feel my temper rise. And that might interfere with my digestion. You would not want that on your conscience now, would you?"

"Not for all the world," Thomas said, smiling, "for that would interfere with mine."

⁓ ⁙ ⁓

Kate was glad as she approached the merchants' hall that she had decided against taking the Wycliffe Bible with her. Such a large parcel would attract the curious—and besides, it was heavy. It was a very hot day. The sweat was already running down between her breasts and the crease between her shoulder blades. If Monmouth wanted to buy the Bible from her, surely he wouldn't mind stopping in at the bookshop—former bookshop, she thought wryly—to pick it up. But when she inquired at the guildhall, the sergeant at arms told her that Sir Humphrey was probably down at the docks.

She paused the briefest moment to consider whether or not it was prudent to go down to the docks alone. Shielding her eyes against the sun that glinted off the Thames, she glanced in the direction of the crates and barrels and sacks piled up dockside. Only one or two men labored in the noon heat, unloading what looked like grain sacks, and they were too busy and wilted to pay her any attention. In the distance she saw Sir Humphrey. She recognized him by his fancy clothes, though in the heat he looked more hot than splendid. Poor man. Kate had seen him twice before when he'd come to speak to John. His wife had come with him once and she'd been likewise absurdly overdressed. From what Kate remembered of the wife's manner, Sir Humphrey probably thought it easier to go about in heavy leggings and padded doublet during the height of summer than to incur his wife's sharp tongue.

Sir Humphrey was coming from the direction of the lone ship docked in the sun-sparked river. Above his large lace collar his face wore an expression of intense satisfaction. He was perusing a small book. He smiled broadly, then quickly secreted the book inside his voluminous doublet, causing her to wonder if perhaps his extravagant dress served another purpose than to please his wife.

Kate Gough, you're a fool! Here was a man who imported Bibles. Why would he need another? What was it exactly that she was going to say to him, anyway? It would have been better to write him a note asking him to come to the shop. She had decided that she would go back and ask the sergeant at arms if she might leave him a message when he called her name.

"Mistress Gough," he said, his calves bulging in their peacock-blue stockings as he hurried toward her, waving. "What news of John?"

"He is out of prison," Kate said, and then added, not knowing what else to say, "but he is not himself."

"Give him time," he said, "I myself have some knowledge of what kind of fear that sparks in a man's soul. The great Thomas More himself searched my house. Fortunately, like John, I got enough warning to burn the damning evidence." He shook his head, clucking his tongue. "I heard some of Garrett's clients at Oxford were caught in the sweep and some even died of the sweating sickness while they were shut up like criminals in a stinking cellar. I guess John and I have been spared to continue the fight."

Kate felt the heat from the sun intently and longed to be away, not wanting to say that John had no fight left in him. "Yes, I suppose so . . ."

"Is there anything you need, Mistress Gough? With John in gaol so long you may be pressed for resources. I know he has a wife and child too . . ." He reached into his doublet and withdrew a small leather purse.

She shook her head at his offer of charity. "We will survive. We still have a few things to sell." She took a deep breath. Here was her chance. "Indeed, Sir Humphrey, I have something in which you might be interested. It is a family heirloom. An illuminated Bible." She lowered her voice, even though now the two lone dockworkers appeared to have deserted in search of shade. "A Wycliffe translation. I thought—"

The expression on his face stopped her cold. "But, of course, how foolish of me," she said. "If Thomas More came back, that's the last thing you would want displayed with your prized possessions. I'm sorry to—"

"It is likewise dangerous for you. I'm surprised that John would allow . . ."

"He tried to burn it with the rest. I stopped him. It seemed such a shame. It is so beautiful, and it is well hidden."

He paused only a moment. "How much?" he said, and she caught a glimpse of the merchant negotiator.

"Ten pounds."

He whistled softly. "You hold it very dear!"

"I know that you could buy a Tyndale translation for pence on the pound, but this is a Bible for the ages. I am sure if you saw it——"

He chuckled lightly. "You should be bargaining for Hansa, Mistress Kate." He smiled at her, a warm, sincere smile above his little pointy gray beard. "I will come by the shop tomorrow and take a look at it."

❧

John Frith woke from a drugged sleep to the image of a severe-looking nun of advanced years hovering over him. The broad face held a clucking tongue and a mouth that moved. "Stay still if ye don't want yer throat cut."

He froze, trying to still even the twitching muscle on his eyelid while she ran the razor's honed edge down his jawbone. As he achieved full consciousness, he realized he no longer lay on the earthen floor of the cellar but on a straw mattress with a reasonably clean woolen blanket over him. He realized, too, with something of a start that underneath that blanket he was naked.

"Where am I, Sister?" he asked when she paused to flick away his scruffy beard from the blade. He gripped the sheet covering him with all his strength, surprised to find that he could. And not only could he grip the blanket, he could tuck it under his armpits and hold it there with purpose.

"This be St. Bart's Hospital. Since ye've decided to open yer eyes and have a look around, I'm thinking ye'll probably survive. It looked unlikely when they brought ye in last week looking more dead than alive. Since I saw some sign of life this morn I thought ye might like a shave. Now I'm thinking it's some real food ye may be wanting more."

"A glass of water?"

She gave a rueful laugh. "Ye're a great one for water. Ye've drunk enough to drink the Fleet River dry since ye've been in here. And peed almost as much."

His face grew hot but he hugged his blanket more tightly beneath his armpits. She poured a beaker of water from a pitcher beside his bed and handed it to him. "When we've finished here, I'll send somebody from the kitchen down with some broth and calf's foot jelly, but best go easy on it."

He took a swallow of water and let it linger on his tongue. He finished off the glass and set it down. She resumed shaving him.

"It be yer great good fortune that ye were too sick to take to the Lollard Tower with the others."

"What possible difference could that make to the pap—to my tormen-tors?" he asked.

"They want ye alive—to abjure. Like the others."

Frith made no retort—just closed his eyes. The twitch had died on its own—probably from fatigue.

Abjure, he thought, knowing full well what instruments of torture were used on his friends to solicit such repentance, knowing, too, that one misstep after a public abjuration was an automatic sentence of burning without trial. If others had abjured, he was sure to be no better than they, no braver than they. His only chance was to escape.

The nun had finished shaving him. She arched her neck back and turned her full scrutiny on him. "There now! Well. That's better. Ye look almost like a man again. And, once those hollows fill out under those cheekbones, a man not ill-favored, I'd say. Not ill-favored at all."

She cleaned the blade and put it back into the little leather case hanging at her belt beside her rosary. "'Twould be a shame to lose such a handsome head in the cause of heresy." She stood and picked up the basin with the remnants of his foul beard floating in the soapy water. "A real shame. They say ye are a brilliant young scholar." That clucking tongue went back into action. "I don't see how a brilliant man can poke his finger in the eye of Al-mighty God."

"But it's not Almighty God," he said with more vigor than he thought his body could summon, more vigor, too, than he should probably use to this woman who had been ministering to him so carefully and who still served that Church. "It's not Almighty God. It's the almighty Church—and therein lies a great difference. It has been taken over by corrupt men. If the people can read the Bible for themselves, they will see that some of the doctrines these men teach are false and self-serving."

"Well, even if I should grant that some of what you say is true, which I do not, a wise man ought to know who to pick a fight with. Especially a bril-liant man with a bright future."

"Sometimes we don't get to choose our fights, Sister," he said wearily. "Sometimes they are chosen for us. But I thank you for the well-meaning advice. I thank you, too, for the shave." He smiled. "And most of all I thank you for the water. All of it."

"Well, you might get the chance to choose. At least this time." She leaned forward as if straightening the blanket. She lowered her voice to a near whisper at his ear. "I'm thinking they'll be coming for ye tomorrow.

The chamberlain empties the slops at midnight. He's usually too lazy to lock the door until he's finished all the wards."

What she was telling him registered too late.

"My trousers?" he said to her retreating back. But she'd already moved on down the ward, past the last two sleeping patients. If she heard him she gave no sign.

～※～

When Humphrey Monmouth came to pick up the Bible, he said nothing about the empty shelves of the bookshop. Tears stung the back of Kate's eyes as she handed it to him. She wanted to hold the Bible to her and not let it go, even as she wondered at this sudden and overwhelming sentimental attachment. It was just that everything dear and familiar was slipping away.

He opened it carefully, his expression almost glowing as he turned the pages, commenting on how the language had changed and the rich pigments of the illuminations.

At least it would be with someone who appreciated it, she thought.

"I shall treasure it," he said.

"I hope it does not bring you trouble."

"It is the Word of God. It should be worth whatever it costs," he said, handing her the money. Then, wrapping it back up, he said, "I'm sorry John is not here. Tell him that a shipment is due to arrive in Bristol Channel September third. It should be safe for him to meet it."

She had not the inclination to say, *I cannot tell him because he isn't coming back, and he wouldn't meet your shipment if he could.* Instead she said, "His memory is bad since he came home. Just in case, give me exact details so I can answer if he asks."

"Lord and Lady Walsh, in Little Sodbury. They will know where the goods will land as always. I will not be going. I fear my presence might put everyone in danger. My house is closely watched. But one of the other merchants, a man named Swinford, will be going. He went with us once before. Tell John that Swinford will leave from dockside at dawn on September first."

"Swinford, Little Sodbury, dawn," she repeated, as if she would really pass on the information.

He picked up the Bible and prepared to leave then turned back briefly. "Tell John to call on me when he feels inclined. I would talk with him. And don't worry about the Wycliffe Bible. You know where it is should you want it back at any time." He inclined his head toward the little leather pouch she held in her hand. "That is but a rental fee. Perhaps you can use some of it to buy more inventory. I will merely hold the Bible for you until such a time as it is safe in England to have such a magnificent thing in your possession."

When he had closed the door and left with the Bible, Kate felt an uncontrollable urge to cry and break something. But, alas, there was nothing left to break except her heart, and she was determined that should not happen. One broken heart in the family was quite enough. Besides, the ghost of an idea was forming in her mind.

September first. Little Sodbury. Swinford. Dawn.

New inventory.

But she had promised John. Was that promise binding now that he had abandoned the business? Abandoned her? What if she didn't sell from the shop? She knew the customers who bought from them. She could call on them directly. Or she could change the name to Gough's Stationer's Shop— this would keep the letter of her promise, if not the spirit—and operate under the same license, and sell paper and quills and sealing wax and such, and Lutheran books with a wink and a nod to her old customers.

She was still scheming when she opened the door to the backroom print shop. The smashed press had been pushed to one corner of the room, where it hulked like some great squat beast, taunting her to action. Littering the floor in crumpled balls lay the reminders of her most recent endeavor. Kicking them aside with more force than necessary, she began to rummage in the storage closet until she found what she was looking for. Hanging on a peg behind a couple of old dried, cracked ink pads was a pair of men's trousers, an old shirt, and one of John's caps.

She had a week until September first, a week in which to contemplate the silly notion. It was a foolish fantasy, but at least the idea of such an adventure gave her something to think about besides the bleakness of her future. She wadded her hair into a ball and put the cap on her head. It felt like a perfect fit.

SEVEN

I was by good honest men informed that in Bristol
there were of these pestilent books some thrown into
the streets and left at men's doors by night, that
where they durst not offer their poison to sell, they
would of their charity poison men for naught.
—SIR THOMAS MORE
ON THE SMUGGLING OF BIBLES

John Frith lay in the dark, fighting the fatigue that threatened to sink him into blissful sleep, listening for the sound of a key turning in the lock. He recited Homer in his head as he'd done in the fish cellar to keep his mind working and alert, trying not to think of Clerke and Sumner dying in his arms, as they begged for water in the fetid cellar, trying not to think of the despair at the end. God had saved him from the fish cellar and that could only mean one thing. He had more work to do.

He'd forced himself to stay awake ever since the old nun left, trying to work out a plan. When none was forthcoming—he'd gone over in his head all the ways Ulysses had escaped his peril and none seemed adaptable to this situation—finally, he'd decided to just wrap the woolen blanket under his armpits and flee barefoot into the fresh, sweet-smelling air of the night. He'd worry about clothes once he was outside. Of course if the beadle were about, and he would almost surely be, he would be picked up soon enough as a lunatic, in which case he could plead robbery, but that would land him in a magistrate's residence giving witness and that was the last thing he needed. My mind is going in circles, he thought, longing for sleep.

For hours now, he'd heard only the snores and groans of his ward mates, punctuated by the creak of a wooden bed frame as some tormented soul thrashed about. When he was sure he could stay awake no longer, the chimes at midnight startled him to wakefulness. Shortly after, just as the old nun had said, the sound of keys jangling in the door made his heart race.

By the time the last chime had sounded, the porter had already lit two rush lights at each end of the ward and was collecting the first of the chamber pots; the clink of his bucket echoed down the ward. In the flickering light, the man was a bent shadow flitting between the beds.

The porter approached his cot and bent to retrieve the pot at the foot.

"Thank you," Frith whispered to his back.

The man, a smallish, old man with a bent back, rose up and looked at him with a mixture of alarm and curiosity.

"You talking to me?"

"Yes, I just wanted to say thank you. It's a very valuable service you perform."

"Sorry to wake you," the old man grunted.

"It's good to be awake. That way I know I'm alive."

The man stood up, holding the chamber pot in his arms, apparently unperturbed by its foul contents. He favored Frith with a toothless grin. "Never thought about it like that," he said, and took a step toward Frith's cot.

"Don't come too close. I've had the sweating sickness," Frith whispered.

"I beint worried about that. I've seen it all. Never caught anything yet. A man's got to piss and a man's got to eat. I carry out your piss, I get to eat."

Frith smiled. "I never thought about it like that."

Frith watched him as he collected the pot of his nearest neighbor. This time he did not go to the outside door but went to the center window, opened it and flung the contents out. He came back and bent to put the pot back in its place.

"I'll leave the window open, so you can get a night breeze," he said.

And the smell it carries with it, Frith thought, but he supposed the porter no longer noticed the smell.

"It's hot enough to roast a chicken in here, and you've got that blanket pulled up like it was January. You feverish? I might could wake one of the nuns."

"They took my clothes away."

"Aye." He nodded knowingly. "Not much chance for a man to keep his private parts private in here. I probably burned yer clothes. If you're contagious they burn your clothes. Some porters give them to the ragpickers. But not me. Everybody might not be as hardy as me. It'd hurt my conscience like a scourge if some innocent person caught the pestilence on account of a farthing I might get." He lowered his voice to an even lower whisper, as if the mention of death might bring distress to some of the occupants who overheard their conversation. "If somebody—you know—and they haven't burned his clothes, then I might—come to think of it, there's a corpse at the end of the hall, waiting to be taken out. His clothes were piled in a nice little bundle at the foot of his bed. I could bring them to you if you'd like. He looked a bit bigger than you, but it'd be better than the blanket."

Frith could not believe his good fortune. "I don't have any money to pay you," he said, "but—"

"No need. There'll be others."

"You are an angel of mercy," he said when the man came back and handed him the clothes.

"Naw." The porter laughed. "I'm just a pisser like you. Wear 'em in good health."

But a few minutes later, before the porter went to the other wing to complete his chores, Frith saw the old man's shadow float to the end of the ward and heard the unmistakable sound of the click of the lock. His heart sank. The nun had been wrong. The porter had locked the door after all.

Fool! It's because he knows you're awake! If you hadn't opened your big mouth! He got out of bed, gingerly, testing the floor with rubbery legs, and put on the shirt and trousers. The old porter was right. They were a bit long, but he rolled the pants up at the waist and tied the yeoman's shirt with the rope belt. At least he had some clothes, if the opportunity should present itself again. Maybe tomorrow night. He would pretend to be sleeping like a dead man—if he was still here tomorrow night, he thought ruefully.

A noxious breeze drifted in from the window carrying the smell of urine and feces. Frith wrinkled his nose in disgust. What did a man have to do to get a breath of untainted air in this world? *Idiot!* He slapped his forehead. *The window.*

Minutes later, John Frith with much wriggling and contorting of his body— much leaner now than three months earlier, but it was a narrow window—let himself down carefully until his bare feet encountered the ground below the window. So relieved was he to be outside the hospital and a free man that he hardly noticed the muck squishing between his toes.

Wearing a dead man's clothes and on legs as unsteady as a newborn colt's, he headed for the Steelyard. He remembered what Garrett had told them about how the books entered England. Maybe he could bargain his labor for passage out of England—and some shoes. The Brethren at the Hanseatic Merchants League would help him get to the Continent where he would join his friend and mentor William Tyndale. Maybe that's why God had saved him from the cellar.

Besides, he knew what fate awaited him if he stayed in England.

— ✣ —

Rain pelted down on the little wherry as it floated up the Thames toward Reading. Kate was grateful for the protection of the heavy cloak John had left hanging on a peg by the door.

It had been hanging there since the night he was arrested. These many weeks, she'd been loath to take it down, wanting to leave it there, until he would come back to claim it. Well, it could at least help to hide her figure, she had thought when she took it down and shook it out, holding it up for closer scrutiny. She was as tall as John . . . maybe with just a little padding stuffed into the shoulder lining . . .

It had worked.

In the pale light of early dawn, the merchant Swinford had not questioned her. To his "Glad to see you're a free man again, Gough," Kate had croaked in a raspy whisper, "But not a well man," and pointed toward her throat.

An auspicious beginning and a sign, she thought, a sign that she was supposed to follow through on her plan. Indeed, it was too late to turn back now. She'd lain awake the night before fretting over her silly scheme, finally deciding to abandon it and go to sleep. But somewhere a rooster's herald of the dawn had wakened her again, so at first light, dressed as her brother John, she'd headed toward the docks, thinking she should turn back, thinking that the merchant would probably already be gone and the docks would be deserted, thinking he would see through her immediately.

But he had only nodded at her and climbed into the little boat tied up at the dock, motioning for her to follow. "We'd best hurry. The weather will slow us down and we're moving upstream."

Then he'd leaned forward to untie the rope from the dock, and Kate had her first moment of panic, wondering if she could copy his surefooted movement.

He held the boat steady. "A man just out of a damp prison cell could get the ague in this drizzle. This time you'd best get behind me. My back'll protect you from the worst of it. In Reading we'll at least get off the river and maybe grab a few hours of sleep. Same place as always. We're to pick up a wagon and some horses. And I think a passenger."

Kate had merely nodded and held on to the dock post with one hand, as she gingerly put one foot in the boat. The strange freedom of movement that the trousers gave her under the heavy cloak caused her to misjudge the distance, and the boat rocked beneath her feet. She sat down hard on the board in the center.

Swinford pushed away from the dock with the oar, and she realized with a sinking feeling that he would expect her to man the other oar. Thank God, she'd often been rowing with John when they were younger, before he married, so at least she knew how. She was supposed to row from the other side, she remembered, so she scooted to the right and picked up the oar. As she dipped the paddle into the water, she felt the drag of the current and matched her rhythm to his. She should just count herself lucky, she thought, that he was not a young man and paused to rest his own arms at those places where the river flowed wider and the current was less strong. But such respites were brief. Soon the boat would start to drift downstream, and he would pick up the oar again.

By mid-morning the rain had begun in earnest.

By noon her arms were aching. The rain had settled to a mist that clung to her skin and breath. The woolen cloak was much too hot for such exertion, but she dared not take it off. Its wool helped repel the water in a way her linen shirt would not. Without the cloak, her shirt and trousers would quickly become wet and clingy. The mist thickened to fog, and they moved closer to shore, avoiding the larger boats in the main channel. Kate was breathing heavily.

But what was worse, she needed to make water.

She averted her eyes when Swinford stood up and, fumbling at the closure of his pants, moved to the edge of the boat. Her face was still flaming when he settled into his seat again.

"You look a bit flushed," he said. "You'd best not overdo in your weakened condition. I can manage alone a while."

"I'd be grateful for the break," she croaked.

But her respite brought little relief. The occasional swell caused by the wake of the larger boats in the channel added to her discomfort. The earthy banks and the rotting reeds had a rank, peaty smell, but she did not feel sick. She was just wet and miserable and even a little hungry. Why hadn't she thought to bring a biscuit? All she had with her was the little pouch of money that Sir Humphrey had given her, the plan being to use some small part of it to pay for some of the goods they were receiving.

The rain started up again, coming down in sheets. It puddled in the bottom of the boat.

"We'd best pull in and find a bit of shelter or at least find something to bail with," Swinford shouted.

Nodding, she picked up the oar and applied it vigorously, ignoring the burn in her upper arm. Once they reached the shore, she could find a private place to relieve herself. For the first time that day, she blessed the rain.

❧

By the time they made Reading, the church bells were tolling compline, and Kate was too tired to even wonder where they were going as she followed her companion up a twisting street to a row of half-timbered houses leaning into the alley. Swinford stopped at the third house and tapped lightly on the door. A woman wearing a lace-trimmed nightcap and shawl over her nightdress answered the door. She carried a candle but shielded it with her hand to keep the light from spilling into the street.

"We'd 'bout given you out," she said in a low voice. "The other one is already here. I've put down a couple of straw mattresses by the hearth in the kitchen for the two of you." As she spoke, she was leading them into the kitchen where the smell of boiled barley and beef lingered, causing Kate's stomach to rumble a little. The woman lit the rush lights on the wall from the candle she carried. Shadows danced along the walls. "There's some bread on the table and soup still simmering in the kettle. It should warm you. I'll bid you good night, then."

But Kate was too weary to eat. She tore off a crust of bread to feed the rumbling in her stomach. She wondered as she lay down on the cot if it was safe to remove her soggy cap but decided that it would look stranger still to sleep in it. She had braided her hair tightly and bound it with a kerchief. Her scalp felt tight and it itched. At least she could take off the coat in the semidarkness of the kitchen. She blessed the kindness of the mistress of the house for leaving a clean coverlet—and for her good housekeeping; the blanket smelled of lye and lavender. She pulled it up to her chin.

"You should try some of this soup. It's tasty," Swinford said.

"I'm too tuckered to eat," Kate said, surprised to find she didn't have to feign the hoarseness now because she had a real rasp in her throat.

She fell asleep to the sound of Swinford slurping his soup and dreamed of black river water and a sheep who bleated pitifully on the shore. On his head was John's soggy tricornered cap.

※

Kate woke early. Stiff from sleeping on the floor and with a sore arm from yesterday's rowing, she put on her cloak and cap and went out into the early light to relieve herself. The rain had stopped, but water drops still clung to the grass and late-blooming roses in the bit of a garden. After finishing her business behind a shed at the back of the garden, she strolled down the lane.

So this is Reading, she thought. *I've heard John speak of Reading.* Not a bit like London, she thought, looking around with greedy eyes. She'd been disappointed that she'd not been able to see more of the fogbound shoreline yesterday, since she'd never been farther upriver than Cardinal Wolsey's grand new palace at Hampton Court. No grand palaces here. Just a sleepy little hamlet, it looked to her, though she knew there was an abbey somewhere near here with an abbot who was sympathetic to the Lutheran cause. If last night was any indication, the townsfolk were sympathetic, too, and the householders here harbored Bible smugglers at great risk to their own lives and properties. She was wondering how far it was to the abbey when she noticed smoke curling from some of the chimneys. The smell of cookfires mingled with the damp earth smell, and she hoped the hospitality of the house extended to breakfast. That thought and the light told her it was time to turn back. Swinford would be anxious to get away.

She reentered the kitchen to the welcome smell of frying salt meat. This time she did not wait to be asked, but took a bit of the bacon that was piled in the center of the long deal table and a slice of last night's bread. A pitcher of milk and some cups were on the table as well. She poured herself a cup and gulped it down, and then cut a piece of the bread, and tucking the meat inside the bread, slid both into the pocket of John's coat. Who knew when she would eat again?

She was wiping her mouth on the sleeve of her coat when Swinford came back. He brought with him a man of about Kate's age. It appeared he was dressed for traveling also but in clothes hung too loosely on him, as though he had, like Kate, borrowed his from an older brother.

"We need to be off, if you're up to it," Swinford said, looking at Kate. "The wagon's hitched and the horses waiting."

"I'm ready," Kate tried to say, but found that she had no voice at all. The words came out in a hoarse whisper. At least she wouldn't have to fake it.

"This is John Frith. He's going with us to Bristol. He was one of the students shut up in the cellars at Oxford for buying books from Garrett. Fresh from the hospital." He grinned and then added, "Under somewhat hurried circumstances, from what I hear."

"Pleased to meet you, Gough. I see we have much in common," the stranger said. "I commend you for your willingness to jump back into the fray. I'm going to the Continent where I hope to be able to assist Tyndale. I'm a translator too. I can't wait to tell him how bravely you and others like you support his work."

He thinks I'm John. And he's commending me for bravery, she thought, noticing that despite Frith's youth and apparent vigor he looked uncommonly pale. His hand held a slight tremor when he extended it to her. She tried to grip it firmly—as her brother John would have gripped it once upon a time.

"I can see we are going to be fast friends," he said and smiled.

It was the most charming smile Kate had ever seen. It warmed her all over.

EIGHT

Will ye resist God? . . . Hath He [God] not made the
English tongue? Why forbid ye Him to speak in the
English tongue, then, as well as in the Latin?
—WILLIAM TYNDALE,
THE OBEDIENCE OF A CHRISTIAN MAN (1528)

ith as much manly swagger as she could muster, Kate
hoisted herself into the back of the narrow wagon, praying as she settled in
the corner opposite John Frith that she would be able to maintain her pose.
They still had a journey of several hours ahead. Swinford had sat in front of
her on the way upriver, and the day had been overcast, the light too poor to
notice that the smooth skin of his companion's cheek had never felt the slide
of a razor's edge or borne even the faintest stubble. But John Frith was sitting close enough that she could see the shadow of a dark beard on his pale
face and smell the wood smoke clinging to his clothes. Arrows of bright
sunlight pierced the clouds, inviting a more careful scrutiny. Trying to ignore the uncomfortable tug of her braided and bound hair, she pulled John's
tricornered hat lower on her forehead to avoid Frith's intelligent gaze.

She need not have worried. Frith gave her a cheerful smile, said, "Have a
nice ride, Gough," and was asleep in minutes, his head slumped forward
onto his chest. Even the bouncing and jarring of the wagon across the rutted

roads did not interrupt his rhythmic snoring. Two hours later, he was still sleeping, having left Kate to enjoy the passing countryside untroubled by her need to posture.

By midday the heat was rising and sunlight was playing tag with piles of clouds. Swinford stopped to rest the horses. Kate relieved herself in a nearby copse, hoping her traveling companions would not choose the same spot. But when she climbed back into the wagon, Frith had not moved and Swinford was holding the reins.

"You're one for modesty, Gough, I'll give you that." Swinford laughed.

"A touch of the runs. I wouldn't want to offend your sensibilities," Kate answered gruffly, as she thought one man might answer another's jibe. She jerked her head toward Frith. "Shouldn't we wake him?" Kate asked. "At least he could stretch his legs."

"Naw, let him sleep. He's had a rough time, that one has. Sleep'll do him good. We'll stop again. If not, he can just piss off the side of the wagon."

Kate tried to banish the notion of Frith "pissing off the side" from her head, as Swinford slapped the reins and the wagon lurched forward. Digging into the pocket of John's cloak, she pulled out the bit of meat and bread and chewed absently. She considered her sleeping companion. He looked innocent, even boyish, in his slumber, despite the darkening stubble on his face—and very pale. His long white neck looked about to break, all slumped over in that position. A tendril of wavy brown hair fell forward, stark against his complexion. Kate resisted the urge to wad up a piece of sacking and place it like a pillow behind his neck.

It was an intelligent face—at least the part she could see—with a determined jaw and a noble brow. He was a translator, he'd said, a Lutheran sympathizer, going to the Continent to meet Tyndale. And though he hadn't said so, not directly, she guessed he was a fugitive. She doubted that the prelates would let the students out free and clear. This one had no doubt escaped from the hospital. Prematurely, if his lack of strength was any indication.

He stirred and stretched. "Sorry to be such a bad traveling companion," he said. "It's just that, well . . . no use going there. I'm glad to be out of that stinking cellar."

"It must have been awful," she said, keeping her hand over her smooth chin.

He waved her off with a smile. "Small price, aye? We're men of the Word, you and I, Gough. Brethren," he said, draping his arm over her shoulder and shaking her lightly.

She felt a jolt go all through her body, a jolt that had nothing to do with the rough bumping of the wagon. Her face flushed with embarrassment. How unlike her own brother he really was, though she would have delighted in being his friend, and perhaps more. His easy charm and his courage tugged at her heart. She wished she could have known him better. John would have liked him too; she knew it. At least the John she used to know.

"You all right, Gough?" Frith asked. "You look like somebody just stepped on your grave." His voice was light, friendly, but Kate saw concern in his dark eyes and felt a stinging in her own, remembering how Frith had congratulated her—congratulated her brother—on his courage.

"Just a bit of road grit in my eye," she growled, and suddenly hoped with all her soul that they would make it in time for this John to meet his ship and make good his escape.

⚜

By the time they reached Little Sodbury, the long shadows had disappeared behind threatening storm clouds. Though Kate's companion no longer slept, he had turned pensive and seemed disinclined to talk. A mask of endurance replaced the cheerful demeanor she'd seen at breakfast. His dark eyes were clouded with pain.

But by now Kate had her own discomfort to think about. It had begun about an hour past with an ache in her lower belly, and with each bounce and jolt of the wagon, it had spread farther into her back. It must have been brought on by the jarring ride or maybe the anxiety attached with what now seemed like a very silly scheme. But whatever had precipitated the untimely arrival of her woman's curse, she was ill prepared to cope with it. She was yet again grateful for John's dark and heavy cloak. Once they got to Sodbury Manor—*please, God let us get to Sodbury Manor soon*—she could figure out what to do. After all, what could they do but scold if they found out she was an impostor? They would surely share the inventory with her for John's sake, if naught else.

Lightning illumined the underbelly of the threatening clouds. The wagon lurched and a little groan escaped her lips. She glanced at Frith. His head was thrown back against the side of the wagon and his eyes were closed. If caught, he would face much more than embarrassment and a little scolding. He appeared not to have noticed either the lightning or her whimper.

"We're here," Swinford shouted. "And none too soon. You two get down and I'll take the horses round to the stable."

A growl of thunder answered, accompanied by a gusting wind. Kate stood up, tried to jump down on rubber legs, felt the warm rush between her legs and instinctively tensed her thighs together to try to hold back the flow. John Frith followed her and seemed almost as unsteady. Surely the gates of paradise would be no more welcome than the entrance of the beautiful manor house with its lit lamps glowing in the window.

Lord and Lady Walsh were standing at the door. "Come in and welcome. We've not much time to waste," he said. "But you've time to take a bit of refreshment before we meet the shipment," she said.

Candles in sconces, hanging from the high-beamed rafters and along the wall, fought back the gloom of the approaching storm. An occasional flash of lightning lit a pair of stained-glass windows set high and on either side of a great chimney, though any sound of rumbling thunder was muted by the thick plaster walls. The candles flickered as Swinford came in, brushing a few drops of rain from his shoulders.

In the center of the hall, a table had been laid with sliced roast meats and fresh-baked bread. A basket of apples and rosy pears glowed beneath lit candles in a silver candelabra. Kate realized that she was ravenously hungry, but the aching in her lower back and belly reminded her that she had more urgent matters to attend to before she fed that hunger.

"My lady, may I speak with you?"

Lady Walsh looked at her expectantly.

"In private, please," Kate stammered, feeling her skin suddenly growing warm and flushed and not unaware of the puzzled expression on Swinford's face. John Frith seemed too tired to notice as he slumped onto a bench in front of the fire.

"But of course," the lady said, moving closer to Kate, who stood slightly apart.

Kate whispered something in her ear. Lady Walsh's face registered only a moment's surprise. "Please, gentlemen, help yourself to the food whilst we wait out the storm. Lord Walsh will give you instructions about the evening's activities. Young Master Gough and I shall return shortly." She smiled warmly at Kate as she motioned for her to follow.

Neither of them noticed that John Frith's head had slumped forward into unconsciousness.

≈≋≈

"Trim the mainsail," the captain shouted as he spotted Sand Point. There was a scurrying of legs up the mainmast as the *Siren's Song* slid silently into

Bristol Channel toward the jutting promontory, its large, square sail suddenly slack-jawed.

They were early. Too much daylight left to see the signal beacons at Worleburg Hill, and still light enough the see the ship's name painted on the starboard side. He ordered the lines draped carelessly over the side to obscure the freshly gilded letters of the *Siren's Song*.

"Drop anchor here," he shouted. The boat rocked gently, its black mizzenmast sail now out of sight too, less than a league from the shallow waters of the inlet. Just another idled fishing boat, plying the rich waters off the channel and not the fastest ship in English waters—that's what the king's men would see. But truth be told, the little thirty-ton caravel with its crew of ten and four black sails could outrun anything that gave chase except a Spanish galleon—and maybe that, too, if the pursuer was too heavily gunned. She was beautiful and she was fast, and she belonged to him.

And that last was why Tom Lasser loved her.

But the lone cannon hidden behind the innocent-looking porthole and speed aside, it made him nervous to be sitting here like some great black swan in plain sight of any curious customs agent. What was more, in the western sky behind them great gray clouds were humping in a line that ran around the bend toward the mainland. His left wrist, broken some years back in a skirmish that he'd been unable to run from, still ached when a storm threatened. It was better than any shaman.

It ached now.

An early September gale at her back could trap the *Siren's Song* in the cove, maybe even drive her landward, stranding her in shallow waters permanently. He thought about breaking out the small boats and off-loading his cargo early, stashing it in the cove, and any other time he would have.

Thunder rumbled in the distance. The mute woman who kept his cabin appeared on board. The first mate eyed her disapprovingly, and, mumbling under his breath, began to fiddle with the anchor rope. Lasser looked at him with a frown and the mumbling stopped. More than once he'd had to set the crew aright about the presence of a woman on board, especially a woman who'd had her tongue cut out by the good men of her village. But Captain Lasser paid his crewmen well enough to overlook their superstitions, and each soul on board had signed or marked with an X his agreement to her presence.

The storm must have drawn her on deck. For the most part, she stayed out of sight in the quarters below. He didn't know about the scrying; maybe she did see visions in still water, but he knew that she was half starved and whimpering when he found her bleeding and moaning in a ditch. The men had used her for their pleasure before they punished her for trafficking with the devil, apparently unafraid that if she was really a witch, she might shrivel their balls to peas.

He had taken her back to his rooms and fed her and sent for a surgeon to cauterize her bleeding stump of a tongue, only to find a few weeks later, when she was healed and he tried to send her away, that she would not go. They must have made a sight on the docks, with him shooing her away as one would try to shoo a stray cat and her just standing there, taking a step every time he took a step, as though they were attached at the ankles. In the end he had waved his arms in the air and walked away.

She had followed him onto the ship.

At first he'd ignored her. But soon when his linen and his quarters were clean, his food actually eatable, he'd come to accept her presence with something like gratitude.

"What do your witch bowls tell you, Endor?" Endor—the name he'd given her, for she was apparently illiterate as well as dumb and could not write her name. "Is it going to storm?"

She pointed to the horizon. A bolt of lightning zigzagged across the sky.

"Right." The captain laughed. "Looks like a sign to me."

The first mate spoke up, his mouth twitching nervously. Tom didn't know whether it was Endor or the storm that made him so nervous. "We could just lash the cargo together and set it afloat. Most of the barrels would wash ashore," he said.

Tom knew the ship's manifest said grain and Flanders cloth, and a few spices, but what really lay in the hold was Spanish wine and English Bibles. He'd planned to off-load some of it in one of the little quiet anchorages in Greenwich or before—the North Sea coast had many out-of-the-way creeks where at low water the crew could walk the cargo to shore—but a customs tidewaiter had joined the ship at Gravesend to keep them honest and stayed with them all the way to London. There had been no chance before Bristol Channel. They were supposed to pick up a cargo here as well—linsey-woolsey, woven and exported without tax by the many cottage industries from Gloucestershire. He'd already paid a bribe of thirty pounds at Mother Grindham's place, Bristol quayside, for the customs agents to be absent when he picked up the cloth. He'd just added it on to the shipping costs—still cheaper for the cottagers than having to pay the king's export tax.

The waters of the cove settled to a dead calm. The sky had darkened now, as the clouds crept closer, their heavy load turning them bruise-blue. Thirty pounds was little enough to pay to avoid risk of being trapped here. His first mate looked at him anxiously, pointed to the western horizon.

"Say the word, Cap'n."

Tom shook his head. "No, I think it'll go around. It'll be dark enough in another hour. When we see the beacon, we'll send the boats to shore with the cargo."

But Tom didn't think the storm was going around. Thing was, he had more than cargo to take on. He'd promised Henry Monmouth that he'd pick up a passenger, and Monmouth had saved his bacon too many times for Tom to let him down if he could help it. Besides, they did a lot of business together and Captain Lasser enjoyed a reputation that said he could be relied upon to deliver. There were other ships and other masters Monmouth could turn to on a whim. One merchant had already built his own "coaster," the *Dorothy Fulford*, boasting he could pay for it in less than a year from his smuggling profits alone. He wouldn't want Monmouth to take such a notion into his head.

He glanced at the spot on the railing where Endor had been standing, but she had slipped below as quietly as a shadow.

"Tell the men to secure the rigging and get ready to ride out a storm," he said.

NINE

our Majesty, your wooing is too much for a simple maid." Laughing,
Anne Boleyn pulled away from the king's embrace, hoping to tamp down his
ardor without inflaming his temper. She was ever mindful of the fine line she
walked.

It was a glorious late-summer day at Hampton Court, a day pregnant
with possibility and hope. On such a day as this, when tiny birds twittered
among the cropped branches of the hedges, Anne almost believed she could
be his queen. On such a day as this, when the smell of sunshine and roses
scented the air, she almost believed Henry to be an honest man.

A breeze ruffled the edge of the ribbons at her bodice, which the king's
busy fingers had undone. The bright sound of women's laughter from somewhere in the verdant heart of the maze rode on that same breeze.

Henry seemed not to hear. "Your hair smells of a thousand flowers and
your lips are cherry ripe . . . cherry ripe . . . just one taste," Henry murmured, his breath moist and heavy on her neck. His fingers fumbled once

again at her laces. "Your . . . little maids . . . as firm as pomegranates, Katherine's are so . . . pendulous."

She pulled away, gently slapping his fingers, kissing them lightly to soften the rejection. How did one refuse a king? She shivered at her own temerity.

"My lord, we should quit the maze and seek other company where I will not be tempted by Your Grace's charm and ardor." She relaced her bodice with a less practiced hand than he'd undone it. "The cardinal could come upon us at any moment. Or worse yet, one of Queen Katherine's spies. Until I am in truth your wife, I shall retain my maidenhead. Anything less would ill become your queen and put in doubt the rightful parentage of your heir."

Henry pursed his lips into a turgid little pout, reminding her of a spoiled boy whose favorite toy had been taken away. "She is not my queen," he said. "She was my brother's queen. I was but a youth when he died and did not know it was a sin to take her to my bed. But it is a sin that might be remedied easily enough. If the Spanish cow were less well connected in the papal courts, the annulment would have been granted long ago."

And your daughter Mary would be a bastard. How does one annul a child? But Anne held her tongue. The only other solution would be to live as the king's mistress and that she would not do. So what if her father was only a knight? Some Howard blood ran in her veins, and the king could create a noble with the stroke of a pen. Had he not made Charles Brandon, his childhood friend, Duke of Suffolk? A reform-minded queen would be good for England. Princess Mary had been raised a Catholic, and England had had enough of popery. The king needed a new heir—one who would not be raised a Catholic.

Again the sound of laughter chimed through the hedges. This time it sounded nearer.

"Let us go, then," Henry grumbled. "With this talk of Katherine, you have spoiled the mood anyway. I assume you will not deny your king your chaste companionship." He said the word *chaste* through clenched teeth.

She followed his silk-stockinged, muscular legs through the hedges, struggling to keep up. "You will attend me in the king's privy chamber—in company as you insist," he said, widening his stride. "The artist's drawings for my new Belgian tapestries have arrived. They, at least, should be to my lady's liking. And it gives me pleasure to parade you before Wolsey. He becomes so apoplectic at the mention of your name that his fat face takes on the aspect of a boiled ham."

"I have observed that the cardinal loves me not," Anne said wryly.

Henry stopped abruptly and laughed. Anne allowed herself to breathe. The storm cloud had apparently passed. He remained still, arms akimbo, legs planted slightly apart, in what Anne always thought of as his battlefield stance, until she caught up with him.

"You are a mistress of understatement. It's not that Wolsey dislikes you. It's just that you are a constant source of embarrassment to him because he has been unable to serve his sovereign in this great matter. It is really Sir Thomas who would conspire against you, if he dared."

They had exited the maze and were crossing the orchards beyond which dozens of men were digging large ponds. At the king's approach, the shovels pumped. Henry paused at the edge of the pond to watch. The afternoon sun cast the shadows of the pear trees and apple trees toward the workers, as though the branches reached out with gnarled hands to grab at them. Henry sat on a bench and patted the spot beside him. "This should be public enough not to compromise your virtue, my lady."

Anne ignored his sarcasm; her thoughts were still impaled upon his last remark. "I fear, you put me in a dangerous place, Your Majesty. It seems I have incurred the enmity of very powerful men."

He gave a half snort. "Thomas? Don't worry about More. He's too busy burning heretics to worry overmuch about anything else." He patted her on her knee. "It's me you have to please, Anne, me alone."

"I'm afraid Sir Thomas might find me objectionable on all accounts," she said softly. She hesitated for a moment, wondering, and then decided what good was having the king's ear, if one did not use it. "I have something to show you," she said. "Not as grand as your tapestries, but I think it is something you should see."

"Well, that piques my interest. Some new poem my lady has written, maybe a small jewel, or some silken token of her love?"

Anne blushed. "Nothing of that kind. There will be time enough for such when our . . . circumstances have changed. Nay, it is nothing but a simple, printed pamphlet."

"A book?" He laughed loudly enough that one of the pond diggers looked his way and then quickly averted his eyes. "My queen will not only be beautiful but erudite. I am a blessed man. Sir Thomas More will not be the only man in England with learned women in his household."

"I'm afraid it is not a book of which Sir More or the cardinal would approve." She reached inside the hidden pocket sewn into her skirt and handed him the small booklet. "I'm asking that Your Majesty please review it in private and keep the source to yourself . . . if it pleases Your Highness, of course?"

He looked stern. "It is not some heretical Lutheran work? I caution you—"

"No Lutheran work. But the work of a man not much loved by Master More. It is a book by one called Tyndale. It is called *The Obedience of a Christian Man*."

"Where did you acquire such a book, my lady?" he said sternly.

"It came into my hands when I visited the Continent. I brought it into England before the present licensing laws were published. I am surrendering it as the law says—to you." She dropped him a full curtsy.

"Wisely done. May all your choices be so circumspect. If your enemies found this in your possession, they would make much of it. But you could have burned it."

"I thought you might wish to read it first."

"Did you read it?"

"Yes, Your Majesty, I read it."

"Well? What did you think of it?"

She hesitated. Henry was no friend to Lutherans either. After all, he'd written the refutation against Luther—as much Thomas More's work as his own, she suspected—that gained him papal favor and the title "Defender of the Faith." She swallowed hard.

"It argues well, but it has some Lutheran-influenced ideas."

He smacked the book against his knee as if to punish it. "Then we shall throw it in the fire with the rest."

"But it also has certain ideas about the right of kings that I think may give voice and weight to the king's own thinking."

"The king's thinking needs no added weight or voice," he said, frowning.

Anne took a deep breath. "Then you are more in agreement with Master Tyndale than you know. That's exactly what that book says. It boldly asserts the divine right of kings over all."

He cocked one eyebrow. "Even the pope?"

"Read it, you will see. The king gives account to God alone."

He took the book from her hand and studied it for a minute or two, then slid it into a voluminous silken sleeve. "Then I shall read it," he said.

From a yew tree above them a pair of crows chose that moment to set up a raucous protest. He laughed. "Methinks the black-robed lot doth protest already." Then, "Let's go look at my tapestry," he said, taking her hand.

As they exited the orchards, the digger closest sighed with relief and leaned upon his shovel.

⌁

Cardinal Wolsey stood alone in the center of the great hall, regarding its great hammer-beam roof and its brilliant ceiling of blue, and red, and gold. A deep sadness descended on his scarlet-clad shoulders. Hampton Court, the greatest palace in all England—and he was about to give it away. What a fool he'd been to upstage the king, even though God knew he'd taken every pain to ease whatever jealousy Henry might feel by referring to this personal holding as just another of the king's many palaces.

"From your palace at Hampton," he'd signed all his correspondence to Henry while in residence there. But after tonight it would be the king's in deed and truly. In one last effort to save his head, if not his office, Chancellor Wolsey was signing over to the king his splendid palace on the Thames wherein he had entertained and suborned many a Roman prelate and foreign prince. A generous but empty gesture, he mused. The king could take any palace with one stroke of a pen, but by surrendering it voluntarily, Wolsey thought to avoid both the stroke of the pen and a stroke of another sort.

He ran his hand over the grooves in the wooden panels of the walls with their carvings chiseled to imitate folds of linen drapery. The same paneling was in his private apartments. From the leaded windows of his study he could look out at the gardens and the winding river beyond. This palace had been, for a humble butcher's son, the culmination of a dream. Now it was all lost: Hampton Palace, the chancellor's seal . . . and he could not bear to think what else. And for what? A woman—not even a beautiful woman by court standards. It was as though she had bewitched the king, who talked of nothing else but his desire to wed her. He was willing to risk papal displeasure and maybe even the threat of hellfire for what he could find between her legs. The word *witchcraft* had been bandied about among the queen's supporters. But Wolsey suspected that whatever dark arts the Boleyn girl practiced had more to do with the gifts of Eve than the devil.

His spies told him she was in the maze today with the king. She might even be seated with him tonight at the king's board. Henry was flaunting her openly now—while his old queen cried and petitioned her nephew Charles, the Holy Roman Emperor, to stop her husband from setting her aside. They were stalemated, but it was only a matter of time. Wolsey could see it in Henry's lust-crazed eyes whenever he looked at Anne and in the confident gaze of her dark eyes. If she held out long enough, she would be queen. And Henry would have defied a pope. There was no place for Thomas Wolsey in such a court. But he was not looking forward to going back to York. He had thought to be in Rome by now, sitting in the papal chair, but that dream had fallen apart.

The slant of light through the windows told him it was almost time. Already the servants were coming to set up the boards. This might well be his last dinner in this grand hall. The king was already decorating the walls. Soon Wolsey would be asked to surrender his chancellor's seal. Tomorrow he would leave for home, praying his enemies did not pursue. Let the jackals fight over the great seal. Thomas Cromwell or Thomas More. Wolsey cared not a rusty bucket of donkey shit. Though he pitied whoever wore the great chain. It had been naught to Wolsey but a chain of burden ever since Henry had decided to set aside his Spanish queen.

"Where shall we put the king's coat of arms, Your Eminence?"

Wolsey stood for a long moment, considering his own crest high on the wall at the end of the hall. Sacred symbols painted on a field of red beneath a cardinal's hat: the cross and the keys to the kingdom rested above the motto *Dominus michi adjutor.* "The Lord my helper," he muttered, pondering the irony of it.

"Your Eminence?"

"Put it there," he said gruffly, pointing to his own crest. "Pack that one up and send it to York. And use the board cloths of gold," he said. "So the king will judge us well."

He departed the hall for one last tour of the kitchens and the cellar. He would choose the wine himself.

～☙～

Thomas More entered the kitchens at Hampton Court on a mission. He wrinkled his nose at the frontal assault on his senses. The place reeked of smoking chimneys, burning fat, and the blood from freshly butchered meats. Good God, the noise alone was enough to unhinge a man's sanity: sounds of banging pans, shouting voices. An acrid smell of smoke burned his nostrils. He coughed to draw a breath. It was like entering hell. But through the blue haze that hovered over the largest kitchen, where a butcher was spearing a deer carcass onto a spit, he spied his quarry and pushed through the harried, sweating workers—some in livery, some in rags—who rushed to and fro within the warren of preparation rooms. A few recognized him and parted before him like the Red Sea before Moses.

Hampton Court was not Sir Thomas More's favorite place, even in the sumptuously appointed rooms above. While it was true Thomas liked nice things about him—pictures, books, a bountiful table—there was a seeming lack of order in excess that unnerved him, and a superfluity of wealth was the hallmark of the court. The whole palace, from its glorious gardens to its ornate chapel, stank of the noxious odors of intrigue and anxiety. Entering the pandemonium where food was prepared twice daily for the hordes of sycophants that marched through its portals stretched his nerves taut as harp strings. He longed to be back at Chelsea in his library after a simple meal with his family, but the king had summoned him to Hampton Court tonight, and so he had decided to put the evening to good use.

He spotted the man he'd come to see, manhandling a log as big as a tree trunk. Thomas struggled to remember the name of the man who'd ferried him once or twice from Hampton to Chelsea.

Albert . . . Alfred . . . no, farther down the alphabet . . . James . . . Paul . . . Peter . . .

"Robert," he called, hurrying in the direction of the workman.

The servant hurled the log into the giant maw of the fireplace that made up one whole end of the room and moved with a bundle of small wood toward the bake ovens along the other wall. He looked up at the sound of his name, pausing long enough to wipe the sweat from his brow with the crook of his arm. "Sir Thomas! I'm surprised to see you here. I mean down here."

"And I you. When I didn't see you at the dock, I inquired and was told to try the kitchens. Have you been permanently moved?"

"When the king comes to dinner, we are all pressed into service if we want to keep our waterman's license. But I'll be finished here and back on the docks if you need a waterman to ferry you home tonight."

"That's good, Robert. You are among the swiftest boatmen on the river. But that's not why I came looking for you. Is there somewhere we could talk privately?"

Robert glanced at the ovens.

"It'll only take a minute, I promise."

"The dresser's room is most like to be empty."

"You lead, I'll follow," Thomas said, following him into a small room where two roasted peacocks sat redressed in their colorful plumage waiting on the ledge to be picked up for presentation at the king's board. Trays of cakes shaped like crowns and gilded with real gold waited for their servers also. One of those cakes would no doubt be placed before him at dinner. He hoped the king would not be looking when he scraped the gold away. Precious metals were for wearing—not eating.

The man began to fidget.

"I'll get right to the point so you can get back to work. The last time you rowed for me, you told me about a man named Harry Phillips, whose father's house you worked in—a 'ne'er-do-well,' I think you called him, a man who would do anything if the price was right. Do you know where I may find this man?"

The servant looked perplexed, though Thomas knew he would not dare to ask outright why a man of his station and reputation would be seeking such a one.

"I have a bit of a cleanup job at Chelsea. The kind of job only a man desperate for money will tackle. It's a bit much for those in my regular service to take on. I believe you said this Harry was a man of learning with some unfortunate but expensive vices. That kind is frequently desperate."

Robert once again wiped his brow with the crook of his elbow. Sweat beads glistened on the hairs of his forearm. From the large rooms behind the dresser's room came a shout—"Where's Robert, we need more wood for the bread ovens"—accompanied by the clanging of pans.

"You go on back to work. We wouldn't want the cardinal's bread to be half baked."

"Aye, we wouldn't that." Robert grinned.

"I'll be down at the docks after the feast. If you'll get me home in time for breakfast with my dame, I'll make it worth your loss of sleep. We can talk more about this Harry Phillips later and whether or not he might suit the job. No great matter."

Roberrrt!

"I'm coming," the servant boomed in the direction of the unknown voice, and then to Sir Thomas, "I'll be there, milord, if I can get away."

"I'll put a word in the cardinal's ear at dinner. I'll ask that my favorite waterman be made available."

But Thomas didn't have to wait until dinner. On the way out of the kitchens he passed the landing leading down the couple of steps to the room where the wine casks waited like fat round pupae in neat rows. Among the barrels he spied Wolsey's bright scarlet cope and cap bent over in inspection as the master of the cellar cut a hole into a barrel, inserted a spout, and prepared to draw the wine into a cup. At the soft hiss of Thomas's slippers upon the stone floor, Wolsey looked up.

"Thomas," he said, beckoning, "come taste this. See if you think it fit for the king's board."

The steward swirled the red wine in the cup, releasing its plummy fragrance. Thomas sipped. It was a fruity, full-bodied wine and carried the faintest hint of the oak in which it lay, like a woman newly risen from her bed, who still carries the fragrance of her dreams upon her skin.

"It is an excellent wine, Your Eminence, a fine burgundy."

"You've a good nose, Thomas." Wolsey's faint smile showed his pleasure that Thomas had liked the wine. "That's what being highborn gains a man. An appreciation for the finer things."

Always the son of a butcher, Thomas thought. Not quite sure in his own taste. Ever choosing the gilded lily over nature's glorious own. That explained a lot about the excess of Hampton Palace.

"This wine was a gift of the Duke of Burgundy when he last visited," Wolsey continued. Then his voice dropped and he muttered as though talking to himself. "Powerful men have wandered the halls of this great palace." And then he seemed to remember he was not alone. "But I've never encountered one in my kitchens before. What brings you to this nether region when all others are strolling the gardens? Some secret plan?"

"You have heard, I suppose, that one of the Oxford students has escaped. He's probably already on his way to the Continent," Thomas said.

"Yes." The cardinal, still preoccupied with the wine, sniffed it again and handed it back to the steward. "This one will do," he said with a nod of dismissal. "Draw it an hour before it is served so it can breathe. The jeweled decanter for the king's board. The silver for the knights."

"And for the others?" the steward asked.

"You choose." The cardinal waved him away. "Now leave us alone for a minute."

With a nod to Sir Thomas, the steward backed out of the cask room.

"'Tis a pity we did not have a watch on young Frith. I have heard that he's a friend of William Tyndale's. You might have run your man to ground quickly, Master More. You could have followed him as a hound follows a fox."

"My man? Your Eminence, I thought that you above all others—"

"Yes, yes, of course. But few have the passion for seeking out heresy that you have. A bit strange when one considers that you are not really a church-man yourself but a . . . lawyer."

Thomas read the word *mere* in the cardinal's pause.

"That is precisely why," Thomas answered, hearing the curtness in his voice and not caring if Wolsey heard it also. "Frith and Tyndale and their kind are breaking the law. The king's own law. I am merely carrying out my duties."

"Yes, yes, of course, Thomas." He waved his beringed fingers airily. "You are wise to do your duty well. That way lies advancement. And there are about to be two posts available. One is the Master of the Stool—an important job. For that one controls access to the king in his most private moments. But somehow I don't think you fitted for wiping the king's arse." He chuckled. "What brings you to my kitchens?"

Though Wolsey was known for his mercurial temperament, he was in a strange mood tonight. Thomas decided he should speak carefully.

"I was looking for one of your watermen, thinking he could ferry me home."

"You came down here looking for a boatman?"

"I was told at the jetty he would be here. He is an exceptionally fast waterman. I promised Dame Alice I would be home for breakfast."

"What is this boatman's name?"

"His name is Robert, Excellency."

"Ah, that one. He has the shoulders of an ox. And he's talkative."

"He helps to pass the time on the journey home," Thomas said warily.

"Anything in particular that you talk about?"

There was suspicion in Wolsey's voice. He'd gotten ever more paranoid with his inability to procure the king's divorce. Thomas decided to be direct.

"He told me about a man named Phillips. A man who is desperate enough to do unusual work. It occurred to me that we need a man on the Continent to seek out Tyndale. It is best to know where one's enemies are at all times."

The cardinal pursed his lips and looked at Thomas with a hooded glance, followed by a knowing smile. "An astute observation."

Thomas nodded to fill the pause. Wolsey leaned against one of the casks for support.

"I'm tired, Councillor. I am beginning to feel like an old man. I will see you at tonight's feast." He crossed the room, leaving Thomas standing in the midst of the wine cocoons, then turned back when he reached the threshold. "You know that other post of which I spoke." His voice was so low Thomas had to strain to hear. "I think it's time for me to retire to York. The chancellorship is about to become available. The king favors you. Says you are a man of integrity," he mumbled. "Though now that I think upon it, you may not be suited for this post either because it involves the king's great hairy arse as well." He chuckled, pausing for effect. "You either have to wipe it or kiss it. Somehow I don't see you doing either. That seems more your rival's strong suit."

"My rival, Eminence?"

"Master Cromwell. Surely you've felt his hot, ambitious breath on your neck. He is as ruthless as you, but perhaps less *principled*. It will be interesting to see who the king favors. The ardent heretic hunter or the Lutheran reformist lying in the weeds."

Thomas was shocked at the cardinal's candor, though not at the announcement. The whole court knew Wolsey was in trouble because he'd been unable to obtain a divorce, but such language could be called treasonous. Thomas wished he had not heard it. And Thomas Cromwell! He could almost laugh out loud at the thought that the hawk-eyed fortune hunter and sycophant would ever get any further at court than Wolsey's aide. His ambition was blatant, but he was clumsy in his machinations. The fact that he held private sympathies with reform was not news either. The cardinal probably suffered this viper in his bosom because of the *common* bond they shared. That the son of a butcher might glory in the advancement of the son of a brewer over Sir John More's son should come as no surprise.

He must make a formal protest at the cardinal's indiscreet remarks. Who knew who might be listening at the door? "Your Eminence—"

Wolsey waved him silent. "By the by, Councillor, the king's whore will be at tonight's feast. You may get your first opportunity to practice your arse-kissing."

TEN

*I am amazed at your foolishness in getting entangled,
even engaged, to this silly girl at court. I mean Anne
Boleyn.*

—Cardinal Wolsey to Lord Percy as
quoted by Cardinal Wolsey's servant

he trumpets sounded. The marshal of the hall raised his white
wand and proclaimed in a tonsil-baring bark above the general din of music
and snarling dogs and laughter, the scraping of chairs and benches, "His
Majesty the King." A general hush fell on the assembled courtiers as Lady
Anne Boleyn entered the great hall at Hampton Court on the magnificent
arm of Henry Rex. Anne arched her back and thrust up her chin in the
proud pose that denied her lower status as the mere daughter of a knight
among the dukes and earls who watched her progress toward the dais.

But Anne did not step with Henry onto the dais. Having finally persuaded him that such a premature action would only inflame her enemies,
she paused instead at the table just below, where the king handed her off to
her brother George. Anne tried self-consciously to withdraw her hand as
the ceremonial kiss lingered overlong. But Henry, like a small boy caught
with his spoon in the honey jar, gave her a wicked smile and held on. *He
revels in flinging it in their faces,* she thought.

She was aware of every eye in the room watching, speculating on the king's public gesture of affection. She was glad she'd worn the yellow brocade gown and the green satin sleeves lined with miniver. The fur was warm in the overheated hall, but the matching black velvet bandeau embroidered with emeralds and golden thread made her dark eyes look brighter. The gown was Henry's favorite and the headpiece and sleeves had been a gift from him.

Henry mounted the dais and seated himself in the high-backed chair on the platform directly in front of Anne. More scraping and shuffling, and the courtiers settled into their seats. *That's it. That's the worst of it,* she was thinking as she smiled reassuringly at Henry. It was a see-it-is-better-this-way smile. He smiled back at her briefly—that mischievous, bedevilment grin—that usually augured ill for somebody. She was wondering who was the target of his scheming this time—her archenemies perhaps—when he lifted his glass and, staring right at Anne, shouted, "Master of the Hall, a toast to the lovely Lady Anne Boleyn who favors us with her presence."

Anne, though she felt her face flush with embarrassment, stared back at him, refusing to drop her gaze in some hypocritical pose of maidenly modesty. He always said he liked her spirit; well, she would show it to him. She stood up and curtsied deeply in one graceful swoop, her elbows almost brushing the floor. A diffident applause broke out among the courtiers. Without removing his gaze from her, Henry lifted his goblet and drained it, then laughed as exuberantly as he drank.

Fill up that majestic belly, Henry, she was thinking, for she knew he would send for her at evening's end and the more he ate and drank, the less trouble she would have fending off his too amorous advances. He would as like as not fall asleep mid-wooing and she would be spared her increasingly awkward and even dangerous evasive maneuvers.

As the musicians began playing and the servants poured wine at the other boards, Anne considered her enemies on the dais. Beneath lowered lids, she watched Wolsey, the man she hated most in the world, the man who had banished her lover from court, watching her from his place on the dais, his face a curious blend of disapproval and disbelief. She noticed, too, how the king ignored him.

How is it, my lord cardinal, to feel the heat of the king's disfavor? If I have any influence you will know more than disfavor. And I will have influence. You banished in disgrace my sweet Percy, sent him to his father with his tail tucked between his legs like some sniveling pup, instead of the glorious youth of my dreams. Well, who is the silly one now, my lord archbishop? If this silly daughter of a knight cannot have a lord perhaps she shall have a king.

Thomas More flanked the hated cardinal on one side. At the toast in her honor he had lifted his glass but had not raised it to his lips. Not an oversight, she was sure. But on the other side sat Secretary Thomas Cromwell, his expression far different from the stoic faces of his companions. He was almost smiling. It was rumored among the courtiers that he had secret Lutheran sympathies, which would explain his singular lack of antipathy toward Anne. Or perhaps he was just another of the many sycophants who always smiled at the king's actions. Whichever, she was cultivating a tentative alliance with him, contriving to gain his approval with smiles and entreaties for his opinions.

Her brother George interrupted her thoughts. "Father would be pleased to see how the house of Boleyn basks in the royal favor," he whispered. "A boon for us all, thanks to you, dear sister. I'll drink to that," he said, raising his own goblet to be filled by the passing steward.

"Shush, George. You gloat too openly. A king's favor can be as fickle as his desires. Much good it did our sister. All she got from her alliance with the king was his bastard. Watch about you and learn who your enemies are."

"Oh Annie, you are shrewder than Mary. She gave it away too freely. The pleasure is more in the chase than the catch. Here, have some of this comfit. It is the same first course as is served at the king's board. We are favored even over Lord Suffolk, the king's jousting partner." He nudged her shoulder and gave a snort of derision. "Look at him. He is stabbing at his dry salet as though it were some peasant's fare."

"He's lucky to be sitting where he is. Henry has been upset with him since—"

"Lady Anne." The majestic voice from the dais boomed loudly enough for everyone in the hall to hear. The music stropped abruptly. "Is your first course to your liking?"

She stood up, this time dropping a perfunctory curtsy, conscious of many stares boring into her. "It is delicious, Your Majesty. Thank you for inviting us."

"Then, please, sit back down and eat it. Keep your brother dear company."

Little gilded cake crowns were being placed before them. "Shall we eat these or wear them?" Henry mocked loudly, and removing the golden coronet he wore, replaced it with the cake.

Beside her, George looked uncertain, then reached for his little cake crown. She put her hand over his and shook her head, then whispered, "The king does not respect those of whom he makes fools."

Nervous laughter wafted through the hall as some followed suit, but she warned George with her eyes. Henry was playing at farce, leading the more vacuous among them to follow his lead so he could later mock them.

"Troubadour, we would have a love song for the ladies. Play."

The king waved at the air with the cake, which he had removed from his head. He pretended to take a bite as, grinning, he scanned the boards to see who would follow. He laughed uproariously when half the courtiers chomped down on the cakes that probably by now were crawling with head lice, then he gestured impatiently for his cupbearer to refill his goblet. Though the evening was young, he appeared quite drunk—but she could never be sure. Sometimes he feigned ignorance or inebriation to lull his enemies into carelessness.

She hoped he was too drunk to notice that Sir Thomas More had ignored the whole fiasco while fastidiously scraping the gilding from his crown cake, as though it were some kind of foul poison, and then eating it. The expression on his face showed that he disapproved of the king's idea of a joke or of gilded cakes or both. Not that she cared to spare Sir Thomas the king's disapproval, but who knew where such a scene might lead? Verily it would end with her at the center being pulled like a bone between the quarreling dogs under some of the boards.

The lute player began strumming once again and the opening strains of a familiar melody wafted through the hall.

"Do you like love songs, Lady Anne?" Henry's voice boomed.

Anne stood up again. She was becoming annoyed at all this popping up and down like a court jester in a box. He was doing it on purpose. He was peevish because she was not beside him as he had wanted.

"All ladies like love songs, Your Majesty. I am no different," she said as gently as she could despite her annoyance, hoping to soften his irritation with her own mild tone.

"Then pray you give your liking or no of this one. Your king has written it and would have it sung for your pleasure."

"My family is much honored, Your Majesty." She curtsied again deeply, watching how the silk folds of her yellow kirtle caught the candlelight to best advantage.

She was ever cautious of her movements, taking care that she did all with grace. She was no great beauty by fair, blue-eyed court standards—as her detractors never tired of pointing out—and she knew it. But she knew, too, where her assets lay and how to accent them. She had pushed her small round bosom high above the square ribbon-bound neckline and was aware that he could see it from his seat to best advantage when she curtsied low. Her knees were becoming fatigued with so much dipping, but even from several feet away, she could almost feel the heat from his desire.

The singer began. The plaintive lyrics floated out across the hall. "Alas, my love, you do me wrong to cast me off so discourteously . . ."

Anne felt her face flame. The king was courting her openly, flagrantly, right here in front of his whole court even when she had warned him. Katherine had many supporters in this room, not to count the many staunch Catholics who feared the growing influence of a reform-minded favorite. Like Wolsey. Like Thomas More. She could feel the resentment they dared not show openly burning as resolutely as her own hatred for the cardinal.

She maintained her posture throughout the song, listening to the lyrics, wishing she were back in the French court, laughing with the ladies-in-waiting, or riding across the flower-strewn meadows of Hever Castle, or huddled with her tutor in the Netherlands, debating theology, or, best of all, stealing kisses with sweet Percy outside the queen's dressing room—wishing she could be anywhere but here being made a spectacle of.

"Greensleeves is my one desire."

Her face felt as though it would crack from the false smile. Her lower limbs were almost numb. Then came the refrain.

"If you intend thus to disdain, it does the more enrapture me."

And when I am your queen, what then? She thought of Katherine on her knees for hours in her papist chapel, praying for her husband's return.

The love song ended and applause broke out among the courtiers and cheers of "Bravo" and "Huzzah." The king waved the guests to silence.

"Lady Boleyn, what think you of your king's musical offering?"

She heard a sharp intake of breath at the board closest, imagined the knowing glances and the nudges, the whispering behind hands.

She lifted her head, her chin jutting boldly forward. "Sire, I think you are a man of many exceptional talents. This is but one example."

He frowned down at her. It was as though the great company disappeared and they two were alone. "God's blood, woman, what does that mean? Stand up and say to your king directly. Do you like the ditty 'Greensleeves' or do you not?" he shouted, enunciating each word carefully, his tone demanding.

Anne raised herself as gracefully as possible, surprised her limbs would even work at all. Gloating expectation laced the silence in the hall. She could almost see the eyes behind her squinting in ecstasy, hear the thoughts that whirled around her. Was this the moment that the king's mistress would finally get her comeuppance? She did not raise her voice. Let the sycophants strain to hear until their ears fell off.

"Everything Your Majesty does is to my liking. The lyrics fall upon my ear unlike any music I have ever heard or am like to hear again—unless, of course, Your Majesty bestows another gift upon us."

He scowled at her as though he were trying to make sense of what she said, then broke into a broad grin and laughed loudly. "Cupbearer," he called. "Fill me up again. My muse has spoken and I must fortify myself."

Some among those assembled responded with subdued laughter. Others were tentative in their agreement.

During the remainder of the meal, Anne did not have to stand again but fiddled with her food in silence, half listening to George prattle on beside her about his ambitions at court. The room grew overheated. She longed to remove the furred sleeves but knew her enemies would seize upon it. She could almost hear their prattling tongues, their snide laughter. "The king sang a love song to his Lady Green Sleeves whereupon she promptly removed them."

Henry finally stood up. Once again there was a scraping of chairs and a scrambling of feet as the courtiers stood. With a loud belch the king left the dais, a groomsman on each side of him to steady him. More and Wolsey followed shortly after but left through separate archways.

Only Thomas Cromwell was left at the king's board. Anne looked up to find his speculative gaze turned on her. When she did not turn her gaze away, Cromwell raised his glass and smiled.

The king did not call for her for two days. But Secretary Cromwell did.

⋆⋆

Kate counted only four in the little shore party gathered on the shingle beach. Five should have been waiting by the signal fire, but in spite of his protests, John Frith, feverish and ill and scarcely able to stand, had been put to bed by Lady Walsh.

"But I have to meet the ship. Sir Humphrey has arranged it. Tyndale will be expecting me," he said, staggering as he tried to stand. "If I stay here, I shall put you all in danger."

Lady Walsh had exchanged glances with her husband, who placed his hand on Frith's shoulder, forcing him back down. "There will be another ship. You cannot go as you are. You'll never stand the voyage."

"William would hold us responsible if anything happened to you. We owe it to him," Lady Walsh had said. "At least, to see that you are cared for until you are strong enough to travel."

Kate was grateful for the warmth of the fire. The night chill penetrated the finely woven fabric of her full skirt and thin shawl, but she was glad to be in a dress again.

"It's your choice, of course, my dear, but I see no reason why you shouldn't act as yourself in your brother's behalf," Lady Walsh had said, as she pulled out a simple gown of soft gray wool. "Here. I think you are my daughter's size," she'd said, shaking out the skirt and then adding a lace cap and kerchief. "I assure you we will not be the only two in skirts to meet the boat. Local women feed their children by selling the cloth they weave in their cottages, and they are not eager to pay the king's export tax."

Kate had accepted the dress with gratitude—as well as the clean rags and belt her kind hostess provided—and joined the little smuggling party with some trepidation. But whatever Lady Walsh had said to Swinford and Lord Walsh, they had treated her as if they had known all along she was John Gough's sister. She wondered if Frith had also been told that his traveling companion had not been who he thought. Though what did it matter what he thought of her? After tonight she would never see him again anyway. Though pity that was. She'd liked him—a lot. She couldn't help but wonder how he would have responded to Kate rather than her brother John. Would he have had that same easy manner, that same charming smile that offered ready friendship?

Lord Walsh and Swinford tended the fire as it spewed hissing tendrils of orange against the night sky. In spite of the curling smoke, the air had that swept-clean smell that it carries after a storm. The rain had stopped, and the clouds, though still backlit in the distance every now and then, were breaking up. A full moon floated among them, like the ghost ship whose shadow they could see riding on the moonlit sea.

"Do you think they see us?" Kate asked, trying hard to keep the excitement from her voice, forgetting all about the discomfort of her woman's curse.

"See us! How could they not, with that great silver orb hanging over us? The customs men can probably see us too."

"Everything will be all right," Lord Walsh reassured them. "This captain knows what he's doing. He's probably bribed the customs people to look the other way."

The moon slid behind a cloud, and the sea and the ship vanished. The world narrowed down to just Swinford, Lord and Lady Walsh, and herself within the small circle of firelight. Even the sea disappeared except for its gentle lapping against the pebbled shore.

"Do you think Master Frith will recover?" Kate asked.

Lady Walsh gave her a knowing smile. "I wouldn't worry, my dear, he's young. He'll—"

But before she could finish her reassurance the moon shed its diaphanous caul and reemerged in the open black sky to reveal that the ship had calved. A small boat glided toward them, riding low in the water. As it neared, Kate made out the figures of two men, their arms moving in rhythmic rowing motion.

She was wondering how four people and two of them women could carry such a heavy load as weighed down the boat when behind her she heard a rustle of leaves. A hay wain pulled by four dray horses appeared. The wagon wheels were rag wrapped as were the horses' feet so that they could move soundlessly through the meadow and onto the beach. The wagon had a driver and three other burly men besides. And surely enough, just as Lady Walsh had promised, there were three women, each with a large bundle on her lap. The driver reined in the horses just outside the circle of firelight. The horses neighed gently, as if to signal their familiarity with the place.

The small boat landed on the beach, its bottom crunching against the pebbles as the two men got out and dragged it onto shore. The inhabitants of the wagon jumped down and began to unload and then reload the wagon, each movement carefully planned and rehearsed for speed and efficiency. Feeling awkward and not knowing exactly where she should fit into such a dance, Kate watched Lady Walsh for some clue. But she was busy talking to the tall man who'd manned the front of the little skiff. Kate could catch only a word here and there but enough to figure he was the captain and Lady Walsh was explaining to him that he would not be picking up his passenger after all.

She saw that the others were forming a line between the wagon and the boat and handing down the cargo to the driver of the wagon who was stacking it. She took her place at the end, closest to the boat where the back rower was handing off the fardels. They began with the lightest bundles on top and by the time they got to the heaviest crates—which Kate supposed held the books, though they were marked as spices—Lady Walsh came to stand opposite her and together they did the work of one strong man.

The captain stood off to the side talking to Lord Walsh. They exchanged papers and Lord Walsh handed him a purse, which the captain weighed with a smile and a toss of his head. Something in his confident manner, in the way the moonlight caught the flash of white teeth in a wide curved smile, treaded on the hem of memory. She was sure she'd seen him before. But no, of course not. Where would she have met a sea captain, and a smuggling sea captain at that?

They were unloading the last one, a small crate marked with the letter *B*. Kate and Lady Walsh reached for it—from its weight, she guessed it held books too—when the captain strode over and lifted it from their hands to Lord Walsh's.

"Take care of this one. It's going to Lady Anne. I was told that you would see that it was personally delivered to Hever Castle."

"You were told correctly. We'll not take it to the church at Worle. I'll take it back to Little Sodbury."

Behind them the horses snorted their impatience.

"They're in a hurry to get this night's work behind them and get back to the stable," the captain said. "And we'd be wise to do the same. Tell the passenger I'll be back on the next moon, if he can wait."

"We'll be looking forward to seeing you," Lord Walsh said. "This is dangerous work, you're doing, Tom, but worthwhile."

The captain shrugged off the compliment. "I'm compensated well enough. The League sees to that. And as to the danger." He smiled and touched the short sword at his belt. "I've a companion at my side more constant than most."

His hand rested on it lightly, almost caressingly. Kate gave a little shudder, thinking how easily he might plunge it into a man's flesh. His cuff flowed over the silver hilt in a white froth of lace, half covering his palm, leaving only the long thin fingers exposed against the metal. *The lace cuff! The long thin fingers resting lightly around metal.* Suddenly Kate knew where she had seen that lazy smile, that swaggering manner—and a lace cuff, albeit somewhat begrimed, not snowy white as this one. She gave a little gasp of surprise.

He turned his gaze on her. "Mistress, are you well?"

"Thank you, sir, quite well," she said, dropping her gaze, hoping to avoid recognition.

"Have we met?"

"I'm sure not," she said, moving toward the wagon.

"Hmm," he said, his face a mask of concentration, then a flash of white teeth and he strode toward her; tucking his finger under Kate's chin, he lifted it to look her full in the face. It was a bold and disrespectful gesture—but what else could she expect from such a man?

"Mary! No . . . not Mary!" he said. And then he threw back his head and laughed and asked like an old friend who happened upon her at some social affair and not an outlaw—two outlaws—courting danger beneath a smuggler's moon, "How fares your brother, the printer. Is he well?"

She jerked her head as though she were shrugging off a fly. He dropped his hand. "My name is Kate," she said. "My brother is out of prison, but he's no longer a printer. He has retired with his wife and child to the country."

The captain laughed. There was a hint of mockery in the laughter. "Well then, Kate, he's smarter than I thought. I feared he had that something in his nature that drives a man to martyrdom as though it were some great prize of honor."

"And you have not that something in your nature? What is the penalty for smuggling Bibles?"

"The same as for smuggling spices and wine. It's all contraband to me—contraband and profit."

"So you will swear whatever oath is put before you if you are caught?"

"I don't intend to be caught," he said, striding away from her.

"Don't let Captain Lasser bluff you, Mistress Gough. He's not as mercenary as he sounds. I've known him to take some risks that no ordinary man would take to serve a more honorable cause than profit," Lord Walsh said.

The captain slapped the lord on the back as though they were equals. "There is no more honorable cause than profit, my friend," he said, as he jumped into the small skiff and picked up the oars. The boat rode much higher in the water now, the cloth being much less weighty than the Bibles. He waved and signaled the other rower to push off.

"There is that risk that profits the soul and not the pocketbook," Lady Walsh called to the departing skiff.

"I never dispute a lady," the captain called back, "even when I have the time."

"God's speed to the *Siren's Song*, Tom," Lord Walsh called, and then turned to the little shore party. "We'd best be off too. The priest of St. Martin's at Worle will give us out and go home."

Kate watched as the little boat headed into the silver wake of the setting moon, heard the waves lapping against its hull. The hilt of the captain's side-arm flashed in the moonlight. She frowned, remembering the feel of his fingers on her chin, and wiped at it with her shawl.

⚜

The eastern horizon had begun to lighten by the time the smuggling party returned to Little Sodbury. Exhausted, Kate followed Lady Walsh to her bedchamber, wondering where and when she would be able to sink into blessed oblivion. They had carried the crates and bundles up the staircase to the octagonal turret in the little church at Worle where they would "rest" for a few days among the rafters of the church roof until such a time as they would secretly be emptied out parcel by parcel, cask by cask, to the various distributors and buyers who would come for them.

The only one they kept in their possession was the small box marked with a *B*, which Lady Walsh now secreted beneath her bed. "It's for Lady Anne Boleyn," she whispered. "And it's not the first one," she added as, rummaging in her cupboard, she pulled out a clean linen shift and handed it to Kate. "They say she's very reform minded."

"But you mean—"

"Yes. And she may one day be queen, if the king has his way. Who knows where that might lead?" She lit two candles from the lamp beside her bed and gave one to Kate. "I've put you in the chamber where Master Tyndale himself stayed when he was tutor to our children. They were well past the age when they needed tutoring, but his ideas were so stimulating, and he was doing such good work in this little room. It's quite cozy. You'll be comfortable there."

She led Kate down the corridor and up a winding stair to a small room furnished with a bed and a desk and a chair. A pale gray light from a narrow window crept into the room, revealing a pen and inkwell on the desk. Probably the very one Tyndale used when he stayed here.

"I'll leave you to your rest, my dear. We'll talk tomorrow," she said. Then added with a weary smile, "It's already tomorrow, I guess. I think I may be getting too old for these little adventures. I'm going to grab a few winks, too, as soon as I check on Master Frith."

Kate collapsed onto the bed and blew out her candle. She lay in the gray light, listening to the stirrings of the servants rousing to their dawn chores, and feared she was too tired to sleep. It had been, all in all, she thought, the most exciting day and night of her life, and how she longed to tell her brother about it. But he would probably only scold her and remind her of her promise. Perhaps Master Frith would be well enough tomorrow that she could tell him about the grand adventure he had missed.

At least now she would have some inventory to take back to London to sell. She would do it discreetly at first, but if the king's favorite had Lutheran sympathies, it was probably just a matter of time before they could sell openly again. Maybe John and Mary could return and John could reopen the print shop. He would be glad she had not abandoned it then. Things could be as they were before.

But as fatigue overtook her the last image in her mind was not of Master John Frith or of her brother John, but of Captain Tom Lasser with his dark eyes and mocking laugh. She'd never met a man so reckless or so arrogant, she decided, so completely devoid of honor, despite what Lord Walsh had said. She pitied his wife—if that unfortunate woman existed—for he was sure to find a hangman's noose at the end of his adventures.

ELEVEN

Turkies, herisies, hops and beer
All came to England in one year.
—From *Tusser's Hop-Yard*
by Thomas Tusser (sixteenth century)

ate woke the next morning to a gentle knocking, followed by a maid carrying a pitcher of steaming water with a fresh towel and soap balanced on top. Kate sat up in bed and rubbed her eyes, uncertain at first where she was. Then she remembered—Little Sodbury Manor. She was waking up in the very room that was once inhabited by William Tyndale, the man whose name she'd seen on so many books.

"Good morning," Kate said to the chambermaid. The girl looked to be barely more than a child. She bobbed a small curtsy in Kate's direction, then poured the water into a bedside basin.

"Good morning, mistress. I'm Tildy. My lady said to see that you have everything you need," she said, pulling a comb and silver-backed hand mirror from the voluminous pocket of her apron, followed by a handful of dried herbs that she crushed into the water. The sweet smell of lavender rose on the steam. From the other pocket, she removed several clean linen strips and placed them beneath the mirror without comment. Then also without comment, she picked up the wad of Kate's soiled linen and slipped it discreetly into the now empty pocket. "My lady said to tell you she will be in the brewery this afternoon and she would like to speak with you. When it suits you."

"What time is it now?" Kate asked more to cover her embarrassment at having someone else do something so personal for her than from any real need to know the time. She supposed this was what it was like to be noble. Well, she for one would rather have disposed of her own soiled linen had she had someplace to do it.

"A little after eleven bells," the maid said, reaching for the chamber pot under the bed. "I am also to tell you that if you go to the kitchen, Cook will give you something to tide you over until dinner." She disappeared momentarily and came back carrying the empty pot. She returned it to its spot. "Is there anything else I can get for you?"

"The young man who came here with us," Kate said, "do you know if he is well?"

"I do not know, mistress, but I can tell you that the older gentleman who came with you left early this morning."

"Left! But where—I was to return to London with him."

"I'm sorry. I don't know where he was going. Only that he took the wagon. I do not think he was planning on returning tonight because I saw Cook give him some provisions. Would you like me to inquire?"

"No. I'll ask Lady Walsh myself," Kate said.

The maid just stood there as though waiting for further instructions. Finally she said, "May I help you dress?"

"Thank you, no. I can manage," Kate said. The girl looked crestfallen. "It's just that I'm used to doing such things for myself," Kate said, thinking she had succeeded not only in embarrassing herself but also the servant girl.

"My lady has said that I should look after you while you are her guest."

"That's very good of you, Tildy, and of Lady Walsh, but I don't expect to be here very long. I thought I would be leaving today."

The girl gave another little curtsy and backed out of the room, leaving Kate to wonder why Swinford had left without her—if he had left without her. Maybe they were just meeting some other cargo, but if that was the case, she would have liked to have gone with them.

But her first task was to find something to eat—she was suddenly ravenous—and then to see what she could find out about the prospects for the young man whose escape from the heretic hunters had been so unfortunately postponed. She was stuffing her wild mop of hair underneath the cap Lady Walsh had provided, when it occurred to her she could find out about

Master Frith and ask in the kitchen for directions to the brewery. But first she had to find the kitchen.

❧ ❦

After Kate had eaten a boiled egg and drunk a glass of sweet milk, milk fresher than any she had ever gotten in London, and learned from Cook that Master Frith had eaten his breakfast—that was a good sign, she thought—she inquired as to the location of the brewery.

"Down the path leading from the kitchen garden and to the left. Ye'll know it by the alebush hanging by the door."

"Alebush?"

Cook clucked her tongue. "You beint from the country, be ye?" And then by way of explanation, "It's the broom used to stir the mash. The yeast left on the broom helps start the next batch working. So they just hang it up by the door till next time it's needed."

Cook must have known Kate didn't understand a whit of what she said. "Ye'll recognize the brewery by the smell. Just follow yer nose."

She was right. As Kate neared the small hut, the smoke coming from the flue in the center of the roof carried a strange smell that became stronger as she opened the door. She entered the room and inhaled the steam from two huge boiling vats hanging over a fire pit in the center of the floor. It was not altogether an unpleasant smell, heady and pungent. She inhaled a bit more deeply. A lethargic, drowsy feeling crept over her, causing her to wonder if the ale they were brewing was so strong it caused light-headedness just to breathe it. She would be careful not to suck in her breath too deeply.

Lady Walsh seemed to feel no effects from the fumes. Her hair bound in a loose kerchief and her face glowing from the steam, she was overseeing the sorting and bagging of small brownish cones into loosely woven sacks hanging from the lowest roof beams. "Here, these are ripe enough," she said, passing a sack to one of the servants. "Add about two pounds."

She motioned for Kate to come in. "We're sorting this year's hop harvest. We grow them ourselves from seeds that Lord Walsh brought back from Flanders." Then she added with a wink and a nod, "Lord Walsh is very particular about his brew—he prefers beer to ale. It's for our own personal use—and that of our tenants and servants, of course. Anything else would be . . . unlawful."

The irony of this statement was not lost on Kate.

"Your timing is excellent. I need a break. I hope you slept well," Lady

Walsh said, taking off her apron and dropping it on the sorting table. The linen was streaked with powdery yellowish stains, and her hands were coated with the same yellow substance. She wiped them on the apron as carelessly as only a woman who never had to worry about laundry and stains would do.

"I'll be back in two hours to help you pour off the first water," she called to the four servants minding the vats. "Come on—stir lively." She made an exaggerated sweeping motion with her hands. "Sing. It'll keep you awake." And then to Kate as they closed the door behind them, "The steam from the malt is a soporific. I'll be lucky if I don't come back to find them all asleep and the mash burned."

As they bustled back toward the manor house, Kate had to step "lively" to keep up. The woman had to be at least fifty years old. How did she have so much liveliness left in her?

"My lady," Kate said, catching up to her and trying not to appear out of breath, "I am truly grateful for your kind hospitality." She was feeling her way, trying to think how best to bring up what the maid had said about Swinford leaving. "But I—that is, the maid said—"

"You want to know when you can get your books and return to London." They had reached the heavy oaken door of the back entrance and Lady Walsh sat down on an oak bench beside a pretty little knot garden. "Let's rest here a minute, enjoy this glorious autumn sunshine," she said, patting the spot beside her. A few yellow and red leaves had gathered in between the knots of herbs. She raked at them with the toe of her shoe, releasing the fragrance of rosemary.

"Tildy told you Swinford left, didn't she? That girl has a sharp eye—and a loose tongue," Lady Walsh said as a fleeting look of irritation crossed her face. "She wants training in the ways of a great house. But at least she was correct in her information. I took the liberty of letting Swinford go back to London without you. He had to leave early to pick up another shipment for Sir Humphrey on the way back, and I knew you needed your rest."

"But how—"

"I hope you're not upset. I realize that it was presumptuous of me. But you can return to London on the morrow. I will send you back with a safe escort. A young gentlewoman doesn't need to be traveling in the back of a wagon like a common washerwoman. It isn't safe and it isn't . . . seemly."

"But that will be such an imposition, and I'm already in your debt," Kate said.

"It is no imposition, I assure you. We have frequent traffic back and forth to London. It's been a while since I've had your particular ailment, but I know you'll feel more like traveling in a few days. You can go as early as tomorrow, if you like." She paused, as though uncertain how to proceed. "There is one thing you could do this afternoon, if you're feeling rested."

"Anything, my lady."

"Would you mind sitting with Master Frith a few hours? He's gravely ill. Gilbert, Lord Walsh's most trusted manservant, watched over him all night, but he needs to sleep a few hours, and I really am needed in the brewery."

"But Cook said Master Frith ate his breakfast," Kate said, not quite certain why she should feel so dismayed at this news. "I thought that meant he was better."

"Gilbert ate his breakfast. We plan to tell the servants that he was well enough to leave."

"Well, of course, I'll do whatever I can. He seems like such a nice man, but I don't know much about nursing."

Lady Walsh looked relieved. There were dark circles under her eyes. Kate wondered how much sleep she'd had. "That is very kind of you. Gilbert has already seen to his personal needs. You just need to be there if he wakes up to give him water or reassure him. Apparently he has a fever in the blood, probably from his ill-treatment in the cellars. I'm afraid his escape and subsequent journey have proven too much for him in his weakened condition."

"But he will live, right? Have you sent for a doctor or a barber surgeon?"

Lady Ann smiled. "I'm afraid, my dear, that we are in a bit of a quandary. His presence here needs to be kept as quiet as possible. There are those in the village who would not hesitate to turn in a friend of William Tyndale's. He's made more than a few enemies among the local clergy. And in this environment of persecution—"

Kate nodded. She understood completely—she might not have a few months ago, but she did now after John's ordeal.

"That's why I'm so grateful for your offer to help. In such a large household—well, you've already seen how servants yap about what they overhear even without meaning to do harm. The fewer people who know of his presence here, the better. That's why we can't ask another of the servants . . . well, you've already seen how prone to gossip Tildy is."

It's not like you have someone to hurry back to, a little voice in Kate's head said. The image of John Frith, wan and pale, his head slumped over as he slept in the wagon, his black lashes against his white cheek, the brilliant smile he'd flashed at "John Gough" whom he thought a "brother," intruded. Before she knew it, Kate said, "I can stay a day or two longer to relieve Gilbert, if you think it will help."

And before she could retract her statement, Lady Walsh grasped her hand. "Oh, would you?"

As Kate pondered the foolishness of her offer, a crimson leaf drifted down, followed by another and another until there was a little garland of them draping the rosemary bushes. Thinking to amend her promise, she inhaled sharply. The air carried the faintest scent of wood smoke flavored with the bitter hops. Lady Walsh stood up, smiling, certain that the matter was resolved.

"You'll not be sorry, my dear. We will make it worth the delay. There is nothing quite like an English autumn in the country," Lady Walsh said. The shadows under her eyes seem to visibly lighten. "Now, if you are sufficiently rested from our little adventure last night, you can begin your duties right away, and I can finish with the brewing." She took Kate's hand in hers, half pulling her to her feet. "I'll take you to your patient," she said.

It's only for a day or two. Kate repeated in her head. *Only a day or two at the most. Where's the harm in that?*

TWELVE

Omnia vincit amor: et nos cedamus amori.
[Love conquers all things: let us too surrender to love.]
—VIRGIL, *ECLOGUES*

I t was there, just out of reach, a light flickering in blind Cyclops's cave, and he struggled toward it, but the monster named fatigue dragged him back—as always. The same voice that had beckoned him to consciousness time and again pleaded, "Master Frith . . . please. I saw your eyelids flutter. I know you're in there," and yet he sank deep, deep, deeper, until the voice, fading and expanding like distant music, sank just below his consciousness.

But he felt her touch, light as gossamer, bathing his brow with cool water. Another voice, a man's voice, strong and guttural, echoed down the dry cistern where his will lay curled and brittle as a winter leaf. "Three days. A man can't live without water. Dip your fingers in the water. Place them between his lips."

Send Lazarus to dip his fingers in water.

Not Lazarus, though. These fingers were small and smooth and cool as pearl, and wet against his hot tongue. If he could swallow them he would surely never thirst again.

"He's sucking the water drops! Quick, dip the corner of the rag in water."

Her fingers slid from between his lips, and he would have cried at such a loss if he'd had tears. He chewed at the rag, tentatively at first. Its rough texture abraded his parched lips. It was not soft and smooth like the other—but wetter. He sucked hungrily, like a starving infant who latches onto his mother's breast for the first time.

"That's it. You can do it." Her hair brushed against his cheek as she leaned forward. It smelled of lavender. He sucked harder.

The water squirted down his throat, strangling him. She lifted him to a sitting position. Gasping and sputtering for breath, he opened his eyes long enough to see the face of the angel who held him in her arms.

"Quick. Run and tell milady he's awake," he heard her say. And then turning back to him, she stroked his forehead as all the while she murmured soothing sounds in his ear.

Where this celestial creature lives must surely be paradise, he thought, and he longed to stay. But the light hurt his eyes and made his head pound. He tried to shape his wooly tongue around the words to ask her if she was real or a mere dream conjured by a fevered brain, but the monster sucked him under until he could no longer see her face or hear her voice.

He would have cried at such a loss, if he'd had tears.

≈

Kate jerked awake with a start. Her neck was stiff from sleeping in the chair. The candle had guttered out, but the room was light so it must be morning. She got up, ignoring the pins and needles in her legs, and leaned over her patient, to feel his brow with her palm.

He opened his eyes. "You are much prettier than Lazarus," he whispered.

"Master Frith, you are awake!" she said, peering into the large dark pools of his eyes. "And your fever has broken." She felt her face relax in a smile.

"I've been awake a while. I've been watching you sleep," he said. "You looked so peaceful, you made me feel peaceful." His voice was low and hoarse. It hurt her to hear it, but an almost smile livened his pale face, softening the hollows beneath his eyes.

She blushed and, suddenly conscious of how disheveled she must look, smoothed her wild hair back from her forehead. "That is probably not a pleasant sight for a man returning from death's portal," she said. "Anyway, it is I who was supposed to be watching you sleep."

"Then it was my turn, wasn't it?" He cleared his throat and his voice grew clearer. "It was a sight sufficient to bring a man back from death's portal."

"You must be starved. It's been three days since you've had anything to eat or drink." She poured a half cup of water and held it to his lips. "Sip slowly."

He drank two swallows, and she removed the cup.

"I remember a few drops of water from an angel's hand. That's why I said you're prettier than Lazarus. You know, in the Bible? Where the rich man is in hell and asks for Lazarus to be sent with a few drops of water?"

"The name Lazarus applies more to you than me, I think," she said, and put the cup to his lips again. "Do you think you could take some nourishment? Maybe some broth?"

"Actually, I—" He tried to push himself up and fell back weakly onto the pillow.

"You're too weak to stand. Just tell me what you want."

His ashen face actually colored a bit and suddenly she understood.

"That's a good sign after so long without water. I'll call Gilbert. He's the one who has been helping you. I just looked after you when he couldn't." As she reached for the bellpull he gave a little sigh of relief.

"So I have you to thank for my return from near death, and I don't even know your name."

"You have Lord and Lady Walsh to thank. And my name is Kate Gough."

"You are the wife of the man who came here with me then."

She hesitated for an instant then refilled the water cup and held it to his lips. "If you don't feel sick, you probably could drink a bit more to give nature . . . inspiration."

He shook his head and lay back on the pillow, his face suddenly drained of expression. *Please don't let us lose him again.* But his breathing was even. He closed his eyes and appeared to sleep.

She heard Gilbert's shuffling gait as he entered the room. "You rang for me, mistress," he said, rubbing his eyes. Gilbert slept in the adjoining chamber. A hole had been punched in the wall and a bellpull installed so that Kate could summon him when she needed him. When he was not sleeping, he kept watch just outside the door.

"Our patient is better," she said. "I'm going to the kitchen to see if I can wheedle some broth while you tend to his personal needs."

If John Frith heard her, he gave no sign.

※

"Play that song 'Greensleeves' again," Anne Boleyn said to the lute player who accompanied her into the herb garden at Hampton Court. "It has a pleasing melody."

Pleasing now, though less so when she first heard it three days ago. But

Henry had sent her a parchment wrapped around a ruby necklace with the words of the song written out in his own hand and a postscript begging her pardon if he had caused her embarrassment. She noticed with satisfaction that the window overlooking the garden was slightly ajar. "Pluck the strings with vigor, so the sound can carry to others who might enjoy it," she instructed.

She was gathering lavender before the winter frosts took it. Her maid had suggested that she place it between the layers of her dresses in the chest in her room and had offered to gather it, but Anne had said she would go herself. The garden was directly below Cardinal Wolsey's study window. He would be leaving for York on the morrow and was probably packing up his books and papers—no doubt a melancholy task. It pleased her to think that the vision of her making herself at home in what was no longer his garden would be one of the last memories of the palace he had so loved, that his memory of his time here would be forever tainted, as were her memories of being in Queen Katherine's service. She'd cried all day when Percy went away.

She felt the cardinal watching her, and looking up she gave him a courtier's false smile and waved. He shut the window. She could not tell for sure if he moved away—the light was such that she could only see the river reflected in its leaded panes—but she thought not. When she saw Secretary Cromwell walking past, she hailed him for the benefit of the watcher at the window.

"Come sit with me for a moment, Master Secretary. I find your company agreeable," she called loudly.

"I am honored, my lady."

They sat together on the bench and talked of the weather, the coming winter, the uses of lavender. Anne broke off a sprig and held it to his nose, flirting shamelessly, when it occurred to her that she really did have something to talk to him about after all.

"Master Cromwell, when last we spoke, you told me of your sympathy for certain reformist ideas, which as I assured you I also entertain. You mentioned some young Bible men who died in the fish cellar. Did the cardinal know that they were imprisoned without benefit of a hearing?"

"There is not much the cardinal misses, my lady. I'm sure it would have been reported to him."

"And you spoke of Sir Thomas's 'interrogations.' Did the cardinal know about those?"

"I would assume so."

"Would you go so far as to say Cardinal Wolsey approved such?"

Cromwell's eyes narrowed. "I would say by doing nothing to stop them, he might be said to have given tacit permission, yes."

Anne pretended to drop her voice to a conspiratorial whisper. "Master Cromwell, wouldn't the denial of due process be an egregious violation of English law—even for the chancellor?"

"If it could be proven."

"I see," she said, "but how could a cardinal make an enemy powerful enough to go to all that trouble?" She got up and continued to gather the lavender, releasing its fragrance into the air. Then keeping her tone light, as though it were an afterthought, "It's such a pity about the young men in the fish cellar. And that parson from Honey Lane. I suppose he has lost his living even though he recanted. One would like to do something to help him and the others too, at least the ones who survived." She paused here for effect, then lifted her gaze and held his. "Master Cromwell, I think I'm in need of a private chaplain. Perhaps you can see if the parson of Honey Lane is agreeable."

Cromwell looked startled but recovered quickly. "I will look into it, my lady. Of course, the king would have to agree."

"And what about the others, what were their names?"

"One was named Betts and one Frith."

"What of them?"

"Betts is still recovering, though whether from the fish cellar or the interrogation it is hard to say. Frith has disappeared."

"Disappeared, you say." She laughed. "Well, good for him."

"Well, it may not be good for him. I know that Sir Thomas is scouring the countryside looking for him. He'll probably try to flee, but they're watching all the ports. He is a very bright young man, but I doubt he'll make it."

"Can we not do something to help him?"

"I'm afraid not, my lady. He has broken the law. If he's caught, he'll be brought in and 'interrogated' until he recants."

A shudder passed through her body. "Then I shall pray for him," she said. She'd forgotten all about the watcher at the window and did not see two shadows move away.

❧

During the next week Kate's patient grew stronger every day, strong enough for her to leave, she thought. When she suggested as much, Lady Walsh said, "Fine, my dear, whatever you wish. You have been very kind. I know you never meant to stay this long, but Master Frith is very restless cooped up in that room. Your company is a sweet diversion for him. But the decision is yours, of course."

So every day she thought, *Maybe tomorrow,* until another week had passed. Leaving was not easy. When she was with him, she forgot about the uncertain future before her.

"Tell me about yourself," he said. "How you and your husband came to be in the smuggling business." So she told him about the print shop and the raid, about the contraband books that had had to be burned and now must be replaced. But she did not tell him that John Gough had capitulated to his enemies—or that he was her brother and not her husband. He would only wonder why she had not corrected him when he first made the assumption, and she did not really know why, except that she remembered the casual way he'd draped his arm across her shoulders, when he'd mistaken her for John. She had not wanted to tarnish that intimate moment of warmth and friendship, had not wanted to tarnish his admiration for her brother. She didn't have to. Master Frith would be leaving for the Continent soon, and Kate would go home to London. Their paths would probably never cross again.

They talked at first of serious things: about the mutual threat they shared, of their common enemies, of their faith, of his plans to join Tyndale and translate and write from that safer distance. Once he cried out in his sleep, and when she asked him if he wanted to talk about his nightmare he told her about the fish cellar. She held him while he cried over the death of his comrades, and she cried too.

He told her stories from Virgil and Homer, his animation growing as his strength returned, and there was laughter too—a lot of laughter. Lady Walsh provided a chessboard, and they played for hours—Kate had forgotten how competitive she was. As his appetite returned and she was employed more and more in the subterfuge of feeding him without betraying his presence, they conspired like children, even sneaking out one midnight whilst Gilbert kept watch, to raid the kitchen. She had not felt so merry for a very long time.

"Kate Gough, your husband is a blessed man," he said one day, after she had finally beaten him at chess, and they had laughed at her exultation in that win. He reached out and touched her hand, a friend's spontaneous gesture of affection, but he withdrew it quickly, snatching it back as though the contact burned his skin. "I wonder if he knows what a treasure he has in you," he said quietly. She longed to tell him the truth, but by then it would have been an embarrassment between them and would serve no purpose.

She could no longer avoid thinking about returning to the empty shop and her lonely room above it. It would seem emptier now. But there would be the books she would take back with her, and she still had the ten pounds she'd gotten for the Wycliffe Bible to buy pens and papers and inks that she could resell. Maybe Winifred and her baby would visit again, and they could become friends.

When she looked up from the chessboard, Frith had lain back on the bed and closed his eyes. He appeared to be sleeping.

She tiptoed quietly from his room.

❧

Another week passed and Kate still lingered, though it was clear her patient no longer needed her. Last night a waxing moon had appeared in her window, reminding her that all too soon the *Siren's Song* would come and John Frith would pass out of her life. Both Lord and Lady Walsh had pronounced him fit for travel.

She had known him scarcely three weeks, and it was as though they had been together forever. His nimble wit and easy laughter made it increasingly hard to leave. She felt alive when she was with him—more alive than she'd felt in a very long time. When he smiled at her, it was like feeling the sun on her face after a long winter.

But she would not think about leaving today. Today she and John Frith and Lady Walsh were enjoying a picnic in the Walshes' private garden. It was Lady Walsh's idea—to take advantage of the last of the late-season sunshine, she said, and cheer Master Frith, who seemed to have grown pensive these last few days. Lady Walsh had packed a basket of cold roast chicken and cherry conserve and fresh bread with soft ripened cheese.

"Cook is getting suspicious, I think," Kate said as she spread a cloth on the little table Gilbert had set up. "She cocked an eyebrow at me and commented on how my appetite has increased of late." She laughed, obviously enjoying the fact that they'd been able to keep their secret from leaking into the village. "Tildy has taken to bringing me a double portion without my even having to ask," Kate said. "I wonder what they must think of me in your kitchen."

"I wouldn't worry about it, my dear. We think you are wonderful, don't we, Master Frith?"

But Master Frith appeared not to be listening to this chatter. He had his eyes closed and was slumped in a posture of indifference. At the sound of his name he opened his eyes. "I'm sorry, what?"

"Master Frith, are you unwell? Is it too cool? Should we go back inside?" Kate asked.

"No. The sunshine feels good. I'm sorry. I was just distracted. Stupid of me when I should be taking advantage of such company as even the gods would envy. What is it you were saying?"

"No need to apologize, John. It is not an easy thing to leave one's home behind, to go into virtual exile. I was just commenting on how wonderful we think Kate is."

He smiled weakly. "Yes. Quite wonderful. I'm surprised her husband is content to be so long apart from her."

His voice was tense, almost curt. Kate wondered if she had done something to offend him, then she suddenly realized that Lady Walsh would not know about Frith's misperception. The fact of her earlier disguise had been so quickly forgotten in the crisis of caring for him that she and her hostess had never really discussed it again. She tried to catch Lady Walsh's glance to warn her, but she was bent over fussing with the little brazier that Gilbert had set up against the light chill.

"Husband!" Lady Walsh gave a little laugh. "Wherever did you get such a notion, John? Kate is unmarried," she said, as she stood up and turned her attention to unpacking the basket. "She is a plum ripe for picking for some fortune-favored man." She looked up, first at Kate, then at Frith. The hand holding the plate of roast chicken froze in mid-task. "Oh my," she said, her teasing smile disappearing. "I seem to have spoken out of turn."

After a moment of excruciating silence, Kate stuttered, "I . . . I think Master Frith . . . may have assumed . . . which of course is understandable given the circumstances that—"

"John Gough is not your husband?" he asked sharply.

"No. He is not. I am unmarried. John Gough is my brother."

"The man who rode with me in the wagon is your brother?"

Lady Walsh coughed lightly. "My dears, I think this meal needs some hot cider. You two start without me. I'll be back shortly."

And suddenly they were alone in the garden, surrounded by the smell of wood smoke and the slant of autumn light—and Kate's deception. She could feel his gaze on her, but she did not look up to meet it as she said quietly, "There was no man in the wagon with you."

"No man in the wagon! But I was not so ill as to be that delusional. There was a man in the wagon. We even talked of our shared trials. I remember his voice was hoarse from—"

"I was the man in the wagon. I dressed in my brother's clothes and impersonated him."

He looked at her incredulously. She looked down at her fingers pleating the edge of her shawl, willing them to be calm.

"Just a bit of road grit in my eye," she said in the hoarse whisper she had used when she said those words to him before. She tried to say it lightly, like a joke.

When he did not laugh, she raised her head to gauge his reaction. Would he be shocked, even angry at her deception? His face was inscrutable. He was not looking at her but was gazing into the middle distance, distracted by some vision in his own head. But of course he was, she thought with relief. He had more important things on his mind than the silly misunderstanding between them. It was as Lady Walsh had said. It must be so very hard to leave behind everything that was familiar, harder still to know that he was being hunted by his enemies. She envied him his travel to the Continent, but she did not envy him his exile.

"Lady Walsh said to start without her," he said, breaking off a sliver of bread. He slathered it with cherry conserve and took a bite, then held it out to Kate. A gesture of forgiveness?

She took a bite. It tasted like wet wool.

"I am sorry that I did not correct you when you assumed . . . but it just seemed easier . . . and what difference—"

He looked at her intently, his eyes studying her face as though he were trying to memorize every feature. She grew uncomfortable under his scrutiny.

"You have a bit of cherry conserve right there," he said, reaching out his hand and wiping it away from the corner of her mouth with one finger. He put the finger to his lips and tasted it.

"It is sweeter now," he said.

It was such an intimate gesture, so laden with implication, that she felt almost faint from the pounding of her heart. *He is leaving on the full-moon tide*, she told herself. *There is only heartbreak here*. It was so unfair. She felt the stinging of tears at the back of her eyelids. *Silly girl*, she chided; *he'll forget you in a week and you him*.

He leaned forward and gently touched his lips to hers. *He is leaving on the tide . . . he is leaving on the tide.* "Marry me," he whispered.

Her breath refused to come. "I beg your pardon," she finally stammered.

"Marry me. I am asking you to marry me, Kate Gough," he said. "I am asking you to marry me. Come with me to the Continent."

THIRTEEN

Hey nonny no!
Men are fools that wish to die!
Is't fine to dance and sing
When the bells of death do ring?
—SIXTEENTH-CENTURY SONG
FROM CHRIST CHURCH MANUSCRIPT

aster Frith has asked me to marry him," Kate said, struggling to keep her composure, "and of course it is impossible."

They were in Lady Walsh's chamber. When the lady had tactfully not returned to the garden and the wind had picked up, Kate had urged her patient to retire to his little room in the attic to rest. "You have been very ill," she'd said, trying to summon reason, which seemed to have abandoned the field. "You are anxious. This is no time in your life to be proposing marriage to women you hardly know."

"*Uno.* One woman," he'd said, holding up one finger. "One very beautiful and very desirable woman. My angel."

She merely shook her head in chagrin and with trembling hands gathered up the remains of their uneaten feast. Over his protests, she thrust the picnic basket at him with instructions to enjoy it in the warmth of his chamber.

She had fled in search of Lady Walsh, who seemed delighted with her news.

"I knew it!" she said, clapping her hands. "I told Lord Walsh the two of you would be perfect together! Just perfect. But why is it impossible? Oh." She looked crestfallen. "You are already betrothed."

"No. No, I'm not. It's just that . . ."

"Well, then, my dear, any other obstacle can surely be overcome. I know a priest in Reading who will marry you without the publishing of the banns—when he hears the circumstances."

"But . . . but, Lady Walsh, John Frith is a fugitive! Leaving on the next full moon. In a week! I would have to leave my home, leave England. And he doesn't even know me—not really. He knows nothing about me, about my life. He doesn't know I have no dowry. He doesn't know what he's doing or what he really feels. It's probably as much out of gratitude as anything. He thinks I saved his life. He called me his 'angel of grace.' "

"And that's a bad thing?" Lady Walsh laughed and cupped both hands around Kate's face and drew her close. "What about you, my dear? What do you feel?"

"That's just it. I don't know. I am very fond of him. Very fond, I'll confess it. He is gentle and charming and so smart. Do you know he reads Greek and Latin and German and Hebrew? I will not be like to ever meet his equal again. But I have only known him three weeks. Three weeks!"

"A woman never really knows any man until she marries him and bears his children. You are fortunate. Most girls never have a choice. My daughters married men their father chose for them. Fortune, or God—we can't always know the difference—has chosen for you. What did you tell Master Frith?"

"I told him he needed to think about the fact that he's been very ill, that he is understandably feeling uncertain and afraid, and that I would not hold him to such a rash proposal."

"Very sensible of you. And what did he say?"

"He said he's not leaving unless I go with him."

Lady Walsh laughed. "Well, there you have it, my dear. His life is in your hands."

⁂

The next morning Kate assembled her patient's breakfast, as she did each morning, from the tray that Tildy brought. Carefully securing the contents against prying eyes in a lady's sewing basket, she put in the boiled eggs—all three of them—and two rashers of bacon and two loaves of bread with a pot of sweet butter from the Little Sodbury dairy. Kate hadn't eaten any of it, only pretending to nibble at the bread while Tildy watched with wary eyes. After what seemed like an eternity, the girl had finished her tidying and left. Looking at the food made Kate's throat tighten. Her stomach, like her heart, seemed to have lost its proper function.

She'd not slept at all.

Her mind just kept reliving John Frith's words and that kiss over and over. But it was foolishness, she told herself. Of course. A young man's folly. Impetuous foolishness. He was probably already regretting it. Of course he would be. Well, she would save him and herself the embarrassment of having to retract a proposal made in haste. She would simply leave the basket with Gilbert and inform Lady Walsh that she was going home. Today.

But when she knocked gently at the door, it was not Gilbert who opened it.

"Somebody will see you," she scolded.

"I don't care," the patient said. "I mean, of course I care, but I was so anxious I'd scared you away I forgot to be careful."

"Step aside, please, and close the door." Agitation and anxiety showed in her curt tone. As he accepted the basket from her, her gaze fell on Gilbert's empty cot by the door.

"Gilbert's not here. I sent him away."

"You may regret that. I see you have prepared the chessboard."

He grinned a devilish grin. "I thought we could play for it. I win, you marry me. You win, I marry you. That way we both win."

His way of acknowledging his foolishness? A clumsy attempt to ease embarrassment by making a joke? "You may have need of Gilbert's company after all," she said. "I've come to tell you, I'm going home today."

She watched his expression carefully for a look of relief, but he set the basket down and ran his fingers through his hair, his eyes suddenly sober, no more smile. "So. It was as I feared. I did scare you away. I should not have been so . . . abrupt. But it's just that there's so little time . . . and when I heard that you weren't married . . ." He paused, his eyes widening as if in sudden understanding. "But of course, there is somebody else. How could there not be?"

The disappointment in his voice stole her breath away, and for a moment she wanted to throw her arms around him and tell him yes, that she would marry him, she would follow him to the ends of the earth. But that would be a silly thing. Kate was not a silly woman. If only there were more time. If only . . . "No. There is not . . . it's just . . . impossible. That's all."

"If there is no one else, why is it impossible?"

She closed her eyes, shutting out his face, searching for the right words inside her head.

"I promise . . . I will be a good husband. I won't beat you . . ." His laugh trailed off. "All right, a bad joke." Then scarcely above a whisper, "You might even learn to love me."

She opened her eyes to meet his gaze, his eyes startling in their directness. *How could any woman with a heart not love you?* she thought.

"I can see you feel affection for me now, Master Frith, but I fear it is an affection born of . . . circumstance. You may in time come to repent your choice as hasty and ill-considered. I could not bear that."

He pulled her to him then. She heard the sound of the chessboard crashing to the floor as though it were far off and not right beside them. But when he kissed her, she heard only the blood rushing in her ears. From somewhere she gathered the strength to push him away. When he let her go, she drew a deliberate breath and waited for her heart to stop racing. Red-faced, he bent to retrieve the chessboard and placed it on the table, then picking up some scattered pieces, he piled them in a heap on the board.

"I have no dowry," she said.

"Dowry! You think I care about a dowry? What have I to offer you?" He took both her hands in his, grasping them with a gentle pressure against her pulling away. "I'm only asking you to consider, Kate. You say I have made a hasty choice. It is you who are in danger of making a hasty choice. Don't throw away a chance for our happiness without due consideration. At least stay until the boat comes. Do that much for the man whose life you saved."

"I didn't save your life."

"You made me want to live. It's the same thing."

She couldn't think rationally, not with him so close, not with him looking at her like that. She pulled her hands away and, bending, picked up two errant chess pieces. She placed the bishop in his proper place on the board, but he took the pawn from her, weighing it with his words. "We are more than pawns, Kate. We are free to make our own choices. Kings and bishops shall not forever determine the fate of free men."

"You're fleeing the wrath of a bishop, aren't you, and the king's soldiers on your heels? How can you be anything but a pawn in a dangerous game?"

"My choice, Kate. My choice not to play by the bishop's rules. A man whose spirit is free will never be a pawn in somebody else's game no matter what the consequences of his choice. My place is with William Tyndale.

And your place will be with me, if you choose it to be so. But either way, it will be your choice."

He placed the faceless pawn on the board in opposition to the intricately carved bishop. Brave words, she thought. Everybody knew where the power lay in such a configuration—apparently everybody but John Frith. He was either a fool or the bravest, smartest man she'd ever known. But her brother had spoken thus and even their father. Now she mourned them both. One had lost his life and the other that same free spirit of which he'd also boasted.

"You are an exceptional man, John Frith. You have paid me the greatest honor of my life. The woman that marries you will be blessed. But I'm not sure . . . I have the courage required of such a woman." *And I cannot think rationally with you looking at me like that.* "I need a proper distance from which to consider what you have said. Shall I find Gilbert for you?"

He shook his head. "I am content to be alone, if I am to be deprived of your company."

"Very well," she said, as she opened the door enough to peer into the hallway.

"You will not leave, then, without saying good-bye?" She felt his fingers caress the back of her neck, smoothing a strand of hair that had escaped her linen cap. His touch felt cool against her hot skin.

"I will not leave without wishing you God's speed. I promise."

❧

"The *Siren's Song* will return in five days by the lunar calendar," Lady Walsh said later that day as Kate helped her mark the dates on the cellar barrels. "You need to give him an answer. If you delay much longer, time will make the decision for you."

"I know. I know." The cellar suddenly felt close, the damp air heady with the sour smell of fermenting apples and too heavy to breathe. "But even if— what about the shop . . . and my brother? I can't just leave the country with-out telling my brother where I'm going. I can't abandon the print shop our father left."

"Lord Walsh could send an agent to look after the property. Where is your brother? We can send a messenger, but you may feel you need his per-mission."

"In Gloucestershire. Clapham Farm. Somewhere near Gillingham Manor."

"Why, that's just in the next shire, within a day's ride of here if you leave early. Of course, you may want to spend one night. I suspect we've time for that. Go see your brother tomorrow, dear. It will relieve your mind. I know it would not be easy to go into exile with unfinished business. I'll send an escort with you."

It had not occurred to Kate that she might be that close. What would John say, if she told him about Frith? Would he tell her to go? Or would he just say nothing with that vacant look he'd had since being released from prison? At least she could see him and Mary and Pipkin before leaving. *Leaving? It's an absurdity, Kate. Lady Walsh said exile.*

"I would be so grateful for the chance to visit my brother if it's not too much trouble. Even if . . . even if—"

"No trouble at all. Do you ride?"

"I'm afraid not. We always lived in London. I had little occasion—"

"No matter. I'll send a carriage with a driver. It will take a bit longer, but you'll be more comfortable. I'll see Lord Walsh about making the arrangements right now."

And before Kate could protest, Lady Walsh had swished out of the cellar and up the stairs, leaving Kate standing alone among the oaken casks. She marked the last barrel with white chalk then followed after, her next move apparently having been decided.

☙ ❧

Hey nonnie, ho nonnie . . . Mary Gough was singing as she drew water from the well. It was the first time she'd felt like singing since coming to her parents' cottage. But it was a beautiful afternoon, cool and brisk, with brief, bright sunlight warming her face, and Pipkin bouncing around her skirts making her laugh with his own monotone contribution of *non . . . non . . . non.*

These last weeks had been hard. It had wounded her pride to return destitute to the home of her girlhood, bringing with her a husband and young child, dependent on her parents' charity for their very bread. To be back in her mother's house, doing things the way her mother did, to swallow without comment her mother's unsolicited advice whenever Pipkin was cross, to constantly have to come to John's defense for a circumstance that her good Catholic parents could not possibly understand: all of it had sucked the joy right out of her.

More than once she'd heard her father mutter as he chewed on a frayed willow twig, "A man's a fool to lose everything like that, and for what? Just so some jackanapes upstart can read the Bible for himself. Couldn't understand it if he could read it, most like. Isn't that what the priest is paid to do?"

Her mother would roll her eyes in the direction of where Mary was kneading dough or sewing or nursing Pipkin—who her mother said should be weaned by now, and maybe he should be, but it brought Mary great comfort to snuggle him at her breast. Heaven knew she got scarce comfort from John these days. Little affection passed between them in the close confines of the four-room cottage.

Indeed, John had taken little interest in anything around him. Most days he just sat staring at the fire as though he were alone in the room, answering in monosyllables whenever her father tried to engage him, until the old man had given up trying. But this afternoon the pattern diverged from the usual. John got up from his stool by the fire and announced that the wood supply needed replenishing before the winter set in hard. Her parents had signaled each other with their eyes as if to say *at last.*

Pipkin had held up his arms. "Go," he'd demanded.

"No, Pipkin," Mary had said, hoping the child would not start to cry. "Your papa has work to do. Come with me. You can help draw water from the well."

So John had departed alone, carrying an axe and an empty bag over his shoulder, and if he was not singing, at least there was a familiar confidence in his stride, a sense of purpose that had gone missing of late. Now Mary and Pipkin were on their twentieth song and their tenth bucket of water—back and forth—his small legs pumping to keep up and her back aching from stooping over so the child could "help" carry the water, then lifting him with one arm so he could watch it splash into the rainwater barrel by the kitchen door.

Each time, he squealed and clapped his hands and shouted, "Pash." Each time as they returned to the well, he tugged with both his chubby hands at the rope while she pulled the bucket up the creaking wheel. She was wearing herself out, and there was still supper to help with. But she was wearing him out as well. Maybe he would nap and she could get some peace. Her mother would look fondly at her sleeping grandson and comment on what a cherub he was—she only called him that when he slept—and John would come home, carrying a large bundle of firewood. He would stack it by the hearth with a smile of satisfaction on his face. Her mother would be pleased. Her father would be pleased. And her husband would have made himself tired enough with honest labor that he might actually sleep the whole night through. They would all sit down at the table for once without her stomach in a knot.

She sighed at this tableau of imagined domestic bliss that she'd constructed in her head, knowing it was just that and no more. "I think that's enough for the washing up. We'd better save some water for the gnomes that live at the bottom of the well."

Pipkin's eyes grew wide. "I'll tell you about them after supper if you'll promise to be good and not touch Granny's spindle." She emphasized the word *not*. The spindle had been a particular sore point of late.

After they had "pashed" the last bucket into the cistern, Mary put the child down and, arching her back to ease it, lifted her face to catch a late-afternoon breeze. Chilly now that the sun was so low-slung. She took off her shawl and wrapped it around the child, drew him against her legs, enjoying the wriggling warmth of his hard little body. Mare's tail clouds, clumped in the sky beyond the hills, were already glowing with the approaching sunset. She would have liked to linger here to watch them turn pink and mauve and gold, but she had chores to do.

John should be back anytime. He'd probably gone to the poplar thicket beyond the pasture. She looked down the road to see if she saw any sign of him, but all she saw was a carriage pulled by four horses. They got little traffic this far off the trodden path, so she was surprised to see the elegant coach, bearing a crest that Mary did not recognize, and more surprised to see the smartly liveried driver rein in sharply in front of the cottage. The chickens around the front stoop left off their pecking and, squawking their protests, fluttered away in a cloud of feathers and dust. Mary grabbed her son by the arm while, with her other hand, she shielded her eyes from the bloated sun to better see the visitors. Maybe she could sneak in the kitchen door and make it to the bedroom her little family shared before the callers saw her. She took a few steps in that direction, still holding Pipkin tightly by the hand.

Then she heard someone call her name. She turned around. Even with the sun in her eyes, Mary could see the curiosity in the discerning gaze of her sister-in-law as she stepped from the carriage with all the grace of a lady to the manor born.

Suddenly the squawking chickens, the muddy path leading to the front stoop of the cottage, the oxen in the plowed field, and the sheep huddled in the pen beside the ramshackle barn all stood out in dismal relief. How shabby it must appear to someone seeing it for the first time. But this was Kate, she reminded herself. No need to be embarrassed. After all, Mary's parents were well-off as far as country folk went. But Kate had always lived in the city. One got used to one's own brand of squalor and tended not to see it.

She should rush out and greet her, she thought, should welcome John's sister to Clapham Farm. But she stood rooted to the ground, wishing she'd changed her apron and put clean breeches on Pipkin. But Pipkin decided for her. Breaking free, he hurtled forward and flung himself in the direction of Kate. Dear, familiar laughter rang out as Kate scooped her nephew in her arms.

"Pipkin, I was afraid you might have forgotten me!"

The sight of her wide smile, the sound of her voice warmed Mary's soul. Yet as she rushed forward to greet her sister-in-law, she noted that she carried no valise.

And that was a relief. This household could not stand one more strain on its tissue-thin fabric of domestic peace.

⚘

"Where is John?" Kate asked after she'd gone into the house, after she'd met Mary's parents, after she'd drunk the cool glass of buttermilk Mary's mother had offered for refreshment, and they were alone in the small bedroom. Mary sat with Pipkin in the rocking chair her father had made and Kate perched on the edge of the bed.

"He should be back soon," Mary answered. "He went to cut wood. He's probably taking his time. It's hard for him here, now that the weather is growing cooler, cooped up with my parents all day."

"But it's working out, isn't it? You look well. Pipkin seems happy." But Kate had noticed little things, like how small the holding was and how dreary and sad looking. Even the sheep grazing in the little enclosure looked more lonely than peaceful. It was hard to imagine her brother here. But Kate tried to keep the anxiety from her voice as she asked, "Is John getting better?"

Mary glanced away, out the window, where the twilight was turning the sky to deep purple, as she answered. "We are fine. Pipkin loves it here. He likes the sheep. He calls them 'woowies.' She patted the child in her lap who after his initial greeting had grown suddenly shy around Kate, as though he were confused by her presence here. He snuggled closer and buried his head in his mother's bosom, refusing to look at Kate until he'd drifted off to sleep. "And John is—" She was interrupted by the sound of John's voice in the other room and Mary's mother calling them to supper. "Well, you are about to see for yourself." She reached out her hand and touched Kate's sleeve beseechingly. "Please, Kate, don't mention anything about . . . you know . . . my parents don't understand, and John is just now beginning to—"

"Maaarry." The mother's voice was insistent.

Rolling her eyes in frustration, Mary laid the sleeping child on the bed between them. Kate felt her heart constrict a little as she realized how much she'd missed him. And if she went away with John Frith she might never see him again, might never see any of them. She gently touched her lips to the child's forehead and followed Mary into the one large room that served as gathering place and eating area.

John was stacking wood beside the hearth. She said his name.

He stood up and looked at her. He still held a stick of wood in his left hand. With his right hand he swept back his blond hair—longer and thinner than she remembered—a familiar gesture he often made when he was confused. She had to fight back tears at the sight of the hard lines around his eyes and the frown lines on his forehead that intersected with the scar above his right temple. How could a man age so much in such a short time? She spread her lips in a smile. He must not see her pity.

"Kate?" he said, wonderment in his voice, as though he, like Pipkin, found her presence in this setting an incongruity. For a moment she was back outside Fleet Prison. The memory of it made her dizzy with despair. This place was paradise next to that.

"Hello, John."

"Kate!" The stick of wood thudded against the hearth as he closed the distance between them in one stride. He hugged her to him with a strength that surprised and pleased her. "We have been worried about you all alone in London. Are you all right?" And then holding her at arm's length and not waiting for an answer, "You certainly look all right. They said there was a visitor. I saw the carriage. I just thought it was some toff whose horse had thrown a shoe or something. How did—"

"A friend loaned it to me. Just for this visit."

"A noble friend. And here I was worried about how my little sister would fend for herself."

The light tease in his tone reminded her of the brother she'd known before everything went so wrong.

"Let's eat before the food gets cold," Mary's mother said, ladling something that smelled of sage and onions onto the plates. "Father, get the chair from our bedroom for our guest." The old man dutifully put down the willow twig he was chewing.

"Where's the pip?" John asked.

"He's asleep and pray he stays that way so we can eat in peace," Mary said under her breath as she took her seat.

"Here ye be, mistress." Mary's father stood behind the chair he'd brought and waited for her to sit as though she were the queen and not the sister of the man he seemed only to tolerate. Amazing what power a noble crest carried, she thought.

"Thank you so much, but I really shouldn't impose. The coachman will probably be anxious—"

"We've enough for the coachman too," Mary's mother said, filling a plate with the steaming concoction and propping a large slice of crusty bread on the side. She handed it to John to deliver to the coachman. "Now sit down, everybody, and eat."

Kate took her seat. Mary's mother was a hard woman to stand up against, and she had to admit the stewed rabbit and root vegetables smelled delicious.

John returned quickly. "Don't worry about the coachman, Kate. I took him a blanket for his shoulders and told him where to feed and water the horses. He'll be fine for a while."

"For a while!" Mary's mother's eyebrows shot up in indignation. "Surely you're not thinking of going back tonight. With all the highwaymen who might be about. There's been reports of wolves in these parts too. You can share with Mary, and John can make a pallet by the fire."

"Yes, please, Kate. It would be cruel to leave and not give us a chance to visit," Mary said. "Mum's right. The coachman can quarter in the barn loft with the ostler. I'm sure he'd prefer that to taking his chances on the road at night. Your friend would probably prefer her coach and team not be put at risk either."

"This is really delicious, Mistress Clapham," Kate said to change the subject.

John put down his knife and looked at her hard. "The coachman should go back without you. London is no place for a woman alone, especially one whose brother was arrested for Lutheran sympathies—"

"We want to hear about your friend. Don't we, John?" Mary interrupted.

Kate understood. It wasn't just talk of religious matters that Mary wanted to avoid. Mary didn't want her here on any kind of permanent basis, even though from the very beginning, when John first brought her to the little bookshop on Paternoster Row, they'd always got on.

He'd met her at a fair in Reading and could talk of nothing but her sweet voice and gentle manner. John had gone there to sell books and buy supplies, and his bookstall was next to that of a balladmonger where Mary and her mother had paused to purchase a broadsheet. Not knowing the name of the song she wanted or all the words, she'd sung a few measures for the vendor. From that very moment John had been enchanted.

"My daughter will not marry at fifteen," her mother had said, but still they must have thought John a good enough catch that over the next two summers they allowed their daughter to make extended visits to her aunt who ran a boardinghouse in Reading.

John found many excuses to make the run to Reading, and at the end of the second year, he'd brought Mary home as his bride. She and Kate had taken to each other like sisters, though Kate guessed that two women in a household was one too many. She had offered to move into the little storeroom above the shop.

And if two was to be avoided, three would never do, she thought as Mistress Clapham hovered. Kate indicated that she did not want a second helping with a shake of her head. She decided to assist Mary in her diversionary tactic. "The coach belongs to Lord and Lady Walsh from Little Sodbury. They loaned it to me so I could visit you."

John raised his eyebrows. "Lord Walsh of Little Sodbury? The one who imports—"

"The same," Kate interrupted with a glance at Mary. Kate could feel her own shoulders tense in sympathy with Mary's. "I met the shipment that you could not."

"My God, Kate, do you have any idea—"

"Let's not spoil this fine meal with arguing," Kate said. "Besides, I have happy news to tell you, John. At least I hope you will think it happy. I am to be married. This time next week I will be the wife of John Frith."

Had those words really come out of her mouth?

"Married!" Mary leaped up from the table and wrapped her arms around her sister-in-law, almost upsetting a tankard of milk. "Kate, how wonderful! Who? When?"

"I'm afraid it is very sudden. John"—how strange it seemed to call him by his first name in that familiar way, when she'd always thought of him as Master Frith—"John is leaving for the Continent within a week and has asked me to go with him."

"But why the haste?" Mary's face clouded for a minute, then she lowered her voice as if imparting some shameful secret. "You're not—"

"No, Mary, I'm not. John Frith is—"

"I know who he is," her brother said flatly, pushing a bite of stew onto his spoon with his knife. "He was a shining star at Oxford. Our supplier, Thomas Garrett—you remember, Kate, the one who was arrested at the same time I was—often spoke of him." He seemed not to notice the scowl on the face of his father-in-law, or maybe he did and that's why he said it, for surely he would know Kate remembered Thomas Garrett. "Frith is a Bible translator, like William Tyndale, a friend of Tyndale's. He's probably going to join him. That or he is a fugitive."

Mistress Clapham sucked in her breath, her eyes popping in surprise.

A wailing sound came from the bedroom.

"Oh my. That's Pipkin," Mary said, relief in her voice. "He'll not hush until he gets what he wants. And I'm the only one can give it to him."

"I'll help with the cleaning up," Kate said.

"Nay. There'll be none of that. You're a guest. You go sit by the fire and talk with your brother. Who knows when you'll see him again." Mistress Clapham nodded meaningfully at her husband. "Squire will help me."

Squire looked a bit surprised but recovered quickly, mumbling, "Quite right," as he picked up a dirty plate and looked at it with a puzzled expression before setting it back down.

John got up and, ducking his head under the low-hanging beam that marked a boundary of sorts between the eating and sitting areas, indicated that Kate should take the bent-willow chair closest to the chimney. He sat on the hearth in front of a smoked ham hanging in the inglenook and dodged a braided rope of onions and bunches of dried herbs as he stuck another log on the fire. The flames sucked at it greedily.

"So you're the keeper of the flame," Kate said, trying to steer the conversation away from dangerous waters.

"And not much else," he answered.

Kate was aware of Mistress Clapham's murmuring and the occasional grunt from "Squire."

She and John talked of small things: the weather when she left London, how pretty the countryside was. *Bucolic* was the word she used; *lonely* was a better word, she thought.

"I sold the Wycliffe Bible to Henry Monmouth," she said when the murmuring in the kitchen died down, and the lantern had been extinguished, her host and hostess having gone discreetly off to bed.

"What did you get for it?"

"Ten pounds."

"Ten pounds! Bless Henry Monmouth. I'm glad I didn't burn it."

"I spent some for food," she said, "but I was going to use the rest of it to buy inventory to keep the shop open. Now I suppose I'll use it for a dowry—if that's all right with you, of course."

"Lulay, lulay thou little child," Mary's sweet pure soprano drifted in. The wood shifted in the firebox. She waited for him to answer. John poked at the fire again, sending up showers of sparks.

"So do I have your permission, then?"

"And if I said no—what then? It's a dangerous life you've chosen, Kate, to tie your destiny to such a man. But no more so, I suppose, than trying to make it on your own, smuggling contraband."

"And is this, then, the life you've chosen? After months of this country life, you are content to stay buried in this backwater, cramped like pickles in a jar?" *When you could be doing so much for the cause our father died for*—but she did not say this. What right did she have to gainsay his choice?

"Content? If a man's not content in his soul it really doesn't matter where he lives. Mary's father has promised us a piece of land. There's a fine stand of poplar down the road a piece. Come spring I should have enough timbers for roof beams and a frame. Things will be better when we have our own place."

"Do you plan to farm then?"

He gave a little half-laugh. "Nay. I'm no farmer. But there are a fair number of illiterate yeomen within the surrounding area. I'm a decent scribe. We'll get by with that and what we can raise."

"I'm happy for you, John. I really am," she said, thinking how he'd settled for so little.

The fire was dying down. No sound came from Mary's bedroom. Pipkin was probably asleep, his cherub's body curled inside the too-small cradle beside the bed or nestled against the warm body of his mother, waiting for his father to join them. It made a lovely picture in her mind. Maybe John had not settled for so little after all, she thought, suddenly bone-weary and a little frightened. How did she know what awaited her on the Continent? She hardly knew John Frith. Here was at least a home and a warm hearth. Here was love and intimacy. But she couldn't think about that now. All she wanted was to sink into sleep. "Are you sure you'll be all right to sleep here?" she asked.

"I'll be fine." He indicated a blanket and a pillow piled in the corner. "I sleep here most nights anyway—if you can call it sleep. I don't want to disturb Mary with my restlessness."

"And why are you so restless?" But she knew.

"It's not what you think," he said, his voice suddenly vehement. "I did the right thing by denying my Lutheran involvement. The apostle Peter once denied our Lord. Three times. And three times, Christ forgave him. 'Feed my sheep, Peter,' he said. He looked down at his hands. "I'm just trying to figure out how to 'feed the sheep.'"

"Don't think I judge you for your decision, John. How can I? When I think of what you have sacrificed for those two sleeping in that room. It's just that you were always my hero."

"It looks as though you may have found a new hero," he said somberly. "And I pray John Frith never has to face that same choice."

She opened her mouth to speak but didn't really know what to say. He stood up. "I'll check on the coachman to make sure he is warm and dry in the stable," he said.

When he did not come back she tiptoed by the firelight into the next room, stripped down to her shift, and climbed in bed beside her sister-in-law. She lay awake a long time listening to Mary's rhythmic breathing, listening for the sound of her brother returning. Finally she drifted off to sleep, trying to summon John Frith's warm smile to chase away her fears.

FOURTEEN

For how many men be there whose sons in childhood are greatly disposed by nature to paint, to carve, to embroider, or do other like things . . . which as soon as they say it, be therewith displeased and forthwith bindeth them to tailors, weavers, cloth-dressers, and sometimes to cobblers.
—SIR THOMAS ELYOT ON THE
LACK OF ARTISTS IN ENGLAND FROM
HIS BOOK *THE BOKE NAMED THE GOVERNOR*

fter his third visit to Hampton Court in as many weeks, Thomas More was glad to be back at Chelsea. It was Friday, and he had finished his early-morning ritual, returned his instrument of penance to its box, and fortified himself to face a scourge of another sort, Dame Alice's tongue. "What's the use of having a husband at court, if he is such a close-mouth," she'd grumbled at breakfast when he professed to not having noticed what Lady Boleyn wore, what she looked like, and other trivialities with which women concerned themselves.

"Gossip is a sin, Alice," he'd retorted in his most long-suffering voice. "And court gossip is especially pernicious."

But even her fractious company and incessant inquiries were more to be desired than being in the cesspit that was Henry's court. Better Alice's whip-lash tongue than watching the king of England fawn over his black-eyed

Lutheran whore whilst his good Catholic queen languished in Greenwich. Thomas entered the sanctuary of his study, and taking up the book on his desk, sighed heavily. Here was another unpleasant duty.

On the morning Thomas was leaving Hampton Court, the vicar-general had quietly pulled him aside. Someone within the very household of a lawyer on the King's Bench had deliberately broken the law. Thankfully, before Thomas could comment on such an outrage, the vicar-general had thrust the little codex in his face and demanded, "What make you of this, Master More?"

A quick glance showed the slim little volume to be an English translation of Erasmus's *Treatise of the Paternoster*. And it was translated by his own daughter Meg! Her tutor, Richard Hyrde, a man in More's employ, had written the preface. But the vicar-general pointed out—even as More's heart was swelling with pride at his daughter's accomplishment—that its author, Margaret Roper *née* More, had neglected to gain ecclesiastical permission to publish it. The vicar-general thumped the title page where the imprimatur *cum privilegio a rege indulto* should be and was not.

"Your daughter has broken the law," the cleric said.

"I—I have never seen this book before," Thomas stammered. "I knew she was working on it, but I had no idea she was close to finishing it. I assure you it will be withdrawn immediately if we cannot gain license to publish. My daughter committed this offense in ignorance, and I beg—"

"See to it immediately. We would not want to have to call it to the king's attention. Not now. Not when you are marked with the king's favor."

Now, in the quiet of his study, Thomas thumbed through the book, noting the clean structure, the clear prose style. If only she'd shown it to him first. Certainly a man "marked with the king's favor" could have gained permission for his daughter to publish a pious little booklet, even in English. But maybe not. The image of Wolsey, who had also once been marked with the king's favor, packing up his study to leave his beloved Hampton Court leaped to mind. Thomas had interrupted him at his study window. The cardinal was watching the garden below where the king's whore flirted with Secretary Cromwell. "Look out for that pair, Thomas," the old man had said. "They're very friendly of late."

It was only a face-saving ruse that the cardinal was retiring to York to take over more of his duties as archbishop. The talk at court was that Henry would not suffer him long. Wolsey had grown too powerful, and he had failed in the king's great matter. It was only a question of time before the lord chancellor would be asked to surrender the seal. There was talk—more of that pernicious gossip—that Parliament might even bring him up on charges of violating the Statute of Praemunire because he was a legate to Rome. Wolsey was a legate to Rome because of his own ambition—in his cardinal's heart he'd no doubt harbored the ambition to one day be pope—but he was also a legate because Henry had asked him to be. Sometimes, in the darkest shadow of his soul, Thomas quaked at what entanglements he'd gotten himself into.

"Be careful of the king's favor, Master More," the old man had mumbled. "It is more easily lost than a woman's virtue."

A servant tiptoed into Thomas's study with a coal scuttle and bent to stoke the fire in the grate.

"Barnabas, summon Mistress Roper," Thomas said to his servant's back. "Tell her that her father would speak with her on a matter of extreme urgency."

⚜

Margaret Roper did not look up when her father's servant appeared at the door. She was unpacking the boxes from the printer. At last. The books! The winged bird that was her heart must certainly burst its ribbed cage with so much fluttering. Her hands caressed the leather bindings—that had cost her a pretty penny. She would have to wear last year's cloak and bonnet to pay for it. But it was worth it, she thought as she turned to the title page and traced the letters there: *Treatise of the Paternoster* by Desiderius Erasmus, translated to the English by Margaret Roper." How pleased Father would be when he saw it.

"What is it, Barnabas?" she said, without looking up.

"You father wishes to see you, mistress."

"Tell him I'll wait upon him anon." Maybe she should not have printed so many, she was thinking. Perhaps the girl in the bookshop on Paternoster Row would sell some for her when she reopened. Her shelves were fair sparse. She might be glad to have the inventory on consignment.

Barnabas coughed discreetly. "Sir Thomas said it was urgent."

"Well then, I'll go now," she said, clutching a book to her chest, suddenly eager to see his face. Whatever his "urgent" matter, this should certainly make him smile.

But when she entered her father's study a few minutes later, she found him in a rare temper. He wore such a scowl as he scarcely ever showed to her—to others maybe, but not to her.

"What is it, Father?"

He held up a book. She recognized the cover with dismay. "Oh," she said. "You've already seen it. I was hoping to surprise you—"

"You succeeded admirably," he said dryly. "I might add that it was not a pleasant surprise."

"I don't understand—"

He slammed the book down on his desk, rattling the ink bottles and quill pens lined up there like little soldiers. It was like a slap across the face. "The vicar-general showed it to me. It seems, daughter, that you have broken the law."

"Broken the law! But how—"

He opened the book to the front matter, shoving it so close to her face she shrank away to see it. "Look. Do you see anything wrong with this?"

She tried to focus on the letters. What could possibly be wrong? She'd given due credit to the author. Spelled the title of the work correctly. She shook her head as she fought back tears of chagrin.

He took down a book from the shelf and opened it to the title page, thumped it with his knuckle. "Here, right here. You did not get the king's permission. It is the law, Margaret. You cannot publish without the Church's permission and the king's seal."

"I am so sorry, Father. I did not realize—but how did he come to even have it? I have only just—you were to receive the first copy. What did you tell the vicar-general?"

"They have their spies everywhere. I told him we would take care of it. We'll have to destroy them if we can't get a license."

All that work—all that expense. "Even the beautiful leather bindings?" She could no longer hold back the tears.

He sighed heavily. "Calm yourself, Margaret." The frowning visage softened slightly. "We can salvage the leather bindings. The printer can bind them with a new title page. I think I can get a license. It is a matter of following procedure. There is nothing theological in Erasmus's work to which the Church can possibly object. It is a work meant only for scholars. Even in English, it is not something that would interest the common sort."

"Father, I'm sorry. I thought you would be pleased. I thought you would be proud of my scholarship. I never thought about—"

He took both her hands in his and gave them a hard squeeze before releasing them. "I am proud of you. But we must be careful. The law can be a valuable tool or a formidable weapon. Now go on back to what you were doing. I'll take care of this," he said with a dismissive wave.

"I was unpacking the books," she said ruefully.

"How many do you have?"

"Four dozen."

"Send them back by Barnabas. See that not one single copy is left out."

She was about to leave when a thought occurred to her. "Father, do you remember the printer in Paternoster Row that I told you about?"

"What printer was that?" he said absently. He was perusing her book, a half-smile playing across his face, apparently his fit of temper past now that he had a plan of action. He was a great one for a plan of action—her father.

"His name was Gough. He was in prison for selling contraband books. I asked you to help him."

"Yes, I remember," he said, turning the page. "I ordered his release."

"Do you know what happened to him? I went by there on my way to the almshouse the other day and the shop was all shuttered up. There was a great chain on the door."

"The shop is probably closed for good. I ordered his printing press destroyed as punishment."

"As punishment! But hadn't he already been punished enough?"

He looked up then from the book and fastened his hazel-eyed gaze on her. "The law is a strict taskmaster, Margaret. Remember that."

"Yes, sir," she said, chastened. But as she slid silently from the room, it occurred to her if the household of the great Thomas More could run so easily afoul of the law, what chance would a lesser man have?

❦

"Master Frith, are you listening?" The cleric frowned at him.

"Forgive me, please," John said. But in truth he had hardly heard a word the man said, some question about consanguinity, he thought. He was too distracted to concentrate. What if Kate turned him down? What if she didn't return before the ship came? He had thought her tied to another man, and when he found that she was not, he had vowed not to leave without her. No other woman had ever moved him so—not even as a youth growing up in Seven Oaks where he'd flirted shamelessly with the Kentish girls and danced the Maypole with the winsome, apple-cheeked Lottie. But when Kate Gough smiled, the clouds parted. He drew comfort from her voice; her touch sent his senses reeling. Though he knew it was wrong of him to ask her to tie herself to a fugitive, to leave her country and all that was dear and familiar behind, he was helpless to do anything else.

He smiled apologetically and reassured the friar who had come all the way from Reading. "I was listening. No. I assure you we are in no wise related. Since we are both strangers in this community, publishing the banns would only be a formality. I'm sorry for appearing distracted. It's just that the woman we are discussing has not yet given me a definite answer and I can think of little else."

"Oh, but I was under the impression . . . Lady Walsh said—"

"Lady Walsh has been a dear friend. She is also very optimistic. She just wanted you to be in residence . . . because of the urgency . . . should Mistress Gough . . ."

"Well, for goodness' sake, man, summon the woman and tell her she must make up her mind. Only yesterday, we received word from Lady Anne Boleyn that the king's men are scouring every port for you. It is extremely urgent that you leave immediately. Even Lord and Lady Walsh will not be able to harbor you once a hue and cry is published."

Scouring every port! And if they caught her with him, what would happen to her? How foolish he had been to place her in such danger.

"She isn't here, I'm afraid," he said. And then before the friar could give voice to what his arching brow exclaimed, John hastily added, "But I expect her back at any time. She went yesterday to bid her family farewell and obtain their blessing."

A discreet knock at his bedroom door interrupted them, and Gilbert appeared. "Master Frith, Mistress Gough has returned," he said. "Lady Walsh has asked that you attend her in her chamber. I will take you there." Then with a nod to the friar. "Supper awaits you in your chamber, Father. Lady Walsh asked me to thank you for your patience and says to ask if you will be so kind as to say a vespers service in the chapel." He paused for emphasis. "She said to say that the service will be a very private affair."

"Will there be witnesses . . . should we need them?"

Were they saying what he thought they were saying? Had Kate already returned and given her answer to Lady Walsh? The physical weakness that he thought he'd beaten threatened dizziness. Was he doing the right thing? If he truly loved her, would he place her in such danger?

"Well, man, don't just stand there," the priest said, giving up a little half-smile. "Unless I'm sadly mistaken, I believe you are about to be married."

Kate met her bridegroom at the altar in the tiny chapel. They stood in front of a table beneath a simple Lutheran cross. Behind them four small benches arranged in pairs held only Lord and Lady Walsh and Gilbert.

The stern expression on the priest's face made her want to run. She could scarcely breathe. Then John held out his hand and drew her forward, murmuring, "I was afraid once you were out of the range of my multitude of charms you wouldn't return."

She inhaled deeply. "Your charms, sir, have quite a long range," she murmured back, and then the priest cleared his throat.

"Who giveth this woman to be married?" the priest intoned, whereupon Lord Walsh stepped forward and placed Kate's hand in John's. He smiled at her and mouthed silently, "I love you." Her hand shook so that when John reached out to place the ring on it—a lovely circlet of garnets donated by Lady Walsh—he had to steady it. She thought she detected a small tremor in the hand that held hers but decided not. Her bridegroom looked as calm as though this were the sort of thing he did every day.

Maybe he does! Maybe he has done it before! Maybe he already has a wife! What do you really know about him anyway? She fastened her gaze on the cross above the altar to keep from swooning. *Lord Jesus, please let this be right.* She drew a ragged breath and the dizziness passed.

It all happened so quickly. The priest mumbled something in Latin that Kate didn't understand and elevated the Host, and Kate realized she was celebrating her first communion with her new husband. Her husband! Her mind could scarcely comprehend.

She was married. She was Mistress John Frith. And tomorrow she would be leaving England, maybe for good.

But first there was tonight to be gotten through.

After the four of them had eaten a light supper in the privacy of the solar with Gilbert alone serving—Kate tasted nothing that she put in her mouth, not even the golden cream pudding that John spooned onto her tongue—she and

Lady Walsh retired to Lady Walsh's chamber. The room glowed extravagantly. Kate had never seen so many candles lit at one time.

"This shall be your bridal chamber, my dear."

Kate opened her mouth to protest such generosity.

Lady Walsh placed her finger on her lips to gesture silence. "I can put up with Lord Walsh's snoring for one night in a good cause. Gilbert will stand watch outside your door to keep the servants away." She reached into a wooden chest and pulled out a fine lawn shift. "Here. This is my present to you."

Kate fingered the intricate lace on the diaphanous material.

"Lord Walsh brought it back to me from Venice. Apparently he hasn't taken a good look at me in some time—which is probably a good thing. It is a trifle binding in the hips." She laughed. "But you will look like a nymph in it. Not that you will have it on for very long."

Kate's knees felt weak. She grabbed hold of the bedpost for support.

"Here, let me help you," Lady Walsh said as she began to untie Kate's bodice, and together they lifted off her dress. She handed Kate a rag dipped in lavender water with which to freshen herself, then discreetly turned her back as Kate employed it. Kate pulled the garment over her body. It felt like gossamer, and she felt naked in it. Little bumps of gooseflesh rose on her skin.

"I know you are nervous, dear," Lady Walsh said, and pinched Kate's cheeks to make her skin rosy. She handed her a sprig of parsley. "Here, chew this to freshen your breath." Then she took a few precious drops from a glass bottle of perfume and dabbed at Kate's temples. "All brides are nervous the first time," she said. "But since you don't have a mother to instruct you and calm your fears, let me."

"I shall never forget your kindness," Kate said, suddenly feeling teary, thinking of her own mother so long gone.

"Go ahead, climb into bed, and I'll brush your hair until it gleams like copper. Your new bridegroom will be unable to resist you. Not that I think he needs any help. He seems quite enchanted with you. You are a very lucky girl."

Kate climbed the little wooden steps at the side of the giant four-poster bed, wondering which side John would prefer. Since she didn't know, she moved over to the far right. She didn't need much room. The small cot she'd grown accustomed to would have fit three times into this one.

She pulled the embroidered coverlet up to her armpits and, while Lady Walsh brushed her hair, considered the twisting vines decorating the carved bedposts and twining in the canopy. Spreading out in the center carving of the canopy was what looked like a giant tree. Two figures stood at the base of the tree and the woman, clothed only in long, flowing hair, was holding out an apple to the man whose torso was half hidden by the trunk of the tree.

Lady Walsh continued, "As for the marital act itself, you need not be worried. Master Frith does not seem at all the brutish sort. He speaks of you with such tenderness." Lady Walsh talked in rhythm with the brush strokes. "And you don't really have to do anything but lie there and relax. The man has to do all the work."

Lie there and relax! She wished she'd drunk the wine she'd been offered at supper. She tried to remember the kiss in the autumn garden, the taste of John's lips, tried to distract her mind by watching the curving vines climb up the post to gather at the base of the apple tree.

"There might be a little pain the first time and then after that"—she gave a self-conscious little laugh—"it can even be quite . . . pleasant."

There was a muted knock at the door. Kate flinched as though she'd been stung. Lady Walsh put down the brush and fluffed Kate's hair, spreading it out across the white linen pillow.

"The gentlemen are without." Gilbert's voice was low.

"Bid them enter," Lady Walsh said, with a little reassuring pat to Kate's shoulder. "The bride is ready."

❧

"I thought they'd never leave," John said as the door closed behind Lord and Lady Walsh.

"I suppose that's the way the nobility does things." Kate swallowed a nervous laugh.

She did not know what to do with her hands. She held them rigidly across her chest. She didn't know what to do with her eyes either. She couldn't look at John. The whole procedure had been excruciating. Lord Walsh helping John undress, assisting him into bed, then the pair of them standing on each side of the bed until the couple was properly *bedded*.

"I think it has something to do with rightful heirs and primogeniture and—"

He leaned over her and stopped her mouth with a kiss . . . "But they are gone now, and we are alone at last," he said.

She clutched the counterpane more tightly. He took her hands in his and gently pulled the cover back. For a brief moment she felt the cold in the room through the flimsy material of her shift, but it did not make her shiver. Her skin was hot even in the cold room. But he quickly covered her up and lay back on the pillow. He didn't look at her, just stared at the roof of the bed, his hands behind his head.

"John, is there something wrong . . . ?" Her voice was very small. She could hardly speak the words.

"No. There is nothing wrong, Kate."

"Then I don't understand." She was trying to keep from crying. It had been such a long day—the journey from Clapham Farm and then the rush to the ceremony. She'd not even been alone with him since her return.

"You are beautiful," he said, his voice scarcely above a whisper. They were both aware that Gilbert was just outside the door. "And I have dreamed about being here together with you like this, but I can't . . . we can't . . . until I know that you fully understand what you are tying yourself to. In the eyes of the Church, our marriage is not valid until it is consummated. You can have it annulled after I leave."

"Is that what you want, John? You said you would not leave without me when you were wooing me. Was it only the chase that excited you?"

He raised himself onto one elbow and turned to her, his face so close to hers she could smell the mead that still lingered on his lips. "I just don't want you to have regrets. You are marrying a fugitive, Kate." He reached out and touched her hair, traced his finger down the center of her forehead, caressing that blue vein she'd always hated. "I don't know what our future holds, but I know it will be shaped for good or ill by the purpose that drives me."

"Have you forgotten why I came here in the first place? We share that cause," she said quietly.

"It's not only that. When I fled Oxford I left all my worldly goods behind—and they weren't all that much—but we're not . . . I'm not penniless. My father has sent me twenty pounds through Lord Walsh, and Lady Walsh has given me a letter of introduction to her friends who run a boardinghouse for English travelers in Antwerp. I think I am resourceful enough, with God's help, to keep a roof over our heads and food on the table even in a strange country." He paused, his gaze searching her for any sign of hesitation. "I love you enough that I will leave without you if you have any doubts."

She smiled up at him in relief. He was so sweet, so almost childlike in his utter sincerity, that if she had any doubts they were all swept away. "I hope you haven't tired of me so soon!"

He opened his mouth to answer. She placed her finger on his lips, stopping his disclaimer. "You will give me beautiful children, husband," she said. "And I have ten pounds to add to your twenty, so we are far from broke. Now let's get this done so we can sleep. It has been a very long day."

A candle flickered in the wall sconce and went out, leaving only the flame burning nearest the bed, but it gave enough light that Kate could see his face.

"Don't be afraid, Kate. I won't hurt you . . ." he said. "I will stop whenever you want."

His earnestness was so touching that it, or nerves, threatened to bring tears. He touched her hair, her face, trailed his hand down her throat—surely he could feel her pulse pounding beneath her skin. "You are beautiful," he said, his voice thick with emotion. And then he murmured something in Latin that sounded almost like a prayer, but it was not from any familiar liturgy, and she did not recognize the words.

He cupped one hand around her breast, gently massaging it. His touch burned like a brand through the fine lawn of her shift. She could no longer control her breath.

With the other hand he lifted her shift and, hovering over her, moved against her in some ancient rhythmic movement that her body seemed to recognize and answered.

Even her bones were melting.

When he entered her, she was surprised that there was any solid part of her to press against, but one sharp stab of pain told her there was nothing left of her maidenly resistance. *And the two shall become one flesh.* For the first time she understood—really understood—what that meant.

. . . one flesh . . . one flesh . . .

His breath was moist against her neck as he said her name and then "my angel," *one flesh . . . one flesh . . .* "my angel of grace," *one flesh . . .* and then she felt his life force spill inside her.

It is over. We are one flesh, she thought as he rolled off her. He sighed and then, murmuring her name again, kissed her one last time, a passionless kiss but a loving kiss, upon her cheek.

I am a married woman now. His seed is inside me. He may have given me a child.

He reached for her hand and rolling onto his side drew her after him until her body curled around his. As she lay listening to her husband's rhythmic breathing she thought how Lady Walsh had been right—on all counts—though she had not mentioned the delicious lassitude that followed the marital act. Kate drifted pleasantly in that little space between wakefulness and oblivion. She wished John had not gone to sleep so suddenly. She stroked his hair gently and whispered his name. He did not stir.

The candle had guttered out, but a full moon was setting just outside the large mullioned double window, spreading its light across the bed. It shone across John's face. She shifted the cover to deflect the light.

Lunar madness. That was what the old wives said would happen if the moon shone across a sleeping person's face.

Maybe he was already a little mad. Maybe they both were. But she was happy in her madness. She snuggled against the solid weight of him as he slept next to her, and she felt safe for the first time in a long time.

The ivy carved in the bedpost twisted and curved in its climb up to where Adam and Eve stood below the Tree of Life. As she closed her eyes and drifted off to sleep, Kate did not see the tiny serpent's head crowning the largest vine, buried deep within the shadow of the leafiest bough.

FIFTEEN

*Thou shalt not uncover the nakedness of thy brother's
wife: it is thy brother's nakedness.*
—FROM LEVITICUS 18:16 (USED BY HENRY VIII
AS JUSTIFICATION FOR ANNULMENT OF HIS
MARRIAGE TO KATHERINE OF ARAGON)

om Lasser scanned the horizon as he guided his ship into the cove. Nothing. Yet it was usually what you didn't see that posed the greatest threat. He'd been around long enough to know a customs agent when he saw one, and the Bristol docks, usually so free, today had been pocked with them. "Thick as fleas," he'd said to the landlord of the pump room where he'd ordered his ale and meat pie.

"It's a man they're looking for this time," the publican said as he wiped the tankard with a dirty towel, "not contraband."

"If that's for me, use a clean towel, please," Tom said. Then he added, "Must have stolen the archbishop's purse to draw so many. Where do they think he'd be running to from the west side of England? Five shillings and a couple of hours would get him from East Anglia across the North Sea Channel, and he's on the Continent. From here, it's five hundred miles around the bottom. Man would be a fool to choose Bristol Channel."

"Or a fox," the publican said, still wiping. "Romney Marsh and that whole east coast is crawling with informers. The spotters say More and the archbishop want this one real bad and are willing to pay. They think he'll lead them to that Bible translator. Just don't be taking on any strange passengers is my advice, Captain." He held the glass up to the light. "That be good enough for you?"

"Good enough, my man, good enough," Tom said, and shoved half a crown across the table, generous compensation for a pint of ale and a clean towel, but reliable sources were hard to find—a clean towel even harder.

So this was the passenger the *Siren's Song* was picking up, he thought as he steered his vessel through the channel markers. Monmouth wisely hadn't told him, just said a passenger for the Continent wanted to leave England because of pressures from "certain quarters." Tom hadn't really wanted to know more. Until now. The stakes had gone up, it seemed. Forewarned was forearmed.

Now, as he scanned the peninsula at Sand Point, something about the too quiet look of it bothered him. It was midday and the sea was calm as a mirror. Nothing, not even a bit of flotsam, pocked the polished surface. Even the scavenger seabirds that usually trailed after the ship, circling and swooping for scraps, were nowhere to be seen. The peninsula was likewise deserted. No sign of his passenger. He looked back out to sea. Something there—he was sure of it. He stared into the distance until he thought he saw the merest speck on the horizon, but it was enough to raise the hackles on his neck. Two crewmen spotted it at about the same time and pointed. "Captain!"

"I see it. Change course," Tom shouted, loping across the deck. "Hoist the sail to windward. Sail south around Sand Point," he said, loosening the ropes to the skiff attached to the starboard side. "Maybe they'll give chase and try to board. Make no protest. They're likely looking for a man, not contraband."

"But what if they ask for you, Cap'n?" the first mate asked as it dawned on him what Tom was about to do.

"Tell them I'm in my cabin, sick with a fever," he said, climbing into the skiff, gesturing for the first mate to lower the boat. "Show them the manifests and the cargo. Offer to take them to me. They'll not want to see for themselves. I'll meet you at Burnham where the Severn empties into the sea. From there she could outrun any customs boat."

"Aye, Captain." The first mate grinned. He loved a chase. "I'll have her there."

"You'd better," Tom shouted as the skiff hit the waterline with a great splash, wetting his shirt. He flung the rope out to be hauled up. "If you don't, I'll hunt you down and hang you from the yardarm."

He laughed to soften the words. But he knew the first mate would hear the threat, as would any other big ears among the crew.

Tom swore under his breath as he settled into the bow of the small boat and picked up the oars. Contraband was one thing. A man could shed himself of those easily enough. An outlaw passenger was something else. He didn't know what the penalty for smuggling a fugitive out of England was but he doubted it was a simple fine. This day's work should go a long way toward discharging his debt to Sir Humphrey Monmouth, he thought as he rowed toward shore.

He beached the skiff and, hiding it behind a rocky outcrop, settled down to wait for his passenger. He didn't have to wait long.

From the shadows of the trees where he waited, he spotted the four of them. *Hell's bells.* They were walking down the beach as nonchalantly as though they were out for an afternoon promenade. The sun sparked off the short sword at Lord Walsh's side. Might as well send out a trumpet blast to signal their presence. Couldn't they have just let the man wait by himself without coming with him to hold his hand and maybe attract more attention? Lord Walsh was a good sort, but a bit too sure that his noble estate could protect him. This was not some little game they were playing. This was not like running black-market wine or illegal Antwerp books where he would be fined or his cargo confiscated and sold back to him by a corrupt official. He could lose his ship over this. No more. He would tell Humphrey Monmouth, he would run cargo only from now on.

As they grew closer, he tried to take the measure of his passenger. The other two were in skirts so the one with the wavy brown hair must be his man. He looked young and more like a yeoman with his porkpie hat and simple peasant's tunic than a scholar. They said he had been very ill, but he looked vigorous enough. He was matching Lord Walsh stride for stride whilst the two women hung back a few steps, deep in conversation.

As they drew near, Tom stepped out from the trees that fringed the shingle beach.

"My word, Captain, you gave us a start." Lord Walsh laughed. "Where's your ship?"

"Well away, my lord. As we should be with all due speed." He tried to keep the irritation from his voice.

"Well, of course. But I'm sure there is no need to be testy. The beach looks quite deserted."

"Looks can be deceiving," he said, holding out his hand to the young man. "I'm Captain Tom Lasser. You are the passenger, I presume."

"John Frith." The young man flashed him a ready smile. "But I'm afraid there are two of us."

"Two! But Sir Humphrey never—"

"Sir Humphrey didn't know. I've married, you see, and I wish to take my wife with me."

Irritated at the presumptuousness of young Master Frith, Tom only half glanced at the woman standing a little apart with Lady Walsh. "I'm afraid that's impossible. Your wife will need to make the journey overland. She can easily and much more cheaply get a boat from Yarmouth. Nobody is looking for her."

"I'm sorry. That's likewise impossible. I'm not leaving without her. If you cannot accommodate us both, I will go overland with her. We'll both leave from Yarmouth."

"Don't be a fool, man. They'd catch you before you even get to Yarmouth." Tom was trying to control his temper. All this and now the cheeky upstart was playing the brave hero in front of his bride.

The woman stepped forward, and Tom got a good look at her for the first time as she said, "If it's a question of money, I can pay—"

The voice. The broad brow with a faint blue line beneath skin so fine it was almost translucent. All too familiar.

She looked straight at him, just the slightest challenge in the tilt of her chin.

"You already have, Mistress Gough," he said, sighing. "One penny plus interest."

"Mistress Frith," she said, taking her husband's hand. And then she whispered to her puzzled bridegroom but loud enough for Tom to hear, "I'll tell you later, John."

"It's not just a question of money," he said gruffly. "I might do it out of *human kindness*."

She had the grace to blush. It was most becoming. As was the stubborn way she went after what she wanted. Had he noticed before how striking she was? He'd only seen her in the gray light outside his prison cell and once again in the shadow of a campfire light. He'd thought her pretty enough. Now in the full sunlight, it struck him that she was quite remarkable with her bright hair and intelligent eyes—green the color of the sea. He grudgingly conceded why Frith might be reluctant to leave her.

"Let's go," he said gruffly, pulling the boat from behind the rock.

The two women tearfully embraced. He pitched an oar to Frith.

"Here, bridegroom, you can help me row, if you've the strength for it."

❧

King Henry always did his best thinking astride a horse, and the ride back from Greenwich, where he'd just come from visiting his brother's widow—that was how he thought of Katherine of Aragon these days, never his wife, never his queen. It was all so clear to him now.

For eighteen years, he had slept with his brother's wife in an attempt to make an heir for England. Each act of copulation a grievous sin, each act more an onerous duty than before, until it was a wonder he could perform at all. And there had been no heir—the surest sign that God was not pleased—just one girl child, Mary, a girl child who might be queen and marry a Spanish prince, or God forbid, even a Frenchman. Their issue would inherit. England's enemies would win the sovereignty that English kings before him had fought to maintain without ever having to spend a ducat of Florentine gold or a drop of blood.

His father had foisted Katherine upon him at the tender age of eighteen, largely because he did not want to give back the dowry her father King Ferdinand paid for her marriage to Arthur. From the first day, Henry had thought to do his duty and was determined to find her a suitable wife. But as the sin festered in his soul so did his distaste for her. For many months the thought of any physical relationship with her had repulsed him. More and more she disgusted him: her pendulous breasts, her Spanish blood, the habit of the order of St. Francis that she wore beneath her robes of state, her excess of piety in general. She never laughed. Not even at Will Somers the court fool—who could make a statue laugh. Not even at Henry's jests—surely a wise wife would. A wiser woman would not answer her husband's jokes with that long-suffering smile that smacked of tolerance and condescension.

Though he had to admit she was not without her virtues, something her supporters never tired of pointing out. She was intelligent, well read—a lover of the new learning coming out of the universities—and could hold her own even with the great Sir Thomas in theological and political dispute. And it was all too plain that she adored her husband, even tolerating the occasional fling like the one he'd had with Mary Boleyn. Tolerated it by spending more hours on her knees praying for him. Somehow that took the edge off a man, knowing that while he was engaged in a little manly "sporting," his wife was home praying for him.

She had been on her knees when he found her this morning. He had greeted her by calling her "sister-in-law."

"I am Queen Katherine, wife of the sovereign king of England, Henry VIII," she had said in her thick Spanish accent, never looking up. "What God hath joined together let no man put asunder."

"You are not my lawful wife, Katherine. You were never my lawful wife. You are my brother's wife."

"How say you 'not lawful,' Your Majesty, when we were married before God and the archbishop? The court at Black Friars did not declare our marriage unlawful."

"With your pitiable display you rendered the court impotent to give a legal rendering. A queen on her knees like a common beggar."

"Your expression of love for me in the presence of the court then, that was not true?"

She still did not look at him but down at her prayer book, studying its jeweled cover as though she would find the answer there. The hands that held the Book of Hours were trembling. He felt a surge of compassion for her that threatened to unman him. Sighing, he turned his gaze away from those trembling hands.

"True or not. It doesn't matter. You were married to Arthur, Katherine. That marriage was annulled at my father's request. The annulment of my brother's marriage should never have happened. Our marriage should never have happened."

"My marriage to your brother was annulled because it was never consummated. You, my lord king, are the only husband I have ever had, will ever have."

Tears welled in her eyes and spilled down her cheeks, large drops of water, like great jewels. He'd once seen a Flanders portrait decorated with such tears.

He could not look at her but concentrated his gaze instead on the figure of the dying Christ hanging above her head.

"Wherein, my lord, have I ever played false to you or failed to serve England?" Her voice was husky with the tears yet to flow. "Have you forgotten the triumph at Flodden against the Scots, how proud you said you were when from the war camps there I sent you the Scottish king's plaid tunic stained with his own blood? Does not such a wife, such a queen, deserve better? Wherein have I ever been aught but a loving and loyal queen?"

She was right, of course, except in one regard. He sometimes wondered if her loyalty to Spain was not greater than her loyalty to England. Ferdinand could not have a better spy in England's court. But he did not say that. He had no proof.

She sniffed, and he noticed how her shoulders stiffened, though her head was still bowed, as though she willed herself to courage. "The pope will never annul this marriage. He will not make a bastard of our daughter," she said. "If my husband will not preserve my honor, God will. You have fallen under some evil spell. God will bring you back to me or you will lose your throne. It has been prophesied. Our daughter will reign within months if you take Anne Boleyn to wife."

"Where did you hear such treasonous talk?"

"My ministers have told it to me. The Virgin has revealed it to the Holy Maid of Kent."

He sighed, trying to be patient. The woman was not reasonable. "If God had blessed our union," he said as gently as he could, "we would have had a male child. I am a king by divine right. To deny me a male heir means God has *not* blessed this union. We lived in sin for eighteen years, and I told you last year: I will do it no longer, with the pope's annulment or not."

She looked up at him then, her tearstained face stricken with grief, but there was another emotion there as well. In her large eyes—Spanish cow eyes, he'd called them, playfully at first when there was still some vestige of harmony between them, before he'd found comfort in other eyes—he saw a steel as hard as the metal in his sword. It was a king's voice that decreed, "Not the pope, not you, not your father, and certainly not your Holy Roman Emperor nephew will make me persist in this sin one day longer, Katherine. You are my widowed sister-in-law. You are not my wife."

She stood up then to face him, her face blotched and red, but her wide intelligent gaze never wavered. "Take your pleasure where you find it, my lord, but know that I am Queen Katherine of England. I will never return to Spain. I will not flee to a nunnery. I am the true and loyal queen of Henry King of England and will be such when I die."

Henry had taken his leave of her then, striding away without even a good-bye.

"When will I see you again, husband," she'd called after him.

"When hell freezes over," he had muttered under his breath, all compassion melted away beneath the heat of her resolve.

He'd mounted his horse and trotted briskly away. The master of the horse had wisely signaled for his riding companions, Neville and Brandon, to follow at a distance.

Horse and rider paused now at a brook. Henry's mount neighed gently and shook its golden harness.

"Drink your fill, Dominican." Henry patted the black stallion on its neck and held his hand to signal "stay" to the courtiers and the master of the horse.

The horse, the issue of a Spanish mare, a gift from King Ferdinand, was one of Henry's favorites—at least something fertile had come out of the Spanish court. He had named the horse himself after the ubiquitous black friars. He thought it a fine joke—less so the prior of Black Friars Abbey, who was as humorless as Katherine.

Behind him, he was mildly annoyed at the whispering of the restless courtiers, the nervous whinnying of the horses, the jingling of the harness bells, echoing the restlessness in his own mind. He should have spent this day hunting boar in New Forrest listening to the call of the huntsman's horn, the baying of hounds, instead of the whining of an unreasonable woman. What did a man, a king, have to do to be alone? He had a wild urge to spur Dominican and make a mad dash through the woods to his left, his cloak flying in the wind, his hat catching on the lowest tree branch, leaving his hair free to blow in the wind. Maybe he would take the road to Hever Castle, surprise Anne—there was a woman who could appreciate a good joke—but he knew they would only clamor after him. Too many of them disapproved of Anne. Too many of them were loyal to Katherine.

Dominican raised his head, and waited, his haunch shivering slightly, for his master's command. Henry gave a light flick of the reins and they waded on through the stream. He waved the court to follow. When they reached the hunting lodge he would send his page to summon Anne to Hampton Court. She would be there upon his return on the morrow.

～✲✲～

"Piety becomes a queen—" a familiar voice behind Anne said, "though not in excess."

Her heart skipped half a beat. Before standing up, she genuflected before the small makeshift altar—a simple cross, an unadorned prayer book, and a kneeling bench in the corner of her chamber. Turning around, she dropped a curtsy.

"Your Majesty," she said, then, "you have been to see the queen?" And before he could answer, because Cromwell had already told her he was going to see the queen, she asked, "How fares Queen Katherine?"

"Very sad, Lady Anne. She is very sad. She was likewise at her altar, probably praying you would be stricken with the pox." His voice was low because the double doors leading to her chamber, the same chamber Queen Katherine would have used had she come to Hampton Court, were open.

"No, Your Majesty. The queen was always kind to me when I was in her service. I remember when—" She checked herself and would not say *when Wolsey sent sweet Percy away.* "Once when I was very ill, she treated me almost like a mother. It distresses me to think what part I must play in her sadness."

Gray light—for it had been a dismal autumn day, a herald of the coming winter—filtered through the mullioned window set above the altar and lent a cold glow to the room. A drop of wax from a lone candle flickering beneath the cross dripped, like a drop of blood, upon the white linen altar cloth. He scraped at the wax with a carefully manicured fingernail. His ruby signet cast a prism of red and purple and yellow.

"Your altar is as plain as any Lutheran altar, Lady Anne."

"It is for my private devotion, sire."

"And *privately* you scorn the liturgy and trappings of the mass?"

"I make no secret of it. Would you care to sit, Your Majesty? I will call for refreshment." He looked unusually tired. He still wore his riding boots.

"No. Come walk with me in the maze."

"The air is chilled. The king might catch an ague."

"The king wishes to be alone with you to talk privately."

He was not smiling. He had been to see the queen and now he wanted to *talk privately.*

"Fetch my cloak," she called to the maid, who hovered with the king's footman just outside the open door, but the maid had already removed the cloak from its peg and was advancing toward her.

He did not touch her as they walked among the tall hedges, did not even reach for her hand, though they were surely alone in the maze. There would be no idlers on such a day as this. Was this a bad sign? Had he decided after all to reconcile with Katherine? Was he giving up on the divorce? Well, she would not be his mistress. She would never be his mistress. She would be queen or nothing. She kept her hands in her pockets to keep them warm.

"I read the book you gave me," he said.

"What book was that, Your Grace?"

"The Tyndale book. *The Obedience of a Christian Man.*"

"What did you think of it?"

"I thought it a book for me and all kings to read."

"Exactly so, Your Highness. William Tyndale is a brilliant man. You would be well served to have him at court."

They walked on, the only sound the occasional brushing of the boxwood leaves against their arms until he broke the silence. "I'll cede brilliance, but there is much in his writing that is troubling."

"Troubling, Your Highness, how so?" She knew what he would say before he opened his mouth. It was what they all said who stood against reform.

"Sir Thomas says he is as heretical as Luther: his emphasis on salvation by grace, denial of Purgatory, and his insistence that the individual is accountable to God and not Holy Church. Odd that More and Tyndale should be enemies, when you think on it. They seem to have much in common in all other respects: both are brilliant thinkers, both admire Erasmus, both are devoted to the new learning in many ways. Two branches of the same tree, it would seem. In the past I have known Sir Thomas to speak of the need for reform, even. I cannot understand why he can think only of Tyndale as fit for kindling."

"It is the Bible," Anne said, feeling her nose run from the cold. She sniffed gently, so as not to give offense, and wished she'd brought a handkerchief. Was this what he had brought her out to talk about? She bit her tongue to keep from asking about his visit with Katherine as she said, "Sir Thomas denies the primacy of Holy Scripture over Holy Church. He would burn the Holy Scripture and its translator in a bonfire that would reach all the way to hell just so some plowman may not read the truth therein."

"The plowman has no need to read Scripture for himself. He is too ignorant. He would misinterpret it. We would be plagued with a thousand false doctrines. Each man his own priest. But I quite agree with Tyndale's statement that the king gives account to God alone. That would mean, of course, that even the pope has no jurisdiction over the king. It has put me to thinking about a new tactic regarding Katherine."

A new tactic? Surely he did not mean that he was going to break with the pope and embrace Lutheranism. That would be a reversal indeed for "the defender of the faith." But whatever the tactic, she thought with relief, it meant that he was not abandoning his pursuit of divorce in face of the Church's opposition.

"You are not giving up then?"

"I am not. My marriage to Katherine is a sin. And I have told her again of my resolve to see it ended. If Tyndale is right, and the king gives account to God alone, then it is even more my responsibility to see the marriage dissolved and to secure the blessing of God and an heir for England. I intend to make you my rightful queen. You will be the mother of my son."

As her heart beat faster, she reminded herself that this was not the first time he'd made such a promise, usually followed immediately by physical advances and demands, demands increasingly hard for her to resist. She was but a woman after all. And he could be exceedingly charming—the most magnificent peacock on the lawn.

"About Master Tyndale," she said, trying to divert him from this usual pattern. "Do you think it would be possible to bring him back to England? It would be advantageous to have such a brilliant man on your council. And there is another. A young scholar named John Frith. Wolsey had him imprisoned unjustly, and I think he has fled England to join Tyndale. Some of your brightest minds are languishing in exile, Your Majesty. Bring them back. England needs them. You need them." And then, knowing how he loved a challenge, "If you can find them, of course."

"Be assured I can find them."

The cold way he said it made her heart squeeze a little.

"Not Sir Thomas, my lord. Do not seek his help in this."

For the first time he laughed, that quick, mercurial burst of staccato laughter that always set her on edge.

"No. This is hardly a job for Sir Thomas. I expect if he could find William Tyndale, he'd already be in chains and facing down a charge of heresy. I have an agent on the Continent. A man named Stephen Vaughan. He's a good man. He'll seek out Master Tyndale and—"

"Frith," she said. "John Frith."

"Don't trouble yourself about Sir Thomas," he said. "I have another plan to bring him around."

"Another plan?"

"I intend to make him chancellor in Wolsey's place. That way I can woo him gently to our cause."

Her heart sank. In all of England there was no greater enemy to her cause and to her person than Sir Thomas More. He was Queen Katherine's greatest supporter, and a man more devoted to the old faith than any cleric. She did not think Sir Thomas More would be so easily wooed.

Henry paused in his striding through the frosty hedges and pulled her toward him. "Now, my lady, give your king a kiss, a chaste kiss upon the lips, for we must be patient, if we are to provide a legal heir for England."

Anne didn't know whether to be relieved or disappointed at this change in him, she thought as she lifted her face and touched her lips to her king's.

SIXTEEN

*[T]he clergy maketh them not heretics nor burneth
them neither . . . the clergy doth denounce them. And
as they be well worthy the temporaltie [secular au-
thorities] doth burn them. And after the fire of Smithfield, Hell doth receive them where the wretches burn
for ever.*

—SIR THOMAS MORE ON THE
PROCESS OF BURNING HERETICS

t first Kate didn't recognize the woman serving them at table
in the captain's quarters—hardly more than a closet beneath the quarterdeck and cluttered with various charts and instruments, none of which Kate
recognized except the sextant. She'd once seen a picture of one in a book her
brother printed. Though the serving woman appeared to be watching them
from beneath lowered lids, she kept her head down, never saying a word as
she removed the empty soup bowl and replaced it with a plate of roasted ca-
pon and a crusty loaf.

"The leek soup was delicious, and it was hot! However did you manage
that?" Kate asked.

The woman signaled her acknowledgment with a nod but did not answer, only turning her back to them as she tidied the rest of the little chamber, leaving Kate to wonder if perhaps the woman was a foreigner.

"She has a firebox in the bow that makes a passable oven. Kind of like a small brazier that you would warm your room with—except larger. She uses it to make miracles, which my crew and I delight in." He gave a little half laugh, half grunt. "The crew almost mutinied when I first brought her on board. But after a few days of her cooking, they decided a woman on board brought better luck than hardtack."

"I can see why," John said, as he sliced a bit of the fowl with his knife and put it on Kate's plate. "It's awfully generous of you, Captain, to give up your quarters like this."

Captain Lasser appeared to take little interest in the food. Kate wished he would take his leave of them. The long ride in the cramped little dinghy—with her perched precariously on the trunk that Lady Walsh had bullied the recalcitrant captain into bringing—wondering where they were going, wondering if they were indeed being taken to the ship or if perhaps he had betrayed them, had left her frazzled. But John seemed to take everything in stride.

John speared another morsel and placed it on his plate. "I guess I had not thought . . . I mean I just assumed there would be a private cabin for passengers."

"This is a merchant ship, Master Frith," the captain said curtly. "As to my 'generosity,' well really, what choice have we? You and your beautiful wife can hardly bunk with the crew."

He pushed back his chair, abruptly. "Endor will see that you have what you need," he said, gesturing at the woman making up the cot—it was hardly more than a bench. "She is a mute, but she is not deaf. She will understand what you tell her." And then with a little half-smile curving his mouth, he added, "Sorry about the size of the bed. It's not built for two . . . but I'm sure you'll manage."

Kate's face burned with embarrassment.

"At least it's not a berth swinging from the rafters," John said cheerfully as if he read no double entendre in the captain's remark, or, if he did, did not think it at all inappropriate. "We'll manage quite nicely, Captain."

The woman, slightly built, thin, with the saddest look in her eyes Kate had ever seen, returned to the table and, gesturing to the captain, raised her hands palms up as she shrugged her shoulders.

"She's asking if there will be anything else," he said.

"No . . . that's quite—" Kate began.

"If she would just light the ship's lantern hanging on the wall . . ." John interrupted. "I'm afraid my wife will awaken in the dark in a strange place and be frightened."

Really, John, he'll think me some helpless little girl, and then she reminded herself that she should be grateful her husband was so thoughtful, and what did it really matter what Tom Lasser thought of her?

The woman's hand removed the lamp and poured a little oil into its base then returned it to its wall clamp with thin, almost claw-like fingers. Kate's memory flashed back to the day she stood outside Fleet Prison—the beggar woman scrambling in the dirty straw for the coin Kate had dropped into her cell had hands like that. Surely not . . .

"Is that—"

He raised an eyebrow. "I'm surprised you remembered. I'm afraid, being a mute woman, she did not fare as well as I did—that and the fact that she was being held on a charge of fortune-telling."

John sounded as close to indignation as Kate had ever heard him. "She's a fortune-teller? But that's—"

"Against the law . . . ?" He flashed a wide smile, the same smile she'd first seen when he mocked her from inside Fleet Prison even as he was begging for his bread. "It's more harmless than it sounds—not witchcraft, not something she does deliberately. She doesn't conjure the devil or anything like that, Master Frith," he said, his amusement growing with John's discomfort. "It's more a gift. I'll show you."

John's usual easy smile was pursed into a small pout. "Really, that isn't necessary, Captain, indeed, I would prefer—"

"She just sees visions in still water." He nodded to the woman, who looked uncomfortable being at the center of their conversation. "Endor, come here. Bring that bowl of water and place it on the table."

Kate was suddenly curious, and anxious that John's attitude not give offense, less to Tom Lasser, she told herself, than to the woman who had served them so carefully. "What can it hurt, John? Aren't you even a little bit curious?"

"Yes, Master Frith," the captain said with a challenge in his voice and another mocking smile, "aren't you a little bit curious?"

"Well, I suppose it can do no harm." John shrugged and stuttered a nervous little laugh, his good manners winning out over his objections.

With a sweep of his lace-cuffed sleeves, the captain exclaimed, "Our lovebirds would see their future, Endor . . . if you will be so kind."

John fidgeted beside her as the woman nodded and solemnly wiped the inside of the empty soup bowl then placed it in the center of the table. She filled it to the brim from the pitcher on the sideboard and, leaning forward, gripped the table as if to steady it, or herself, and closed her eyes. John signaled his disapproval of the whole procedure with a lifted brow and tightened lips, but Kate was glad that he made no verbal protest.

The captain grinned. *He is enjoying watching John squirm,* she thought, and was about to signal that she had changed her mind when the woman's eyes popped open and stared into the bowl.

The ship rocked gently in a swell.

Endor shook her head ever so slightly and closed her eyes again.

"Really, Captain . . ." But the captain lifted two fingers to his lips in a shushing motion.

They all waited for the water to grow still again. No one spoke. The only sounds were the creaking timbers above as the sailors went about their work and a scratching noise beneath the floors. Rats in the hold. Kate gave a little shiver. All ships had rats—didn't they? She was suddenly very grateful that John had asked for the light.

Suddenly, like a puppet on a string, Endor jerked her eyes open and again stared into the bowl. Kate was wondering how she could hold them so wide and unblinking, when without warning the woman gave a troubled grunt, gesticulated violently, and pushed the bowl aside. Some of it sloshed onto the white linen cloth. She shook her head vigorously and, without waiting for permission, opened the door leading to the main deck and ran from the room. A few minutes later they heard footsteps running overhead.

Captain Lasser gave a nervous little laugh. "I guess her gift cannot be summoned at will. Don't read anything into it. She was just embarrassed that she saw nothing in the water."

But Kate noticed that the mocking smile had disappeared.

"Yes, I'm sure that's all it was," John said. He sounded relieved that the whole silly charade was over.

"Will she be all right? Shouldn't we go after her? She was upset," Kate said.

"No. She's just gone up on the poop deck for a bit of fresh air. It's her favorite spot."

But Kate wasn't so sure. She wished she could talk to the woman. Ask her exactly what it was that upset her. She leaned forward and looked at the still water, but all she saw was the reflection of her own troubled face. The ship rocked gently and that image too disappeared, but Kate felt an uneasiness stirring in her stomach.

Whether her queasiness was caused by the ship's motion or Endor's reaction to whatever she had seen in the water, she wasn't sure. But she was sure she regretted that last spoonful of leek soup.

⹃⹄

For the remainder of their first evening at sea, and for a good part of the next, Kate lay in the narrow bunk and wanted to die. For the first couple of hours John held her head as she threw up into a basin not only the leek soup but everything she'd eaten for the last week.

"I don't want you to see me like this," she moaned the first time. By the time she got to the dry heaves, she no longer cared. When she had nothing left to throw up, she lay exhausted on the bed while John went up to rid the little cabin of the foul contents of the basin. She was thinking that being captured might not be so bad if she could just get her feet on dry land again when John returned. He carried in his hand a mug of something hot and steaming.

"Captain Lasser says this will help," he said, holding it up.

"He does, does he? If you were sick too, I'd suspect him of poisoning us." She raised her head and shoulders, supporting herself on her elbows but unwilling to commit to sitting up. "What is it?"

"Ginger brew," he said. "The captain says if it's seasickness, it will settle you," he said, putting it to her lips.

Her stomach clutched, but she sipped the spicy, pungent brew more to please him than because she had any faith in it.

"Come on. That's my girl," he coaxed. "Captain Lasser says you should drink it all. Says it'll help you find your sea legs."

Don't treat me like a child, John. "I don't want to find my sea legs. I don't ever plan to use them again." And then between sips, "How long did you say it was going to take us to get to Antwerp?"

"Four, maybe five days, depending on the wind."

"Two hours," she moaned. "It takes two hours to cross the Channel. If we'd gone that way we'd already be there."

"Or in the Tower," he said soberly. "Come on, drink up. We'll be settled in our new lodgings and will have made new friends well before Christmas. You'll never have to set foot in a boat again."

Kate drank the spicy, honeyed mixture. She had to admit it soothed her innards. She lay back and closed her eyes. But if her stomach was more settled, her thoughts were still churning. Christmas in another country across the sea with her new husband. It all seemed unreal. Kate knew a little about Antwerp: knew that it was a great city of the Holy Roman Empire—probably bigger even than London—and the publishing capital of Europe. Many of the Tyndale books bore the imprimatur of Antwerp. Thank God Lady Walsh had given them the names of a contact that would help them.

"John, do you know where—"

"Shh. Don't start worrying. I have a plan. I have friends there. You will love them, and they you. Just rest."

After about five minutes, she felt his lips brush her forehead.

"Better?" he asked.

She managed a nod.

"I think I'll go up on the quarterdeck and give the captain a report. He seemed so anxious to help. You know, he really isn't a bad sort."

Kate did not open her eyes but waved him away. The cabin was quiet now. The sea was calm again. And so was her stomach.

She didn't even awaken when John returned to the twilit cabin an hour later.

꧁ ꧂

Kate did not awaken until the next morning. The cabin was empty. She could tell the morning was well on by the light streaming through the lone porthole. She stood up gingerly, surprised to find the dizziness and nausea had departed. Poor John. He must have slept on the blanket left in a huddle on the floor. A surge of emotion flooded over her as she remembered how dear and tender he had been to her. How could she have found such a perfect husband?

A bowl of fresh water and a bar of Castilian soap—apparently the well-heeled captain liked his little luxuries—waited on the table where last night's dinner had been served. She pushed the image of the steaming soup from her mind, lest her stomach rebel. But she was thinking that she really should eat a little something when Endor brought another mug of the ginger concoction. Kate shook her head in protest, but the woman pointed to the mug and nodded vigorously. Then she held up two fingers and uncovered a few buns and a bit of cheese hidden beneath an oiled cloth.

"I don't understand."

Endor pointed to the cup, made a drinking motion, then to the bread.

"You want me to drink this first, and then I can have the bread?"

Endor nodded.

Well, it had served her well enough the first time, she supposed. She drank the brew, surprised to find that it was not as noxious as she had thought it last night. Endor cut off a hunk of cheese and, placing it with the bun, handed it to her.

Kate took a bite and chewed slowly, relieved to find that her stomach made no protest. "Do you remember me?" Kate asked, licking the crumbs from her fingers.

The woman nodded.

"I am glad you are safe." And then a thought occurred to her. How did she know the woman was safe? She was clearly a servant but what other duties did she perform for the captain? "I mean, you are here of your own free will?"

The woman gave a little knowing smile and, nodding, clasped her hands together and touched them to her lips.

She is in love with the dashing captain, Kate thought, pitying her. It showed in the soft, misty expression in her eyes. Then she remembered something else about the woman in Fleet Prison. She had been obviously pregnant. She wondered if the baby had been the captain's and what had happened to it.

"My name is Kate and your name is . . . Endor?"

Again the woman smiled and nodded and pointed to the sunlight streaming through the porthole. Then she pointed at Kate and to a ladder that Kate had not noticed before because of the clutter piled in front of it. She had assumed that the only way up was through the door onto the main deck that Endor had used last night.

"That leads directly to the upper deck? Is my husband there?"

One quick nod affirmed both questions. Endor spread her arms in a sweeping motion across the table, moved her hands in a quick circular motion in front of her stomach, and gave three mock pulls on a bell rope. Kate understood completely.

"Dinner is at three bells. We will be ready." She was about to ask about the baby. "When last we met you were with child; may I ask——" But the woman had already picked up the chamber pot and was hustling out the door. Either she didn't hear Kate or anticipated the question and deliberately chose to ignore it.

As she pulled a clean linen shift from her trousseau that consisted largely of the cast-off garments that once belonged to Lady Walsh's household—though they were superior in construction and material to anything Kate was leaving behind in her little rooms above the shop in London—the scent of dried lavender mingled with the briny smell of the sea, and was soon joined by the aroma of the smooth white soap. She pulled the clean garment over her head, then giving a good shake to her second-best skirt, she climbed into it. A quick tug on the comb through her tangle of curls and she gave it up, leaving it free-flowing beneath a simple cloth cap.

The sun beckoned and she felt refreshed—all trace of the sickness gone. God bless Endor and her magic elixir—maybe she'd found her sea legs after all. She stuffed another of the sweet buns into her mouth and one for John in her pocket. As she maneuvered her clumsy skirt up the ladder, she had a fleeting wish for the discarded pants she'd left behind.

⁓✠⁓

The young courtier was dismayed when he got the summons to attend the king at York Place. Being summoned to court was always gut-wrenching, and when court was at York Place, it was especially so. The London palace was the property of Cardinal Wolsey, Archbishop of York, but was often used by the king, and being summoned there was a little like an invitation to the Star Chamber at Westminster. As Stephen Vaughan gave his horse over to the groom at the gatehouse, he did a quick mental inventory to think if he'd given insult or injury to any powerful persons of late. He could think of none.

He was fencing with shadows. As he well knew, the king was capable of calling a man to travel miles on a mere whim, to play a game of chess or listen to his latest song. Or it could be something as simple as wanting Stephen to plan a masque for court or marshal a tournament. But it had been a while since His Majesty had sent for him, and Vaughan had supposed the king had found himself another general dogsbody. And that was just as well. He hated being among so many hypocrites and hangers-on, not to mention the anxiety of always wondering whether he was being called to answer for some perceived, or trumped-up, misdeed or if he might—God forbid—stumble in the discharge of whatever duty the king had summoned him for.

"His Majesty sent for me," he said to courtiers lounging outside the Presence Chamber. They were playing dice and did not look up. "He's in the cardinal's chamber."

"Is the cardinal with him?"

"With him!" one of them snorted. "The cardinal's in York, licking his wounds."

"Licking his wounds?"

"You haven't heard?" The speaker looked up then and added, "But then, how could you? Haven't seen you around for a while, Vaughan. You in some kind of disgrace too?"

Stephen ignored the note of derision in his voice. The others laughed, a little nervously, Stephen thought. There was a low snigger as one of the dice players muttered, "His Majesty is probably busy measuring for new tapestries. I've heard he plans to change the name of this one from York Place to Whitehall. Has a nice ring to it. What I would give to see Wolsey's face when he hears!"

The dice clattered on the table.

"Snake eyes. Here, you want to see Wolsey's face?"

The loser flipped a gold sovereign bearing the cardinal's visage in the direction of the winner, who grinned and waved the coin in the air. "Face and head. Stamped in gold on the coin of the realm. How the mighty have fallen."

"Not far enough. Arrogant bastard." But it was hard to tell if the loser was referring to Wolsey or his gambling companion until he grumbled, "'Tis only His Majesty's good grace that lets that whoreson of a Smithfield butcher keep his head." And then, as if he suddenly remembered Stephen was standing there, he nodded abruptly. "Go on up. His Majesty said to keep an eye out for you. He's with his armorer, but he said to send you up anyway."

Stephen took the stairs two at a time, his short sword clanging against the stair rail.

"Vaughan, come in," the voice bellowed like a bull.

It was the king's voice, and it was not a joyous bellow.

But to his relief he soon discovered that it was the armorer who was to bear the brunt of the king's displeasure.

"Look at this, Vaughan," the king shouted, and clanged his sword against the codpiece of a full suit of majestic armor behind which the master craftsman was cowering. "Does this look to you like a suitable covering for the king's manhood, this . . . this . . . paltry codpiece? You must not think your king much of a man, armorer."

"It was an error, Your Majesty." The armorer was wringing his hands, visibly shaken. "The apprentice must have misread the king's . . . splendid proportions. He is an ignorant fool. I will see that he is beaten."

"And what about you? Who will see that you are beaten for not inspecting the armor before presenting such an insult in our presence?"

The armorer turned white as death. "Your Majesty, please . . ."

"Oh, get out of my sight. And take this *thing* with you." The king kicked the armor with the heel of his boot. The clang reverberated to the rafters. The armorer cringed as though he'd been struck. "Fix it," the king snarled. "And bring it to my palace in Richmond a fortnight hence. And don't disappoint me."

"Yes, Your Majesty. I will see to it," he said, backing away. "It will be as majestic as your—"

"Go on. Get out!" The king waved him away. "Leave the sword."

He picked up the two-handed sword and wielded it overhead to the right, then to the left. Stephen pitied his adversary. "Great Harry," as the people called him, was known for his prowess with a two-handed sword.

"Nice heft to it. 'Twill do to slice a Frenchman open or an insolent armorer."

Quick as lightning he tossed the sword to Stephen, who luckily caught it by its gilded hilt and not its honed blade. Stephen carefully laid it aside.

"You see what fools surround me, Stephen." The king sighed but smiled at him warmly, ignoring the craftsman struggling to wrestle the offending metal suit out the door.

Stephen did not know how to answer or if he should trust the smile. He bowed. "You summoned me, Your Majesty?"

"Yes, what was it . . . ?" Henry paced long enough to set Stephen on edge then gave an "aha" gesture and settled in an armchair. He indicated that Stephen should sit on the bench beside the fireplace. "I have a little errand for you, Master Vaughan."

Stephen sat on the bench, grateful for the warmth for it was a cold day and York Place, for all its grandeur, was not as cozy as his two-room lodging in Cheapside. He listened, trying mightily to concentrate as Henry outlined his plan for bringing back a scholar in exile to serve at court, wondering what part he would play in such a scheme.

"His name is William Tyndale. He is a brilliant man. He has fallen afoul of the law—and Sir Thomas—with some of his Lutheran writings, but I think he can be persuaded to come home. Back to England and the true Church. That'll be your job, Vaughan. Tell him his king, his country, is in need of him. If he will agree to the terms which I have written out, he shall receive a full pardon."

"But he is on the Continent, you say?" Stephen said, trying not to sound anything but pleased to serve his king. "How shall I find him, Your Majesty?"

The king shrugged as though he were merely asking Stephen to go to Lincoln's Inn or do a little search of the local taverns. "He is thought to be in Antwerp. That is where most of his illegal writings come from. You might start with a printer named Johannes van Hoochstraten. He uses the alias Marburg for Tyndale's works." He got up and, rummaging through a chest, drew out a packet wrapped securely in linen and bearing the royal seal. He handed it to Stephen.

"In there you will find sufficient funds to keep you while you are out of the country and specific instructions as well as a pardon for Master Tyndale should he agree. I shall expect a report every two weeks. You may report to me through Master Cromwell at the treasury. Mark your correspondence 'for the king's eyes only.'"

"Yes, Your Majesty. I shall find him." Stephen wished he were as confident as he sounded. "Just give me a day or two to put my affairs in order."

It was as though Henry had not even heard him.

"You will leave immediately. Don't wait for the tide and don't go down to the docks. We wish to keep your mission known only to us. A royal boatman will take you out to meet a ship. Just show the captain the king's seal on that package and say you are his messenger. No captain can refuse you. You'll be in Antwerp by tomorrow."

Leave immediately! For the brief time it takes an arrow to reach its mark, Stephen considered protesting. He had affairs to attend to. Who knew how long he would be gone. Finding a man who did not wish to be found in a city such as Antwerp—assuming he was even in Antwerp—was no easy thing. But he did not ask for more time. He merely nodded and, backing out of the king's presence, promised to do his best.

"One more thing, Master Vaughan. I almost forgot," he said, ringing for the servant that was to take Stephen to his ship. "There is another scholar that may be in Antwerp, a friend of Tyndale's. He is also a fugitive, but he has found an advocate in Lady Boleyn. His name is . . . Frith . . . I think. If you encounter him, extend the king's grace to him as well. Tell him to come home to England. He has friends here."

Stephen nodded his assent, but backed out hastily, lest it occur to the king to add yet another name to his burden.

SEVENTEEN

[The clergy] have with subtle wiles turned the obedience that should be given unto God's ordinance unto themselves.

—WILLIAM TYNDALE,
THE OBEDIENCE OF A CHRISTIAN MAN

om Lasser considered the woman leaning against the quarterdeck rail, her proud profile raised to the sun's rays, bright hair blowing in the wind. She should be standing in the bow, he thought, like Fair Helen, the face that launched a thousand ships.

"I see your sea legs are still working," he said.

She turned her face away from the sea, toward him, and smiled. "As long as I have Endor's magic concoction."

"I think you've brought us good luck and fair winds," he said, pointing to the full sails.

"God brought the fair winds, Captain, not I."

He supposed she was right. A man made his own luck, but he couldn't command the winds. They had rounded the toe of England in two days. Two more days and nights had put them into the Straits of Dover, the narrowest Channel crossing leading to Calais and close enough to the English shore to hear the terns nesting in the white cliffs. They had been challenged only once, when they neared the bend that led to Rye, but the tide and the wind had been favorable and the ship had been able to outrun the small customs boat.

"Is that wide estuary the mouth of the Thames?" she asked, pointing to where the sea met the river's brackish waters.

"It is," he said, giving a fair turn to the wheel to steer the *Siren's Song* east toward the Continent. He was in an uncharacteristically good mood. A firm breeze gave a light chop to the sea and the sails were full. England still lay to the west and vigilance was still required, but one sharp turn eastward should put them on the docks at Antwerp by nightfall, just one more legitimate merchant ship among the many hundreds that accessed the port each day. But they were not there yet. He was careful to steer in mid-channel, avoiding the English coastline.

"London is just up the river," he said, "if you sniff the wind you can probably smell it."

They'd reached the Thames estuary at low tide. Another stroke of luck, he thought, too many mudflats for the London tidewaiters or the customs officers to bother with.

"It smells like home," she said, a sadness creeping into her voice. He had a sudden urge to smooth the little frown line that formed around her mouth. He was trying to think of some glib remark to make her lift her face to the sunshine in that pose he'd just admired when her husband joined her at the rail.

Tom felt a moment's discontent as he watched John Frith slip his arm around his wife's waist, as easily as though it belonged there—which of course it did, he reminded himself.

"The *Siren's Song* has done her job well, Captain. It has been a good voyage. We are grateful to you and your fine ship. Ulysses could not have done better."

Tom laughed. He couldn't help it. He liked the man, liked his easy grace and optimism as though nothing ill had ever touched him. Amazing. Even after all he'd been through, and Tom knew what he'd been through. They'd shared a few pints of ale together and swapped enough stories that Tom would remember him as an amiable companion—and the woman too, he realized, watching her.

"May I ask you a question, Captain Lasser?" she said, her wide mouth tensing in concentration as though she were not sure she really wanted to.

"Ask away," he said, thinking she was going to ask about the working of the ship, the places he'd been. She'd been full of questions since she found her "sea legs."

"What happened to Endor's child?"

That took him unawares. Her husband, too, from the startled look on his face.

When Tom didn't answer for a startled moment, she continued, "I thought . . . that is, when I saw her outside Fleet Prison—"

"You thought right," he said, interrupting her to relieve her embarrassment. "She gave birth to the child before I could get her out. It was stillborn. A little boy."

"Oh." The puzzled expression crumbled into pain. "That is so sad."

"It was probably just as well," he said abruptly, probably too abruptly, but he was anxious to relieve her obvious distress and himself of the subject. His answer did neither. Her expression hardened into anger.

"That is a cruel thing to say about a child—or about its mother!"

"Maybe. But it's the hard truth. Life can be cruel. Often is."

Her expression did not change.

He sighed, sucking in the salt air. "Endor was raped. The child would have never known his father."

Just the cold hard facts. That was all he could bring himself to say. Even that made the rage boil up inside him, bringing bitterness to his mouth. Rage—and guilt. He gazed out to sea, watching as a seabird dived into the waves and came up with a wriggling fish in its beak. Predator and prey— the way of all things.

"A child is a gift from God." She said it with indignation, with fervor, as though she were a lawyer before the King's Bench pleading for the life of the child.

But he would not back down. She might as well know the bitter all of it. Life would not be likely to treat a woman kindly who was married to a refugee.

"This child was a gift from a man, one among many who raped her, cut out her tongue, and left her to bleed to death in a ditch." Her hands flew to her mouth, her eyes wide with horror. He almost repented his brutal words but he could not stop. "Why, Mistress Frith, would any woman choose to keep such a 'gift'?"

One small cry escaped her mouth. Her husband hugged her to him. "The captain saved her, Kate," John said gently. "He took her to a surgeon and they cauterized her bleeding tongue."

Her bleeding stump of a tongue. Tom could still hear her screams. And when it was over he'd left her with a little money in a rooming house. Alone. To fend for herself. Hardly the follow-up act of the Good Samaritan.

"Still, to lose the baby," Kate said, some of the anger drained away, some of the misery returning. "It was her *child*. It might have given her comfort."

"I don't think so," Tom answered as gently as he could in the face of such naïveté. "Most like she would have watched her little boy starve."

"He would not have starved," Kate answered levelly. "I think you would not have let him starve, Captain."

"Don't be so quick to make me out the hero of some romantic legend, Mistress Frith. There are few men among us who are really heroes."

"I disagree, Captain." This time it was her husband who objected. "You are to be commended. You took her in."

But he would not accept this, could not. "When Endor was arrested with me—she used to follow me around whenever I was in London. They said she waited by the docks for the *Siren's Song*. I'd give her a little money, buy her a meal—anyway, she was with me when they arrested me for smuggling French wine. Fine French wine. That was a bottle you enjoyed last night. I'd just lost at cards, and I didn't have the money to buy them off. So they threw me in the Fleet and Endor with me. If it hadn't been for Humphrey Monmouth, we'd both still be there. When she got out, she was so weak, I took her on board just for the night. We were to lift anchor the next morning." He gave a rueful little laugh. "You see, she's made herself pretty much at home. She did it. Not me."

"Still a heroic act," John said and then added, breaking into a broad smile, "You know Sir Humphrey, then? So you are one of us?"

"One of you? Oh—" He laughed. "No. Sorry to disappoint you, but I'm no follower of Luther."

"You hardly behave like a good Catholic," Kate said frostily.

"Must a man be one or the other? I'm a ship's captain. I don't pretend to be a theologian—and except for your congenial husband here, I've never met one of any stripe that I would care to pass an hour with."

"Then why risk—"

"A little risk lets a man know he's alive. Besides, Sir Humphrey was a friend of my father's. I'm a second son. Destined for the Church . . . well, as you said . . ." He pointed to the sea where the sun was glinting off the water, showers of diamonds with each ripple. "Have you ever seen a cathedral as glorious as that? Sir Humphrey lent me the money to make the gap to buy the *Siren's Song*. I work for him, and he happens to be working for . . . the Lutherans or heretics or whatever you want to call them."

John did not answer readily, his gaze having wandered out to sea. He pointed back toward the London shore. "Captain, is that something we need be concerned about?"

Tom saw it in an instant. A pilot ship had left the estuary and was headed toward the main channel with all due speed. "Could be going to meet that galleon riding south of us, I guess."

But the small boat didn't turn south. It continued on, straight for them.

"All hands on deck," Tom yelled. "Hoist the mainsail." There was an immediate scurrying of legs and hands and elbows as the mainsail was unfurled. "The lateral too," he shouted. If they turned slightly north they could easily outrun it. But at that precise moment great Neptune sucked in his breath, and the wind died. Not even a hiccup. The sail hung slack-jawed.

The small boat was manned with six oarsmen and she was gaining on them.

"She's flying some kind of flag," Kate said.

"It's the Tudor green and white. We'll have to let them board if they want. Get below."

"But—"

"Get below," he shouted. "We don't know what they're looking for. You don't need to incite their curiosity."

So close, he thought. So close, as the small boat pulled alongside.

"Request to board, Captain," a man standing in the bow shouted.

"Who makes the request?"

"King Henry of England, Captain. We have a passenger for you."

He groaned inwardly. *Just what I need. Another passenger.*

"Permission granted," he said.

Probably just some courtier not wanting to wait for the tide. They would be in Antwerp by nightfall and he'd finally be rid of the lot of them—even the woman who kept popping up at every turn of the bend and was beginning to pop into his head at odd times and unbidden. She was another man's wife, but with any luck he'd never see either of them again.

❧

A tap on the door and Thomas More did not look up from his desk. He'd been closeted in his study since early morning, hard at work on the polemic text of his answer to William Tyndale's *The Obedience of a Christian Man*. It was the translator's most insidious, most heretical work besides his New Testament with its vile Lutheran glosses.

"What is it, Alice?"

"I've brought you something to eat," she said, swinging open the door with her wide hips as she carried in the tray.

"Just leave it," he said tersely. He did not look up. He heard her deposit the tray on the table beneath the window behind him, but he was not to get off so easily. The next moment he felt the brush of her cap against his neck as she peered over his shoulder.

"What is it that occupies you so? I suppose we have to get used to this preoccupation now that you are wearing the great chain of office." Her ample bosom swelled with such pride it threatened to break the stitches of her bodice. "Don't cover what you're writing," she said. "I have a right to see—unless it is some private matter of state that you must not speak about?"

"I don't have to cover it. Your Latin is not that good. Not that I have any reason to hide it."

"Then what does it say?"

"It is an answer to Tyndale's latest heresy. It says that William Tyndale and his like are heretics. It says that their perfidious writings, which seek to make every man his own priest, will kindle the flames that consume their loathsome bodies should they return to England's shores. It says that we will seek them out in their fox's holes and bring them to account for their unpardonable sins."

"That's the weighty business of the lord chancellor! Not war with France or new taxes or—" Her gray eyebrows knitted the seams of her forehead in indignation. "It is no wonder you have no appetite. I can make out some of those words. My brothers used to scrawl them on their slates when the tutor wasn't looking. That's the language of baseborn men. Hardly noble enough for the discourse of the chancellor of England. Anyway, how can it matter so much?"

He picked up the pen and, stabbing at the inkwell, sighed. "You do not understand, Alice. This is more important than one man's hearth and home, more important than one kingdom even. This heresy pouring into England from this one man and his friends with their English Bible could bring down the Church. To weaken it is to destroy it. Not I—nor any good Christian—can stand idly by and let that happen. The Church must be protected at whatever cost."

"I'm no Lutheran, but I fail to see how reading the Bible can—"

He waved her to silence. "You don't understand, Alice. Wherever the Bible is read in the vernacular, ignorant peasants misunderstand its lessons.

It incites them to murderous rebellion. There must be discipline and order in all things. Without order there is the kind of chaos and unrest afflicting the Rhineland. The Church is the established order. Its truth has come down to our days by continual succession for fifteen hundred years. If you do not see the importance of defending that, then God help you!"

She bristled at his tone, as she always did when he said to her, "You do not understand." And he had said it twice. He should have been more judicious in his choice of words for the sake of familial harmony.

She gave his manuscript a little shove. "One would think it was the Church of Thomas More and not the Church of Jesus Christ. Methinks the Good Lord can protect His Church if it needs protecting without the sacrifice of your dinner."

"You just don't—"

She flounced out of the room in a huff before he could repeat the offending words but returned before he'd written two more lines, slapping down a roll of sealed parchment in front of him. It bore the seal of Cuthbert Tunstall, Bishop of London. He tore it open and scanned it quickly as she left the room without a word.

The student John Frith, whom Sir Thomas wished to interrogate, had apparently slipped the net. All inquiries had yielded naught. The bishop speculated that he might have joined his former tutor, William Tyndale, on the Continent. If only they'd been able to put a spy on his trail!

If only! Bumblers! Thomas threw down his pen angrily, blotting the last word. He couldn't do it alone. The hair shirt scraped against his back, which was still irritated from its morning scourging. He got up gingerly and went over to the window and looked out at the landscape. Winter was setting in. The trees were already bare, and there had been a hoarfrost last night. Soon the Christmas revelries would begin at court. God, how he hated those! Maybe he could plead an ague. He thought of Cardinal Wolsey, banished from court, and wondered how he was bearing his exile. Thomas had not thought Henry had it in him to take on such a powerful man. It had to be the influence of the Boleyn woman.

He lifted the lid off the steaming platter on the tray before him. Lampreys.

He had no fondness for lampreys.

He put the lid back on the stewed eels and returned to his desk. He didn't have time to eat anyway. There was much work to do, and Holbein was coming this afternoon to work on the portrait of the new chancellor of England in the proud bosom of his family.

❦

Lampreys were likewise on the menu in the archbishop's quarters in York, in the north of England. Unlike Thomas More, Cardinal Wolsey had a real liking for the eels, especially when he had the best French wine to wash them down. Though he had to admit the edge was taken off his pleasure in them by the surroundings in which he had to consume them. His apartments in York were not nearly so grand as those lost to him in London. But he was not the sort to wallow in it. At least he had gotten out with his head. He might not be chancellor of England anymore, but he was still a Roman cardinal, and if he played his cards right, he might yet find a home in Rome. So England was lost to him. What was England but a provincial little island with a small-minded despot for a ruler who had a taste for tarts? The cardinal had his eyes on a bigger prize.

As he spooned the lampreys in their rich broth into his mouth, he thought of Sir Thomas More who, his spies had told him, had been offered the great chain of the chancellor's office. Well, he wished him well of it, though he doubted the most brilliant legal mind in England possessed the kind of cunning the job required. If Cardinal Thomas Wolsey had tripped up on the king's great matter, Sir Thomas surely would. It would be interesting to watch it play out, but if his plan worked he'd be well away before then.

Apple tarts and clotted cream and a fine soft cheese followed the lampreys, but after the first bite of sweet tart cream and mellow cheese burst on his taste buds he chewed absently. Before consuming it all, he called for writing materials and a messenger. Belching loudly, he pushed aside the half-eaten cheese, wiped his mouth on the edge of the tablecloth, and picked up the quill.

To His Holiness, Pope Clement VII
From God's loyal servant in England Cardinal Wolsey
Regarding the serious threat to the Holy Roman Catholic Church in England . . .

When he had finished his letter, he sealed it with his cardinal's seal and handed it to the messenger. "This is for Carpeggio's eyes only. Bid the messenger be swift of foot."

Captain Lasser must have concluded the passenger was no threat, Kate thought, or he would not have invited him to dine with them in the captain's quarters. He was far too mercenary to bite the hand of Humphrey Monmouth by betraying them. Still, she was apprehensive. How could she help it? Her world was changing so fast apprehension was a constant companion these last days.

In the space of one week she had gone from being a single, lonely woman without prospects to a new bride. A married woman! With a whole new world of adventure opening before her. It seemed like some impossible dream. But she knew how fast it could all be snatched away. The vision of the misery of the Fleet was not an easy thing to forget. With a fluttering in her chest she watched her new husband open the door of the cabin that had been their bridal chamber for the last five nights—not as sumptuous as Lady Walsh's chamber, but its intimacy afforded some delights.

She had to admit the passenger certainly didn't look like a threat. He was a youngish man—older than John but younger than the captain. His neatly trimmed reddish beard had not a streak of gray, though when he removed his cap his hair was lightly thinning at the crown.

"I'm Stephen Vaughan, emissary of King Henry," he said in a friendly manner as he extended his hand to her husband.

"John F—"

"Gough. From Antwerp. Master John Gough and his wife Kate," the captain interrupted.

So perhaps the captain *didn't* trust him completely.

"John and his wife are in the export business. They are returning home from visiting family."

How smoothly he lied, she thought. She could almost believe this herself.

Endor tapped the captain on the shoulder and extended her open palm toward the table in a gesture that said the meal was ready.

"Come sit," he said. "I'm famished."

"Very gracious, Captain Lasser," the newcomer said as they crowded around the small table. "I had not expected . . ."

"You are welcome. Now let's eat."

Endor had managed some savory meat pasties and a mash of turnips on her small cook box—probably their last meal on the ship. It was good that the captain was sharing it with them, she thought, and the thought surprised her. But John seemed to enjoy his company, and she had learned to suffer it. In spite of his occasional sarcasm, she liked his ready wit, and when the talk inevitably turned to his sea adventures, she never found him boring and self-serving. He possessed a cynical but honest view of the world and his role in it. And there was Endor. She still was unclear about his part in that, but she had ceded to him a grudging admiration.

"Gough?" The newcomer looked thoughtful as he took a drink of the cider his host provided. "Didn't there used to be a bookseller down by St. Paul's Churchyard by that name?" Kate noticed how his hazel eyes glinted as though he teetered on the brink of discovery.

"Distant cousins . . . very distant. We hardly knew them," she said quickly.

She felt her face flush. The captain looked amused.

I don't lie as easily as you, she wanted to say, but she just looked away, a little angry at the expression in his face, but grateful when he jumped in to divert the conversation.

"So you are the king's agent, Master Vaughan," the captain said. "That must be exciting work." He plunged his knife into the center of the meat pie, releasing a little puff of aromatic steam.

"Exciting, yes, but sometimes a little off-putting. Like today. Called upon without even a moment's notice."

"Must be some urgent business, then."

"All the king's business is urgent."

"Very hush-hush, I suppose?" John entered the conversation, eagerness in his voice.

"Not so much this time," Vaughan answered between bites. "I am to make inquiries, and I might as well begin now. That's why I mentally stumbled on your name."

He paused for a drink. John and Kate exchanged a look then looked quickly away lest he notice.

"The man, men actually, that I'm looking for are learned, probably connected with the book business. One is named William Tyndale, and the other is a young scholar by name of . . . Firth . . . no, that's not . . . Frith. Yes, Frith, that's his name."

Kate's throat closed. She did not look at John. She did not look at the captain, but down at her lap.

"I thought you might know them. It is thought they are in Flanders since they are bookmen and Antwerp is a printing center. At least that's what I'm told. I don't read a lot myself—don't like the smell of ink."

The table swayed in front of Kate, the turnip mash suddenly turning to wool in her mouth, the aroma of the meat pie nauseating.

The stranger appeared not to notice as he helped himself to another bite, exclaiming, "This is delicious, Captain. I left in such a hurry I didn't even have a chance to eat. The king can be a demanding master." And then before putting it in his mouth, "If you encounter either of them, William Tyndale or this John Frith, you can leave word for me at the glovers' guild."

"So you are a glover in your spare time, when you are not on the king's business, then?" Captain Lasser asked.

Kate marveled at his casual manner. Of course, he had much less at stake than they. He would only incur the displeasure of a patron. John would lose his freedom, maybe even his life, if he did not recant. *Recant.* The word took her breath away. She recalled her brother's dilemma with a more urgent understanding.

"It is a family business," she heard the stranger explain, his voice riding a receding wave. "My father was a glover. My older brother runs the business, but I am a journeyman in the guild."

"Why does the king want these men? Have they committed some offense?" John asked.

Kate hoped Vaughan did not notice the breathless quality in his voice. His voice sounded small and far away, riding the same wave as the other. The bite she'd just eaten threatened to return.

The captain motioned for Endor to fill up Vaughan's empty cup, then added casually, "The Goughs are in the wool trade. They would not likely travel in the same circles."

Kate stood up unsteadily. She'd just lost her sea legs.

EIGHTEEN

ate was well enough by the time the *Siren's Song* approached the estuary that she could appreciate the sunset. It would be their last at sea, and surprisingly that filled her with sadness. The reflected afterglow washed the tanbark sails of dozens of ships with red and mauve and orange and tinted the water a shimmering sea of myriad colors. The sight nearly took her breath away.

"They look like giant butterflies hovering over the sea," she said to John.

"River," John corrected her. "Antwerp actually fronts on the river Scheldt and not the North Sea, like London on the Thames."

"The river Scheldt," she repeated, trying to wrap her tongue around the strange word.

Master Vaughan joined them on the quarterdeck. "The prettiest—and busiest—port in all of Europe," he said. "You must be glad to be getting home, Mistress Gough. The color has returned to your lovely face. I'm glad you are feeling better."

"Much better, thank you," Kate said.

And that was no lie. For apparently the king's spy believed their story. It looked as though they had made it, and that, she realized, was largely due to Captain Lasser. She watched him steer the ship into the river channel and upriver toward the harbor, a small smile livening his face as his eyes searched for the channel markers. This is truly a man who has found his calling, she thought, noticing every detail: the way his full sleeves blew in the sea breeze, blue-white against the ocher of his suede doublet; his captain's stance, arms akimbo, legs spread wide for balance. She tried to picture him in a priest's robe with his black hair trimmed in a tonsure instead of pulled back and tied with a riband, and almost laughed aloud. If ever a man was ill-suited to the Church, Tom Lasser was. He probably had a woman in every port.

Endor had come out of her little hut to watch them enter the harbor as well. She held her face up to the fine spray thrown up in the ship's wake, and Kate was both gratified and surprised to note that she wore an expression of contentment—almost bliss. She is happy, Kate thought. Even in her circumstances, she is happy. Kate almost envied the wounded woman that contentment. Was that what suffering did? she wondered. Place you in such pain that with its lessening, contentment came more easily. Or maybe just being in the presence of the man she loved was enough.

The last of the ship's sails was trimmed and the vessel slowed, rocking gently in the wakes created by the traffic. A few minutes later, it bumped against the jetty with a grinding noise and a great creaking of ropes on pulleys as the anchor dropped and the gangplank lowered to the dock. The afterglow had deepened, bruising the sky in streaks of deep orange and purple and casting the warehouses along the wharf in shadow. People rushed hither and yon, shouting in a language she did not understand and hustling between wagons and carts that waited to be loaded and unloaded. Everywhere horses clip-clopped and whinnied and drovers cursed at them impatiently. The sounds of commerce overwhelmed her.

Strange voices.

Strange buildings.

She had a sudden yearning for home, for something, anything, that was familiar. Even for the cramped cabin in which she'd spent the last five nights, nestled with John like two spoons in a wooden cupboard.

John reached down to pick up her trunk, waiting at her feet.

"I'll get that, sir," one of the sailors said, and before John could thank him, he heaved the heavy box onto his shoulders and started across the gangplank with it. It was their signal to follow. This is it, she thought, with a moment's panic.

In her anxiety she forgot all about Endor until the woman approached her and groping for Kate's palm pressed something into it. Kate looked down in surprise at the crude tin medal Endor always wore on a string around her neck. She recognized the emblem: a door with two women, an older woman standing behind a younger woman who held a child in her lap. The mother of the Virgin Mary. The grandmother of Jesus. Saint Anne. The patron saint of childless women. Kate felt a fierce tugging at her heart. A sacred amulet for a woman who had lost a child, a gift to a woman who desired a child. How could she know that desire? Kate had not told her. But it was a rare woman who did not desire children. Perhaps Endor was just acting on supposition.

"Thank you, Endor, but I don't want to take your medal. You will be lost without it."

Endor frowned and mimed putting the necklace around her neck and pointed to Kate.

"Put it on," the captain said. "She wants you to have it. She will not be satisfied unless you take it."

So. He had been watching. Kate bit back her tongue to keep from asking if he knew the importance of this particular saint to a childless and impoverished woman such as Endor, but of course she could not with Endor present. She put it on. "I shall treasure it and always remember the kindness of the woman who gave it to me," she said. "I feel protected now."

Endor nodded somberly, as though she had just encountered a catastrophe and was satisfied she had done all she could do. That expression of satisfaction made Kate suddenly remember the night Endor had run from the room after gazing into the bowl of water. The gift was a sharp reminder that she might need protection—as if she needed a sharp reminder with the king's agent standing so close—and there was something soothing about the weight of it. Not that she felt protected by the cheap piece of tin, but that she felt comforted by this woman who had so little and seemed to care so much.

"Well, Captain, thank you for your . . ." John couldn't say it properly, not with Vaughan so close. "Your . . . kindness and your hospitality." He reached for the captain's hand and shook it heartily as if trying to say with the handshake what he could not say with words.

"Yes, Captain Lasser, we are most grateful," Kate added, trying to tell him with her eyes what she could not say.

"I make this port often. If you need passage sometime in the future, just look for the *Siren's Song* or inquire on the docks."

He said it casually, offhand. A mere pleasantry. A polite answer. As though they were just two passengers he might or might not ever encounter again—which of course they were.

The pressure of John's hand at her back guided her onto the plank. "Steady now," he said. "It's the wrong time of the year to go swimming."

There was no trace in his voice of the kind of anxiety she felt. And, she realized as she stepped carefully onto the dock, no trace, either, of the man who had carried her trunk. She scanned the crowd. He'd had brown hair, hadn't he? Yes, brown hair. And he'd worn a blue kerchief knotted around his head instead of a cap. John's hand was still at her back, the pressure firm and insistent as he lengthened his stride.

Vaughan shouted after them, "Don't forget, Master Gough, if you should see Frith or Tyndale, tell them I have an offer of pardon from the king."

"Keep walking," John whispered as they hurried toward the most crowded portion of the dock. "Pretend you don't hear. Next he'll be asking where we live."

Somebody jostled her and stepped on the hem of her skirt. She felt it tear but kept up her pace. "John, he said *pardon* . . ." she said between breaths, "an offer of pardon from the king . . . maybe we should go back and—"

"Or maybe it's just a trick," he said. "Keep walking."

A few minutes later they looked back to see that Stephen Vaughan had disappeared into the crowd, but John did not slacken his pace. Kate was beginning to get a stitch in her side, but she soon forgot about that discomfort. She stopped abruptly, almost causing him to stumble.

"My trunk, John," she wailed. "All our things. What happened to the man with our trunk?"

"Don't worry about your trunk. We may have been lucky to get out with our lives."

Dusk had descended quickly and with it a chill that threatened frost. The foot traffic had lessened as well. Even the dockworkers had deserted, no doubt anxious to find a warm hearth. She pulled her cloak tightly around her, moaning inwardly—all her pretty things. Bad enough to start a new life among strangers, but with nothing but the clothes on your back! *Stop whining, Kate.* She tried to sound braver than she felt. "Do you know how to find the house we are to go to?" she asked.

"I was going to ask the captain," he said ruefully, then looking around at the rapidly thinning crowds, "It's probably not safe here after dark."

"What does *Antwerpen Grote Markt* mean?" Kate asked, pointing to an arrow with the words burned into it.

"Town Square. That's where the guild houses are. We'll ask there for directions."

By now they were a couple of furlongs from the docks. The dim outlines of the ships bobbed in the distance. She could no longer tell which one was the *Siren's Song,* but it didn't really matter. They turned in the direction of the pointing arrow, leaving the river behind them. At the end of a narrow, winding street, where the smells of cookfires and roasting meat mingled with the night smells of the river, a lantern beckoned on a lamppost.

As they headed for it, Kate heard footsteps keeping pace with them.

"John—"

"I know. I heard it too. Walk faster."

"I can't walk any faster."

And just then, "Master Frith, wait up. I have your trunk." It was the voice of the sailor who took their trunk.

"I have been trying to catch up to you. Captain said to follow you and see you get where you're going. I almost lost you back there."

If Kate had breath enough, she would have sighed with relief.

❧

Endor's body jerked as she slept on her pallet within the small enclosure in the bow of the ship. The dream was always the same.

She was running down the narrow alley that was Rottenhouse Row. Running hard. Breathless and afraid. They were behind her, gaining on her, their footsteps loud, loud, louder, pounding, pounding. Like her heart. Five of them.

There had been a sixth with them behind the tavern where she'd gone to deliver the bread. She saw the knife blade slice across his throat, heard the gurgle of his blood, watched in frozen horror as it spurted from his neck.

I won't tell, she cried. *I won't tell,* as they grabbed her. *Ye won't tell. Nay, witch, ye'll not tell.* One bent her arm behind her back. *Please, please, let me go. I won't tell.* But they raped her one by one, their brutish bodies smothering her, hurting her until she lay choking, gagging on her own shame and vomit, as the last one stuck a fist in her mouth and pulled on her tongue until she feared he would rip its roots from her throat. But that was not his plan. One crude chop and another and another—as she struggled to wrench free while they held her—all with the same knife he'd used to kill the man. Then there was nothing left in the whole universe but the taste of rusty metal and blood and an agony that seared itself into her brain as surely as white-hot metal sears flesh.

She always woke trying to cry for help with words that could not form— only helpless, shame-filled moans.

It always took a minute, one breathless, terrible minute before she realized where she was, before she felt first the boards beneath her and soft wool blankets. Not in a ditch then, not lying in her own blood, the world fading around her, wondering when she'd last said confession, thinking she was going to hell for how could she confess without a tongue, thinking she already was in hell. One long minute thinking her heart would not beat again before she remembered. She was safe. She was in the enclosure that He had built for her. It was a blessed place—the only space she had ever owned.

It had only taken one week for the dream to find her there. But at least the waking was better. He had provided her a hammock like some of the crewmen slept in, but she preferred the nest of warm wool blankets on the floor. In her whole life she had never slept anywhere but on the floor or the ground, but she was glad for the hanging bunk. It made a good shelf to store her things. Though she could not see them in the darkness, it was good to know they were there: the bone-handled hairbrush given to her by her sister Meggie before she was sent away to work in the kitchens of the great house, a second shift, one spare blouse, and a cloak He had bought her for cold days. Her things—even the rags she used on her bleeding days folded neatly in the tin bucket she used for washing them—where nobody else would bother them. A private place. A safe place. With a door that latched.

The ship rocked gently now and then still sheltered in the harbor. Pulling her blanket up over her head, she curled herself into a ball, but knew sleep would not return this night. Her fingers groped for the amulet that always gave her comfort after the dream, and then she remembered. Saint Anne was gone; she had given her to the girl. The still water had shown her the girl needed it more. God had already given Endor a protector.

Endor. That was the name he'd given her when she followed him onto the boat. *Tell me your name,* he'd said, and of course she could not say, *Ella. My name is Ella.* He'd given her that little half-smile and said, *I shall call you*

Endor. Now she thought of her name as Endor. Endor had a protector. Ella did not. Ella was dead.

The night was still and cold. She opened the latch to let in the heat from the cook box, which sat just feet from her door. Its live coals banked in the ashes never went out. They would keep her warm on the coldest night. The ship was very quiet. The men had all gone to the tavern on the shore. She was glad. They would relieve their lust in the brothels. None ever approached her, but when they were at sea on the long runs to the eastern ports, sometimes she saw their hungry glances. She knew they thought she was bad luck, only suffered her because He made them—and because she baked good bread from the fine milled flour in the barrels below, flour destined for the kitchens of the noble and the powerful.

Through the crack in the door she could see the black sky reflected in the black sea. She could not tell where one stopped and the other began. Wrapping her blanket around her, she went out onto the deck. It was her favorite kind of night, moonless, crisp and clear. Great crowds of stars spangled a black sky. God must live on one of them, she thought. There had been no stars on the night Ella died. God was not watching.

In the ship's quiet, the scurrying of little feet from the ship's bowels where the cargo lay in boxes and crates seemed louder. But the rats did not frighten her like they had the girl. They were just more hungry creatures. Whenever one ventured into her enclosure, she beat it with her wooden clog until it returned to its place. Everything had a place. The enclosure was hers, and she would allow no intruders. Their appointed place was in the hold among the wooden barrels filled with fancy goods for the rich who did not pay the king's taxes. If she closed her eyes she could hear their futile gnawing. They would not get into the iron-banded barrels, and it would take a heap of gnawing to get into the sewn canvas sacks. Most would have to be content with the tiny grains of spillage.

It was the way of all things.

But still the sound made her sad. It reminded her of Jemmy. Her brother used to catch the rats on the London docks and bring them home in a handmade cage he'd rigged. The money he made from selling them to the lord mayor's chief rat catchers they used to buy bread. When there was no bread they ate the rats.

Jemmy had always looked out for her. He used to hold her hand when they were in the streets. The first thing she'd ever seen in the still water had been the portent of his death. Just a wee girl, maybe five or six summers, she had looked into a puddle after a rain and seen the hangman's noose. One week later they had hanged Jemmy with two other cutpurses. Ella had cried for two days, and she had learned the pictures in the water never lied. Endor wondered how long it would be before the girl or the man—she could not tell which, since she had only seen the stake—would meet her trial.

❧

Kate wrinkled her nose as the woman opened the door to the upstairs rooms: one small sitting room, a garderobe, and a bedroom and all flooded with that wonderful watery light that hovered over the whole city. "It smells of turpentine," she said to John. "But I guess we'll get used to it. It's clean and certainly has a bigger bed than we're accustomed to."

"That's the only thing that makes it undesirable." He grinned. "I don't like the idea of even the possibility of so much space between us."

"Shh," Kate said, feeling herself blush as she looked at the austere woman who showed them the chamber.

The woman was the sister of the man who'd owned the studio. According to Mistress Poyntz, the hostess at the house where they had gone last night, he'd died right here in this room and less than a month gone.

"I'm not sure I'll like living in a dead man's studio—" Kate had started to protest when Mistress Poyntz had told them about the rooms early that morning, but Mistress Poyntz had tried to reassure her. "I've seen it. I'm sure you'll be comfortable, my dear. It's nice and spacious, good light—the brother was a very well known artist—and Catherine said she would put in a feather bed. It will just be temporary until somebody moves out of the English Merchants' House. The English merchants never stay long. You can't keep sleeping on pallets in the parlor as you did last night."

Kate looked around the pretty chamber, thinking maybe she could put the idea out of her head after all. It was a nice room, nicer than her room had been above the print shop, nicer even than her room had been during her stay at the Walshes'.

"We'll move the bed away from the windows over next to the easel where the sketches of that really ugly woman are displayed," John said.

"John! The landlady will hear you. We can't afford to insult her," she said softly from the corner of her mouth. "Lady Poyntz says lodgings are very expensive here and this woman is accommodating us."

"Don't worry. She probably speaks only Flemish." Then in a louder voice, looking over Kate's shoulder, "We'll take it," he said in English then repeated it in her language.

She answered something that sounded like gibberish to Kate and he fumbled in his pocket.

"You speak Flemish, too?" Kate asked in wonderment.

"After a fashion. It's just Low German—not that different from Dutch." He handed the woman one of their precious coins.

Kate sat on the settle beneath one of the wide windows and ran her hand across its bright cushions. "We should go back to the English Merchants' House and get our trunk, I suppose." She noticed a paint smear on the piping around the damask edging. Noticed too that the rooms were very well appointed for an artist's studio. He must have been successful. She supposed ugly people wanted their portraits painted too.

Catherine, the woman who was to be their new landlady—Kate couldn't remember her last name, started with an *M,* she thought—was rummaging in the cupboard. She brought out clean towels and a cake of Castilian soap, placed them on the table beside the bed.

"We can get it later," John said, with a familiar gleam in his eye as he sat down on the bed. He patted it with his hand. "Let's test this new feather mattress as soon as she leaves. See if being on dry land has a deleterious effect on our lovemaking."

Kate glanced at the woman, who was digging out an extra coverlet, releasing the sharp smell of herbs into the air to mix with the turpentine. She appeared oblivious.

Kate pulled a face mimicking shock and murmured, "Why, Master Frith, for a theologian you are quite the ardent husband."

The woman handed them the coverlet and smiled, her eyes showing unusual merriment. "I hope you will be happy," she said in careful but perfect English. "It is good to have joy in this room again. Quentin would have been pleased too. He did not paint ugly women only. You may see his work in the cathedral. The altarpiece is very well known. People come from miles to see it."

John's face turned the color of the crimson bed hangings. "Th . . . thank you, Mistress Massys. It is very . . . Christian of you to take us in during your time of mourning. I did not realize you spoke English. And so well. We are mindful of your loss and will treat your brother's studio with respect, I assure you."

Kate stifled a giggle. It was good for John to get caught out once in a while.

Catherine Massys nodded gravely, but her eyes still sparkled. "Thank you for that assurance. I shall look forward to seeing you at the Bible study at the English House. Though not tonight, I expect."

As she was speaking, she moved mercifully toward the door. "If you require anything else, Merta, my maid, will deliver your breakfast each day. Just tell her. She does not speak English, but that should be no problem for you of course."

She closed the door as John was still sputtering an answer.

He lay spread-eagled across the bed as Kate burst out laughing. "John, how can we ever face that woman again?"

"Let's not think about that now," he said. "Let's just be glad we're safe and we have a roof over our heads."

"And not to mention this lovely bed," she said, lying down beside him and then as quickly getting up again.

"Now what?" he wailed as she walked across the room and turned the easel around, then began to strip down to her shift.

"I'll have no ugly duchess watching over us," she said. "She might mark our unborn children."

NINETEEN

. . . old crones who still wish to play the goat and display their foul and withered breasts . . . who industriously smear their faces with paint and never get away from the mirror.

—ERASMUS OF ROTTERDAM (PROBABLY THE
INSPIRATION FOR MASSYS'S SATIRICAL
PORTRAIT OF A GROTESQUE OLD WOMAN)

t was as John had promised. By Christmas Kate was beginning to feel at home in Flanders. She'd gotten used to the constant clamor of polyglot curses and riotous greetings, the sounds of rolling carts on cobblestones and the jangling of harness bells outside their little town house chamber. And they had only to latch the wide glass-paned windows and fasten the creaking wooden shutters to banish all the world.

Each morning, after they had breakfasted on Merta's fresh milk and buttery hot cross buns, John left to go down to the Grote Markt, where among the many guild houses he found ready employment as a translator. Leaning out the window, Kate watched him down the narrow winding street until with a sweep of his hand and a quickly blown kiss he turned the corner and passed out of sight. On dreary days she puttered around the little apartment like any common hausfrau, sweeping up crumbs, plumping the cushions, spreading the counterpane on the handsome feather bed, giving it an affectionate final flourish with a sweep of her hand—for it was indeed a very fine bed.

On clear crisp days she ventured as far as the marketplace, her basket on her arm, walking as purposefully as the strangers she encountered until she reached the tented stalls. Then she would wander from pavilion to pavilion, indulging her senses with the exotic goods they offered: fingering a fine piece of Venetian lace, gasping at the colors of a tapestry from Bruges, inhaling the spicy smells of cinnamon and anise and dried fruits. Once she even bought a bit of bound fabric with a carefully stenciled cartoon of a fountain and unicorn and the silk threads to embroider. John deserved an accomplished wife and the tapestry would look pretty hanging above their bed. It seemed like a good idea at the time.

She bought fresh bread and cheese and sometimes hot soup to keep warm on the little brazier Catherine Massys had sent "to break the early morning chill," though Kate seldom felt that chill. She enjoyed lingering abed with her new husband, snuggled deep in the feather bed—until the morning sun warmed the room through the east-facing windows. But it was the market bookstalls she could not resist. Antwerp was the printing center of the world. She spent hours browsing—so many books in so many languages, and more than one of the vendors carried English books. Yesterday she had seen a book she wanted to buy, but today it was gone. She wondered if the book-seller could understand her inquiry.

"Luther?" she asked, enunciating slowly.

The vendor nodded, dug under the pile, and handed her a book which she could not read, but she recognized the German language.

"English?" she asked.

"Yes," he said clearly. "I have it in English. I have lots of English. The English merchants buy from me. I buy directly from the printers."

He reached into a large sack and pulled out three different works. "I have Tyndale—it says Hitchens but that's just another name Tyndale uses—and Erasmus's *Adagia* and a book of Luther's sermons." She reached for the book of sermons. It was the one she'd seen yesterday.

"You do not display them? I thought I saw this one yesterday."

He shrugged. "Not in large numbers. This is still a Catholic town even though the city fathers usually look the other way for the sake of trade."

She paid for the book of sermons—a gift for John, who would enjoy comparing it to his German copy. She was learning that the translation of a language was as much art as science. "I suppose I should hide it beneath the cheese," she said.

"Oh, you'll not be bothered. Foreigners are seldom harassed here." He shrugged. "We're all foreigners. Without our trade this city would shrivel like an old man's—" He blushed to the top of his balding pate, blushed as only a fair-skinned man can blush. "What I mean to say is we mind our business, and they mind theirs."

"I'll take this one too," she said, picking up an English translation of Homer's *Odyssey*. The sermons were for John. The Homer was for her. John quoted Ulysses so much she wanted to share the great heroic adventure, wanted to glimpse the lure of *wine-dark seas*.

What a wonderful place to live, she thought, walking home. John had chosen well. Here in Antwerp they were just two more foreigners in a city of foreigners. London seemed very far away.

Sometimes she and John walked down to the docks at sunset to watch the ships come in: Portuguese caravels, Spanish galleons, Venetian merchant ships, all carrying the colorful insignia of their nation's origins. Whenever she spied an English ship, she strained her eyes to see if it might be the *Siren's Song*. She would think briefly of Endor hunched over her little bake oven, and would become aware of the cheap tin medal nesting between her breasts, next to her skin, beneath her chemise. She thought, too, of Captain Lasser standing on the stern scanning the horizon with his hawk's eyes.

But tonight there would be no time for walking down by the river. Tonight they were going to the English House.

⚹

The English House was even more welcoming than usual. A chilly drizzle had settled along the twilight streets of Antwerp and the blazing hearth promised warmth and conviviality. The hall was ablaze with candles, and ivy and holly twined the wooden rafters of the hall. As she handed her mantle to the housemaid, delicious smells drew her gaze to the linen-draped buffet.

"If that table had voice it would surely be groaning beneath the weight of so many Christmas puddings and roast meats," she whispered to John.

"And we will do our part to relieve it of its burden, sweet wife."

The welcome sound of English voices also greeted their senses. Not one strange syllable among them all. English laughter is even different from other laughter, she thought, feeling a rush of gratitude for this little island of home. They were greeted as old friends, and truly by now, Kate had come to recognize some familiar faces among the eight or so merchants who gathered there on this particular night, though the clientele had a tendency to ebb and flow with their business endeavors. Of course John laughed easily with them; he worked with them every day.

It was polite for a company of mostly men. Lord Poyntz saw to that. The ale was sufficient but not overly abundant. So Kate was content to enjoy her food in silence as she listened to the current of manly conversation rippling about her. She couldn't help but wonder about the wives they'd left behind in England.

As always, Mistress Poyntz seemed glad enough for feminine companionship in this company of men. After supper, while the merchants engaged in theological debate or tales of smuggling Bibles past the customs officials, or played at cards or chess, the two women sat with their embroidery. Their hostess laughed as Kate stabbed at the fabric folds that were looking more crumpled with each day.

"You will learn it, my dear, never worry. What's a little crimson stain here and there? A mere blossom in a *millefleur* field." She lifted the fabric to her dainty mouth and bit a silken thread, then asked, "How do you find your lodgings? Are they pleasing?"

"Quite. And our landlady is very accommodating, though we seldom see her."

"That could be a good thing," Mistress Poyntz said. "Not that Catherine Massys isn't a very nice person . . . She comes here from time to time. She is a friend of one of the merchants and quite an intelligent woman. But you are after all still newlyweds and deserving of some privacy."

"She speaks English surprisingly well," Kate said, feeling herself flush at the memory. "I'm afraid John and I were a trifle . . . free in our conversation, thinking she would not understand."

"Oh dear, I'm truly sorry. I never thought . . . but whatever you said . . . I am sure poor Catherine is thrilled to have you as tenants. She was devoted to her brother, but she worried that his studio would become a sort of shrine and be invaded by his students. Now she can plead her tenants' privacy whenever some artist wants to nose around his studio. Quentin was quite famous. He did the triptych in the cathedral and was very well known for his portraits—one of them was even praised by the great Sir Thomas More." She made a little face. "We know Sir Thomas because he negotiates with the merchants."

Kate's alarm must have shown in her face.

"Don't worry, my dear, that is the be-all and end-all of our relationship with Sir Thomas More. He comes to Antwerp frequently, but he will *never* be invited to the English House. Anyway, he and the Dutch philosopher Erasmus—do you know of him?"

Kate nodded, indicating that she did.

"Well, Erasmus and Sir Thomas More are the greatest of friends, I understand, and they both have a fondness for Flemish culture." She motioned for the housemaid to clear the table. "Quentin even engraved a medal for Erasmus. Though I don't much care for his work. Quentin's . . . not Erasmus's. Quentin's work is very . . . literal. Very exaggerated. Almost grotesquely so. What do you think of his Christ descending from the cross?"

"The panel in the cathedral? I haven't seen it yet. Though there are some sketches left behind in our bedchamber . . . I know what you mean about exaggerated. The sketches are of an old woman in old-fashioned dress, really exquisitely dressed—one can see every thread in the embroidery of her horned headdress—but she is so . . ."

"Ugly?" Lady Poyntz laughed.

"Who would commission her portrait?"

"Who indeed? But I don't think that one is really a portrait—at least not of anybody we know. It is supposed to make some kind of point about the vanity of old women."

There was something sad and very sobering about that . . . about the vanity of old women as though old women could not, should not even try to, be beautiful. She glanced at John, wondering if he would find her beautiful when they were old, trying to picture him with gray streaking his hair. But the dimple would still be in his cheek. He would still speak with the same animation with which he was conversing with John Rogers. The house chaplain was assuring him that, yes, he was in touch with William Tyndale and would be happy to inform him of his friend's presence in Flanders.

Mistress Poyntz excused herself and went to the kitchen to supervise the putting away of the plate. The candles flickered low in their sconces and Kate, sighing in obvious frustration, put down her embroidery. John glanced in her direction lovingly and, rising with smiles and handshakes all around, bade the merchants good night.

The drizzle had settled into fog as they walked the few blocks home. He reached for her hand. His touch was warm and comforting and the voice of the town crier assured them that it was nine of the clock and all was well—though he assured them in Flemish. But Kate was learning the language a little.

"You seem pensive," John said. "Did I tire you by keeping you in that raucous company overlong?"

"No. Well. Maybe a little tired. But it was a fine supper, and I like Lady Poyntz." The smell of the fog rolling in from the river, the taste of it in her mouth, was familiar. It reminded her of England. "John, did you know that Sir Thomas More is the negotiator between England and the merchants and that he comes to Antwerp sometimes?"

"So that's what's bothering you."

He gave a little sigh. She imagined the vapor of that sigh mingling with the fog, sweetening it with his breath.

"No, I didn't know. But I'm not surprised. This is an important city. It is expected he would come here from time to time."

"What if he should see you?"

"He wouldn't know me. He might recognize my name, but . . . I'll be watchful. Don't worry, my angel. I'm small fish. The mighty Sir Thomas wouldn't bother with me. It's Tyndale who has to be worried. That's why he moves so frequently. Though Lord Poyntz says he's trying to convince him that the English House is the safest place for him. There he would have immunity from arrest by German authorities, and no one is allowed in except by invitation." He squeezed her hand. "Don't worry. We are safe," he said, unlocking the door to the stairway that led to their second-story chamber.

By the time the town crier had called ten of the clock and all well, John lay sleeping beside her and she snuggled in the crook of his arm. The beating of his heart against her cheek comforted her. She was about to drift off to sleep herself when she remembered the sketch of the grotesque old woman she had turned to the wall. *Will you love me when I'm old, John,* she whispered. *Will I be your angel then?*

John's gentle snoring gave no answer. But as Kate rolled on her side and tried to sleep, she felt a surge of compassion for the woman who'd sat for that sketch.

※

"Go on. Touch it if you want," the king whispered in Anne Boleyn's ear. "When you are queen you will have your own and a saltcellar to match"—he flashed his quicksilver smile at her—"with rubies as big as your eyes."

Anne pulled back her hand. She was not queen. Not yet. Not as long as Katherine of Aragon was his legal wife. But as she withdrew her hand, her fingers caressed the pearls circling the base of the beautiful covered bowl. It was by far the most exquisite piece of plate she had ever seen, rock crystal, gold, sea-green enamel, and all inlaid with precious stones.

It was the Twelfth Night masque and Henry had declared to Anne that this year's revels would be a joyous celebration of his intent. This time she had agreed to sit at the great table beside him. The gilded mask gave her some anonymity, though all the court would guess whose eyes looked out from behind the jeweled feathered mask. But since the protocol was less stringently observed for a masque, Anne had agreed.

Light and color filled the hall at Hampton Court. It seemed to Anne, as she glanced down the boards from her elevated place of honor, to be an almost heavenly vision: the troubadours strolled among the guests, strumming their lutes; cupbearers filled golden goblets at a fountain pouring fine French wine; heady smells of perfume and beeswax mingled with the succulent smells wafting up from the kitchens below. The candlelight danced, and the light shifted to reveal a jeweled cuff here, a lace collar of spun gold there, a silver snood woven fine as a spider's web: an incandescent swirl of color shifting in light and shadow. Two liveried heralds bearing trumpets appeared at the back of the hall.

"My lords, attend ye," the marshal of the hall shouted, and the processional began.

Servant after servant bearing great crystal bowls upon red velvet cushions tasseled with gold marched down the hall as the cry "Wassail, wassail!" echoed down the boards. "Wassail, wassail!" to the pounding of fists upon the boards. The candelabra hanging from the rafters shook, making the lights dance. As the cupbearers and sewers began to serve the Twelfth Night libation, a choir began to sing and the voices hushed until each cup had been filled. Then the king stood and lifted his own golden cup.

"Wassail," he cried and laughing drained his cup. Anne lifted her own cup. One sip of the spicy, sweet wine and she imagined she could feel it going to her head. She put the cup down. There was the dancing to get through. Her senses needed to be sharp.

"Your Majesty's master of the revels is to be commended," Anne said. "I have never seen such pageantry."

"This is nothing," he said, laughing. "Wait until you are crowned my queen; then you shall see pageantry. Come, let's show them how well their sovereign dances."

Her heartbeat quickened as, taking his hand, she let him lead her onto the stage that had been built for the six dancing pairs, each couple carefully selected, carefully dressed, carefully choreographed. At intervals the couples emerged from behind the painted cloths that formed a backdrop to join the dance. Each was dressed as the king and Anne were dressed, in cloth of gold slashed with Tudor green, their elaborate sleeves decorated with Tudor roses, the men in velvet, feathered caps, their ladies in pearled coifs of green velvet attached to snoods of fine gold mesh. All the dancers wore identical gilded and feathered masks.

"Your Majesty, for such a powerful athlete, you are light of foot," she said as the pipers joined the harpists, and the last couple emerged. A great tree had been erected in the center of the stage, and they danced around and around it, until Anne felt almost dizzy.

"See, already they have lost us," the king said. "They are laying bets on which is the king."

A series of painted cloths to resemble arches formed a backdrop. As the couples circled the tree, they wove in and out of the cloth archways. The pipers played faster. The dancers moved in and out among the arches, in and out, around the tree, faster still, among the arches, around the tree—and suddenly the king grasped her waist and pulled her behind the real archway, a stone archway above the stairway leading to the kitchens below.

Henry let escape a staccato laugh as with a wave of his hand another couple looking almost identical to Henry and Anne joined the dance.

"Come, we'll go out through the kitchens and enter the hall from the other side."

He was like a small boy at play, so pleased with himself. Breathless from the dancing, she had to run to keep up with him, as they dodged sewers and cooks carrying trays and stirring pots who paused only briefly to drop a curtsy with a smile and a nod or a "high-ho, Your Majesty" as if it were every day their sovereign sprinted through their workplace.

"Who was that dancer, Your Highness, so much like you in height and weight and bearing?" she gasped between quick breaths.

"Not as good a dancer, though, sweet Anne." He threw the words over his shoulder at her with no hint of breathlessness. "Say ye not nary as good a dancer."

"I did not dance with him, Your Majesty, how should I know?"

He laughed at her impudence. "It was Edward Neville. From the privy chamber. See that you do not find occasion to dance with him."

He was still running and she still breathless when they entered the hall and removed their masks.

⚜

After the king had had his fill of merriment and dancing, after all wagers had been satisfied as to which masked dancer was the king—and nobody winning except Lord Neville, who gleaned all winnings by his proxy Charles Brandon, Lord Suffolk, as reward for his part in the foolery—and after the feasting was done with its divers courses of turtledove, swan, peacock and plover, garlicky beef, neats' tongues, and spiced whale meat, which Anne did not care for but tried to eat anyway because it was a great delicacy, after the confections and subtleties were presented to huzzahs and bravos—these she also did not care for and found somewhat sacrilegious; there was something profane about the Virgin and Child made of sugar—Henry was still sober enough to suggest they retire to his chamber.

"Your Majesty, the evening waxes full and I must plead fatigue. Besides, it is unseemly for—"

"Lord Neville will be there. As will Charles Brandon and of course your lady's maid. Your virtue and your reputation will remain intact. I agree we must be circumspect. I have a gift for my closest confederates to mark this occasion. Surely you may be counted among the king's close friends."

So with feet weary from too much dancing, head aching from too much wine, and stomach bloated beneath its tight stomacher from too much feasting, Anne put on a docile smile and followed the king to his chamber. Where did the man get his stamina? He was not mortal. He'd eaten and drunk and danced more heartily than anybody at the revels, and he appeared to feel none the worse for it. As they passed the hallway leading to her chamber she thought longingly of her bed. And besides, she did not think Charles Brandon, the king's boyhood comrade and husband to his sister Mary, approved of her. No doubt Henry was trying to win him over by insinuating her into the king's most intimate circle, but she was too weary to play the charmer. However, he had mentioned New Year's presents. One did not refuse a king.

⚜

Henry was as good as his word. He had gifts for everyone: finely honed swords for Lord Neville and Charles Brandon, poetry manuscripts in his own hand for Brandon and Neville along with garters banded with the Tudor rose and jeweled buttons, even leather gloves of finest lambskin for Anne's maid.

"And take this for your lady wife, our dear sister Mary, with the message we forgive her for her wanton disregard of our favor in marrying you."

His expression matched his icy tone as he handed Brandon a small package. Anne wondered what was in it. As much as he loved his boyhood friend, Henry had planned a different kind of marriage for his widowed sister Mary Tudor, one of political advantage for the Crown. Brandon dropped his head in acknowledgment of his gratitude at being reinstated in the king's good graces. But Anne felt a moment's pang for the disgraced Mary, who had not been invited to the Twelfth Night revels. If Brandon could be restored to the king's favor, why not the king's sister Mary? She felt a flash of anger for Lord Suffolk, who had left his wife behind in the dismal cloud of her disgrace.

But one did not refuse a king.

"There is one more gift, for our special friend, Lady Anne."

He bade Anne close her eyes and placed a small velvet envelope in her hand. But before she closed her eyes she'd seen the look exchanged between Neville and Brandon and it was not a look that warmed her heart. She fingered the little envelope, trying to recapture her excitement at the thought of another present from the king—too flat for a ring or even a jewel of any size. It felt like a small square with sharp edges.

"Don't look yet," he said. "Just open the envelope."

She slipped her fingers in the velvet pouch and took out the small flat thing, feeling the smoothness of its surface and the sharp pointed edges. She heard a little intake of breath from Neville or Brandon, she didn't know which.

"Open your eyes, my lady, and look at your king's gift."

Anne opened her eyes. And what she saw distressed her so she could not stop the welling tears. She dropped her gaze so the courtiers would not see.

It was a miniature portrait of Henry, beardless as he was now, so it was a recent likeness. He had shaved his beard for the Christmas revels. It was a perfect miniature likeness, his little-boy mouth, his chin slightly cleft above its fleshy throat. He was wearing a simple surcoat and a featherless black hat and a single gold chain. The watercolor image was set against a dark blue background and framed by a thin gold circle within a red rectangle. And it was within that rectangular border that Anne found the source of her tears.

Gilt angels at the corners, both top and bottom, carried golden letters on a scarlet background: *H K*. Top and bottom. She could see them clearly through the tears.

Henry and Katherine.

"Your Majesty, I cannot accept this. I do not deserve such a token of your and the queen's generosity." The hated object swam before her, the king's image distorted through her tears. "I feel the evening has quite overcome me. I must bid you good night."

She curtsied as quickly as she could and backed out of the chamber, then picked up her skirts and fled from the king's presence. The sound of his rage pursued her down the hall.

"I'll have that painter whipped for such an insult," he shouted.

But all Anne could think about was the smug look on Charles Brandon's face.

TWENTY

This is not my doing; but would to God I could in this way, give liberty to enslaved consciences and empty the cloisters of their tenants!
—MARTIN LUTHER ON HEARING THAT NINE REFORMED NUNS HAD ESCAPED FROM AN AUGUSTINIAN CONVENT. KATHARINA VON BORA WAS ONE OF THOSE NUNS. (1523)

During the winter Kate went out less. Catherine Massys turned the lower floor, where Quentin's art school had formerly met, into two small shops. A chandler leased one, and she ran the other herself, offering artist's tools for sale: pigments and canvases and sable brushes. It was a good way to be rid of some of her brother's inventory, she said. The artists in his school had come to rely on him for supplies, but she didn't intend to give them out for free.

On cold, gray days Kate enjoyed sitting with her in the shop, struggling over the unicorn tapestry. They talked of women's things: the new caps offered for sale in the shop window across the street, the slight measure the Venetian cloth merchant gave when measuring silk, but they talked of other things too.

It was from Catherine Massys that Kate learned just how much greater a foothold the religious reformists had gained on the Continent than in England and that Dr. Martin Luther, the man who started it all and whose theology Kate had come even more to embrace since her exile, was a married man.

"Sometimes his wife travels with him," Catherine said, "and the children too. I saw her once."

"But I thought Luther was a monk. A priest," Kate said.

"You do not approve of priests who marry?"

"No. I mean, I suppose I always thought of him as too . . . devoted to marry. The lonely monk in his cell. Of course, I see no reason why the clergy shouldn't marry. Saint Paul said it was better to marry than to burn."

"Burn?" Catherine's brow bunched when she didn't understand some English idiom.

"With lust," Kate answered. "Feel tempted by . . . you know . . ."

Catherine smiled and nodded. "I understand. Burn. Like fire burns. An all-consuming love. English is a poetic language," she said. Then, "Do priests marry in England . . . or do they just . . . burn?"

"Some marry." Kate thought of Cardinal Wolsey, who rumor said had a wife, and Bishop Cranmer, who was said to carry his wife around with him in a box. "But they keep it secret." Kate picked at a knotted thread. A small hole was beginning to appear in the tip of the unicorn's horn where she'd picked it once too often. "What's she like, this wife of Martin Luther?" she asked, tugging at the fibers as if that could make the hole go away.

Catherine shrugged. "I only saw her from a distance. She is younger than Dr. Luther by half. Small oval face, plain clothes. Eyes wide apart, and looking more wise than pretty. Her mouth a little . . ." She pursed her own mouth into a pout to show what she could not say. "Her name is Kate, like you. Kate von Bora. A great family, but they disowned her when she broke her vows."

"Broke her vows? She was a nun?"

"She ran away from a cloistered house with eight other . . . nuns. After converting to Luther's ideas."

An apostate nun and a renegade priest living together openly as man and wife. Kate wondered how they managed to stay out of prison.

"She must really be committed to the Lutheran cause to marry a man twice her age because of his writings."

"Or maybe, as you English say, she just 'burns' for her Martin."

"Maybe," Kate said. Her face flushed just thinking about the way her heart leaped and her flesh quivered at John's touch. She was aware of Catherine's amused smile.

"I'm glad you are happy here with your new husband," Catherine said, then added after a brief pause, "and I'm glad you're living in my house. I think we might become friends. I meet with a few women every Friday. We study the Bible together. Maybe you would like to join us. Two of the women speak some English. They would like to practice on you."

"Do you meet at the English House?"

"No. We meet here. The Flemish women would not be admitted to the English Merchants' House, and besides, they sometimes bring their children."

"Is it safe?"

Catherine shrugged. "Safe enough. Nobody will bother us. The authorities consider us harmless, just gossiping hausfraus."

"I'll look forward to it," Kate said. She stood up and moved to the window, watching for John to turn the corner. "I've been meaning to tell you, I saw the altarpiece in the cathedral. Your brother was very talented. The figure of the dead Christ looked so——"

"Very, very dead?" Catherine's mouth pursed of its own accord this time. "Quentin was talented. But sometimes I think his pictures to be a little too . . . real."

"The sketch in the studio of the old woman——"

"If it . . . disturbs, I will remove it. It was an oversight to leave it. His sons took away all the paintings. The unfinished sketch, they perhaps didn't think it was to be valued."

"No," Kate said. "Don't take it away. I've come to live with it. Like a melancholy but kindly ghost. Was it the portrait of a real woman?"

"No. At least I don't think so. I think it was meant as a commentary on old woman's vanity."

"Old woman's vanity! What of old man's vanity!" Kate said, without taking time to edit the scorn from her voice. "Quentin Massys should have painted their withered calves in fine silk stockings and skinny haunches sheathed in gold brocade, their squinty eyes leering out of pockmarked faces at every full bosom that bounces in front of them——"

Catherine's sharp little laugh echoed in the shop.

"Forgive me," Kate said, realizing too late how rude her comment sounded. "I didn't mean it as an insult to your brother." Having abandoned the delicate unicorn's horn, she stabbed at his neck with her needle. "I should learn not to give voice to every opinion that walks through my head."

"No. It is . . . honest talk. Quentin admired honest talk. He preferred people with opinions. He hated empty faces. He would have painted your portrait with your eyes wide with . . . umbrage. It was just the kind of thing he did best—any kind of emotion. The portrait of the moneylender and his wife, in it the greed shows in their faces."

The stamping and neighing of a horse drew Kate's attention to the window. "It appears you have a customer. I should probably take my opinions and my round-eyed umbrage upstairs. John will be home soon. He should not have to seek out his wife when he comes home. I'll look forward to Friday," she said over the jingle of the bell above the shop door.

～※～

Kate was able to meet only a few times with Catherine Massys and her little group of Bible women before the torrential rains began. But it was enough for her to know it was something she wanted to keep doing. Though they prayed and sang and even debated in Flemish, two of the women spoke fair English, translating for Kate when the discussion of the Lutheran Scriptures became lively, even asking for her opinion. And she could guess at the content of their prayers. Some of the women silently mouthed affirmation of the words Catherine prayed out loud. Kate knew enough Flemish to know that the words were not from any prayer book or Roman liturgy. These prayers were ardent and earnest and personal. She could tell by the way they hugged their children to their hearts as they prayed.

The second week, at Catherine's suggestion, Kate brought her Tyndale Bible and after Catherine read from the Gospel of John—from Luther's German Bible since there was no Flemish translation—Kate read aloud from the Tyndale English Bible. " 'I am the Vine. Ye are the branches . . .' "

The third week Kate taught them to sing one of Luther's hymns that she had copied from John's translation. The little choir numbered a dozen women's voices and made quite a joyful noise unto their Lord, singing each verse of "A Mighty Fortress Is Our God" first in English and then in German with more sincerity than melodious tone. As they sang the last verse, Kate was reminded how much she and John had in common with its German author and his Kate—not the least of which was the danger they all courted. These women, who suckled their young as they worshipped, were developing a kind of liturgy of their own. And Kate was sure it was not a liturgy of which the Church prelates would approve.

"We will not be harassed in Antwerp as long as we do not celebrate the mass," Catherine had assured her, but still when they were singing and the large iron knocker sounded on the barred shop door, Catherine waved the women to silence. Kate could see the fear in their faces, and she was afraid too. In England a man could be whipped or worse for saying the Lord's Prayer in his own language. What would John say, she wondered, if his wife were arrested for illegal worship? Would he be proud of her or would he be angry? One thing was sure, he would be worried. She could spare him that at least. Sometimes she wished she knew less about the dangerous waters he and William Tyndale waded in.

The fourth week the rains began and the deluge continued unabated until the low-lying streets and gutter sewers flooded. The women could no longer meet. Only the highest streets farthest from the river stayed dry. One soggy day wept into the next. Each day, fewer and fewer desperate or hardy souls ventured into the waterlogged streets, and most of the first-floor shops had to close.

Since she could no longer keep the shops open, Catherine Massys went back to her home in Leuven. Quentin's son sent a servant to collect the six shillings in rent. He spoke no English. Watching his futile attempts to sweep the water from inside the shop each time he came, Kate was glad their little nest was on the second floor. She looked out her large windows at the empty, flooded streets and thought this must be the way Noah's wife felt and wondered if the rain came down in sheets like this across the Channel in England. John inquired, and word from the English House was yes, it was raining in England "like the end of the world." The Thames could not hold all the runoff from England's rivers and the undercroft at St. Paul's was below water. That meant the print shop was probably flooded too. She wondered what she would find when she went back there—if she ever went back there.

On the fourth week of the rains, the rain dwindled to a drizzle and the street below Kate's window drained sufficiently to be almost navigable. Kate put a sign on the door of the shop, directing the women upstairs. If they came they would be welcomed, and she intended to be prepared. As she scrounged among John's papers for discards, he looked up from putting on his coat. "What are you looking for?"

"Just a few pieces of paper and bits of charcoal so the children can draw Noah and his ark."

He frowned. "I thought that was over now that Catherine has gone back to her parents' house in Leuven."

"Why does it have to be over? Anyway, some of them don't know that

Catherine is gone, and they may come since the rain has let up." She held up a paper with scribbles all over it, one that had obviously been edited and re-copied. "Can we use the back of this?"

He glanced at it briefly, then nodded and rummaged in the pile until he found two more. She kissed him to show her thanks and started to slice what was left of last night's loaf in thin enough slices that there would be at least eight—enough for the children if they all came. There was still a teaspoon or two of conserve that hadn't molded. He glanced disapprovingly at the thin smear of jam she was spreading, though she knew it was not the conserve he begrudged.

"Kate, meeting with Catherine and those women was one thing. But I'm not sure this is such a good idea. I don't think—"

"You worry too much."

"If suspicion is aroused they will come after the leader. With Catherine gone, they might think you are the leader."

She sighed in mock exasperation. "We're just a group of hausfraus, John, meeting to gossip. What harm in that? I'm just telling stories to the children, teaching them a few English words, while the women talk of other things."

"What *things*?"

"Women's things." She wiped the knife on a bit of cloth and turned her gaze away. "Certainly no learned discussions like you and the chaplain have." And then she added, to soften the hard edges of the deception, "Sometimes we sing a little—one of Luther's hymns or—"

"Luther's hymns! Kate—"

"Please, John, Don't be cross. Do you not think I worry about your activities? This is very important to me. It gives me a way to make a contribution while you are occupied with your great cause."

He frowned then, cupping her face with his hands, kissed her lightly on the forehead. Looking at her soberly, he said, "You make a good point. Who am I to deny you? But just be very cautious, Kate. You must be ever watchful of what you say. The Church's spies are everywhere." He reached out and snatched the paper from her. "Don't use this. It would lead them right to our door."

Spies! A little shudder passed up her backbone. Of course, the paper showed his translations of contraband material. "I should have thought of that. I promise to watch for dastardly spies and hand out nothing," she said lightly, to hide her unease. "Now shoo. Maybe they have some work at the Kontor for you today."

But by midday the rains began again in earnest and continued on into the next month. No Bible women came. Kate was almost relieved.

Business in the sodden Grote Markt slowed down to a terrapin's pace. The traffic on the river Scheldt slowed, too, and the merchants had less for John to do. They had a little bit of savings to get them through, and they were dry and high, and most days the water was not so high that the milkman's horse and cart could not get through. Venturing out between the downpours, Merta still provided them with fresh bread and cheese curds. Only a few market stalls were open, but one day John found some withered turnips for sale from a street vendor huddling under the cathedral eaves and another day some dried apples. The English House was on higher ground, so Lady Poyntz sent word for them to come there and eat whenever they felt like braving the wet and the cold.

They made do. There was only the two of them. But that was something else that was beginning to bother Kate. Her courses were as reliable as the clock on the Merchants' Guild Hall, though heaven knew it was not for lack of opportunity that she did not conceive. Each time she and John lay together, she thought, *This time. This time there will be a child*, and she remembered Pip and even the tiny babe the woman had left in her care and how the child looked out of wise blue eyes, awakening a longing in Kate that would not go away.

By the end of February, the rains had almost ceased and the Bible women had returned, grateful they could still meet in Catherine's absence. But business at the Kontor had not resumed fully, and John was showing signs of restlessness.

"Have you had any news from Chaplain Rogers or your friend Tyndale?" she asked one day as he stared listlessly out the window to the empty streets below.

"Funny you should ask, sweet wife. You must have read my mind. I was just thinking about him. The last news anybody had of him was that he was in Worms. But it is thought that he plans to come to Antwerp to print his second edition and work on his Old Testament translations." He continued to stare out the window as if at any moment Master Tyndale might emerge from the clouds. "The rain has lessened a bit," he said. "I think I'll go over to the English House and see what news there is."

You've just come from the merchants' guild, if there were news you would have heard it, she thought, but she did not say it.

"Do you want to come with me?"

"No." The thought of spending one more evening in the company of a group of men and only the ragged unicorn to occupy her did not appeal. "I'll stay here in the dry."

"You're not feeling poorly?"

"No. I'm fine. I just am not in the mood to get wet. You go on. I should probably write a letter to my brother and Mary. Let them know we are safe and settled. Mistress Poyntz said she would send it with her correspondence to Lady Walsh."

That was no lie. She'd been putting off the letter for weeks, wanting to tell them when she did that she was pregnant. But she might as well go ahead and do it.

His lips pecked her cheek. "If you're sure then," he said, smiling broadly as if the clouds had parted, and the sun had come out. He was already shrugging into his cloak. "I'll bring you some food back, and I won't be long."

After he left she sat for a long time in the gathering twilight, listening to the intermittent splatter of the rain against the windows. Finally scolding herself for having wasted the natural light, she lit a candle and gathering quill and ink sat down to write at the little corner desk where John worked.

Dearest brother,

I hope you and Mary and Pip are well. This is to let you know that my husband and I arrived safely in Antwerp and have settled in. This is a very big city. Its streets teem with beasts of burden and creaking carts and people shouting in many different languages. John has found work with the English merchants here. I have joined a kind of Bible class for some local women and their children, which was thriving until the winter rains. We hear it is flooding there as well. I hope the water has not gotten into our father's shop, though there is little left there to ruin. Lord Walsh promised he would see that it was boarded up and protected against vagrants until we decide what to do with it. Have you started building your new home yet or are you still with the Claphams? I suppose . . .

She sat while the candle spit and danced with her pen poised above the paper trying to figure what it was she "supposed," until sighing heavily she finally put down the pen and blotted what she'd already written. She would finish it tomorrow.

She went to bed alone, sinking into the feather mattress like a stone, missing John. She was still awake when she heard his footfalls on the stairs.

As he bent over her and kissed her lightly, she put her arms around his neck and drew him closer.

"I'm glad you waited up," he said, laughing. "I missed you."

She slapped him lightly on the face, a lover's pat. "I didn't wait up, you oaf, you woke me up with all that happy whistling. I don't think you missed me overmuch."

But how could she feign discontent with him here, beside her, nibbling at her ear? She lay awake for a long time after they made love, listening to the sound of the rain and the even rhythm of his breathing, wondering if tonight they had made a child.

⌁

Anne Boleyn had fled after New Year's. She had summoned her brother George and demanded he escort her to their father's home. She would not stay at Hampton Court and be made a laughingstock. The king had of course come after her, riding all the way to Hever Castle, bringing with him Charles Brandon and Lord Neville, "so they could witness his contrite apologies," he'd said. Did he not know these two who had witnessed her humiliation would be the last people she wished to see?

But how could she not forgive him when he braved the cold and the rain to bring her a new miniature likeness, the same as the other but with the offending *H K* painted out and a diamond and emerald necklace besides and three bolts of crimson cloth of gold? What woman could withstand Henry Tudor in all his glory, especially Henry Tudor bearing gifts? He had decked out his horse and himself in such finery as would make the sun blush in envy.

"I see from your attire that you have not been hunting, Your Majesty."

They stood in the hall looking out over the rain-sodden garden. Her heart skipped a little, whether at the aggressiveness of his suit or the splendor of the suitor she wasn't sure.

"I am hunting." He flashed his smile at her. "Some quarry deserves more splendid dress."

"Am I no more than prey to be stalked, then, my lord?" she said quietly, just out of earshot of Neville and Brandon.

"Such prey as is worthy of a king. And I am yours. Quarry worthy of a queen." She could feel her heart beating in her temple. She wanted to swear at him and beat his chest with her hands. She wanted to brush her lips against his and feel the pressure of his need against her body. She did neither but mustered her will to stand before him in the presence of his henchmen as demurely as any maid.

He pressed the miniature into her hand. "Someday there will be *H A* in gold on all of the king's portraits. Henry and Anne." He paced a bit. Looked away, out the window to yew trees in the garden where the rooks sheltered from the rain. The smile disappeared as quickly as it came. "Will you be satisfied then?"

"I will be satisfied, my lord. I am always happy in your presence. Shall I return now with you to court?"

She longed for court. Though she had her enemies there, anything was better than this nun's existence in her father's house. She had begged her father to take her with him when he went to the Continent as he had done before, but he had refused, saying the king might desire her company.

Apparently the king did not. He frowned. "It is probably best you bide here for a while. Cardinal Carpeggio is on his way from Rome. I remain hopeful that in spite of Wolsey's bumbling it will still be worked out and a standoff with Rome avoided. The cardinal should not see us together. He needs to be convinced of your virtue and that our marriage is right."

"And what of Katherine? Is she convinced?"

"She will never be convinced. Though I have not been in her bed for two years, yet she hopes. I cannot convince her that our union was a sin. If she would take herself to a nunnery then it would be easy to make the case for us to marry. But she will not."

"Is she still at Greenwich then? Still in the royal apartments?"

"She is. Until this matter is settled, I can ill afford to have the King of Spain and the Holy Roman Emperor on my neck. Charles is coming to see his 'most favored aunt.' Ferdinand will never be assuaged, but Charles seems a reasonable sort. I am actually on my way to Greenwich to meet with him."

"So the princely robes were not for me, after all."

"Do you think I would dress this way for a private conversation with another man? Such is not my inclination." He laughed and raised her hand to his lips. "A lady is foremost in my heart."

Under the watchful eyes of the Duke of Suffolk and Lord Neville, he kissed her lightly on the cheek as he bade her farewell, as chaste a kiss as her father had given her when he rode off to his ambassador's duties.

"You will let me hear of the meeting's outcome?" she called as he strode away, then, "God's speed, my lords."

But God was apparently not in the mood to give good speed. When next she heard from Henry, it was the middle of February. He was hunting in the rain in New Forrest. He sent her a brace of coneys and a deer "killed by the king's own hand" and a message that the cardinal had sent word that he was delayed by frozen seas and flood tides and did not know when he would come. Henry said nothing of his meeting with the queen's nephew, but told her with winsome words how he longed to have her by his side. Pretty words. She crumpled the message and threw it in the fire and wondered if Katherine had accompanied him to Richmond. He might not be sleeping with her, but he still traveled with her. The people still hailed her as queen. She'd heard the women sometimes lined the streets when she passed in procession, calling her "good Queen Katherine" and throwing flowers at her feet.

By April the sweating sickness had broken out in London. Henry sent word that she should stay away. If the cardinal did not come soon and exercise his legatine rights to let the English archbishops decide, then he would be driven to break with Rome and do it himself. At any rate, he said, as he would be in progress from one duchy to the next, wherever the sweating sickness was not, she should remain at Hever. But he said he was sending her a special gift, the anticipation of which lifted her spirits somewhat. But her flagging spirits soon returned. What good were diamonds and gold, if one had no place to wear them?

And when her special gift finally came, it had nothing whatsoever to do with diamonds and gold.

TWENTY-ONE

nne Boleyn, as she did each day, kept watch from her chamber window for the king's livery. She was not alone. Her sister Mary Carey had decided to bring her children to Hever Castle because the sweating sickness had reached the Careys' manor in Pleasance Park. When her husband William had come down with it, she'd packed them up and fled. But Anne, in spite of her loneliness, had not been pleased to see her. She was aware of Mary watching her with a catlike expression as she watched for Henry.

Her little niece, named for the queen—how like Mary to flaunt it; did she think the whole world blind?—played with her dolls at their feet while the other, aptly named Henry, slept in the nursery. One of the dolls bore the painted visage of Queen Katherine and the other Princess Mary. This irritated Anne considerably. When she looked at the child playing at her feet, she imagined she could see Henry's petulant mouth and intelligent eyes, and she felt something very akin to jealousy—which fact surprised her. Why should she care that he'd slept with her sister, unless she was growing fonder of her splendid Goliath than she had ever intended?

She had spent the last twenty minutes explaining the nature of her relationship with the king, trying to make her sister understand that she, Anne, had chosen a different path. Mary missed the point entirely.

"You mean to say you have not lain with him yet?" she chortled.

"I am not as easily put on my back as you, dear sister."

For her answer, Mary reached down and smoothed the doll's dress. "Don't ruffle the queen's gown, poppet. Your father is very fond of both the queen and the princess." She smiled at Anne innocently. "William gave her the dolls. He was given them by the queen's own usher as a gift for . . . his daughter."

Anne resisted the urge to slap her. What if Henry should visit while she was here? Would seeing her with his child playing at her feet rekindle attraction? They had avoided the awkward subject of his relationship with Mary Boleyn. "You slept with my sister" is not something one hurls at a king. And the king was much too chivalrous to bring it up in her presence.

"I'm sure Lord Carey misses his children terribly," Anne said archly. "It is probably safe to return home now. It has been a fortnight, hasn't it? Aren't you worried that your husband may be dying and you are not there to comfort him?"

Mary shrugged. "He has his royal grants to comfort him."

Grants that you earned on your back, Anne opened her mouth to say, but was interrupted when her watchful gaze fell on a lone rider approaching the entrance, dressed in a plain brown cassock rather than the Tudor livery. Anne turned away, not knowing whether to be relieved or disappointed. It had been two weeks since her last message from the king in which he'd promised her a special gift. But all things considered, if he was going to bring the gift himself, she'd just as soon he wait until Mary had departed.

A soft tap at the door interrupted this wishful thought.

"If that's a servant with refreshment, I hope it doesn't bear the taint of vinegar. I am sick to death of the smell of vinegar." Mary wrinkled her nose. "It permeates the very air we breathe."

"Small price if it keeps the pestilence away. It was the king who insisted it be used at Hever."

"Well, he was ever a coward whenever sickness was abroad. If you're thinking he'll come calling, I would not wait by that window overlong. He's probably holed up in some wilderness lodge with only Brandon and Neville for company," she said as Anne opened the door.

"Lady Anne," said a steward, "there is a priest without. He would speak with you."

"A priest!"

"He says he is a parson from Honey Lane. He says to tell you he was sent to you as a gift from the king. To give you spiritual comfort during these difficult times and to offer prayers for your well-being."

Behind her she heard Mary's snicker. "And to think all I ever got were a few paltry land grants and some fine clothes."

"Tell the parson from Honey Lane I shall meet him in the chapel presently," Anne said, trying to ignore her sister. "And that I am much moved by His Majesty's dear regard for my physical and spiritual well-being."

"I wouldn't be too moved, dear sister." Mary sank into the wide window seat and gazed out the window. "And if I were you I'd be very careful to whom and what I confess." Then she looked back at Anne, all trace of humor gone from her face. "After all, you are my sister. I would hate to see you bring disgrace or worse upon yourself . . . upon us all."

But Anne was in no mood for such sisterly advice. "You must be confusing my litany of sins with your own. I have not entertained half the French court between . . . as intimately as you. Flirting is not a sin. But you need not worry. I only confess my sins to God. As this priest well knows. The king knows my mind on such matters too. He sent this particular parson at my request. But you were never one to take such things too seriously, were you?"

She threw this last over her shoulder as she exited and looked back to see if the barb had found its mark.

Mary frowned, her eyes still sober. "And you may take them too seriously," she said. "A simple maid might drown in such deep waters as you are wading in. Take care, sister. Take great care."

But Anne was not worried. The hated Wolsey was gone, and she was almost sure Thomas Cromwell was already on her side. She would circle herself with reform-minded priests like this parson from Honey Lane and the scholars from the fish cellar who had been so ill-used. Once they were safe at court, they would be in her debt. Such friends would drive the wedge deeper between Henry and his Catholic queen. No. Anne was not worried. Why should she be when the king of England had promised to make her his queen?

By mid-May the floodwaters of the Scheldt River had receded; the merchants were once again in full industry; and Kate was pregnant. But she had not yet told John. She wanted to be sure.

"You have that look about you. You are carrying right enough." Mistress Poyntz looked wise in her certainty, especially when Kate told her she had been queasy in the mornings, and just last night she'd had the strongest urge to have a paste of goose liver when she'd hardly ever been fond of it. She confessed this as she helped herself to another helping of the hearty fish chowder bubbling in the great kettle on the kitchen hearth.

"Sorry to be so greedy. At this rate, I'll grow as fat as the goose that sacrificed the liver," she said, sopping her bread in the creamy soup. "This broth is delicious!"

Mistress Poyntz, who was plucking a chicken for roasting, laughed. "There's plenty." She gently nudged the pile of feathers with her feet into a wide-mouthed sack, then lowered her voice because the wide kitchen door was open to the adjoining solar. "You may be eating for two, you know."

But there was no need to lower her voice. John, as usual, was engaged in animated conversation with Chaplain Rogers about the theology of the Eucharist, in particular their views that the Roman doctrine was all wrong. John's voice intruded through the open doors, louder and more excited than usual.

"To argue for the Real Presence of Christ is a superstition. The baker doesn't make the miracle of the mass, God does." She heard the thumping of his fist on the table for emphasis. "The miracle is in the change wrought in the recipient, not the physical attributes of the bread and wine."

To which Rogers responded, "I'm with Luther on most things. He's dead right on the theology of justification by faith and not works, but in his defense of the Real Presence in the Eucharist, I quite agree with you; he's wrong as wrong can be."

Since there was nobody to dispute the other side, they carried on both sides of the argument with an almost sporting zest.

While Kate agreed with their espoused view that the bread and wine were symbolic and did not literally turn to the blood and flesh of Jesus Christ in her mouth—she wasn't sure she could swallow it, even to save her soul, if it turned to the real thing in her mouth—she sometimes wondered why this was such a sticking point for all sides. The miracle of the mass was not being denied. She would have expressed this view to Mistress Poyntz, but she had finished with the plucking and moved on to deal with the hapless bird's innards. Kate helped herself to another half bowl of chowder. But she ate it with distraction as she thought about the conversation going on in the next room.

Wasn't the true miracle of the mass in the transformation of the participant's heart, in the forgiveness of sin? But where was the harm in believing it also became the real blood and flesh? Either way, it was an act of obedience, an act of worship. She sipped her soup and thought of the children who came with the Bible women, how gladly, how quickly, they absorbed the simple truth of love that Jesus taught. Love God. Love your neighbor. What really was there left to argue about?

But she dared not say this to John, who was more and more absorbed by such finer points of doctrine. He had even mentioned writing and publishing a polemic on the subject of the Eucharist. She wished he wouldn't. Translating the Bible was dangerous enough. That could be done in secret, even anonymously—in point of fact, she'd wondered why Tyndale signed his name to his translations. But to sign one's name to a direct challenge to any doctrine of the mass was like laying down a gauntlet to the supporters of the old faith. Men had been burned for less.

Would John be more discreet if he were a father? She sighed. Probably not. Luther was a father six times over, and it hadn't stopped him.

But it had stopped her brother John.

᠁ ᠁

"What news have you from England?" Kate asked after a dinner of roast chicken. She and her hostess were back in the kitchen polishing the plate. The kitchen wench was fine enough for scouring the pots, but Mistress Poyntz always saw to the polishing of the pewter and silver herself. Kate always helped.

"Not good news, I'm afraid, my dear. The rains had scarcely ceased before the sweating sickness broke out. First the floods, now pestilence. And if that weren't enough, the cloth workers rioted on May Day to protest the presence of foreign workers. Several Frenchmen were killed—in Shoreditch, I think."

She paused in her recital to call for one of the servers to take the great mastiff dozing by the kitchen hearth into the garden, then resumed her vigorous rubbing of the great platter with a paste of vinegar and salt. "The king's soldiers had to be brought in to restore order. From what I hear it was a bit of a massacre. Isn't it a shame what God-fearing folk will do to other God-fearing folk when their livelihoods are threatened?"

Or even when only their opinions are threatened, Kate thought. But the word *Frenchmen* had set her mind working in another direction, conjuring the young Winifred who had left the blue-eyed child on the floor of the book-shop to chase a cutpurse. Madeline. The child's name was Madeline. *Her daddy's a Frenchy* the woman had said. But she said he worked as a waterman in Southwark. The riots had been in Shoreditch and with cloth workers. She dismissed the thought.

Mistress Poyntz handed the platter to Kate to place in a drying rack by the fire. "You and Master Frith are fortunate to be well away from England now. Bad omens and ill tidings are everywhere. A great fish beached itself upon the shore and died; the astrologers are working overtime to explain some strange lights in the night sky; and some nun in Kent has prophesied that the pestilence and want are God's punishment against the king because he's trying to annul his marriage. Of course the Lutherans blame the Catho-lics and the Catholics blame the king for abandoning his Catholic queen. The king says it's God's punishment because he's living in sin with his brother's wife, with whom he no longer lives in sin—" She broke off with a little laugh. "Instead he lives in sin with Anne Boleyn."

"She's one of us, you know," Kate said, removing the last of the dinner plates from the drying rack and polishing it with a warm scrap of linen.

"One of us?" Mistress Poyntz took the plate from Kate's hand, and placed it in the cupboard.

"A protestant," Kate said. "She protests some of the doctrines of Rome."

"You mean she's a Lutheran?" She looked at Kate in surprise.

"Lord and Lady Walsh say she reads Luther and William Tyndale."

The servant had left the door open to the late-afternoon sunshine. Kate looked out into the bit of kitchen garden where the mastiff was lifting his leg, aiming expertly at a rosemary bush. His business done, he lumbered back in and resumed his place on the cool hearth. He was old and spoiled by the many patrons of the English House, who had numbered six merchants for dinner today, and Kate had smiled to see each slip him a morsel from the table when Lady Poyntz wasn't looking.

"Well then, if Anne Boleyn should become Queen of England, that would be quite something, wouldn't it?" Mistress Poyntz said. She placed the gleaming platter in the center and stood back to admire her filled cup-board. "That would mean quite possibly the king's heir would be raised as a reformer. I'm sure Princess Mary is Roman Catholic to the core." She lowered her voice as if the walls had ears. "Speaking of Master Tyndale, we have had correspondence from him. He had to flee Cologne when the printing house he was using was raided."

Kate listened in amazement. Lady Poyntz was better than the town crier.

"He's been moving about ever since, trying to keep ahead of the English spies who would of course sue the German authorities for his immediate arrest if they found him. He's in Worms now, but he's coming to Augsburg in June to meet with Luther and some of the German reformers. Prince Frederick has called a special meeting of the diet to hear a sort of statement of faith from the Lutherans, to see where there may be points of reconciliation. I think your husband and Chaplain Rogers are hoping to seek him out there and bring him here to safety."

"John hasn't mentioned that to me," Kate said, a little taken aback that this woman should know more of her husband's plans than she did.

Lady Poyntz patted her hand reassuringly. "Don't let that little oversight trouble you, dear. They've only been planning it for a week. I'm sure he will. They don't tell us wives everything—only what they want us to know. Lord Poyntz will just suddenly announce that he's to be gone for weeks on end . . ."

She droned on about some business adventure her husband was involved in, but Kate only half heard. It did trouble her. Not the fact that John had not yet mentioned it, but the fact that it sounded dangerous. And she would be separated from her husband for the first time since leaving England.

❧

It was a sunny June day at Chelsea and well past three by the sundial in the garden. Margaret Roper had waited long enough to be summoned to a picnic with her father. On beautiful Fridays in June they usually dined down by the river. She had told William when they married that every day of the week belonged to him, except Fridays. Friday afternoons belonged to Sir Thomas.

She always looked forward to their conversations, but especially today. Today he was sure to mention her book. It was now officially published, bearing the king's license, and they were free to discuss it. When no summons came, she decided to take matters into her own hands, and went in search of Dame Alice. She found her in the great kitchen, harassing the cook.

"Where's Father? It's Friday. It's a beautiful day. Has he been summoned to Westminster again?"

Alice removed the lid from the great soup kettle hanging in the fireplace and ladled herself a taste. She frowned. "It needs salt and more flavor, maybe a touch of sage," she barked. "And this time send some *cool* buttermilk with Sir Thomas's dinner. It will not hurt you to go down the ladder steps into the cellar. Send the boy." She gestured with a nod of her head toward the urchin tormenting the rooster that strutted around the open kitchen door. "He has little enough to do to keep the hearths in summer. He wants exercise."

"So then Father is at home? Why are we not—"

"You can ask him yourself." She was busy ladling the soup, adding a crusty hunk of still-warm bread, wiping a pewter tankard for the buttermilk with the snowy linen of her apron. "He's in the study. As always. You can take his food in to him, not that he's going to take time to eat it. He even neglects his devotions. I am that vexed with him."

It was clear that she was "that vexed" with something.

"I suppose we should be patient," Margaret said. "We should have expected now that he's lord chancellor the king has full claim on his time—"

"Fiddle-faddle. 'Tis not the king's business keeps him in his study night and day. The king is off on a hunting trip. Has been since March. 'Tis his own obsession. Heretics—heretics roasted, fried, or flambéed—that's all he thinks about. I think he would send them all to hell himself, even your husband, and be glad of it if he had the power."

"William is no heretic! Just because he keeps an open mind . . ."

The boy returned with the buttermilk. The cook had wisely disappeared into the pantry until the storm that was Dame Alice in one of her moods blew over. She snatched the pitcher from his hand, sloshing a milky drop onto the table. The boy retreated as his mistress filled the tankard, then assembled the tray and thrust it out at Margaret.

"Here. See if you can distract him from this obsession."

A few minutes later, Margaret knocked tentatively on her father's study door.

"Who is it?"

She recognized the tone he used when he did not wish to be interrupted.

"It's Margaret, Father. I've brought your dinner," she said above the scratching of his quill. She did not wait to be told to enter but shouldered her way into the room. The habitually tidy chamber was in disarray with books haphazardly strewn across every surface, some facedown and opened as if marking a place, manuscript pages spread out to dry. Even the window ledge was covered. She had never known him to be so careless with his books.

"Just put it down, Meg," he mumbled. "I'll eat it later."

"Where?" she asked pointedly.

He looked up then, and she was shocked to see his face. Dark circles ringed his eyes. His cheeks sagged.

"Father, are you unwell?"

He put down his pen and began shifting some of the books to clear a space on the corner of the desk. "I'm fine. Just busy."

"Alice prepared the tray herself," she offered as she set it down.

He picked up the goose quill, dabbed it in the inkwell.

"Shall I sit with you while you eat?" she asked, and bent to remove a couple of open volumes from the chair.

"Don't touch those," he said curtly.

She saw that the one on top bore Tyndale's name.

"You are writing a refutation of Master Tyndale? I thought you finished that weeks ago."

"It is another. The heretics do not sleep; neither shall I. That devil Tyndale skips about the Continent, wreaking havoc as he goes. In the meantime I must provide an antidote for the poison flowing from his pen."

A skin was already forming on the creamy soup as it cooled. "Surely Master Tyndale stops to sleep and eat."

"There will be ample time for that later," he said evenly, but she could tell she was trying his patience.

"What about the king's business?" she asked.

"The king has no greater business than the pursuit and burning of heretics," he said flatly.

She looked around the scattered books in the room, hoping to see hers. "I've obtained the king's license to publish my translation," she said.

"I know," he muttered. "I have a copy here." He cast a cursory glance around the room. "Somewhere."

He'd already returned to the document before him. He wrote rapidly, rarely stopping to consider or pausing to scratch out a word, as if everything he wanted to say flowed fluently from his brain as effortlessly as rain.

"It's Friday. I was hoping we could share a meal and . . . perhaps discuss . . . my translation."

He did not even look up. "There will be other Fridays, Margaret. We will discuss it later."

There could be no answer to such a profound dismissal.

TWENTY-TWO

There is no bond on earth so sweet, nor any separation
so bitter as that which occurs in a good marriage.
—MARTIN LUTHER

ate was on her hands and knees scrubbing the deal floorboards
of their bedroom when she first felt the pain in her back.

"It's nothing," she said aloud to the sketch of the ugly old woman. Then
she muttered into the answering silence, "We should get a cat. At least I
could talk to something that moves."

You'll be glad enough for the silence when the baby comes.

Now she was hearing voices—her mind carrying on both sides of the
conversation. She was more desperate than she thought.

I should practice singing a lullaby. That way John won't come home unexpect-
edly and hear his mad wife talking to herself. She started to hum, and then she
realized she knew no lullaby. And she didn't know anything about babies or
their care in general—not the first thing. Maybe John knew. He seemed to
know everything, though she thought surely there must be some knowledge
one could not get from books.

She scrubbed at a patch of green paint on the varnished boards, scratching at it with her fingernail. That patch of paint had been bothering her for
weeks. John had even mentioned it once. She brushed a line of sweat from

her brow with her forearm and scrubbed harder. If she hurried, there was still time to finish this and freshen herself and get to the town market before he came home. She went over the list in her mind: wine, a good bottle of French—she'd been saving a sixpence a week since she'd first begun to think she was pregnant—and beeswax candles, and fruit and cheese and freshly baked bread and maybe a bit of smoked fish and a pie, yes, custard pie from the pie shop at the end of High Street, an extravagance but it was to be a celebration.

She tried to imagine the look on John's face when she told him. *John, you are going to be a father.* No, too blunt. The poor man might swoon. *John, I think I might be pregnant—I don't know for sure. It's been ten weeks.* Better. Less final. Give him time to get used to the idea.

She scraped the last bit of green and wiped it on her apron. *What if he doesn't like the idea?* He would never say; he would be too mindful of her feelings. But she would know. She would be able to read it in his eyes.

Another wave of pain struck across her back and into her groin—familiar but more insistent. It felt almost like . . . She stood up carefully and going into the garderobe checked for bleeding. One small bright spot, that was all. Not that uncommon, Mistress Poyntz had said, warning her about what to expect. She sat down on the stool and waited a few minutes, then checked again. No more blood. Probably just a warning that she should leave off the hard work.

She emptied the pan of mop water into the street below the window, careful to look each way, shouting in her halting Flemish "look out below," before she flung its contents. She'd been more careful with her slops and dishwater ever since she'd hit a dandy alighting from his carriage. She suppressed a giggle, remembering the indignant look on his face and the bits of egg clinging to his pointy beard and fine starched ruff as she shouted her apologies. She'd had one brief moment of fear—before John charmed away his choleric humor—that her hapless victim might challenge her husband to a duel. Imagine having to kill a man—or be killed—just because your wife was clumsy with a pan of dirty dishwater. It was good they dueled with words and not swords, though John had assured her later, with a bit too much bravado, she thought, that he could handle himself with a blade.

There was enough time to freshen herself. The shadow from the jeweler's shop across the street was short, its glass emblem in the shape of an oversized diamond still glinting where the sunlight hit it. She splashed a little fresh water into her bowl, and lathering some soap, applied it to her hands and arms and face. God bless Quentin Massys for installing an ingenious series of lead pipes and a hand pump—a luxury most did not have. They never drank the water, preferring the fresh, clear water from the public well only a couple of furlongs away to the dank taste of the piped water, but it was fine for washing up and would be a godsend when the baby came.

She was running a comb through her hair when the hard pain hit—a pain so sharp it snatched her breath away. She had to clutch at the bedpost for support. That felt like more than a warning. Maybe she should forget the market, go to see Mistress Poyntz. She would know what the pains meant.

Another pain bent her double.

And another.

A warm rush between her legs, and Kate Frith knew there would be no celebration when John came home. A third pain crumpled her into a ball on the floor.

～⛭～

John Frith heard Kate's sobs from the foot of the stairs, which he took two at a time. He'd never heard his wife cry, not once, not even when the floods came, not even during the long winter nights, when he feared she was so homesick, and now here were these great wrenching sobs that did not cease when he flung open the door to find her dressed only in her shift and curled into a ball on their bed.

"My God, Kate, are you hurt? What's the matter?" he asked, fearing what every good husband fears, that some intruder had broken into his home and violated his most prized treasure.

But a hasty glance showed the chamber to be undisturbed, more tidy even than usual. He sat down beside her on the bed, and she raised her head to look at him, her attempt at an answer no more than a shake of her head. Her eyes were red and swollen with crying. Her hand clutched at the cheap tin amulet Endor had given her as though it were a lifeline and she a drowning woman—a veritable picture of despair. This was his fault, he thought miserably. He'd been too distracted, had not paid enough attention to her, had thought her stronger in mind than she was simply because she never complained.

He brushed one damp strand of hair away from her eyes and touched her chin, lifting her face. "What is it, my angel? Have you had bad news? Have you hurt yourself in some way?" He became aware of a sickly, sweet smell in the room. "Are you sick?"

Then he spotted the dress crumpled in a heap on the floor, its crimson stain gleaming darkly.

"I am going to get a doctor. Don't move. I'll be right back."

She rose up then and reached out her hand to grasp the sleeve of his shirt. Her voice was raspy with so much crying. "No. It's too late. What can a doctor do now?"

"Too late? What do you mean?" But a glimmer of understanding was beginning to dawn.

She took a deep breath as if the very air held some quality of strength. "It was a child, John. I lost our baby."

"But—"

"I should have told you," she said softly, "I wanted to wait until I was sure," and then the tears started again.

God, how he hated those tears! He could not bear to see her cry. "I don't care about the baby," he said. He gathered her to him and kissed the top of her head, but she pulled away and looked up at him, searching his eyes as if she were rifling through his soul and did not like what she found there. A deep frown creased her forehead, and the faint blue line on her brow was no longer faint, but stood out like a cord. He could almost see it pulsing.

"You don't care about the baby!"

"That's not what I meant. Of course I care about the baby, but its soul has returned to God. I only have one of you."

Her face remained a mask of misery and something else—concentration perhaps—as she asked, "You don't think the baby's soul is in limbo then?"

"I don't believe in limbo; you know that. Every human soul exists with God from the beginning, and the innocent soul returns to God. What could be more innocent than an unborn child?"

Not exactly the doctrine of Holy Church, but it made more sense than what they taught—and it seemed to give her comfort. She sighed a ragged breath, but the tears had ceased. Finally, he'd said something right. "Will you be all right? Shouldn't we call a doctor anyway?" He looked down at the bloodstained dress. "Will the bleeding stop on its own? Are you in pain?"

"What good can a leech do?"

He did not refute the logic of that. "Merta. I'll get Merta then. Or Mistress Poyntz. They'll know what to do."

She put her hand on his sleeve as if she wanted to give him reassurance, comfort. "John, there *is* nothing to be done. It is nature's way," she said between sniffles. A long pause. "I'm sorry . . . but I . . . wanted it so . . . so much." Each word was an effort, and the sobs began again.

He put his arms around her then, noticing for the first time how fragile she felt. He'd always thought her such a strong woman. Had she lost weight? That seemed hardly possible when her appetite had been so ferocious— Of course. Now he understood.

"There will be others, Kate. We will have another, you'll see. My sister miscarried at least twice, now that I remember." It had seemed such a casual thing when it was reported. He wondered if there had been so much blood, so many tears. "But you must get healthier first. Lots of good red wine to build you back up."

That made her cry even more.

"Really, angel, you shouldn't take on so. You'll be even weaker."

She gave one little shudder and the sobs lessened. He held her until she fell asleep, then he got up and cleaned the mess on the floor, bundling the dress up so she would not notice it the first thing when she awoke.

As he was mopping up the blood from the floor, he noticed that the splotch of green paint on the floor had disappeared. It had been bothering him for weeks. Now it seemed such a silly thing.

~ ❧ ~

In the weeks after the miscarriage John was more attentive. They went to the English House less and walked down by the river more. He held her hand and called her his angel, but he'd made love to her only once since she lost the baby and then so carefully she'd almost missed it.

"Really, John, I'm not some porcelain doll."

"You need to conserve your strength."

At least that was his excuse. Or was it that he really didn't want a child, didn't want the responsibility of a child, thinking it would take away from his work? But she tried not to think of that, tried to be cheerful for his sake. Sometimes she would go for several hours and not think about the lost child. Then she would wonder about it and why she could not be the one to bring it into the world and what that might mean. But not wanting to worry John, she kept these thoughts to herself.

By the time John announced he was going to Augsburg to the conference convened by the emperor to hear the Lutheran Confession and possibly find William Tyndale, Kate had forgotten all about the trip. Disappointment must have shown in her face.

"Why don't you go with me?" he asked.

But Kate wasn't altogether sure that a trip on the water was what she most wanted right now.

"They say the Rhine River Valley is spectacular. And since I translate for the Hansa Counting House and Augsburg is on one of the Hansa trading routes, we should have no trouble getting cheap passage."

When she didn't answer immediately, remembering how seasick she had been on the *Siren's Song*, he seemed to be reading her mind. "As I recall you're pretty good at river travel." He smiled broadly and the tucked wing of her injured spirit fluttered a little, threatened to unfold.

She remembered their time together in the tiny little berth on the *Siren's Song* when they had made love to the rhythms of the sea, how close they had seemed, just the two of them against the world.

What was that concoction Endor had given her to drink? Ginger tea. Yes. That was it. She remembered seeing the ugly little root in the spice market. She would lay by a goodly supply—just in case.

⚘

The trip to Augsburg was a disappointment, though the Rhineland scenery had been as spectacular as John had promised, and there had been no sea-sickness. The boat was smaller than the *Siren's Song*, having only one square sail and a crew of four. It was one of the boats especially built by the Hansa shipbuilders for the merchants of the Hanseatic League who traveled the inland waters, so in spite of its size, there was a passenger compartment— with a bed big enough that John, after kissing her affectionately good night and snuggling with her briefly, could turn over and sleep the rest of the night without ever touching her. Babies were not made that way, she thought, as she lay awake long after she heard him snoring.

John was frustrated because William Tyndale did not attend the confer- ence as he had hoped. The weather was hot, and Kate was stuck with a smelly crowd of mostly men outside the hearing room doors, straining to hear the discourse while John scanned the crowds in the vain hope of spot- ting his friend. This did not make him the most agreeable of companions, and he was incensed that the conference had been moved to a smaller venue and that in the end the "confession" had been summarily rejected.

"They didn't want the people to hear their paltry refutations or the strength of Luther's argument."

But in spite of his disappointment, she had to admit he tried to be attentive and not preoccupied, so much so that she wondered if she was becoming a burden to him.

They were sitting on a bench on the docks, in the shade of a warehouse, watching for a ship to come in to take them home, as they ate bread and sausage and drank some bitter-tasting brew that John seemed to relish. The smell of it reminded Kate of the Walshes' brew house. She wrinkled her nose and took a sip. At least it was wet and she was thirsty.

"Really, when you think about it, why should Tyndale have come? I mean, if he's a fugitive because of his religious beliefs, wouldn't it be foolish of him to attend a conference where all the officials of the realm have assembled to consider the doctrines they are hostile to?"

"Very perceptive of you, wife. That's exactly the way Jan Hus of Bohemia was captured after having been promised safe-conduct to a papal council." He took a bite of the sausage. "You're not eating. Is it too spicy for you? Shall I get you something else?"

"No. John, I'm fine. Really. What happened to Hus?" she asked, taking a small bite to placate him.

"Once he got to the conference he was betrayed, arrested and burned without trial. Luther learned from his Bohemian predecessor. He seldom ventures out of Protestant Saxony where he lives under the protection of the prince."

"Then how can it be called a Lutheran confession without Luther to confess it?"

"He sent his approval of the document by his friend Melanchthon."

That had been another disappointment to Kate. She was curious to see the great Martin Luther and maybe even his wife. It was said Katharina von Bora often traveled with him.

"Where does he live? Is it far? Do you think we could get an audience with him?"

"One seeks an *audience* with the pope," John said, tossing back the mug and reaching for hers, still half full, and the rest of her uneaten sausage. "I understand Luther meets with anybody regardless of status or reputation who wants to discuss the doctrine or even just to ask a favor. Now that I think on it, he might even know where Tyndale is."

"But if you can't find Tyndale how could you find Luther?"

"Easily. Luther doesn't have to hide as long as he stays in Saxony. I introduced myself to some members of the Lutheran delegation—we had an interesting discussion on the nature of grace. Anyway, they told me Luther lives in an old Augustinian convent in Wittenberg."

"How far is that?"

"I don't know exactly. Way northeast of here. Too far. At least from here."

That's just as well, Kate thought. She'd had enough of spicy meat and bitter German beer. She was even looking forward to the English House. At least the food was good. But first they had to find a northbound ship. They'd only booked passage one way, thinking to catch another merchant ship on the way back. They had been told at the Kontor, the countinghouse of the Hanseatic warehouse looming behind them on the docks, that there were frequent ships plying the Rhine route between Augsburg and Antwerp. So far today there had been only one ship headed north and that one had no room for passengers. But Kate could see two more on the horizon that were coming from the south. She hoped one of them could accommodate them. The larger of the two ships was coming closer. It had a familiar look to it, though she couldn't be sure.

"John, is that—"

"I think it just might be," he said, stooping to pick up the chest at their feet. She shaded her eyes with her hand as the *Siren's Song* sailed closer.

"Yes, it is. Come on. Let's go down to where she's off-loading cargo."

"But there's no passenger cabin. Remember that tiny little bench of a bed."

"I remember," he said, his eyes glinting. "As I recall we made it just fine." And then added, "If you're too cramped, I'll sleep on the floor."

"But Captain Lasser had to give up his own quarters—"

"He'll be glad to have us. We got to be pretty good friends."

"While I was puking my insides out. That's what I recall."

She didn't understand her reluctance. The other journey had been pleasant after she got over her sickness, but there was just something about Captain Tom Lasser that made her anxious.

"Would you rather wait for another?" he asked.

"No," she said, feeling silly. "Who knows how long we'd have to wait? After all, it's just a way to get home."

TWENTY-THREE

*[Thomas More has] the best knack of any man in
Europe at calling bad names in good Latin.*
—BISHOP FRANCIS ATTERBURY,
SEVENTEENTH-CENTURY ANGLICAN

homas More left the Star Chamber, carrying the excitement of
a hound with a fresh scent in his flared nostrils. The new Bishop of London
was proving a much more valuable ally than his predecessor. Cuthburt Tunstall had been a friend and a man of learning, but he had lacked the necessary stomach for the job, whereas Bishop Stokesley had reminded Thomas
that to attack with words was worthy, but such a threat as heresy could
really only be burned out. Thomas couldn't agree more. The real work was
about to begin.

Today they'd made great headway. They had secured a public confession
before the court from a man named George Constantine, a chief distributor
of heretical translations and tracts. After some persuasion in More's private
garden at Chelsea and a little rest in the stocks at the porter's lodge, Constantine had been generous in his Star Chamber testimony, giving up the
names of his contacts, not only in England but in Antwerp as well. John
Frith, the author of a bold and blasphemous tract that referred to the pope as
the Antichrist in Rome, was one such name. Another brilliant young mind
lost to the influence of Luther—that *cacodemon,* that shit-devil.

Indeed, it came as no surprise to learn that Frith was in Antwerp, since he was known to be a protégé of Tyndale's, or that there was a nest of heretics there, especially in the English House. He had long suspected it, but the English Crown had no authority in Flanders. Though the Catholic authorities would be happy to cooperate, merchant treaties protected the inhabitants of the English House from interference by all foreign authorities. What they needed was a spy inside, and now they had one. Henry Phillips was both a coward and the kind of pond scum that would betray his own father for money. Just the kind of man they needed. What Henry Phillips couldn't be bribed into doing, he could be intimidated into. But Bishop Stokesley had learned something else through his network of spies. Something very troubling.

Thomas passed through the heavy doors of Westminster Hall, shrugging off the ever-present crowd of supplicants in New Palace Yard . . . *Sir Thomas More, I have been wronged! Sir Thomas. I seek justice . . . you are known to be a man of justice . . .* A woman who would not be ignored pressed through the throng and thrust a package into his hands . . . *A gift, Sir Thomas, for rendering a just verdict in my husband's case.* He paused long enough to give it back to her—he must avoid at all cost the appearance of bribery; Wolsey had done enough damage to the office of the chancellorship—but she was as quickly gone as she appeared. Preoccupied with what he had just learned from Bishop Stokesley, he thrust the object inside his robe of state and forgot about it. He had more important matters to ponder.

According to the bishop, the king was making independent inquiries concerning some of these same men he knew Sir Thomas and Stokesley were pursuing. That worried Thomas somewhat. Why would he not have informed his chief advisor that he'd sent a man named Stephen Vaughan to ferret out Frith and Tyndale? He feared England's sovereign was becoming more open-minded than he need be. No doubt, the influence of the Boleyn woman.

Or maybe it was simply that the king did not fully trust his new chancellor, even entertained some remorse at his choice. Thomas had only to recall the king's visit to Chelsea a fortnight past to know the source of the coolness between him and his sovereign. Thomas had been pruning roses as he waited for the king's messenger to bring documents for his signature, when Henry turned up with the documents himself. Thomas should not have been surprised, he thought now; Henry liked to catch his courtiers off guard. He was at his most dangerous then.

"Thomas," he had said in his best hail-fellow-well-met voice. "I had a yen for some witty companionship so I thought I'd bring these personally." He waved a sheaf of parchments above his head.

Thomas wiped his hands on his smock, self-conscious in his plain dress, thinking how ill-prepared his household was to entertain the king, whose entourage would be waiting on the small barge in the harbor expecting hospitality. But the king knew that. It had been part of his strategy all along, to gain the advantage.

Henry commented on the beauty of Chelsea's broad lawns as if he'd just dropped in to pay an old friend a visit. "We can sit at that pretty picnic table beneath the willow. No need to trouble your lady with hospitality." He draped his arm across Thomas's shoulder as they walked, laughing and joking about the court fool's latest jibe. "You should have seen the look on Brandon's face when Will Somers mocked him."

But Thomas knew that when the king was affable and jocular to put a man at his ease, it was then the man should be most on his guard. They sat down on the garden bench in the dappled sunlight, and Thomas perused the court documents, signing them one by one: an order for increased provender for the royal stables—the spring rains had laid waste much of the pasture; a new tax to be levied on exported wool—the cloth merchants would not like that one, but it had been passed by Parliament at More's urging; mostly mundane, everyday things that a messenger could have brought.

"Oh, I believe there is one more." Henry had pushed the rolled parchment in front of him. "You have a peaceful haven here, Chancellor," he said, gazing out at the river. "You are a lucky man."

Thomas looked at the petition with its gold illumination and its regal black script. This was no routine matter of state. It was a document admonishing the pope "to declare by your authority what so many learned men proclaim," that the marriage of Henry and Katherine of Aragon is unlawful and should be set aside, freeing the king to marry again. It was followed by twin columns of names, names of scholars from the universities and renowned churchmen. Some, like Thomas Cranmer's, he was not surprised to see. Others like Bishop Stokesley's made him waver for a moment in his resolve. Which loyalty took precedence? Crown or Church? But with Thomas there was no room for doubt. There could be no compromise. He put down his pen and pushed the document aside. To repudiate the Spanish queen would be to repudiate everything she stood for. And she stood for a Catholic England.

"Your Majesty, it is with much regret that I must remind you I cannot in good conscience sign this."

Henry looked at him directly, his eyes narrowing to slits. The muscles in his jaw made a tight little line of knots. He said nothing. A jay in the tree above them squawked some kind of protest—or warning.

"Your Majesty has long known of my views on this matter."

Henry's smile tightened. He withdrew the petition and, furling it tightly, shoved it inside his doublet. "We would not ask you to go against a matter of conscience, Master More. I had thought perhaps you could merely lend your signature—one among many, all men of conscience, for this last effort to present to the pope—as a favor to your king."

Last effort? Did that mean he was giving up if this petition failed to persuade His Holiness that the marriage should be annulled?

"Exactly so, Your Majesty. One of many. The signature of a layman will not be missed."

"Layman or not, it is the signature of the chancellor of England." Henry allowed himself one abrupt slap on his knee before assuming a more nonchalant demeanor, as if it didn't matter at all that his chancellor was an impediment to his heart's greatest desire. "But it is a small thing. If this does not work, I may seek a better course of action."

He had not chosen to make his chancellor privy to what that better course of action might be, but Thomas didn't have to ask. There were those advisors surrounding the Boleyn woman who were pouring poison into the king's ear, telling him the pope did not sit in authority over an anointed king, telling him England could break with Rome.

The king had taken his leave abruptly, and had not spoken directly with Thomas since. But be that as it may, Thomas was not going to be distracted by that memory or deterred from his purpose. Today they'd made headway. If they could break the back of the smuggling chain and burn a few of the providers, the world would be restored to its proper order.

Thomas hailed his waterman lounging by the landing of Westminster Stairs. As they rowed away toward Chelsea, he remembered the package inside his jacket. He took it out and unwrapped it under the watchful eye of his waterman.

"A gift for your wife?" Richard, the waterman, asked.

"No, a gift from a woman for whose husband the court ruled favorably."

"Oh?" Richard looked surprised.

"A just ruling," Sir Thomas answered the unasked question.

It was a silver vase of unremarkable quality. It would bring a few pounds in the marketplace. He would sell it and give the money to the almshouse. He wrapped the vase back up, and closed his eyes to sleep a little during the long trip home.

～≽≼～

Captain Lasser considered Kate Frith as she ate her fish stew with less enthusiasm than he had remembered. Noting the restlessness in her hands, he thought her changed in some way he could not quite fathom. He wondered if she was happy in her life of exile. Her husband seemed much the same as before, as though he'd drunk some magic elixir from a perpetual fountain of cheer. He wore that same infectious warmth of personality that made him a hard man to dislike—though there was that something in Tom's mind that tried. Really tried.

"So you found employment with the Antwerp countinghouse? Is it sufficient? I could speak—"

"Oh no, I assure you we are managing. Even though the Kontor is just a subsidiary countinghouse, they have more than enough work, but it's not the work I want to be doing. As soon as my friend Tyndale returns to Antwerp, I'll have more than I can do."

"I'm surprised Tyndale could afford to pay you. I mean . . . I know his translations and tracts sell; I've shipped enough of them, but they are cheaply bought, and he probably has some trouble finding printing at market rate given the risk to the printer."

"Oh, I don't expect pay. Some things one does just for the good of it," Frith said, a little pompously, Tom thought. "I'm hoping to save enough so that when he does come to Antwerp, my wife and I will have enough to manage. So far there's just the two of us."

Tom noticed the way Kate closed her eyes at his words, just a slow blink really, but she also looked away from her husband, as though she could not bear to hear those words.

Embarrassed at intruding upon some private pain, Tom too glanced away. Outside the porthole, where blue sky should have been, sheer cliffs rose in a wall of rock. "We're entering the gorge. The channel is narrow here. I'd best go up on deck." Then he added, "You might want to come with me. The view of the cliffs is as splendid as any cathedral."

"I want to visit with Endor a while," Kate said. She did not look at her husband as she added, "You go on up, John."

It sounded to Tom like a dismissal, but John seemed not to notice as he gave his wife a perfunctory peck on the cheek and followed Tom up the ladder.

※

"I am pleased to see you again, Endor. Have you been well?" Kate said after the men had left.

Endor nodded solemnly and, breaking into a smile, reached for Kate's hand and patted it as if to say yes, she was well and also pleased. She picked up Kate's wine cup, with a question in her eyes.

"No. No more wine. But I would like some water." Then realizing that fresh water might not be easily come by at sea, she added, "If you have any."

Endor smiled and nodded, then taking Kate's cup placed it beneath the spigot of a small wooden keg mounted on the wall. Kate had assumed it contained ale.

"Will you sit with me a moment?" she said as Endor handed her the water.

Looking surprised but pleased, Endor sat at the table opposite Kate, not settled back in the chair but perched on its edge like a bird about to take flight.

"I think about you often." Kate reached inside her bodice and pulled out the emblem of Saint Anne that hung around her neck. "I have this to remind me of you."

Endor smiled and nodded.

Kate returned the necklace inside her chemise, feeling the cool metal as it slid between her breasts, then placed her palms straight down on the table to stop the fidgeting of her fingers. Her index fingers rubbed ever so slightly against the smooth ridges in the boards of the table. Not knowing how to begin, she inhaled deeply of the sea air mingled with the smell of linseed oil and old wood. Endor looked at her expectantly. The muted sounds of the water, lapping against the ship's hull, punched into the silence.

"We have something else in common now, Endor," she said. "I too have lost a child."

Endor's hands reached across the table and covered her own. They were rough and strong and comforting. The cup of water sat just to the right of their joined hands.

"It was a great grief to me," Kate said, trying to keep her voice from breaking.

Endor nodded and closed her eyes, then gave her head a little shake as though shaking off the memory.

Kate slid her hand from beneath Endor's and picked up the cup, took a sip. It was clear and cool and still full almost to the brim. She could see her own eyes reflected in it as she lifted it to her lips. There was no other way to say it but to ask. Just ask.

"Is that what you saw in the water before, Endor? Did you know that I would lose my child?"

Endor's eyes grew wide, her mouth pursed into a tight line. She withdrew her hand from the table and scooted closer to the edge of her seat, poised ready for flight. Kate remembered how upset she had become before. She should not ask her to do it again. It would be a sin, not just a stain upon her own soul but on Endor's soul as well. And it was prohibited. Like trafficking in English Bibles, a burning offense. Thou shalt not suffer a witch to live, the Bible said. But surely Endor was no witch. She only had a gift. Maybe it was God who gave her the gift. There was nothing evil about her.

Kate set the cup down in the middle of the table.

"Will I have another child?" she whispered.

Endor did not move. This time it was Kate who stood up and turned away upset. She should not have asked, had determined that she would not. The words had just slipped out. "I'm sorry. I had no right—"

A tug on her sleeve urged her back down. Endor nodded, then wrapping her hands around the base of the cup, pulled it toward her. She stared into the water. Kate held her breath, but Endor just gave a little shake of her head. Then she closed her eyes and stared unblinking into the cup again, her face a mask of concentration. Kate was unconscious that her own eyes were unblinking in sympathy with Endor's until they began to burn and water. Endor smiled, her sharp little chin nodding rapidly. She held up one finger.

"One child," Kate said, her breath scarcely coming. "You saw one child."

Endor nodded then pointed with two fingers to her eyes, then to the porthole, then back to her eyes.

Kate shook her head. "I don't understand."

Endor pointed to her eyes again.

"My child will have . . . eyes—"

Endor pointed to the map on the wall mounted beside the water keg. It was a blue map of the world.

"My child will have . . . blue eyes!"

Again the sharp little chin bobbed. "But John has brown eyes and mine are green . . . how . . . oh, what does it matter? I don't care if it has purple eyes. Thank you, Endor. Thank you," she said, hugging the woman to her.

Endor nodded and shrugged as if to say it was a small thing.

⁓ ⁓

Later that night, Endor lay awake contemplating the spangled velvet sky through the slice of night outside her open door as she listened to the night sounds: the scraping of anchor ropes against the hull, the creak of the boards, the laughter of the night watch as they played at dice. Not these familiar sounds but a little pinch of guilt chased away her sleep. Since that last time when the captain had asked her to gaze into the bowl, she had prayed for the gift of second sight to be removed. It brought great trouble to her heart. Not trusting in the prayers, she had not looked long enough into still water again to see the visions.

Until tonight.

Endor could feel the woman's pain in her own heart. How could she not give what comfort she could? And yet it seemed that the silent and unknowable God who had flung those millions of stars across the heavens had heard her prayers after all.

For all Endor had seen in the still water was the reflection of her own blue eyes.

⁓ ⁓

The cabin was dark when John came back. The moonlight, filtering through the porthole, lent a ghostly presence. Kate was asleep on the narrow bed, her hair spread out across the pillow. Except for the rhythmic movement of her breathing, she might have been a dream. He lightly touched her hair. She stirred but did not waken. He yearned for the feel of her body next to his, just as he imagined the Greek lord of the underworld must have yearned for Persephone, or David for Bathsheba, Menelaus for his stolen Helen. She was almost irresistible.

Almost. For all John Frith needed to quell his manhood was the memory of the bloody dress lying in a sodden crumpled heap on the floor and the vision of Kate's face, red and swollen with tears, the sadness in her eyes that lingered still. He knew she thought it was selfishness on his part whenever he pulled away, selfishness because he was so caught up in his work and his goals that he did not want to share his life with children. That was why she kept bringing up Luther, reminding him without putting it into direct words that the great Dr. Martin Luther had children and he still found time to work.

He spread the blankets on the floor and lay down on them, trying not to disturb her. He did not want to see the accusation in her eyes when he turned away from her. He could hear her even breathing, softy exhaling into the stillness of the room, as he lay awake, listening, too, to the sound of the ocean's breath as it kissed the ship. He longed to press his mouth against hers, sucking her breath into his body, drawing her spirit in to make it one with his. He wanted to possess her soul so that there could be no division between them.

He slept fitfully and dreamed he was Ulysses, alone, shipwrecked, floating on a wide plank in an endless ocean. He drifted toward a longed-for shore that he could see but never reach. Just before dawn, he woke to find her lying beside him on the floor. She whispered his name and he opened his arms to her. She was Bathsheba. She was Persephone. She was Helen. She was irresistible in her wooing.

TWENTY-FOUR

I shewed you that I neither was, nor wolde be curious of any knowledge of other mennes matters, and lest of all eny matter of princes or of the realme.
—SIR THOMAS MORE IN A LETTER TO
ELIZABETH BARTON (AKA THE HOLY
MAID OF KENT)

he chapel of the English House was John's favorite place in Antwerp—next to the studio he shared with his wife, of course. Sometimes he came there because he sought a simple, sacred space. But today he'd come seeking Chaplain Rogers to report on the Augsburg conference called by the Holy Roman Emperor to facilitate peace among the warring religious factions in the realm. The chapel was a tiny chamber at the dead end of a narrow passage leading to the main hall of the English House. It had a simple altar and two narrow rows of benches, a shaped window in the old style, and a heavy wooden door that opened into a walled garden where one could take one's devotions if the life of the house intruded on the quiet, which it seldom did. Its walls were thick.

Rogers was all ears, still nursing his disappointment that circumstances had prevented his going. "You didn't really miss anything—it's all there." John pointed to the Augsburg Confession. "They printed it in both German and Latin. I brought you the Latin. I couldn't get my hands on the German.

I expect all the copies were done away with after it was read aloud in German, over the protests of the diet who tried to prevent its reading."

"How was it received by the emperor?"

"I don't really know, since I wasn't allowed in the small chamber where it was read, but I know it was read because the reader spoke in a strong, clear voice that carried beyond the doors. When he got to the abuses at the end concerning false teaching, there was great applause and cheering—at least outside the chamber."

Rogers held up the document and translated: "'The churches among us teach with great consensus . . .'" Then after scanning the twenty-nine articles, he asked, "Do you agree with the document?"

"For the most part. Certainly on the key issue of salvation by faith and not works, which strikes at the heart of the whole Roman penitential system, and I agree with permission for the clergy to marry, of course, but I'm not sure that private absolution for one's sins remains within the Church. I'm more inclined to every man his own priest, a kind of priesthood of the believer as the early Lollards taught, but what I really don't understand is why Luther refuses to see the fallacy in the doctrine of transubstantiation." He shrugged. "Of course, it really doesn't matter since the diet refused to consider any of it." And then John suddenly remembered his manners and the reason Rogers had begged off at the last minute. "What about your ailing friend? Is he better?"

"He will recover, God willing."

"Well, you made the wiser choice by staying here. When you have studied that hastily printed document, you will know as much as those of us who made the journey. That copy bears a rough facsimile of Luther's signature and seal, so it is probably worth keeping for all its poor quality and may be a document of some importance one day. It lays out the reformed position pretty clearly even though it falls somewhat short to my thinking."

"No sign of our mutual friend at the conference, I suppose?"

"Not a hair."

Rogers's hands curled the papers into a roll and slapped it gently on John's shoulder, his eyes alight with pleasure. "Well, we heard from him in your absence. We can expect him any day."

"You mean—"

"Tyndale knows you are in Antwerp. He says that he's coming here to work on his Old Testament translation and that you and I can be of help to him."

"That is great news. Great news." Before he could stop himself, John had jumped up, grasped his friend by the shoulders and given him a hearty shake that almost knocked him off his feet.

Rogers laughed. "Yes, it is great news."

John could feel the anticipation rising. At last.

"Say nothing about his coming, except to your wife, but caution her. We must be very discreet. Only yesterday, someone knocked at the door inquiring for Master William Tyndale. The porter tried to get rid of the man, but he was fairly insistent, almost belligerent. This was the second time he'd been here. Now that I think on it, the first time was about the same time you arrived. Said he was an Englishman, a glover by trade, and was seeking a fellow Englishman."

John felt a vague stirring of unease.

"This time he sounded a little desperate, insisting he had a message for Master Tyndale from His Royal Majesty, Henry VIII, King of England, that he'd been informed he was here, and he wasn't leaving until he spoke with somebody in authority. Mistress Poyntz finally called me to persuade him to leave."

"Do you remember the man's name?"

"I don't think he gave his name."

"Did he have a neat little red beard, shaped in a point, and thinning hair? Tallish, lightly built, a little older than me?"

"Yes," Rogers said in surprise. "Do you know him? Should we not have turned him away?"

"It is good you turned him away. His name is Vaughan. Stephen Vaughan. He was on the same boat that brought Kate and me to Antwerp. If he's still here after all this time, he is a spy for somebody, rightly enough, but it may not be the king. Thomas More, most likely."

"This is a bothersome development," Rogers said, laying the *Confessio Augustana* on the altar, and running his fingers through his hair as if he could comb out the irritant. "I have assured Tyndale of protection."

"Should we warn him away?"

Rogers considered for a moment. "No. I think not," he said. "He would be as safe here within the walls of the English House, safer probably, as anywhere in Europe. It shall be his sanctuary. We shall see to it."

"Sanctuary." John nodded in agreement. "If ever a man deserved it, William does."

It was mid-afternoon and the smells from the kitchen wafted down the passage and through the open door. "He'll have a safe place to work here—and be well fed at the same time."

The chaplain laughed. "Can you stay and break bread with us?" He picked up the rolled document and waved it invitingly. "We can discuss the *Confessio Augustana* in detail." When John hesitated, Rogers added further inducement. "This is Monday. Rabbit dumplings."

"I know," John said. "I smell the succulent little creatures simmering with their dumplings, but tempting as both the conversation and the victuals are, I promised Kate I would not be long."

"Ah, marital bliss." He hesitated and then asked, "Is it still?"

"Still what?"

"Bliss?"

John groped for a witty answer, wondering whether more than idle curiosity had prompted his friend's question.

"Most days," he said. "Most days, I feel that I am Adam and she is my Eve, and I cannot imagine life without her. But sometimes . . . it can be . . . well, you have a double portion of joy but sometimes a double portion of pain as well."

"So would you recommend it, then, to those of us who are single?"

"Ask me again in thirty years," he said with a smile. Then as an afterthought he added, "Say nothing about this Stephen Vaughan to Kate. I do not want to worry her needlessly. She's been . . . a little anxious lately."

"It will be our secret," Chaplain Rogers said.

◆

It was late in the day and Kate was in the Thursday street market to purchase fresh bread and pickled herring for tomorrow's Bible class. The lesson was from the story of the miracle of the loaves and fishes, and the food would be a kind of object lesson for the children. She was headed for the fish market when the man hailed her.

"Mistress Gough, Mistress Gough."

Who would know her in this strange city by that name, unless . . . She turned to see Stephen Vaughan hurrying toward her. It was too late to run. She turned her back to him, pretending to be preoccupied, examining apples from the top of a pyramid piled high on a vendor's cart, hoping Vaughan would think he was mistaken when she did not respond. Aware of him standing close by, observing her, she questioned the vendor in her halting Flemish about the freshness of the apples. The vendor, from whom she'd purchased fruit often, answered her in English, "Clinging to the tree this dawn."

She felt a light tap on her shoulder. "Mistress Gough, how fortunate and well met. I had despaired of seeing you again."

She turned around then, thinking there was no recourse but to brazen it out. "Sir, you must be mistaken . . . Oh, I remember. You are the young man whom we met on our return from England. Master . . ." Kate said, trying to buy time.

"Vaughan," he said.

"Yes, Stephen Vaughan, right? I would have expected that you had long ago terminated your . . . reluctant errand and returned to England."

"My business for the king is not complete, alas. That's why I am so happy to encounter you. I neglected to get directions to your residence when we parted."

"Directions? But why—"

"I found your husband to be very amiable company, and since he is a resident of Antwerp and a fellow Englishman, I thought he might be able to help with my errand. I inquired at the mercer's guild for an exporter named Gough, but nobody seemed to know him."

"He is not with the mercer's guild. He is with the . . . he deals . . . in rare metals." She shifted her basket of foodstuffs. "I really must be going, Master Vaughan. My husband will be expecting me."

"Let me escort you home. I can carry your basket." He reached for her basket, but she held on with some force. The tug-of-war that ensued would have been comical had she not felt so threatened.

"No. That is . . . most . . . kind of you . . . but I have to make a couple of stops on my way." And then, when she saw that he was not going to be so easily gotten rid of, added, "You may call tomorrow. We live in a cottage on . . . Rutted Road Way. Number three. About one mile east of town. Just ask anybody." She pulled away quickly, thinking to join the crowd of shoppers in the busy heart of the street.

"But wait, I—"

"I'll tell John to expect you. Tomorrow around midday."

In her haste she brushed too closely against the apple cart and a mound of rosy orbs cascaded to the ground between her and Vaughan. Behind her, the vendor swore, berating the unfortunate Vaughan as if the accident had been his, demanding payment for the bruised apples, threatening to call the authorities if he did not pay. Ducking behind a parked wagon with a load of hogsheads, she darted through the square, not stopping until she reached the other side of the market to scan the crowd. No tall thin man with a red pointed beard in sight. But just in case he was following her—after all, if he were an agent of the king, who knew how skillful he might be?—she headed in the opposite direction from home.

The basket was heavy on her arm by the time she turned into her street and, checking once again, ducked into her doorway.

John met her at the door at the top of the stairs with a worried look on his face.

"I was just about to come looking for you. I thought you'd gotten lost."

"Worse than that," she told him, putting down her basket and unwinding the kerchief that bound her hair. She had worked herself into a sweat with so much hurrying.

"What could be worse than that?" He smiled, pulling her to him and kissing her on the forehead.

"Stephen Vaughan," she said, pulling away to look him in the eyes. "The spy who came over with us. He's still here and he's looking for you."

"I know," he said, thinking badly of Mistress Poyntz for gossiping. "But don't worry. It's a big city. He won't find us."

"He found me!" she said.

"You saw him?" His eyes clouded, his brow furrowed slightly. "Where? When?"

"Just now. In the marketplace. He hailed me by the name Captain Lasser gave him, remember? Gough. He called me Mistress Gough. He asked for you. Asked where we lived."

"What did you tell him?"

"I lied. I just made up the name of a street."

"How blessed is a man with a wife who is not only beautiful but clever. Even if he does find such a street, he will be asking for somebody else." He took her hand and lifted it to his lips. "Don't worry, my darling. Antwerp is a big city. We'll not likely run into him again, and if we do, he doesn't know who we are—thanks to the good captain."

But in spite of his assurances, she saw him casting furtive glances out the window.

"I don't think I was followed. I was careful. That's what took so long."

"See, what did I say? Beautiful and clever." He took the lid off the basket and peeked in. "Now, what can we find in here to eat? I gave up rabbit stew, just to dine on bread and cheese with my beautiful and clever wife."

"Just bread. No cheese. I was too busy trying to get away." A vision of the disturbed apple cart popped into her head and she remembered. "But we have some nice, crisp apples."

"And a bottle of good beer that Mistress Poyntz sent," he said. "Life is good. Don't worry. I'll take care of you," and he kissed her, a long satisfying kiss that made even her scalp tingle.

"Umm. Life is good," she said, "but you'd better enjoy the apples. They may be the last we have for a while." Then they laughed together as she told him about the upset apple cart.

But though he pretended not to be worried, she couldn't help but notice how his eyes searched the street outside the window. And when it grew dark and they lit the candles, he closed the shutters, shutting out the breeze on a warm summer night. She thought about Stephen Vaughan and prayed he would not be watching from the shadows when the Bible women came on the morrow.

⚜

It was hot in the great hall at Chelsea, so Dame Alice had directed that dinner should be served outside in the courtyard. She inspected the dining board. All was as it should be: the second-best plate, pewter not silver, laid on snowy white linen, a simple meal of jellied herring and lamb slices kept cool in the cellar on a bed of mint leaves, accompanied by cucumbers and onions pickled in vinegar infused with herbs from her own garden and imported peppercorns, and bread and butter churned just this morning. There was a simple egg custard, dusted with fine white sugar, to complete the unpretentious meal that should suit a Franciscan brother from Canterbury.

She hesitated, then picked up the great bowl of custard and turned back toward the house. The Franciscan might think the white sugar from France an extravagance. There was time to swap it out. She could substitute a cheese and fresh pears instead. She pirouetted again—as much as a large-hipped woman wearing a farthingale can pirouette—and set the custard back down. No, this was the chancellor's board and a visitor, even a humble visitor, expected something extra.

It was a fine line she walked as hostess for a great man, never knowing who would show up at her table. Thomas had a habit of inviting to dinner at Chelsea whoever suited his fancy, be it a justice from the King's Bench, some visiting artist or university scholar, or a beggar he'd decided to feed—whether from charity or intellectual curiosity she could never tell.

Sometimes he invited all of them at the same time. It could be a real challenge, though lately it was a challenge that she missed.

After he was made chancellor, she'd gone out and bought better linens, an elaborate gilded saltcellar, carved spoons, more silver, all in the expectation they would have a surfeit of royal visitors. But Sir Thomas invited few courtiers to Chelsea and the king had visited only once, staying with Thomas in the garden the whole time and then leaving in a huff before she could even get the fine saltcellar from out of its wrappings.

Lately, preoccupied with his writings, her husband had taken his meals, what meals he took, in his study. At least he would be joining his family for this meal, since they were to have a guest, and there would be erudite conversation and cheerful spirits. That was a good thing. She had not heard Thomas jest in a while. He must have exhausted his wit in his writings, along with that finely honed sarcasm—which she missed even though it was more often than not directed at her.

An occasional welcome breeze from the river ruffled the board cloth and the strings of her everyday bonnet—no use in getting fancied up for a Franciscan—but the breeze brought with it the rank smell of the Thames in summer. She pondered for a moment whether the Franciscan would find finger bowls of fragrant flowers floating in lavender water an extravagance, and decided she didn't care. They would help dispel the smell of seaweed and dead fish wafting from the river.

Or maybe that odor was wafting from the herring. She picked up the platter and sniffed. No, whatever fishy smells the herring gave off were quite overwhelmed by the sharp aroma of the jellied wine that bathed them.

She was just placing the last of the flower bowls, hurriedly assembled by two kitchen maids, when she looked up to see her lord chancellor coming toward her, the brown-cassocked brother in tow.

"Alice, this is Richard Risby of the Francisan Observants at Canterbury. He will be stopping with us tonight."

Alice bowed her head to acknowledge the introduction. "You are welcome to join us for a humble family meal. Others of our household will be joining us shortly."

The brother nodded. "Chelsea hospitality is legendary, Dame Alice. I thank you." His eyes quickly scanned the food she'd spread out. "Ah, egg pudding with French sugar. My favorite," the cassocked visitor exclaimed, rubbing his hands together. "Sometimes in the refectory we grate a little cinnamon onto it."

Apparently vows of poverty did not extend to the Franciscan larder, Alice thought, but while she was trying to think of a comeback that didn't give offense—she was never as quick-witted as Thomas—the others of her household appeared as if by magic.

"My daughter Margaret Roper," Thomas said, and spreading his hand to casually include the others who were settling at the other end of the long table, added, "and her husband, William, and my two other daughters, my ward, and Alice's daughter," not bothering with their names. "Come. Let's eat before those thunderheads building on the other side of the river decide to join us. Margaret, you sit next to our guest. I would have him see how well versed my daughters are in the classical languages and Holy Scripture."

They were soon all seated. The More household was nothing if not disciplined and well ordered. Being late to dinner or anything else would not be tolerated. Thomas had no doubt got that from his old father of whom Alice was not fond. She blamed those few flaws she saw in her husband's character on John More and devoutly wished Thomas tried less to be like him. She was glad they were not suffering his company today. Though he took most of his meals at Lincoln's Inn, he often came to Chelsea whenever there was to be a guest of note. But a cleric would not interest him.

Alice sat on the other side of Margaret and she could hear them jabbering away in Latin, God bless 'em, while Thomas looked on proudly. She didn't know for sure, but she was guessing from the heavy look of concentration on Risby's face that he was hard-pressed to keep up with Margaret's erudition.

"Perhaps we should converse in English so that others might enjoy our conversation," he said. "You are to be commended, Master More, on the superior education you have given your daughters, though one wonders . . ."

Here he wisely did not voice the words that, Alice suspected, were forming on his lips, something about the waste of learning on women, a sentiment with which she did not wholeheartedly disagree.

"One wonders if half the ordained brethren could speak so well," the Franciscan muttered as he reached for a second helping of the egg custard.

"Yes. One wonders." Thomas smiled and winked at Alice.

That wink to her was as good as a kiss from any other man.

"What news do you bring from Canterbury, Brother Risby?" Thomas asked, as the sewer put the platter of lamb in front of him. Alice was relieved to see he took a large slice. Now if he would only eat it.

"News of a holy maid. The whole countryside is murmuring of her miraculous visions. Have you heard of her?" the Franciscan said.

"If you mean the mad nun of Kent, then yes, I have heard somewhat."

"Mad? How say you mad, sir?" The brother held his spoon suspended in midair. Alice watched in dismay as sauce from the herring dripped on her fresh cloth.

"Elizabeth Barton? All England has heard of the young maid's visions," Margaret said. In English.

Alice poked her in the ribs to remind the girl of her manners. She might be able to read and write Latin and Greek but she didn't know a lady should never interject herself into a conversation between men. Well, almost never. Except for the sake of a good argument.

"*Holy* visions, Mistress Roper," Risby answered.

"Mad visions, some say," Sir Thomas corrected evenly. "Somehow a rhyming doggerel of her prophesy reached the king's eyes—through Master Cromwell, one suspects—foretelling of grave happenings to his person and his kingdom should he persist in . . . certain matters. The king asked my opinion of it."

"What thought you of it?"

"I told him it seemed but the harmless ranting of a simple mind."

"To prophesy against the king . . ." Margaret said, "wouldn't that be treasonous?"

"It would be. Unless of course it was the harmless outpouring from a simple mind gone mad, or a simple mind being manipulated by unscrupulous persons, or a maid who had merely lost her wits."

"William says—"

"I do not wish to hear what William says, Margaret. This talk about Elizabeth Barton is foolish gossip, and you know gossip and the carrying of ruinous tales is not permitted in this household. We will speak no more of the maid of Kent and her . . . visions."

With this pronouncement his gaze lingered on Margaret and then moved to Alice and finally to his son-in-law Roper, who colored visibly and jabbed at Margaret under the table. Alice had a moment's sympathy for him. To be a member of this household and not be held in Sir Thomas's good opinion was not a comfortable place to be. It was a testimony of Thomas's fondness for Margaret that he'd allowed the marriage at all.

"Now let's talk of things that better serve digestion. Speaking of news from Canterbury, I have some for you, Brother Risby. One whom you may know, Bishop Cranmer, has lately come into the king's good favor. What think you of him?"

"I think . . ." Risby paused as if choosing his words carefully. The clouds had humped menacingly on the horizon and a wind had risen. It ruffled the leaves above them and whipped at the tablecloth. "I think Thomas Cranmer is no friend of Queen Katherine."

A large raindrop plopped into the center of the custard bowl.

"I think a storm is about to break over our heads," Thomas said, rising. "We'd best heed the warning. Everybody grab a dish," he shouted and picked up the platter of lamb.

The Franciscan grabbed the custard bowl and followed Sir Thomas. The party gained the shelter of the house just as the heavens opened up.

The lamps burned late in Sir Thomas's study that night. Alice knocked at the door at bedtime.

"Go on to bed, Alice. I'll see our guest to his chamber."

Alice was sure she had heard the name Elizabeth Barton before she knocked. Apparently the prohibition on gossip did not extend to the master of Chelsea.

TWENTY-FIVE

If those things which I have written be true, and stand with God's Word, why should his majesty, having so excellent a guide of knowledge in the Scriptures, move me to do anything against my conscience?
—WILLIAM TYNDALE UPON BEING
OFFERED THE KING'S CONDITIONAL PARDON

ugust passed in a flurry of excitement. Tyndale had finally come to the English Merchants' House, and John was happily at work with him on his Old Testament translation. Kate spent more time than she wanted hunched over her ragged embroidery with Mistress Poyntz. Kate's poor unicorn more closely resembled a deformed donkey than a regal, magic beast—but if she wanted to be close to John, she had to be where he was. And every day, except Tuesdays and Thursdays, days he still worked at the Hansa Kontor, he was happily engaged aiding the great translator at the English House.

Kate knew her husband was an Oxford scholar, but it was gratifying to see a great man like William Tyndale desiring his assistance. The men labored late and long, arguing even during meals over just the right word to convey original meaning. "Simple, man. Keep it simple! It's Scripture, not Virgil. A plowman would not know such a grand word, Frith. Save the classical allusions for your next polemic. Your erudition will enrage More and his cohort." And then he'd laughed, as though it were some scholarly contest with "More and his cohort" and no matter of life and death.

John always gave in with hardly any resistance and with good humor. Kate thought his respect for Tyndale teetered on the edge of worship.

"He's not Jesus Christ, John," she once said when they were back in their little studio chambers. "You are brilliant. Stand up to him. I thought your choice was better than his." Though she couldn't remember the particular word in dispute and hoped he did not call her on it.

"He may not be Christ, but he certainly has Christ in him. More of Christ than any robed cleric I've ever known. Do you know what he does on Tuesdays and Thursdays while I'm at the countinghouse? He goes out into the streets of Antwerp, down to the poorest part of the city, and seeks out the hungry and the hurt, just to give them a bit of food or a warm shirt."

"Isn't that dangerous? What if he should be seen?"

"He says nobody knows what he looks like. He's quite clever the way he just blends into the crowd. Pulls his cap down, his collar up, and goes out over the garden wall behind the chapel in case somebody is watching the house. I saw him on the street the other day and almost passed him by, thinking him just another yeoman laborer. He was sharing a pie with a hunchback beneath the shade of a plane tree. They were laughing together as though they were old friends—a hunchback beggar and the greatest linguist in England, maybe all of Europe!"

Kate had never seen John happier. It was gratifying to see him completely engaged in the labor he loved, gratifying, too, to know that as absorbed as he was, he wanted her nearby. Tyndale, Chaplain Rogers, and John had set up a little workshop marked off with a carved wooden screen in one corner of the solar. John's worktable was positioned so that he could see where Kate sat with her books or her embroidery or even the English House accounts with which she helped Mistress Poyntz, who complained of being burdened with "so much ciphering." (It seemed little enough for Kate to do in payment for the many meals they took at the English House, and it gave Kate blessed relief from the hateful embroidery.) But if she wandered into the kitchen to help or into the garden or went with Mistress Poyntz to her bedchamber to see some newfangled fashion, John would look up, his pen dripping ink, and smile as she reentered the room. "I think better when I can see my beautiful wife. You give me inspiration."

And so pleasantly the summer passed into autumn. She still didn't quite know what to make of the infamous translator. That he was brilliant, she was sure. Driven, surely, one might even say obsessed. Indeed, it seemed that his desire to bring an English Bible to England was all he ever thought of—a worthy life goal to be sure and one deserving of personal sacrifice, even peril. The man was truly much to be admired for his courage, and yes, even though she was reluctant to admit it to John, not wanting to encourage him overmuch in his bond with such a dangerous man, there was that gentleness of spirit that seemed to abide in him.

But what troubled her about him was that same singleness of purpose that she so admired. After all, there were other things in life—like family and children and music and beauty. She hoped Tyndale's fervor was not something one could catch like the pestilence. For if it was, her John surely stood within reach of it. And who knew how that might end?

❧

It was Tuesday, and John was hoping to wind up his work at the Kontor early. The days were growing shorter, and Kate liked him to get home before dark. Glancing up from the bill of lading he was translating for a German merchant, who waited patiently in a chair beside his table, he saw with satisfaction that his chamber in the countinghouse was almost empty. Only one man waited, standing with his back to John's table watching the late-afternoon shadows creep across the street.

John stamped the German's papers with the official Hansa seal and handed them to him.

"*Danke. Herr Frith.*"

"*Ich freue mich, von Nutzen zu sein.*"

The man standing in the arched doorway stepped aside to let the German pass.

"*Hoe kan ik u helpen?*" John said, looking up, addressing the newcomer in the more widely used language in Antwerp.

The light from the open door lit the man's face in profile. John's heart flipped over and then plummeted into his boots. The door closed behind the German merchant, leaving the two of them alone in the room.

"So we meet again . . . Master Gough," Stephen Vaughan said in English as he turned to look John full in the face.

Master Gough. Maybe he hadn't heard the German call him by his real name.

Vaughan moved over to the writing table and without invitation took the seat the German had vacated. "How fortuitous that I should encounter you by chance," he said. "I met your lovely wife a few weeks ago. She invited me to your home, but alas I must have . . . misunderstood the address."

The tone of his voice, the little pause before the word *misunderstood,* signaled that he knew he'd been given the wrong address on purpose.

"I apologize if my wife gave offense. A woman alone encountering a slight acquaintance, well, you can understand how she might think it imprudent to disclose where she lived . . ." John heard the nerves in the sharp little laugh he gave and hoped Vaughan did not notice. "So . . . well. It is good to see you again. Now, how may I be of service? You said you were a glover, right?"

"Oh, I'm not here on mercantile business. I'm still making inquiries. This seemed like a good place to inquire—especially since you are in the *export* business, as I recall."

John ignored the barb and feigned surprise. "Still on the king's business, then? It's been almost a year. Or is this some new inquiry?"

"No. Same inquiry. This has been a difficult one to resolve. But I think I've about run my quarry to ground." He paused, then smiled broadly. "One of them, at least."

There was no mistaking his meaning.

"Well then, congratulations," John said, still pretending ignorance as he glanced out the window hoping to see anything that might allow him to conjure some distraction. The Kontor was a great square of a building with as many chambers as a rabbit warren. If he could just make it to the courtyard . . . "I'm sure you are anxious to complete the mission and return to England."

"Don't look so anxious, Master Frith. I'm not here to arrest you. As I told you on the boat, I'm an agent for the king, and I have been commissioned to make you an offer of pardon."

"Pardon for what and from whom? To whom do you report?" John asked, not allowing himself to be drawn in by the man's easy reassurance, wondering if he could take him—he was taller than John but of slender build, and he was not wearing a sidearm.

"Not to Chancellor More, if that's what you are thinking. My correspondence to the king goes through Thomas Cromwell. For the king's eyes only."

"And Tyndale?"

"The same. The king is prepared to offer both of you safe passage and his protection—if you will return to England."

"Why? In exchange for what?" But John thought he knew. "I will not recant. I will not be put on parade with symbolic faggots for burning pinned to my cloak. I will not ride an ass backward down High Street while the priests incite people to abuse me with refuse and stones."

Vaughan laughed. "I don't blame you. But be assured, you will not be made a mockery nor asked to recant your past deeds or even your beliefs—at least not in public spectacle. His Majesty is aware of Master Tyndale's superior talents and of your reputation as a scholar. As a scholar and linguist himself, King Henry is much impressed. He thinks your intellect and talent will be an . . . asset to his court."

"He is not influenced by More's and Wolsey's hostility toward our endeavors?"

"Wolsey no longer wields any influence. And as for More . . . well, the king makes up his own mind."

"How do I know this is not a trick? How do I know that you are who you say you are?"

Vaughan reached into his surcoat and took out a rolled parchment, unfurled it, and placed it on the table in front of John. "You will see it bears the king's signature. I trust you can read the Latin," he said, smiling at his own joke.

He waited patiently as John read. What the man said appeared to be the truth. It was a full pardon—but with royal strings attached, asking only that "Master Frith" cease heretical writings from this point on and that "Master Tyndale" halt his illegal translations and that the two men devote their wealth of talent and intellect to the service of their king.

"Lest you think the document a forgery, please consider that it would be a treasonous offense to forge the king's signature and seal."

"It appears to be as you have said. But I will have to think on it," John said. "I will discuss it with my wife. Surely you understand that."

Vaughan shrugged acknowledgment. "I assume you are living in the English Merchants' House. As you probably know, I have not been allowed admittance there. Will you be here tomorrow?"

"Thursday. I will give you my answer on Thursday."

"Very well," Vaughan said. "Very well indeed." He looked thoughtful and drummed his fingers on the table as though considering his next words carefully. "I would not presume to give you advice on the matter. I'm just the messenger. But be assured, Master Frith, I have no authority to arrest you and no desire to do so. I will not pursue you further whatever your decision. I cannot say the same for others."

He spoke with such sincerity that John almost believed him.

"You may show the document to your wife. And I would suggest if you know of William Tyndale's whereabouts that you show it to him as well. You would do your friend a great service. The chancellor is known to have his own spies."

He stood up and walked to the door and, tipping his cap with a smile, said, "Thursday."

Minutes later, John left the Kontor with the king's invitation and statement of pardon in his pocket. He did not go home, but went straight to the English House.

❧

By the end of the following week Stephen Vaughan was back in London, again being escorted into the king's presence, again wearing a dread as heavy as chain mail when he entered the gates at Whitehall. But in spite of the fact that after his meeting with Tyndale, he had written the king of an unlikely successful outcome, Henry was in a good humor. Pity the poor messenger who must intrude upon that good humor, Stephen thought, but so be it. He'd fulfilled his commission as messenger. How could he be held responsible for its outcome?

"Your Majesty." Stephen bowed first to the king, then a slighter bow to the Duke of Suffolk. "Your Grace."

"Vaughan. At last." The king pushed back his chair and stood up.

He's put on weight, Stephen thought, noting the way his doublet strained across his chest. The year's activities must have included more sedentary sports than jousting. Then he noticed the chessboard set up between Henry and the Duke of Suffolk.

"Leave us, Brandon. We would speak with Master Vaughan privately. He has been on business for the Crown." And then with a glance at the chessboard, he added, "Don't worry. We will not disturb the board. You're going to lose anyway."

As Brandon got up and swaggered away, Vaughan wondered what fool would dare to best the king at chess—or at any game for that matter. Brandon might, he thought. After all, he'd on occasion beat him in the joust and dared to marry the king's sister without permission. But apparently he'd been forgiven. Stephen hoped Henry was still in a forgiving mood.

"Sit, sit. Take Suffolk's place," Henry said. "And tell me what news you have. Cromwell reports that you found Tyndale. Your letter showed him to be an agreeable sort. You said he was visibly moved by the offer of pardon."

Henry closed his eyes as if searching his memory. " 'Water stood in his eyes when he read the gracious words,' I believe you said."

"Aye, Your Majesty. The man was visibly moved by your offer of mercy."

"And what of the other? The scholar Frith? Did you find him also?"

"He arranged the meeting with Tyndale."

"Good man. Good man. I can't wait to see More's face when he comes face-to-face—never mind. Are they without? Of course, there will needs be a Church official present to affirm the king's pardon; Cranmer will be most easily bent in that direction. In the meantime they will be housed in the Tower. Comfortably, of course."

"Your Majesty." Vaughan coughed to clear his throat of a sudden choking sensation. "They did not return with me."

Henry picked up the black bishop, Brandon's bishop, and fingered it thoughtfully. Then set it back down. He cocked one well-combed eyebrow at Stephen. "Then when may we expect them?" he said quietly.

"As I told you in my letter, although both men were much moved by Your Majesty's mercy—Tyndale sent this reply." He reached into his pouch and withdrew a roll of parchment, handed it to the king across the chessboard.

"Do you know its contents?"

"I do not, Your Majesty . . . It is addressed to Your Majesty, and it is written in Latin. I do not read Latin."

That was a lie. He knew what the document said. Both Tyndale and Frith had made it clear they would not be returning to England under the king's conditional pardon though he had practically begged them. They were good men, and he could tell somewhat tempted, Frith in particular. He'd arranged the meeting, even suggesting that perhaps once they were back in England, they could persuade the king of the importance of an English Bible. After all, why had he extended the pardon if he were not in some sympathy? Perhaps the Boleyn woman was influencing him in favor of the Bible cause.

Longing to be dismissed, Stephen watched as the king unfurled the parchment and began to read. The more he read, the more tightly his mouth pursed. His skin turned a mottled red color.

Stephen's choking sensation returned. *He could die of apoplexy, and I'll be blamed.*

"I shall translate for you, Master Vaughan," Henry said, and began to read aloud, each word clipped and hard with derision. " 'If it would stand with the king's most gracious pleasure to grant only a bare text of the Scrip-

tures to be put forth among his people.' What kind of criminal dares to bargain for an offer of mercy—by God, he'll rue the day he might have been
saved from the fire and spurned it."

He rolled the document into a tight narrow column, his ringed fingers
clutching it as if it were Tyndale's neck, and then slapped it down upon the
chessboard, sending the pieces flying.

Vaughan leaned down to pick them up.

"Leave it," he barked. "Footman," he shouted, and when the footman
appeared, "Summon Master Cromwell," and then looking hard at Stephen
continued, "And what of Frith?"

"He is of a mind with Tyndale," Stephen said soberly.

Cromwell entered the room, his robes brushing against the rushes on the
floor. His gaze traveled briefly over Vaughan. "Yes, Your Majesty?"

"Master Vaughan is to be paid. His work is finished here."

Moments later, Stephen left Whitehall with a pouch full of relief and a
few gold crowns for his efforts. Not extravagant pay, but adequate. It was
the best possible outcome for his failed mission. But he doubted and fervently hoped Henry would not seek his services again. A second disappointment might not be forgiven. The king was a hard man to cross. He was glad
he was not wearing William Tyndale's boots—or even John Frith's.

❧

Anne Boleyn was still at Hever, still waiting. It had been months since
Henry had summoned her. Some days she thought she would simply die of
boredom. Some days she even sought out the priest Henry had sent her, who
instructed her in patience and in the finer points of the reformed faith.

"It is true the old queen has her followers, but so do you, my lady. And
you have the king's ear. You will be a great agent for the faith. You have
many supporters."

And as if to prove his point, on a dry day in late September, when it
seemed her garden like her life had lost its bloom and her youth was slipping
away, Thomas Cromwell showed up at her door with a summons. Henry
Rex desired her return to Hampton Court with all due speed, and he had
sent a high court official to escort her.

TWENTY-SIX

*But if I had served God as diligently as I have done
the king, He would not have given me over to my grey
hairs.*

—CARDINAL WOLSEY
UPON HIS ARREST FOR TREASON

he daylight was fading as Thomas Wolsey was led from the
small barge that brought him to the traitor's gate of the Tower of London.
As the cardinal walked up the water stairs, the torchlight painted his
shadow along the curtain wall that fronted on the Thames. In the flickering
light, he appeared a man of diminished stature; a twist in the stone stair
leading into the Tower keep and his shadow loomed large; two more stairs
and it was but a wraith. Had he been a more thoughtful man, he might
have paused to ponder what this fickle rendering might portend. But he was
not and did not.

His chief concern at the moment was the chronic burning of his innards
that had erupted into conflagration when the king's soldiers arrived with the
summons from the Crown. It was all he could do to hold himself and his
dignity upright as he entered the gaoler's comfortable quarters.

During the trip back to London, he'd allowed himself to think that he
would get no worse than a warning from the king. He'd always been able to
bend Henry to his will. The king might rule over life and death in this

world, but as the pope's representative in England, Wolsey ruled over life and death in the hereafter: "whatsoever ye shall bind in heaven." And that was a powerful tool to hold over a man's head—even a king's. The soldiers who had arrested him in the chapter house in York had certainly shown him due deference, calling him "Your Eminence," even helping him to pack a chest and bring two of his servants. They waited now with his belongings outside the gaoler's quarters.

When the constable entered, Wolsey swallowed the taste of gall rising in the back of his throat. He had no love of Sir William Kingston. With the Tower's elaborate fees and extortions from prisoners, Wolsey considered its constable an unscrupulous opportunist and exploiter. Constable of the Tower was one of the most lucrative posts in England—outside the Church. It was like a small fiefdom: every ship that sailed upstream to London had to come through Tower Wharf and leave a tithe of the goods they were carrying. Everything that grew on or wandered onto Tower Hill or swam under Tower Bridge belonged to him. And then of course there were the fees he charged prisoners for his "suites of iron." If the cardinal had been a more thoughtful man, it might have occurred to him that the constable might have felt perfectly at home at the Vatican. But he was not and he did not.

"Constable Kingston, I trust you have an explanation for this indignity visited upon a servant of Holy Church."

"It is as a servant of the king that you are here to answer, Your Eminence. You will be our guest until your . . . until the king's mind has been satisfied as to your guilt or innocence on the charge of praemunire—of serving the pope above your king."

"That will not take long," Wolsey said. "There is no evidence that I have ever been anything but His Majesty's loyal servant." But the griping in his gut reminded him of the letters he had written to Carpeggio. What a fool he had been to put his thoughts in writing—and to advise an alliance between France and the Holy See! Whatever demon had overtaken his mind! But he knew the demon's name. Ambition. He had thought to be called to Rome by now, beyond the reach of Henry's wrath.

"That may be," the constable said, "but you are to be our guest for that duration, however long it takes. I see that you have brought two servants. You are to be allowed only . . ."—he consulted a sheaf of papers on his desk—"one servant. And as I have no set tariff for a cardinal, I would say you rank at least equal to a duke, so you are assessed twenty pounds per annum for your board. Of course, you will not be our guest that long, I'm sure; such charges are usually dealt with expeditiously. We will say ten shillings a week for your board."

"So much?" The pain in his gut cut a swath across his wide girth. "May I sit? I am not well."

The constable kicked a chair in his direction.

Wolsey heaved himself into it and added, breathless from the passing pain, "You are well paid for your service to the Crown. But you might as well know I am as poor as a beggar. Our Lord's poor servant. I have not a farthing to my name. All my secular tithes, rents . . . fees have been stripped from me."

The constable smiled and leaned forward to finger the luxurious ermine of the cardinal's red cope.

"Even the clothes on my back belong to the Holy Father, who, I might add, will not be pleased at the treatment of his servant." He paused for effect and lowered his voice almost to a whisper—as he always did when asking this next question. "Have you no thought for your soul, Sir Kingston?"

But the constable appeared unfazed. It was a sign of the times, a sign of Luther's malignant influence, that such a threat no longer froze the hearts of those who heard it. Pope Clement himself was being held prisoner by the Holy Roman Emperor.

"In that case, Cardinal," the constable said, without looking up from his papers. "You'd best let your servant return to York. He'll not like the pauper's fare we serve here. Nor will you, I suspect." Here he looked up and smiled as he said, with just the slightest hint of sarcasm in his tone, "Though I will do my best for our Lord's poor servant."

"I have not much appetite of late, anyway. Where will I be quartered?"

"We had thought to put you in the Bell Tower. But that is reserved for better-paying guests. Don't look so frighted, Eminence. A man of your fame will not be put in the dungeons. Though I'm afraid you'll find the Beauchamp Tower a little less than what you are accustomed to at Hampton Court or even York."

But it was not until he was led into this windowless chamber by the surly warder who'd actually spat on the floor in front of him, that the full force of this dire circumstance began to dawn on the cardinal. He held his pomander ball to his nose and inhaled. His father's butcher shop in Smithfield carried a more pleasant odor than this hellish pit, but he suffered it in silence. He would not give them the pleasure. He knew that every word he said was being reported to the constable and from the constable to the king. At least his clothing chest had been brought up, though there was no sign of his servants.

"Bring me a clean piss pot if you please, warder. And a pitcher of water. I shall try not to overburden you with my presence." And then after a pause he added, "Any good deed you can vouchsafe for the Lord's servant in his hour of need will not go unnoticed in heaven. I shall pray for your soul."

"Save your prayers, Cardinal. I've no need of 'em. I say me own prayers. But I'll get yer water and empty yer piss pot out of Christian charity. My English Bible tells me 'to love my enemy,'" he said as he shut the door behind him.

So, what Wolsey had feared might happen, had assured himself would never happen, had happened: the King of England had decided to break with Rome. Otherwise he would not have dared arrest a cardinal. The Boleyn woman had simply bewitched a king, and it was becoming increasingly apparent that Henry would do anything to have her—in the carnal sense of "having" her. One had to admire the woman in one sense. He had known princes who lacked the whore's cunning mind and great lords too craven to make such an absolute gamble for power. If the wench had opened her legs for her king as her sister had done, then this crisis would have been averted.

But it was not her virtue she was guarding, he was sure. Reports of her behavior at the French court were widely gossiped about, and he'd seen her with young Percy with his own eyes—admittedly not making the beast with two backs, but close enough. Yet for all her cleverness, the vixen had no idea what chaos she had wrought. If Henry could treat the most powerful man in England in such an abominable fashion, and set aside a beloved queen, did she think herself invincible? The king would tire of her soon enough. But he feared he would not be around to see her get what she deserved.

The warder returned with a pitcher of fresh water and, wrinkling his nose, picked up the chamber pot.

"I thank you, good sir," Wolsey said, affecting a rare, humble demeanor.

Imagine the hands that touched such filth handling the Holy Scriptures, he thought as he crossed himself and murmured, *"Benedicte,"* in the warder's direction.

The warder returned a few minutes later to find him on the floor doubled over in pain and, moved with compassion, went in search of a pallet and a doctor, thinking as he went that it would not be good for such a famous man to die on his watch.

❧❧

On Anne Boleyn's first night back at Hampton Court, dinner was an intimate affair, served not in the great hall but in the watching chamber leading to the presence room and the royal apartments. Only the senior courtiers were present. Anne had a moment of anxiety as she took her seat beside the king, remembering New Year's, the last time she was in the royal apartments, and how some of these same courtiers had witnessed her humiliation. But if any remembered, they wisely made no reference to it. Only Brandon had the gall to mention—under the pretent of welcoming her back—her absence at court.

As she toyed with her pigeon pie and honeyed neats' tongues, she commented that Henry had not chosen to replace the tapestries in this room. The renovations at Hampton Court since Wolsey's departure had not stopped with the commissioning of the Abraham tapestries but had extended to every nook and cranny, as though the king were out to prove that the once-reputed great palace of the cardinal was not so great after all. The wood carvers and carpenters could be heard hammering the great vaulted ceiling of the Royal Chapel day and night. Already the gilding of some of the beams was in progress. In the chapel, more than any place in the palace, Anne felt the pull of her Lutheran sentiments. She hated the gaudiness of it, preferring the simplicity of the altar in her bedchamber, could not imagine saying her prayers in the queen's seat that bowed out from the balcony overhanging the main chapel. She imagined Katherine sitting in that exalted place, murmuring prayers that fell sodden with tears upon the ornate altar behind the rood screen.

"I keep the tapestries in here because they remind me of the cardinal," Henry said. "Especially one of the Petrarch Triumphs: *The Triumph of Fame over Death*. Wolsey is about to see if that is true."

"Is the cardinal ill?"

"I do not know about the current health of the cardinal, but he is at this very hour being placed under arrest for treason."

"Treason! Wolsey? The mighty cardinal who mocked all England with his arrogance?" She wanted to add "mocked even the king," but she bit back the words.

"I doubt that he is in a mocking mood now," Henry said.

"What is the charge?"

"Praemunire."

Anne had no love for the cardinal. Indeed, she celebrated his downfall; as long as Wolsey lived she would not feel safe at court. But there was something chilling about how quickly Henry turned on favorites: first his queen of many years and now his trusted friend and advisor. And the charge itself, praemunire, had that nebulous trumped-up feeling. It was a spurious charge; of course the former chancellor had ties to Rome. He was a cardinal. That was why Henry had chosen him—because he had influence with the pope, and now to turn that seeming strength against him seemed unjust.

"Will such a charge not be difficult to prove to Parliament?" she asked.

"We have intercepted certain papers . . . documents from a papal legate . . . this wine has turned sour . . ." He spat it back into the cup, spraying the white linen cloth with little red drops. "Bring me another, throw that cask out," he shouted to the cupbearer. "Wolsey was brokering a separate peace between the pope and the French. It will cost him his head. Now we shall see if fame truly triumphs over death."

How easily he dismisses Wolsey, she thought. As if there had never been a relationship between them. But what was that to her? Her enemy had fallen, and that had to be a good thing.

"Speaking of chancellors," Anne said, reminding herself not to celebrate the downfall of one enemy when she had so many, "I see that Master More is absent."

"His father was taken ill suddenly." Henry motioned to the sewer. "Take this great mound of grapes away. They said Sir John More fell ill from a 'surfeit of grapes.'"

"Then he should recover," Anne said, eyeing the grapes, wishing she had taken a bunch before the king commanded them to be taken away. She looked at the disappearing platter. "I never heard of anybody dying from a surfeit of grapes," she said, "perhaps it was a surfeit of *grape*."

Henry laughed at this uproariously. The courtiers closest followed suit. She noticed Brandon did not laugh.

"Sir John More is known to be a man of strong discipline and not inclined to excess of any kind. A man of sterling character and sound judgment," Brandon said archly.

"Like father, like son? Would you not agree, my lord Suffolk?" Anne asked.

"Exactly so."

Henry scowled. "I know little of the father's, but the judgment of the son might be called to question," he muttered, but he did not say it loudly enough for the others to hear. Anne wisely did not remark upon it. But might it just be that the new chancellor was following the same path as the old? That was a thought that gave Anne considerable satisfaction.

The king signaled for the court musicians to begin playing, but as the pipers' and harpists' notes floated through the room, he remained silent, not singing along as he sometimes did. He seemed preoccupied. When the performance was ended and the last elaborate confection removed, he announced loudly enough for all to hear, "The groom will show you to your rooms, Lady Anne. Your ladies are already there. From now on, when you are at Hampton Court you will sleep in the queen's royal apartments."

Then he looked out over the assembled courtiers, no more than a dozen or so of the favorites, and his eyes held a direct challenge. Nobody was brave enough or foolish enough to pick up the gauntlet, not even the Duke of Suffolk.

Anne was unprepared for the grandeur she found as she entered the royal bedchamber and closet reserved for the queen at Hampton Court. The rich tapestries and silver sconces on the wall, the damask bed hangings, the golden candlebra and elaborately carved writing table in the queen's closet, the bathing chamber with its great stone tub lined with linen, rivaled even what she had seen at the French court. As lady-in-waiting to Queen Katherine, Anne had once assisted the queen out of a similar tub at Richmond Palace, had been often in her well-appointed apartments, but nothing at Richmond was as grand as what the cardinal had built. No wonder Henry had coveted it.

As she entered the room, two women standing at each side of the door curtsied. "Welcome, my lady. The king has asked us to serve as your ladies during the queen's absence. I am Lady Margaret Lee, I am Lady of the Privy Chamber, and this is Lady Jane Seymour."

Anne noted Margaret's careful words, "during the queen's absence." *You're not the queen and we all know it. You are just another of the king's favorites. But just in case, we will serve you willingly and well.*

Anne did not resent Lady Margaret's caution. How could she? The woman was just being prudent. Anne had seen both ladies before at court. Of Margaret Lee she approved. She was an older woman with a cheerful demeanor and married to a respectable knight: a good choice, Henry must have thought, to guide and guard a young queen. But about Jane Seymour, Anne was less pleased. She was Anne's exact opposite: pale and blond, and not very well educated, preferring embroidery over discourse or gaming. Anne doubted she could even write her name. She had been hoping for a better-suited companion.

"May we help you prepare for bed, my lady?" And without waiting for an answer Margaret began to remove Anne's bandeau and snood, letting her hair fall to her waist. As Lady Margaret brushed her hair, Anne watched Jane lay out a chemise of finest lawn so diaphanous that it left little to modesty. Anne had seen Katherine's nightdress. This was not Katherine's nightdress.

"I hope there is a goose-down counterpane to keep me from chilblains," she said.

Lady Margaret smiled. "There is a velvet dressing gown if my lady desires it."

"My lady desires it," Anne said flatly.

Her attendants retired to their ladies' chamber shortly after seeing her to bed, whereupon she'd promptly got out of bed. Wrapping herself in the blue velvet dressing gown, a deep, pure blue, the color of the Virgin's robe in the stained-glass window in the Royal Chapel, Anne considered where to say her prayers. A cursory glance told her there was no altar, but she was not inclined to go tripping down the gallery in her nightdress to the royal pew above the papist chapel. She would ask Henry on the morrow if she could fashion a simple altar in one corner of the room. In the meantime she would have to make do. Her English Bible told her to "go into her closet" but she figured that was just a way of saying that a pious Christian did not make a public show of her prayers, so in the end she just knelt beside the canopied and curtained bed, pulling the rich velvet of the robe between her knees and the cold, stone floor. Anne was not a great believer in the mortification of the flesh.

She had just finished her prayers and was reciting the "Our Father" when she heard a noise coming from the queen's closet. Maybe she should have chosen that room after all; maybe the words were to be taken literally and the Spirit was here to admonish her.

But it was no spirit, holy or otherwise, that stepped from behind the paneled wall. It was a man of very solid flesh.

"Your Majesty, I did not expect you tonight. I mean, the hour is late. My ladies are sleeping. What if they should waken and—"

"Then we shall have to be very quiet," he said, and began to remove his doublet.

He had stripped down to his long shirt and hose before she could find the words, "Your Majesty, I must protest."

"Then you must protest quietly if you do not wish to wake your ladies."

Anne felt a moment of panic. She knew that it was not just her virginity at stake, which she had protected thus far through divers methods, but her future. She backed away from him.

For a moment the expression on his face almost frightened her. "My lady, I have given you gifts that would beggar a prince, surrounded you with heretical priests of your choosing against the wishes of my counselors and advisors, and are you not at this very moment ensconced in the queen's own chambers? Have I not made my intentions clear? God's Wounds, woman, will you not lie with your king in the queen's own bed?"

She took a step back and inhaled deeply. If she refused him now, might she be going too far? But had not her sister Mary been thus rewarded? Before she was cast aside? And she had even borne the king a bastard. That thought gave her courage.

"But I am not the queen, Your Majesty. And until I am, I will not lie with the king."

He reached out then and roughly pulled her to him. He kissed her hard, his breath coming fast, and groped beneath her robe, his hand hot on her breast through the thin film of her chemise. Her body wanted to give in. She had not felt such temptation since Percy was sent away. Sweet Percy. That thought steeled her will.

"Your Majesty, I cannot. It would be a sin—"

His breath in her ear was as hot as his hand on her breast, as hot as her skin felt beneath the too warm velvet robe.

"Then at least," he said huskily, "give your king a hand."

"That much I can do," she said, and her fingers began to work, practicing a skill she had learned at the French court, a skill that she had perfected with Percy. "That much, and no more, I will do," she whispered as the king's seed spilled into her hand.

TWENTY-SEVEN

 y mid-autumn the translators were well into the Pentateuch, translating directly from the Hebrew that looked to Kate more like dancing lines than real words. What must it feel like to know that your work was so important that lives would be changed because of it? At times it was hard not to envy her husband his brilliance and sense of purpose. She dared to wonder if she could have learned to read the Hebrew, or at least the Greek, if she'd had his teachers, even daring to think that he might teach her the classical languages as her brother had taught her to read English. But once when she had peered over his shoulder and inquired about the dancing squiggles, he had answered impatiently. "It's really not an alphabet, Kate. It's a bit more complicated than that."

"But the Greek letters that William translated the New Testament from, that's an alphabet, right? *Alpha* for the letter *A*?"

"Hmm." But he had just kept on writing without looking up. "There," she said, pointing to a bit of Greek text among the papers scattered on the writing table. "That's *beta*, right?"

He looked up then and kissed the hand pointing to the Greek text. "Are you thinking of teaching your young scholars Greek?" He laughed.

"I might," she said, bristling a little. "Or maybe you could drop in some Friday and give us the benefit of your brilliance."

"I just might," he said. "But for now could you fetch your thirsty husband a cup of cider?"

She brought him the cider, thinking that at least he had stopped protesting her involvement with the Bible women. Of course, he didn't really think of them as Bible women, she thought and felt a little guilty that she had deceived him. She didn't talk much about the reading of the Scriptures, the serious discussions or the fervent prayers. Or how they held hands and sang their closing hymn. Instead, whenever he asked her how her meeting went, she distracted him with tales about the frivolous things they chattered about, the gossip they exchanged before their worship began: some witty remark that Hulda had made about the baker's pious wife, or Caroline's complaints about her husband's wandering eyes. It was less than open disclosure. And she felt a little guilty about it. Sometimes. But not now. Not when he was asking her to fetch and carry for him. Not when he was humoring her like a child.

❧❦

By All Saints' Day, Kate had the English House accounts in good enough order to pass inspection at the Hansa Countinghouse, so Kate returned to punishing the ragged donkey-unicorn beast. But the thing had become an embarrassment. Even kindly Mistress Poyntz had suggested maybe she should start another, now that she had practiced so much on this one, but still Kate was determined to persevere—until the incident with the needle.

She was brushing her hair getting ready for bed and trying to count in her head the days from her last bleeding. She'd a letter from her brother John, just yesterday, informing her that their house was finished, he and Mary and little Pipkin were doing well. He had enough business as a scribe to keep them in the victuals they couldn't raise, and she might be happy to know that he'd not abandoned the reform movement but had been inspired by her to start his own small yeoman Bible study. He was teaching the local populace to read and had set up a rudimentary printing press to print sheets of English Scripture as a text.

Then one more bit of happy news he'd added at the end, she was to be aunt again—along with a question, when was he to be uncle?

When indeed? It had been months since she'd lost the child. Why had she not conceived again? Since that time on the boat, it had certainly not been for lack of trying. The old midwife she'd consulted had said a woman was more fertile on certain days, but alas she could not remember which days she had said. *Stupid, Kate, stupid as a cow, You can't remember something that important, and you think you could learn Greek.*

John's exclamation of pain interrupted both her self-recrimination and her hair brushing.

"By all the gods on Mount Olympus, Kate, are you trying to kill me?"

It was the closest she'd ever heard John come to swearing—at least in English. The brush clattered to the floor and Kate whirled around to determine the cause of his abrupt invocation of pagan gods.

He was pulling her needle out of the heel of his left hand—thank God and all the angels, it was not the one that held his pen.

"Let me see it." And then upon close examination, "It's only a pinprick," she said, relieved. "It went in and came out clean, see," she said, holding up the needle, "not even a smear of blood."

"Well, it hurt like—"

"I'm sorry. It was careless of me to leave it in the chair," she said in a tone that one would use to placate a pouting child, and she kissed the almost invisible wound.

But five minutes later he was still sucking on the tiny red spot where the needle went in as though it were a mortal wound. This from a man who'd endured the horror of the fish cellar prison for months and come back from the jaws of death, never saying a word about his pain or his fever or even the danger, and now carrying on about the prick of a needle! Nevertheless she clucked and fussed, washing it with a little vinegar and dabbing it with honey as her mother used to do her scrapes and cuts when she was a child.

When she had finished and apologized yet again, he'd held up the little tapestry that had been balled around the offending needle and glared at it. "What *is* this thing, anyway?"

"Thing? What do you mean, *thing*? Isn't it clear? It's a . . . a unicorn."

"Oh. Well. Yes." He squinted, turning it sideways. "I suppose, now that you tell me."

"You know, John, not everybody in the world is as brilliant at everything they do as you are," she said, trying to hide the hurt in sarcasm. "Some of us need a little practice to do even something as insignificant as a little needlework."

Now it was his turn to apologize, which he did prettily enough, telling her with genuine surprise in his voice that she was a woman of many talents.

"Name one," she'd said, fighting back tears that suddenly ambushed her. It was such a little thing. "I cannot spin or weave or play a musical instrument. I cannot sing. I cannot do any of the things the wife of a brilliant man should be expected to do. Just . . . name . . . one."

"You can read and write and cipher," he said, looking at her in puzzlement. "How many women can do that? You may not sew a fine stitch but you are the perfect wife for a scholar." And he'd kissed her, lightly, affectionately, on the head, in the same manner in which she had kissed his wound.

But those are not womanly gifts, she'd wanted to say. Not womanly gifts at all. The womanly things she just couldn't seem to get right—not even the most basic thing, such as motherhood—and she was not to be allowed, it seemed, to do the unwomanly things of real importance.

He stroked her hair gently, then she felt the weight of it lift from her neck as he kissed her neck, just a nibble at first, and the comforting kiss became something more, as his tongue began to explore her ear. He tossed the offending tapestry to the floor and then kicked it aside. "You are the perfect wife for this scholar," he said, pulling her to him.

His hands—both his left and his right—seemed to have sustained no impairment in their function. She had just enough time to think, before her mind surrendered to her body's more urgent needs, that it was gratifying to note, in this one area at least, her husband found her womanly function more than adequate.

⁂

The next day she confessed her failure again to the sketch of the ugly duchess. "It seems John is to be denied an accomplished wife," she said in disgust as she picked the tapestry up from the floor and started to throw it away. Then she had a second thought. This creature, or this needlepoint picture of a creature, ugly, imperfect as it was, she had made with her own hands. It did not exist before she made it. The pucker in the flank wasn't so bad, but the hole in the horn could not be fixed. Yet he had a beautiful eye, just a tiny spot of white silk floss in the blue of the eye, to catch the light. She'd been proud of that eye. There was a grief in just throwing it away. She smoothed out the tapestry and covered up the top part with the edge of her hand. There, that was not so bad. A few more stitches on the wide body to fill in the skimpy parts—someday she might cut off the part with the horn. It didn't have to be a unicorn. Maybe it just really wanted to be a horse.

"Kate Gough, you are as mad as the painter who sketched that other ugly portrait," she muttered aloud.

But she could not bring herself to throw the embroidery away. She folded it up carefully and put it away until she could think more on its redemption.

◦◦◦

The bells of St. Mary-le-Bow tolled mournfully as Sir Thomas walked behind the coffin of his father. It was a blessing that the burial ground of the church in St. Lawrence Jewry was close by the patriarchal home in Milk Street. It was a cold, gray day and Thomas was chilled both in body and in spirit and feared of giving out. He was not prepared for this day and felt oddly cut loose from his moorings, adrift on a choppy sea. In Sir John More's eightieth winter his demise could hardly have been unexpected. But it was. Thomas had never imagined the world without his father in it.

The sad procession passed a few boyhood landmarks that prodded the heaviness around his heart into a hellish foreboding. How could this be? How could this lion of the King's Bench, who had stood sentinel for all of Thomas's life against the forces of disorder, this staunch defender of duty and discipline and law, be felled by a bout of indigestion? Where was the order in that? It was for Thomas as though his metaphor for God the Father was dissolving into vapor. The Father lived as long as the father lived.

He had walked down this very lane, past the church of St. Mary Magdalen, which now took up the mournful tolling with its one bell, so many years ago. It was an image buried deep in his memory, reborn as fresh as yesterday, his boy's hand in his father's larger one, on his way to be page in the household of John Morton, Archbishop of Canterbury and Lord Chancellor of England. As they walked his father had lectured him upon his duty. A grand opportunity for a boy, he'd said, to enter the service of the most influential man in England, admonishing Thomas to acquit himself well, not to embarrass his father, to do his duty, and one day he would be a great man too.

They'd passed the tall stone fountain in West Chepe. It had been a dismal, dreary day like this and like today there were few waiting at the fountains to fill their buckets with water from the Tybourne River. There had been a burning on Tybourne Hill, a Lollard heretic, his father had said, as Thomas wrinkled his nose at the lingering smell of smoke and seared flesh, explaining that Lollardy was a form of anarchy, an evil bent on destroying the order of the world. It was the first time Thomas had ever heard the word.

As the procession turned up St. Lawrence Lane on its way to the church, they passed Blossoms Inn. A few curious travelers watched as the mournful procession passed. Thomas recognized only the innkeeper, who removed his hat and bowed his head. He and his father had stopped on that day so long ago and shared a cup as the father continued his instruction to the son. That was the day that Thomas first became aware that John More had his son's future mapped out as carefully as he laid out a legal argument. A future which, he was later to be reminded, was to be bound up with law at Lincoln's Inn and not theology at Oxford.

When Thomas thought he could not take another step—he had not slept or eaten in the three days it took his father to die, the very picture of the dutiful son keeping watch at his father's deathbed—his daughter Margaret suddenly appeared at his side and offered him her arm. Together they completed the short journey that ended in the churchyard. There was not much ceremony, not the ceremony one would expect of a great man—his father had left instructions when he realized that he was dying. A requiem mass was celebrated by the parish priest, and thirteen mourners—thirteen as in the number of Christ's Last Supper—gathered around the tomb. Thomas watched, almost numb with disbelief, as his father's coffin was duly sprinkled with holy water and lowered into the stone tomb.

It would not occur to Thomas until much later, after they had returned to the house in Milk Lane for a funeral feast attended by some very important people and presided over by his father's now widowed fourth wife, after Thomas had lain sleepless for most of the night in his boyhood room, trying to wrap his mind around the realization that his father was not asleep in the great carved bed in the room below but in the cold ground of St. Lawrence chuchyard, after he realized that he would no longer pass his father in the halls of Westminster and kneel to pay his respects, that his father's ambition had been fulfilled upon seeing his son Chancellor of England.

And now Thomas had to write the rest of the story himself. He had fulfilled his duty to his father. He was free to serve the Church.

❧

"What do you think, John?" Kate said to her husband's back as he was bent over his desk. She waved Catherine Massys's letter of invitation in front of him. "Do you care if I go?"

He scanned the letter, frowned, and handed it back to her. "Are you sure this is something you really want to do?"

Translation: I would rather you didn't.

"It would just be for a few days. She says I can travel both ways in the company of Quentin's son and his wife. It will be perfectly safe. Leuven is only a day or so south of here."

"A hard day. And of course I would care. I would miss you. What about your women's . . . meeting?"

"Quentin's son is leaving on Saturday after the Friday meeting, so I would only miss one. Just think how much work you could get done without me to distract you."

"You never distract me." He smiled and kissed her lightly. "It is the work that distracts me from you."

"You are a silver-tongued flatterer, John Frith." And she swatted him lightly on the shoulder. "But I've become so accustomed to your sweet talk I don't think I want to be without it. I'll just tell Catherine I appreciate the invitation to visit, but I can't be away from my husband that long," she said.

"That's good," he said.

But that night as she watched John laboring by candlelight over his translations, she reconsidered. "It would really only be for a few days. You would hardly have time to miss me," she said.

"I will miss you the minute you are gone."

He put down his pen and stretched. She walked behind him and massaged his neck, feeling the firm tight muscles relax beneath her fingers as he closed his eyes and moaned in relief. "You know, sweet wife," he said between *umm*'s and *ah*'s "I think I already miss you, and you're only thinking about going." But when her fingers stilled, he picked up his pen and went back to work.

༺ ༻

The day after his father's burial, Sir Thomas More took to his Chelsea bed complaining of heaviness in his chest. All Dame Alice's poultices and potions were of no avail to him. He lacked the strength to get out of bed. In his feverish dreams he was a boy again, lost and wandering in a dark wood, calling for his father who did not answer.

But on the fourth morning, his son-in-law Roper brought the news that, while the lord chancellor was involved with his father's death and bound up in his grief, Cardinal Wolsey had been tried for treason and sentenced to lose his head. When Thomas heard that Wolsey had cheated the executioner by dying on his way to the block, he smiled. At least the old reprobate had been spared the indignity of the headsman and managed to confound the king's best-laid plans, yet again.

Thomas called for Barnabas to help him dress, and staggered, coughing and sputtering phleghm, down to his study. He drank Alice's broth to get rid of her and then took up his pen. The fact that Wolsey had been convicted meant only one thing: Henry had decided to break with Rome. Maybe not today, or even tomorrow, but someday soon. Thomas More knew he would be called upon to choose between Crown and Church. This time the choice would be his. In the meantime he would fill the world with such a fury of refutation against the heretics that William Tyndale's ears would burn as though the flames already scorched them.

Thomas would find his path through the dark wood. An imagined flame of a human bonfire would light the way.

TWENTY-EIGHT

The true heart of a wife [is the] preciousest gift that a man hath in this world.
—William Tyndale
on the Seventh Commandment

homas Cromwell left the king's privy chamber more chagrined than he was when he entered. The meeting with the king and the agent he'd brought at the king's request had taken an unexpected turn.

Cromwell had not been happy when Henry asked him for the name of someone whose absolute loyalty and silence could be counted on, someone with open ears and a way of ferreting out information, someone on whom he could rely to go to the Continent and collect good opinion on his "great matter" to present to the pope. That could mean only one thing: if the king was still seeking influential testimony, then the break with Rome was not as imminent as Cromwell had hoped.

Sir Thomas Elyot's name had come quickly to mind. Not that he was that reliable. But he was a noble acquaintance who needed employment, and Thomas Cromwell knew the value of granting favors to financially embarrassed parliamentarians. The king seemed pleased enough with the choice, instructing Elyot to report to Master Cromwell for any expenses he might incur during his mission. Cromwell liked the sound of that. It was good that he was to be the paymaster; it would put the fellow even more in his debt—and keep him informed.

Thinking that was the end of the matter, Cromwell had bowed and was about to take his leave when Henry stayed him with his hand.

"You may be wondering, Master Cromwell, why in light of our recent conversations with you and Archbishop Cranmer, we are still seeking testimony in this matter. We are not. As you have advised, we have chosen another course."

"But Your Majesty said—ah, I see. It is a ruse. Very clever of Your Majesty."

He'd been worried for a moment. He cared not a saint's knucklebone for the Boleyn woman, but getting shed of the Catholic queen could only be a good thing for the cause of reformation. And getting rid of Rome would be a good thing for the treasury—all that wealth, all that land and gold and silver owned by the Church and shut up in England's monasteries and cathedrals. "Just think if the Crown had control of that, Your Majesty, and that neither the king nor his kingdom nor its archbishops nor bishops nor even its humblest parish priests would any longer be subject to Rome's tyranny."

It was an action bold enough to take the breath away.

Even Phillip the Fair of France had not dared go so far when he'd quarreled with Pope Urban, installing instead a French cardinal as the head of the Church in France. Cromwell had advised Henry against that historic precedent by pointing out the disastrous results. Christendom had wound up with two popes for a while—one in Rome and one in Avignon and then a third to overrule the other two.

"One supreme head," he'd advised the king, "of both the temporal and the sacred. Then the king could grant his own divorce." That was the seed Cromwell had planted in Henry's head, the seed Cranmer had watered, and now it was close to sprouting in spite of Chancellor More's fanatic clutching at the old order.

"You are right, Master Cromwell. Gathering testimonials is only a pretense," the king said, idly examining his hands, adjusting his signet ring as though the matter were not important at all. "Master Elyot's real mission is to seek out William Tyndale and John Frith. You will brief him on this mission in secret."

Cromwell paused as he tried to figure what this might mean. He'd thought the ruse was simply intended to throw the Roman prelates off their guard, so as to catch them by surprise when Parliament declared Henry

VIII, King of England, the supreme head of God's Holy Church in England.

"I do not understand, Your Majesty. Forgive me, but I thought that had already been done; Stephen Vaughan has already found them and brought back their answer."

Cromwell was later to remember the look on Henry's face and see it again many times in the next few years. It was a flash of anger, shocking and swift in its approach, like ragged ground lightning on a clear summer day. Just as dangerous and just as fleeting.

"Found them and lost them." He waved his hand as if waving away a gnat. "Vaughan's was a separate mission. Masters Tyndale and Frith have spurned the king's grace. If you locate them again, you are to assist Sir Elyot—they are probably still hiding somewhere in the Low Countries, though they may have sought other cover by now—in bringing them back." And then he added, "By whatever means necessary."

"If I may ask, Your Majesty—"

"To stand trial for heresy, of course."

"Of course," Cromwell answered. But he really didn't understand. He'd thought the king had been influenced in their favor by Anne Boleyn. Her influence was why he had offered them grace and favor in the first place. If he had now changed his mind because of the insult to his vanity, why not rely on the spy Thomas More and Bishop Stokesley had sent? Henry Phillips was a notorious ne'er-do-well. If anybody could trick them out of the protection of the English Merchants' House, it would be he . . . unless the king no longer trusted Chancellor More.

"Your Majesty, Chancellor More has already an agent working on this, as I am sure you are aware."

"Chancellor More is distracted."

Why not fan the flames of More's ill favor? Cromwell thought, as he said, "Distracted from the king's business?"

"It just may be that though he is a layman, Chancellor More's purpose lies more in Pope Clement's interests than his king's. Is the mission clear then?"

"Quite clear. Find Tyndale and Frith and bring them back by whatever means required." Then sensing that this meeting had come to an end, he bowed. "Will that be all, Your Majesty?"

"That is all, Master Cromwell."

As he left the privy chamber with Elyot in tow, it occurred to Thomas

Cromwell that the king's favor was as mercurial as his moods. He would do well to remember that.

❧

A spider had spun its web wide between two bushes in the courtyard of the English House. John Frith pondered the web's gossamer symmetry, the strength of the almost invisible filament that anchored it to the bush nearest the bench on which he sat with William Tyndale. The sunlight slanted across the web, gilding the silken ribs of the gossamer edifice. It was a thing of beauty, not unlike the intricate splendor of a rose window in a great cathedral, John thought. A thing of beauty, but at the heart of that intricate beauty a black-robed spider devoured a struggling firefly at its leisure. John would have freed the hapless insect, but it was too late. The head of the firefly was already being slowly digested by the spider.

It was a sobering metaphor for what he had just offered to do.

"I would like to wait until my wife returns," he said to William Tyndale. "She has gone to visit Catherine Massys in Leuven."

Tyndale looked down at his ink-stained hands; the interlocking fingers worked and his knuckles cracked. "I understand," he said. "You know, John, you do not have to go at all. We can wait; we can find another way. I had hoped to get some return indication from Stephen Vaughan as to His Majesty's mind after receiving my letter. It may be that he is open to being persuaded to let the Bible be legally distributed. But you are a fugitive just as I am. The risk would be considerable for either of us."

"If Thomas More traps me, the cause will not suffer as it will if he catches you," he said. And then lightening his tone to reassure his friend, "Besides, I am small fry. They have forgotten about me. And consider this, my friend"—he slapped Tyndale on the shoulder—"though you may write better than me, and translate faster, I am a better talker."

Tyndale laughed. "I cannot deny the verity of that." But the laugh soon died as he said soberly, "First you'd have to gain the king's ear. He has given safe-conduct to Robert Barnes, after Barnes sent him a gracious letter requesting that he be allowed to return to take care of business. Safe-conduct with no strings attached." He too was watching the spider feed on its prey. He added, "But Robert Barnes has never incurred Thomas More's wrath."

"Thomas More only knows my name, not my face. He wouldn't know me if he encountered me on the street. I know Robert Barnes. He is a good man. I can go under disguise—maybe as his servant. That way the safe-conduct would cover me as well."

"If you are going as anybody's servant, you'd best keep your mouth shut." Tyndale allowed a small smile. "Servants don't spout classical allusions for curses."

But John didn't take Tyndale's good-natured baiting. "When is Barnes leaving?" he asked, making up his mind.

"This afternoon. A Hansa shipment is due to leave for the London Steelyard in about five hours—I'm proud to say it'll be carrying something besides Flemish weavings. Barnes told me he planned to be on it. You could be in London tonight. If all goes well you might even be back before your wife returns. If you decide to go."

"Even if I can't gain the king's ear, I can spy out the lay of the land. I can surely get to Cromwell. We get such conflicting reports. Some say that More is losing his influence, that the Boleyn woman has influence over the king. It might be that some persuasive argument would win him over. He must at least be open to the idea. Why else would he have offered us pardon and a place at court?"

"Take Chaplain Rogers with you," Tyndale said.

John shook his head. "Two would be in more danger than one. I'll go alone. But, please explain the safe-conduct to my wife so she'll understand why I left without telling her. Tell her I'll be back as soon as I can and that I would like her to stay in the safety of the English House until I return."

"Never fear, John. We'll keep her safe. You just watch out for yourself. Kate's too young to be a widow."

⁘

Kate listened to Catherine Massys's rhythmic breathing and longed for the sound of John's gentle snoring. This was her last night in Leuven, and she was eager not just for the comfort of her bed but for the comfort of her husband's arms. But she was glad she had come; she had particularly enjoyed meeting with Catherine's friends. They were a group of very brave women.

Because they had to be more secretive than in Antwerp—which was bigger, an important business center, and more tolerant, less watchful of such activity—a sharp edge of excitement sparked the Bible study of the women of Leuven. Children were not allowed. They might carry tales away. The women were mostly older, except for two: one who was unmarried and one who, like Kate, was childless. They received Kate into their sisterhood with smiles and hugs. Kate soon learned that these women took their faith as seriously as life and death. Kate marveled at their boldness—and their recklessness. Even Catherine squirmed when Berta, the oldest among them, after reading the Bible lesson railed against the black-robed Roman charlatans. Did it never occur to Berta that the stranger they trusted might be a spy for the Church?

But Kate suspected they all knew this was no silly girl's game they were playing. As Kate had helped Catherine arrange pillows in a circle on the floor in her room—"an upper room," Charlotte, the pretty blond fräulein, called it—the women spoke of the ruses they used with their husbands. One of the regulars, a woman named Dora, had not shown up. Her husband had found out about the meetings and given her a black eye and threatened worse. It would be a while before she would be back. "But I know Dora. She will find a way," Catherine had said soberly. How much they must have been like the earliest Christians, Kate thought—before a powerful Church hierarchy hid the simple, pure message preached by an itinerant Galilean carpenter in undecipherable language, carved stone, and hammered gold.

Now remembering the woman whose husband had beaten her, Kate lay awake in the quiet darkness of that same upper room and breathed a little prayer of thanks for her gentle husband who had once jokingly promised "not to beat her." To Dora and many women like her it was no joke. Yet even Kate's husband, who believed as she did and risked his life to prove it, disapproved of the women's meetings and would have been more content if she stayed at the English House sharpening his quills and fetching him cider.

Was it a sin for Kate to want more? A sin to want to participate in a direct way in the cause? The priests preached—even some of the reformists—that women bore the curse of Eve, and so theirs was the lesser role. Was it a sin of pride that made her want to take the risks they took, make the difference they made? A sin of pride to think she even possessed the courage? That same sin—if sin it was—had put her on the river dressed like a man to do the work of a man, and God had rewarded that act by uniting her with John. And then another thought occurred to her that squeezed like a hot pincer on yielding flesh.

Could it be that her woman's pride was the sin that caused her baby to die in her womb?

Was that God's punishment? Rewards for good works, punishments for misdeeds: that was what the priests taught. *But you don't believe that, Kate Frith. A God of grace and mercy, even a God of justice, would not punish your innocent baby for your sins*. And then another thought pushed its way in. *But God might think such a willful woman not fit to be a mother.*

No. (Did she say that out loud? Catherine mumbled in her sleep and turned over.) Kate rejected such a notion out of hand. The Lutherans believed in grace, rejecting the image of God as harsh harvest lord with a whip in one hand and a bag of coins in the other, and she agreed with them.

So why were her warring thoughts keeping her awake? Maybe because she was too stupid to figure it all out, maybe because she was a woman—no, if she was stupid, it was not because she was a woman. She'd been reading the translated pages of the English Old Testamant that John and Tyndale had been working on so hard. She'd found women there: strong women, like Judith and Deborah and Esther. And in the New Testament, too, there were Dorcas and Phoebe and Lydia of Philippi to whom the Apostle Paul addressed his letter: "I thank my God for every remembrance of you . . ." Brave women who also met to study and pray at great personal risk.

One thing was sure. She did not have to deceive John as these Leuven women deceived their husbands. It was wrong to deceive him. She would tell him the whole truth, how their numbers grew with each meeting and how they were just as determined and just as serious as he and the fellows who had been locked up with him in that Oxford cellar. He would not forbid her. Of that she was sure.

She fell asleep imagining him sleeping alone and wondered if he lay awake, missing her.

TWENTY-NINE

The spirit of error and lying hath taked his wretched soul with him straight from the short fire to the fire everlasting. And this is lo Sir Thomas Hitton, the devils stinking martyr, of whose burning Tyndale maketh boast.

— SIR THOMAS MORE
ON THE DEATH OF THOMAS HITTON

e . . . is . . . breaking . . . the law! Your father, the greatest defender of the law in England, is disregarding it as though he is the giver of the law and not its keeper. The law is clear. All people charged with heresy are to be turned over to the secular authorities."

"But he is the secular authority," Meg Roper said as quietly as she could, to calm her usually mild-mannered husband.

"There are procedures—lawful, established due process—which he is flouting." He pounded the table. Some of his morning porridge slopped out.

"Shh, William. The servants might hear you," she said, wiping up the spill.

He lowered his voice, but only a little. "He's becoming deranged, I tell you. He has a morbid obsession with burning. First, there was that leather seller Phillips that he and his boot-licking bishop unlawfully interrogated at his 'tree of troth' in Chelsea's own garden and continued to do so in clear violation of the law—even *after* the man was found innocent by a jury. And then that priest named Hitton—the first burning in eight years. Eight years, Meg, England had been free of the taint of smoke, and then your father is made chancellor."

"But that is just coincidence."

"It was an illegal search that put Thomas Hitton in the fire, and Thomas More delighted in the burning of a man whose only crime was that he had letters in his pockets to people your father called 'the heretics beyond the sea'! Letters, Meg. A man was tied to a wooden stake and burned because he carried *letters* to William Tyndale."

Meg remembered uncomfortably the time when she had wandered into the garden uninvited and been scolded for her intrusion by her father, whom she had always thought the gentlest of men, and how more than once she'd heard strange cries coming from the porter's lodge, another place where she and the rest of the household had been forbidden to go.

"It's all lies, vicious lies, spread by his enemies," she insisted. "Every great man has enemies. He is lenient enough with your reform views. How can he be as bad as some are saying?"

"Don't be so blind, Margaret. The great Thomas More himself searched Petite's Quay and imprisoned John Petite, a member of Parliament and a burgess of London, even when he found no banned books."

William tore off a hunk of bread and pointed it at her to punctuate his words. "Somebody better stop him. Somebody better talk to him. Even Wolsey didn't break the law with such abandon. And Cuthbert Tunstall might have been a toady for the pope, but unlike Stokesley, he drew the line at torture and burning. When your father's victims tell what he's doing, he just gives that little smile of his and says that he is only trying to save souls. Between him and the new Bishop of London, there won't be any souls left to save."

"Would you like some more porridge?" she asked, hoping to change the subject. "I'm sorry that's all we have. Cook is busy making black puddings. You like black puddings."

But he would not be so easily diverted. It was as though a dam had broken, and the words just kept pouring out. She had no idea he carried such resentment for her father.

"I know of a Cambridge book dealer named Nicholson who swears that Sir Thomas beat him for five days—five days—whilst he was tied to a post in his garden and had cords tied around his forehead until he fainted. You'd better talk to your father, Meg. You have some influence with him. Talk to him, if you love him. He's becoming drunk with his own power."

"I'll talk to him," Meg promised, just to shut him up. She was sure her father would have an answer for each and every one of the scurrilous charges.

"When?" he asked pointedly.

"When the time is ripe, William. I'll confront him with the rumors, and then you'll see he'll answer all your charges."

"Maybe to your satisfaction," he said, "but I doubt to anybody else's." And then he left the table abruptly without even giving her the usual peck on the cheek.

⁓ ⁑ ⁓

The shocking news that John had gone to England without her, back into the mouth of danger without even consulting her, made Kate angry. Then it terrified her. When he returned a week before Christmas looking so ragged and unkempt she hardly recognized him, he hugged her so joyfully, she wondered if he was oblivious to the abandonment she'd felt, the terror he'd put her through.

"There are more of the great unwashed masses than there are of prosperous men, my love," he'd said. "The trick is to blend in among them without looking like a vagrant. Just your everyday yeoman laborer here," he said, "anxious to get home to his wonderful wife," and he kissed her. He smelled of the road, but his lips tasted honey sweet.

"I even counterfeited a license to show that I am in the employ of one Sir Sidney Stottlemeyer," he said when they separated. He reached into his leather pack and handed her the document so that she could appreciate his joke. "A beadle outside of Westminster actually said he knew the man, even though I just made up the name. 'Great gray-haired worthy knight,' I said, 'with a mole right at the tip of his nose.' 'Yes, yes, I remember him well. Give him my regards,' the poor fool said."

She examined the official-looking document he'd forged in his fine hand, wondering at her husband's courage and resourcefulness. "Why did you need to show a license? We were never asked for such a document. I don't recall our apprentice carrying one."

The smile vanished and a look that said as much of anger as she ever saw on her husband's face took its place. "That's the beneficent Chancellor More's doing. He's pushed a law through Parliament stating that any healthy person found outside his native parish without a license to beg or proof of employment shall be stripped naked, tied to a cart tail, and whipped publicly through the streets until his body is bloody."

Kate had a sudden vision of her brother's back with its striped scars, followed by a vision of Margaret Roper defending the charity of her noble father. The old familiar anger welled up inside her.

But anger could not long survive John's innate good nature. He laughed as though it were all some great game and not a matter of life and death, as he pulled off the stained jerkin and sliced open the lining with a knife. Letters, dozens of them, came pouring out. "Each one is stuffed with money," he announced proudly, "and words of encouragement and great affection for our cause." His eyes were bright with excitement.

He'd come back alone, he said, not waiting to travel under Barnes's safe-conduct because he wanted to deliver the letters—and to see his beautiful wife, of course. He'd not been able to see the king, he said, but it would probably have done no good anyway. As chancellor, More was hell-bent on burning every reformer in Christendom. When John started naming names of Bible sellers, Bible buyers, and Bible readers who had been interrogated by Sir Thomas More and Bishop Stokesley, her heart nearly froze with fear.

"Do you remember hearing us talk about a man named Christoffel van Ruremund?"

Kate shook her head.

"He is . . . he was . . ." John said, "a Dutchman running pirated unbound copies of William's New Testament into England. He wasn't one of us, but he didn't have to be. As long as William gets the Word out, he doesn't care who gets the profit."

"You said 'was'?"

"More caught him. Shut him up in the Tower. He died there after one of the chancellor's 'interrogations.'"

Her breath caught in her throat. "How did you hear that?"

"There's an inn down by London Bridge, the Sign of the Bottle, where the Bible men meet. I don't know if you knew about it. Your brother probably did. They told me about Christoffel and a few of their other customers. The innkeeper's wife warned me that the place was being watched by More's spies." He paused and took her by the shoulders, hugged her to him. "Don't ever talk to strangers about what we do here, Kate. Even the women you meet with. Sometimes I wish you would just be content to—"

"You know I wouldn't," she said before he could give voice to the protest she did not want to hear—especially now when he'd taken such a risk and not even consulted her first. "You're the one who takes chances. You're the glib one, preaching to every John and Tom that will listen to you, running off into the dragon's lair."

"It's just that the fewer who know us, know what we do . . . well, suppose this Christoffel broke under interrogation—lesser men have."

She thought of her brother, who had broken under the same wrath, and the shame and the horror she'd felt for his suffering.

"If he knew where we were . . ."

Tears stung her eyes at the thought of losing both her brother and her husband to Thomas More's frenzied hatred. "Promise me you'll never do that again," she said. "Please."

He pulled her to him, kissed the top of her head. "I went down to Paternoster Row. I saw your print shop."

She looked up at him, genuinely interested, though she knew his ploy. He was trying to divert her. He had not promised. But she determined that if he went again, he would not go alone.

"It still has a sign, GOUGH'S BOOK AND PRINT SHOP. A bit rusted and in need of paint."

"Was anybody occupying it?"

"No. It had boards across the windows and doors. And a faded notice that said it had been sealed up because of the plague, with a crude drawing that was supposed to warn away those who can't read—that's what kept the vagrants out, I suppose. The notice bore Lord Walsh's seal. I recopied it and put a new date on it."

"But you didn't go inside." She had a sudden wash of longing to see the little shop and climb the stairs to her old room beneath the eaves.

"Of course I went inside. That's where I stayed while I was in London. I pried a board loose and went in through the window fronting the alley." He grinned at her. "I slept in your little bed, though it would have suited two better."

"How long were you there? Where else did you go?"

"I didn't stay in London long, just long enough to find out what I needed to know."

"And what was that?"

"That if the Boleyn woman ever opened Henry's mind as we thought, that window has closed. Last April he called together some of the clergy and they even discussed licensing an English Bible. Some, according to my sources at the inn I was telling you about, actually had the courage to argue for it, but More won the day. As long as More is chancellor, there will be no legal Bible," he said soberly. "And yet, the Bibles are everywhere, from Gravesend to Bristol, from the noblest castle to the meanest hovel. One day, not soon, but one day—it is a freedom the people mean to have."

"But how can they have it if the king doesn't allow it?"

"They have shown they are willing to risk everything for it. What can a pope, a king, or even an emperor do in the face of that? When the numbers become too large, they cannot but give in. Else there will be nobody left in England to pay the taxes and fund Henry's wars."

He sat down on their bed and pulled off his boots. "It's good to be home," he said, lying spread-eagled across the bed. "You haven't told me about your trip?"

But he had already closed his eyes.

"I met a lot of Catherine's friends. They were really—I'll tell you about it later," she said. "When you are not so weary."

⇝⇜

By virtue of his role as chancellor, Sir Thomas More was the only layman present at the Convocation of Clergy summoned by the king and since the purpose for the convocation ostensibly concerned the treasury, it was his reluctant duty to read the proclamation. They were all there: Archbishop Warham of Canterbury, Tunstall, the new Bishop of Durham, and Stokesley, his London replacement, along with a host of bishops, abbots, and priors, many of whom Thomas could call by name.

With a rustle of silk and a whispering of fine black wool, they took their places in the hall at Westminster, nodding heads covered with purple and black coifs and tippets lined with ermine, tight mouths murmuring behind ringed fingers. The atmosphere in the hall was heavy with their dignity and laden with the odor of rich perfumes, but it reminded Thomas of the air just before a storm. Wolsey's arrest had been for them the sound of thunder on the horizon.

They were waiting to see if the storm cloud had dissipated, and they had every right to believe that it was so. The cardinal, in spite of his arrest for conspiring with the pope against the king, had been laid out, upon his timely death a few short weeks ago, with the full dignity of his profession: miter, crosier, ring, pallium, and vestments. He had lain in state for all to see, his bier well lit by wax tapers while canons sang dirges. Though it was noised among the clergy that the king's whore had given a New Year's masque at court to honor "The Going to Hell of Cardinal Wolsey," still the fact that he had been buried with a cardinal's honor showed that the king was still in the pope's thrall.

It was Thomas's unfortunate task this day to disabuse them of that notion.

He stood at the front of the hall and waited as the murmurs ceased and all eyes turned toward him, then he announced with that efficiency for which he was known, that he was here to represent the Crown. A few murmured their displeasure that His Majesty chose not to honor them with his presence when they had traveled so far along winter-ravaged roads at his request. It was not a good omen and they knew it.

He picked up the papers from the table in front of him and, clearing his throat of the clot of resistance to his task, began to read the charges. Every eye was trained on him: every ear strained for every word. Thomas did not lift his voice. He never lifted his voice. It had long been his observation that the helpless shouted. Thomas had no need to shout.

Without emotion and in an even tone that did not suggest how much he abhorred the reading, he delivered the king's declaration. It charged that the pope's nitpicking delays concerning the king's marriage had raided the treasury of £100,000, and restitution would be exacted from these assembled English representatives of the Holy Roman Catholic Church. Every priest and prelate who had abetted the late cardinal's praemunire was likewise culpable to the cardinal's treason and therewith subject to imprisonment in the Tower and confiscation of property.

A collective intake of breath, an exchange of anxious glances, even a few utterances of outrage, but no one gave direct challenge. Cowards all, Thomas thought as he resumed the reading. Had he worn the miter and not the chain of office—toward which his father and his fleshly nature had driven him—he would not have remained silent in the face of such an outrage as did Archbishop Warham. There was none among them, save perhaps Bishop Fisher of Rochester, who had the backbone to stand firm. But even he remained silent in the face of such blackmail.

Thomas continued. If they should in their wisdom pay the sum of £100,000 to the treasury, then no further investigation or charges would be forthcoming. The Crown would be satisfied.

Thomas was not surprised to learn two days later that they had agreed to pay the king's extortion. Nor was he surprised when two weeks later Henry VIII, King of England, stood in front of Parliament and demanded he be recognized as the sole protector and supreme head of the English Church and clergy. This time Bishop Fisher of Rochester argued mightily. Thomas, feeling the weight of the great chain of office burning him like a brand, remained silent. *Qui tacet consentire videtur.* Thus with his silence Thomas gave consent to the destruction of his church in England.

That night he spent prostrate on his chapel floor at Chelsea with the blood from the welts on his back congealing, self-inflicted wounds to placate a disappointed Christ. But tomorrow, he would be strong. He would renew his efforts to seek out the real enemies to his church, those who sought the destruction of the Holy See. He would do that for the Christ he'd disappointed. As long as he lived—if he lived—he would hunt them down. Hunt them at home. Hunt them abroad. Thomas More, priest, would offer up the heretics as his atonement. The smell of the smoke would waft all the way to heaven.

THIRTY

*[Richard Bayfield] being both a priest and a monk . . .
fell to heresy and was abjured, and after that like a
dog returning to his vomit and being fled over the sea,
and sending from thence Tyndale's heresies hither
with many mischievous sorts of books . . . the monk
and apostate was well and worthily burned in Smithfield.*

—Sir Thomas More
on the burning of Richard Bayfield

For the next few months, through the long winter and much of the
next year, the little band of translators, fortified by the letters of support
John had brought back from England, worked diligently. The days and
nights fell into a quiet routine built around his work.

Kate and John moved into the English House at Tyndale's insistence, but
Kate refused to give up her Bible classes. The studio had not been rented, so
Catherine Massys agreed that the women should keep meeting there. Kate
was delighted that their number was growing and wanted to share that delight with John, but somehow she didn't think it wise to bring the subject up.
He had only reluctantly agreed to the meetings when Kate protested having
to move in with the Poyntzes. It simply was not safe to be anywhere else,
he'd said, not with more and more fugitives fleeing England. Sooner or later

they were bound to run into someone like Stephen Vaughan, known to be back in Antwerp, who recognized John or even Kate.

Vaughan claimed to be no longer an agent of the king, but they didn't fully trust him. He'd warned through an English merchant, with whom he'd established an uneasy friendship, that one of Tyndale's distributors had been seized in England. George Constantine had broken easily under More's weeks-long interrogation, giving out names of shipmen, printing houses, and the secret codes placed on the shipping crates of contraband freight. Vaughan claimed to be afraid for his own safety since Constantine had reportedly given his name as a sympathizer with the Antwerp refugees.

Even Tyndale went out less after being warned by the same merchant that the king had ordered Thomas Elyot, the new English ambassador to the imperial court, to seize the translator and bring him back to England. Tyndale had guarded his image carefully during the years he'd been in exile, but there were now many who would recognize him. He still ventured into the poorest sections of town to do his charity work, though less frequently. Sometimes John went with him, but Kate was never allowed.

Their discussions were many and lively over what this scripture might really mean in the strictest translation or whether the "poorest, unlearned plowman" in England might understand this word choice better than that word choice. On more than one occasion she bit back her opinions until she thought she would choke on them. She did not want to embarrass John. They were becoming more and more a closed society. She slipped quietly out on Friday mornings, hoping not to call attention to her leaving, lest they suddenly decide that her meetings posed too great a risk. They wouldn't even allow her to carry copy to and from the printer's, for fear she'd be followed.

When the days shortened, she began to dread the winter. She had less and less claim on John's time. But Kate could not honestly say that her husband neglected her. He was filled with energy, and even in the poor privacy of the English House, when their chamber door was barred he showered her with affection and certainly passion enough to make a child—to make a houseful of children. The fault must lie within her, she thought.

At first light he always slipped from their bed to begin work early. On those cold mornings she would entreat him to come back to bed. "William says we should begin early to save the cost of candles," he always reminded her. And then with a kiss upon her forehead, he said, "Go back to sleep, my angel." But she did not go back to sleep on some days. On Fridays and now on Tuesdays, she got up and dressed, slipping out through the chapel garden to go to the little studio apartment where the numbers of both women and children were growing. But she was ever mindful that she was not followed. John would never forgive her if she brought harm to his work or put his friend in danger.

Tidings from England grew ever more disturbing. With each new ship, frightened refugees brought stories of burnings. One of the victims especially weighed on her spirit. Richard Bayfield was a former Benedictine monk who had embraced reform and trafficked in both the Lutheran reformed materials and Tyndale's books. Like others before him, who had been forced to abjure, he had fled to the Continent. She remembered the first time she'd met him. It was the summer before, and he was in a jolly mood, having just run a successful cargo in through the east coast, through Colchester and down into London right under the nose of the chancellor's spies. He'd laughed and toasted the successful run with several merchants of the English House, and the translators had even abandoned their labors to join in the celebration. It seemed as though God truly smiled on their efforts.

But when Bayfield had come again in November he seemed a different man. This time the scene was somber. He'd come, he said, to report misfortune and failure. The ship had been seized at St. Katherine's docks just downriver from the Tower. He had escaped being captured by dumping the contraband Bibles in the estuary when he spotted the tidewaiters below the bridge. Having once recanted, he'd said with shame, they could burn him without trial upon a second offense. Tyndale had told him not to worry about the Bibles, quietly suggesting that the printer could replace them but not a good man and that More must have a spy somewhere close if he'd known the destination of the shipment. Perhaps Bayfield should take a respite.

But Bayfield had shaken his head and said, "No. No respite. I have to atone for . . . the other."

Kate knew what he meant, and she admired him for it. She thought of her brother and the sadness that had come upon him after he'd abjured. The shame she had felt for him. She wanted to remind Richard Bayfield that he need not, indeed could not, atone for his own sins. As a follower of Luther, surely he believed in the free forgiveness of sin through grace and not works. But she never got the chance to offer that comfort. At Easter, he'd been seized bringing contraband into Norfolk and summarily executed.

Three weeks later they got news of the burning of a London leather seller, by name of John Tewkesbury, for possession of Tyndale's books. From that day forward, such was her husband's anxiety for their well-being that she became a veritable prisoner in the English House.

"I might as well be in the Tower," she said angrily when he forbade her to go out.

"I don't think so, my angel." He looked up from his work. "Here you have a very sympathetic gaoler," he said, putting down his pen. "Come. We'll take a turn behind the walled garden."

"I do not wish to take a turn around the garden. I am not some child to be placated," she said. "I know, John, how important your work is. I know, too, how hazardous it is. And trust me. I will not speak of your work here."

"I do trust you, Kate. It's not that. I fear for your safety. It is only a matter of time until your activities are discovered and censured. Inquiries will be made. More's spies are everywhere."

"The other women know me only as Kate. They do not even know your name. If, as you say, there is risk, then it is to me alone, and I have chosen to accept it. It is little enough. It is not some great contribution as you and Tyndale are making, but it is my contribution." She thought of the woman in Leuven with the black eye, the Dora who would find a way. "I will do this, John. I will find a way. The women are counting on me."

She put on her cloak and threw up her hood against the late spring chill, and then she kissed him. "I love you, John Frith," she said. "Now, I am going to my meeting, and I will be back in time to sharpen your quills and refill your cider cup."

He did not try to stop her.

❧❦

Pleading heaviness in his chest, Sir Thomas More did not attend the king's Christmas revels, though he was sure his absence would be marked. He simply could not bear to see the Boleyn woman flaunting her influence before the court, nor could he bear the sight of smug Thomas Cromwell, growing fat on the king's favor. He spent those nights instead closeted with his latest guest in the porter's lodge—happier progress there. After the "tree of troth" and a few days in the stocks had softened his resolve, the prisoner Constantine had leaked information like a rusty bucket. Tonight the chancellor had instructed the porter to allow his escape. A rodent scurrying to his vermin's nest, he would be followed as he made his way back to Antwerp.

"You say Master Constantine has gone over the wall?"

The porter grinned. "Aye, my lord, I fear I was negligent."

"Well done, Barnabas. But we'd best mend the stocks, and lock up well. Our prisoner might want back in," Sir Thomas joked. Then his tone shifted. "We'll need the lodge readily enough. We're entertaining a barrister of the Middle Temple tonight, by name of Bainham. Methinks lawyer Bainham wants instruction in the ways of the true faith. It is not near so broad as he would have it be. He has written that 'if a Jew, Turk, or Saracen do trust in God, then he is a good Christian man.' Can you imagine that, Barnabas? A good Christian who would pray with Jews and Turks and Saracens!"

Barnabas shook his head in disbelief. "Is he to be persuaded with argument first, my lord, or interrogation?" he asked.

"Argument and prayer. We may be able to save his soul without harming his body. But he has gone far to the other side, I fear. He questions the truth of the Eucharist." He groped within the deep pocket of his voluminous robe and held out a rolled document. "Here is a writ for his arrest. Tell the sergeant at arms if he cannot find him in chambers at the Middle Temple, to look in the bed of his new wife."

"He is newly married then?" The porter's expression of dismay suggested that his enthusiasm for the interrogation was waning.

"Hold to the faith, man. The fact that he is newly married counts for naught. Don't waste your sympathy. His new bride is not some sweet innocent learning the pleasures of love from her new husband. She is the widow of a notorious heretic, a writer of materials almost as injurious to Holy Church as Tyndale's own."

The porter took the writ and Sir Thomas turned back toward the main house. "I shall be in my study. Call me when our guest arrives. No matter the hour."

But when he entered his hall, Sir Thomas went to his study only long enough to retrieve the little knotted rope from its resting place. Then he turned toward the chapel. It was long after midnight by the time he lit the lamps in his study and began to write.

❧

The next morning, Meg Roper knocked tentatively at her father's study door.

"Who is it?" The voice was sharp, impatient. Its unfamiliar tenor made her think at first that some other man sat at her father's desk.

"It's Margaret, Father. I've brought your shirts."

"Come in," he said. Then nodding at the bundle she carried, "Put it on that chair beneath the window. There are two more wadded up beneath the stool."

She retrieved the soiled shirts, noticing that one of them was still damp with sweat and stiffened blood, noticing, too, how thin he had become and how gray his hair and skin, as though all were of one color. She lingered, not knowing how to begin, hoping he would invite her to stay. He did not, but turned his attention to the polemic he was writing. She could tell by the furious way his hand moved the pen, the scowl on his brow, that it was another of the hate-filled answers to one of Luther's or Tyndale's works. Why did these men have to carry on such a public argument? Why couldn't they exchange their vitriol in private and spare other souls the pain of listening?

He was so absorbed he didn't appear to be aware that she was still there, until he mumbled pointedly, without looking up, "Was there something else, Margaret?"

"One of the shirts, Father. There was so much blood, I couldn't wash it clean. Was that all your blood?"

He put down his pen then and looked up at her, sighing. "Well, whose else would it be?"

"But it was spattered so—"

"You understand the ritual of the mortification of the flesh. We've talked about this before. You know why I do it," he said, scolding in the same tone he'd used when as a child she'd been negligent in translating her Virgil.

Verily they had discussed it. And she did understand, but not really. The Church had condemned the practice of self-flagellation, though some of the monks still practiced it in secret. When she'd first asked him why he did it in face of the Church's teachings against it, he explained that it was a sound doctrine and that the Church had come out against only the public display of the practice. Monks and priests had been parading through towns, whipping up the crowds as they whipped themselves. They created spectacle— spectacle that attracted criticism. Some of the flagellants were even selling their own bloody garments to superstitious peasants as miracle cloths.

Her father had laughed when he said that, and added he hoped she didn't have intentions of selling bloody pieces of his shirt. He wanted to keep his devotion private. That's why he didn't use the Chelsea laundress. Margaret had not minded. She'd been laundering his bloodstained shirts for years. But never had they been so bloody. This was no token ritual.

"Why would you ask such a question, Margaret? If it's all my blood? Have you been listening to devilish rumors?"

"I just worry about you. As the blood on your shirts increases . . . your joy seems to be seeping out."

He smiled weakly. A smile that if it was meant to reassure fell short. "There will be time for joy later. When the hard work of the Church is done."

"The Church! You are chancellor, Father, not archbishop."

"Don't be impertinent to your father, Margaret. It is a sin. But my duties as chancellor are not unlike the duties of archbishop. The state cannot exist without the Church. What is good for the Church is likewise good for the Crown." His voice dropped off here, as though he was distracted by some unpleasant thought.

"I'm sorry. I did not mean any disrespect. It's just that there are rumors . . . that perhaps you are . . . too zealous in holy matters. More zealous than the law allows."

His voice hardened. "You would presume to instruct me in the law, daughter? I have taught you more law than manners, apparently."

She felt her skin grow hot beneath his withering glance. They were suddenly not father and daughter but adversaries. His eyes were cold, his voice controlled, completely devoid of that warmth and merriment she usually saw when they were together. It occurred to her, but only briefly, to think how she would hate to face such a prosecutor.

"Of course I would not . . . it's just that . . . William says—"

"Ah, William says." The look he gave her was so fierce it almost took her breath away. "What else does son-in-law Roper say? The man whose false theology I have allowed to infect my own household simply out of love for my daughter—tell me, daughter, what else does William say? How ill does he repay me?"

Meg clutched the bloody shirts to her bosom, unaware that one had left a stain upon the pale blue silk of her bodice, unaware of anything except the shame and remorse she felt for causing her father pain.

"Nothing, Father. William has nothing but the highest praise for you. He is very proud of you, as are we all."

He paused and looked out the window of his study where the season's first snowfall was beginning to cover the ugly, scarred earth of a killer frost.

"Winter is come again," he said as though that fact surprised him.

"Aye, Father. It is," she said, relieved that the subject was ended. Nothing had changed; she had not persuaded him, but she had kept her promise.

"You will need a new cloak," he said. "The chancellor's daughters should be arrayed as befits their station."

"You are very generous," she said, thinking, how could the rumors be anything but false? He was a loving father and a just man. Was not his tolerance of William's reform tendencies proof of that tolerance?

"Would you allow me to put a soothing ointment on your back?"

He laughed at that. "Well, that would somewhat undercut the act of atonement, wouldn't it?" It was good to hear his laughter. She was trying to remember the last time she'd heard him laugh, when they were interrupted by the porter's sudden appearance at the door.

"Your guest has arrived, Sir Thomas," he said.

"I'll be right there." Thomas answered, leaping up from his chair. She watched in amazement as he hurried after the porter with all the energy of a youth.

❧

Barrister James Bainham proved not to be easily persuaded. Kate watched the stunned expressions on the faces of the translators as the merchant informers told how he had been subjected to More's tree of troth, then racked until his body was crippled and ruined, and yet he had not recanted. But the news that his new wife had been thrown into the Fleet for not producing the Tyndale books when their house was searched, accomplished what his physical torture could not. He abjured.

Kate remembered her brother, how he had recanted for the sake of his wife and child. *Would John do as much for me?* she wondered. *Would I want him to?* The merchants and translators and some of the refugees—the few who could be trusted—were holding weekly prayer meetings now for the sufferers back in England. Praying that she would never be faced with such a choice, Kate thanked God that John was not in England.

THIRTY-ONE

By March, Kate was sure that she was pregnant. The first morning she was sick, she laid it to the venison she'd had the night before—she'd thought she'd detected a gamey smell beneath the heavy spices the cook sometimes used to salvage what was marginally salvageable. John had left their warm bed in the emerging dawn to go down to the scriptorium, as they jokingly called the cluttered section of the hall that Mistress Poyntz tried to hide behind a screen. Kate was struggling to lace her bodice when without warning the nausea overwhelmed her. Before she could grab the chamber pot from beneath the bed, she splattered the offending venison onto the rush-strewn floorboards. She lay back on the bed until the nausea passed, then cleaned up the mess and went downstairs to see if John needed her.

For the next few days she was able to stomach only stale crackers and weak cider. John had at first made a little joke about her sudden fondness for communion wafers, and then he'd started to worry. Kate ameliorated his concern by telling him that married life was making her plump, and so she thought that if she ate less, she might not lose her figure. Whereupon he'd slipped his arm around her waist and told her he'd love her if she grew as fat as the baker's wife.

By the time the thawing earth had birthed the first snowdrop, Kate no longer blamed the venison. At first she dared not hope and didn't share her good news with anyone, not even the women in her study group—but more than once, John had come upon her daydreaming and commented that she seemed far away. "Just thinking how lucky I am to have such a talented husband," she would say, or, "I'm dreaming of the coming spring." This seemed to satisfy John, who would go back to writing his own work.

He'd been working on the polemic for days, whenever he was not reading copy for Tyndale or translating passages. In it he argued that the doctrine of Purgatory was a recent construct of the Church, with no basis in Scripture, and that the bread and wine of the Eucharist were merely symbolic of the body of Christ. Kate understood the argument against Purgatory; it was the scaffolding on which the sale of indulgences was based, the means by which the common people were exploited and enslaved by a corrupt Church hierarchy. She didn't, however, understand her husband's insistence on spending so much time on the symbolism of the Eucharist. Even the Bible men, or "new men" as some called them, could not agree on the doctrine of transubstantiation. What did it matter if the participant thought the wine really turned into blood, as long as he thought he was taking into his body the spirit of Christ in an act of obedience? But John was utterly devoted to developing the fullest argument possible against the Real Presence of Christ's body and blood in the bread and wine of the Eucharist. He already had enough to fill two volumes, and he was still writing.

The masculine environment of the merchant boardinghouse was not a proper home for a new baby, she decided one day as the translators argued good-naturedly. The child needed a proper home. How to tell John? Unlike her, he loved the environment of the English House. But then he'd been trained at Cambridge and Oxford. The close living of the dormitory brotherhood suited him. Indeed, she feared that the news of the coming child might not be wholly welcomed by its theologian-turned-husband-about-to-turn-father. With the passing months, he'd seemed more relieved than bothered by their childlessness, laying it to God's will each time she brought it up. Well, now that this child was an accomplished fact, and one he'd taken an active role in accomplishing, she would just remind him that this was also God's will.

By May, she was certain enough that she began to clumsily stitch crib clothes, and confided in Mistress Poyntz, beseeching her to purchase suitable fabrics. When Mistress Poyntz returned from the market, she summoned Kate to her room and laid the soft linen for swaddling cloths out on the bed.

"I couldn't resist this," Mistress Poyntz said, and it was almost as if she read Kate's mind. "No, you will not pay for this. This is a gift."

Kate fingered the silk and lace of a tiny little bonnet with disbelief. It had been three months—two weeks past the time when she had lost the other child. It was going to happen; they were going to have a child. The tears welled in her eyes and spilled over, running down her cheek. She sniffed and brushed them away.

"You have to tell him, you know," Mistress Poyntz said, reaching for her hand.

"I know," Kate said between sniffs. "I was just waiting until—"

"Until you were sure you wouldn't lose this one. But you can't really ever be sure of that, my dear, not until you are holding the child, and he is tugging at your nipple like a hungry little savage."

"I'll tell him," Kate said. "When the time is right, I'll tell him."

❧

It was the last straw, Sir Thomas thought, as he strode from Parliament House down to the Westminster Stairs to hail his boatman. The session had ended and he had lost. Cromwell and the king had won it all. Parliament had made Henry the sole power in England, stripping the bishops of everything—even the power to arrest heretics. That, too, now rested with the king. If Chancellor More wanted someone arrested for heresy, he must go through Cromwell and not Bishop Stokesley. Hah! That was a fool's errand.

A commission was to be formed of half lay men and half clerics who would decide all Church matters, including cases of heresy. With Cromwell's Lutheran sympathies and the Boleyn woman pushing the king for leniency, there was little likelihood of maintaining recent progress. Thomas More's campaign for the protection of the one true Church had stumbled badly.

By arguing for the bishops, who were too craven to plead their own cause, and against Henry, he had risked everything. He had already lost the king's favor over the great matter of his divorce. Now with this failed parliamentary campaign in favor of the bishops' maintaining their power and privileges, he had incurred the king's wrath. But so be it. Thomas More had been true to that which mattered to him most in the world. There would be no coward's stain on his honor. Consequences be damned.

He had to call the boatman twice. "Richard!" Sharply the second time, accompanied by a swat on the shoulder from a rolled-up writ.

The boatman, who was sleeping on a bench beside the stair, jumped up. "Begging your pardon, my lord. I had not expected you so soon."

"My business here is finished," Sir Thomas said curtly. "Take me home."

If the boatman heard any finality in his voice, he did not voice it.

As the boatman rowed silently up the sun-dappled Thames toward Chelsea, Sir Thomas did not notice the perfume of apple blossoms in the air or feel the warm breeze against his skin. In his heart it was still winter. He plotted his next move in his own great matter, and he was glad his father was not alive to see it.

⌁

"I am sorry it has come to this, Thomas," the king said two days later, after the clergy had acquiesced in Convocation. (They had little choice given their craven natures, Thomas thought. Cowards all—except Bishop Fisher, who alone had stood with Thomas against the tide. Even Stokesley was strangely silent.)

Thomas found the king in the garden at York Place, playing with the dogs beneath a shower of pink petals. Wordlessly, Thomas handed him the white kid bag containing the chancellor's seal and chain of office. Judging from the laboring of Henry's breath, His Majesty's body was overheated from the exercise, but his voice was chilly.

"I had thought, by appointing a layman chancellor, to avoid such adversarial circumstances," he said, falling heavily onto a bench beneath a canopy of blossoms. He indicated that Thomas should sit beside him.

"It is my health, Your Majesty, which as you know has not been good since my father died. I cannot under such circumstances serve Your Majesty as Your Majesty deserves."

Henry laughed, but Thomas knew that laugh. He'd heard it when he refused to sign the king's petition to the pope. It was a laugh that carried no mirth.

"Pretty words. You are a complicated man, Thomas," Henry said, accepting the bag, then flinging it on the bench between them as though it were a small thing and not the symbol of the second-most powerful man in the realm. One of the great mastiffs came up to him, and he scratched it behind its ears. The dog stood at attention.

Thomas said nothing. When no persuasive argument could be made in one's defense, saying nothing was the least objectionable option.

"I miscalculated in making you chancellor, Master More. I had grown exceedingly weary of stumbling over clergy, always at my head and foot and side, whichever way I turned. I thought with your appointment to be rid of this unceasing intrusion into affairs of state." He sighed, exhaling such a great breath the dog's hind leg quivered. "But now I see that you have more clergy in you than any archbishop I know."

He stopped scratching the dog's ear. The dog sat obediently at his master's foot, so quietly he might have been carved in stone. His companion, a bitch with skin the color of smooth ale, lay some few feet away, watching, her ears peaked as if waiting for a signal.

Even the dogs will not challenge his discipline, Thomas thought. *You have not as much sense as they do.*

"It is my health, Your Majesty, only my health, which prompts me to surrender the seal. I simply wish to retire in peace," he said quietly.

"And I wish to abdicate the throne and move to France to be a bootblack to Francis I," Henry said just as quietly, each word heavy with sarcasm and threat.

Then the king stood up and, whistling to his dogs to follow, strode back into York Place, leaving Thomas alone on the garden bench with the white kid bag holding the abandoned symbol of power.

※

"You *are* getting fat as the baker's wife." John laughed as he patted his wife's gently protruding stomach beneath the light linen of her summer shift. "But I'm glad the sickness has passed. I like seeing you eat again," he said.

After she'd told him her news, he'd gone down to the kitchen to pilfer a bit of dried apple and cheese and bread—"and buttermilk if there is any, please." He'd come back with it all, the buttermilk too, and now they had it spread out between them on the bed in a midnight picnic. He watched her now as she munched.

"What are you looking at, John Frith? Haven't you ever seen a woman eat before?"

"Not like this," he said, laughing as he reached up and wiped the milk mustache from her upper lip, then licked his finger clean.

She leaned across the spread of food between them and kissed him. "I love you, husband," she said.

"You say that now," he said, nibbling a slice of dried apple, then offering her the other half. "But when the child comes, you'll only have eyes for him . . . or her."

"Well, I won't, but if I did you'd hardly notice. You have your work and your friendship with William and Chaplain Rogers and the gang of merchants that promote your cause."

"Our cause," he corrected her. "And I will notice."

"I was afraid you wouldn't want the baby," she said, abandoning her food lust, suddenly hungry for reassurance. "That's why I waited so long to tell you." She watched him carefully, alert for the flickering glance, the lowered eyelid. She would know if he lied to her to protect her feelings.

His gaze did not waver. "I want only what you want," he said. "And I will try with all my heart to be a good father."

That was a good enough answer, but somehow, unlike the victuals of the midnight picnic, it left her vaguely unsatisfied.

≈

She was in her fifth month when he told her he was leaving to go back to England. It was mid-July and hot at midday. John had taken to walking with her in the shade of the garden each day, at first so careful and solicitous of her that she felt cramped until she reassured him that this time would be different.

The roses were in bloom and there was a turf bench beneath a plane tree. "Let's linger here a minute before we go back in," he said. "Tyndale is out on one of his charity runs, and Purgatory can wait."

He spread his handkerchief so she would not get grass stains on her skirt and held her hand as they sat side by side on the grassy bench.

"I felt the baby kick this morning," she said. "It was the strangest thing, a little like a butterfly flutter. My heart fluttered with it."

"How do you know it wasn't just bilious humors from all the strange foods you've been eating lately? You said you didn't like pickled herring, and last night you ate your portion and half mine."

"Your half went to the baby. Apparently he—or she—likes pickled herring. You don't begrudge it, do you?"

He laughed. "I can begrudge you nothing. You could have taken it all—you know that."

"There! It's happening again. Feel it?" She placed his hand on the place where she felt the fluttering. It stopped abruptly.

"He doesn't like me."

"Of course she likes you. You are her father."

"I didn't like my father. I thought he was an ogre."

"But you are not an ogre."

"Neither was my father."

"Daughters always like their fathers."

"How do you know it will be a girl?"

"I don't," she said. "Does it matter to you?"

"Only if it matters to you."

That answer she also found unsatisfying—as if his only interest in the child were secondary.

"Can I get you something to drink? Or more pickled herring?"

She smiled. "No, we are prepared," and she reached into the pocket of her skirt and brought forth a new apple. "It's a bit tart, but refreshing." She held it out to him.

"Of course, Eve, I'll take a bite of your apple," he said, then grimaced as he crunched down on the sour apple.

She laughed. "I expect Eve's were sweeter," she said, "but mine bear no curse. It seems our child has a taste for sourness. Last week it was sweet. I sucked honey from the comb as wildly as John the Baptist."

The noonday sun pressed the roses into releasing their fragrance. Kate inhaled, *smell that, little one*, as she spoke wordlessly to the child in her womb. This was a moment of perfect joy, she thought, if only she could keep it forever. John was unusually quiet as she reached over and kissed him lightly on the cheek.

"Kate, I have something to tell you," he said. "And I don't want you to get upset. It won't be good for the baby."

The perfect moment was gone as quickly as it came. The apple tasted bitter in her mouth. The roses wilted in the heat.

"There has been another burning," she said. "No. Don't tell me. I do not want our child to hear such words." She could not bear to hear them either. Ten men had been burned since Thomas More was named chancellor. Each telling had made her heart clutch with fear. Each telling had prompted smoke-filled dreams that startled her awake in the dark of the night.

"No. It's nothing like that! Indeed, it looks as though things may be turning for the better. Parliament has stripped the English clergy of its connection to Rome and placed it under the jurisdiction of the king. The best news is that Thomas More has resigned the chancellorship in protest. Also, the bishops no longer have the power of arrest and interrogation in matters of heresy. That now belongs to Henry."

"You mean he is both king and pope?"

"Something like that."

"Well then, that should make him happy. He can grant his own divorce. Though I can't believe the bishops went along with that. Even the Archbishop of Canterbury?"

"Warham is in very ill health. They say Cranmer is being groomed for the post. He is one of the Boleyn faction—very reform minded."

"But that is wonderful news! Why should I be upset?"

He reached for her other hand so that he was holding them both. "Since things are improving, Tyndale and I think it might be time for me to make another effort. I'm going back to England. Just a quick trip. I'll be back well before the birthing. If I can get to the king or Thomas Cranmer or even Cromwell, I'm sure I can convince them to extend this new atmosphere of tolerance to letting the Bible be licensed in England."

Snatching her hand away, she jumped up from the bench, her precious burden momentarily forgotten in the heat of her anger. "No. I will not hear it! You will not go! Is Thomas More dead? Is that new Bishop of London—Stokesley—that you said was more dangerous than Tunstall, is he dead?"

"No," he answered quietly. "They are both very much alive. But both are in disfavor. Their influence has been severely curtailed."

His carefully modulated tone infuriated her, as though he were explaining a concept any simpleton should understand. She turned on him then. "You are a fool, John."

He looked at her as though he couldn't believe his usually even-tempered wife had turned into an obstreperous shrew.

"Calm yourself, Kate. It's not good for the baby."

"As long as Thomas More draws breath, you and your friends will be hunted down and given no more consideration than a hound gives its prey. There are many in England who cling violently to the old faith. You and everything you represent are anathema to them. Let William go if he thinks it is so necessary."

"Shh, Kate. Lower your voice. The whole of Antwerp doesn't need to hear our discourse. Tyndale cannot go. He is a bigger prize than any of us."

"And you're expendable, is that it? Does William Tyndale have a wife? Does he have a child?"

The heat in the garden suddenly became unbearable and rose up from the ground in shimmering waves. Kate struggled to get her breath. She felt her knees go weak. John caught her as she fell.

When she came to herself, she lay on the turf bench, and he was on his knees beside her, bathing her brow with a cool rag. She tried to sit up, but her head was still swimming. Mistress Poyntz was there as well. "The baby . . ." Kate murmured, "is the baby—"

"The baby is fine, my dear. You just swooned in the heat."

John's face hovered over her. "Everything will be well, Kate. I will not go if you don't want me to. I promise," he whispered. But the misery in his face reminded her of the way her brother John had looked when he told her he'd abjured. She knew that in the end, it was not her decision because she could not bear to see that look on his face every day of her life.

THIRTY-TWO

She is of middling stature, with a swarthy complex-
ion, long neck, wide mouth, bosom not much raised,
and in fact has nothing but the king's great appetite,
and her eyes which are black and beautiful . . . She
lives like a queen and the king accompanies her to
mass and everywhere.
—DESCRIPTION OF ANNE BOLEYN
WRITTEN BY THE VENETIAN AMBASSADOR (1532)

t is a noble sacrifice you are making, Kate," Tyndale said as they watched the boat sail out of the harbor.

John was waving at her from the deck, and she was frantically waving back, trying to keep from crying out to him to come back. No. It was a mistake. All a mistake. She needed him. Their child needed him. She should never have agreed to let him go.

"He would not have gone if you had naysayed it. I am sure of it. You are the joy of his life. Try to be of good heart. He will take no foolish chances and will be back before his child is born."

He was the only joy in my life, and now he is gone, she thought, as she watched the ship sail out of sight until she could no longer see John's waving figure, wishing that she had Tyndale's certainty, wishing she, like Endor, could see the future in water. She stared into the murky green liquid of the harbor, but all she saw among the floating bits of debris was the rippling reflection of a fat woman standing beside an old man. For a moment she was startled, not recognizing the reflected silhouettes.

"I wish John had your gift for disguise," she said, noticing the slump of Tyndale's shoulders, the general weariness in his posture, the powdered gray streak in his hair. "You could probably go right up and knock on Thomas More's door, and he would not know you." She hoped her words did not betray the resentment she felt in her heart.

"He wouldn't know me. He has never seen me."

"Then why does he hate you so?"

"You know the answer to that." He smiled at her kindly. "It was part of your argument against John's going. Everything we believe in, our very existence, the way we question the Church's received wisdom, received from powerful men and not from God—there is only one revelation of God, and it's not a man sitting on a throne in Rome but a book of ancient Scriptures interpreted by every man as the Spirit of God leads him—that belief is anathema to Thomas More and all those who uphold the 'whited sepulcher' that the Roman Church has become. They cannot suffer that belief to live—or those of us who teach it—" He broke off with a sigh and, putting his arm around her, said, "What you need to hear from me right now is that when we said that someone should make a return trip, I did offer to go. It was John who insisted that he should be the one."

That did not make Kate feel better. "We'd best get back," she said. "You to your work and I to . . . my worrying."

"John told me about the women's Bible study," he said. "I think it's a wonderful thing you're doing. I understand. But it is not without risk."

"Don't let that trouble you," she said, feeling the words in her mouth dry as wool. "I've given it up. For the safety of my child. It's no longer just me."

He patted her shoulder in a gesture of comfort. She was not comforted.

She was even less comforted later that night when she was tidying John's desk, and found stuck within the pages of his *Disputation on Purgatory* the carefully forged papers that would have established his identity as a Hansa merchant. She prayed fervently that he would notice they were missing before he was called upon to produce them.

❧

So far so good, John Frith thought as he disembarked without challenge on the Essex coast and hailed a small cargo packet to ferry him to Reading. His first mission was to visit the prior at Reading Abbey who over the years had acted as a conduit for funds and information, both of which the Antwerp contingent needed badly right now. The translators had sold their winter coats to pay the printer for the last printing, counting on this trip to replenish both their funds and their wardrobes.

He could get a bath at the abbey and a shave, God willing, he thought as he wiped the sweat from his brow and scratched at his ragged beard. He had purposely let it grow as a disguise against the spies and Channel watchers that dotted the coast. Maybe the prior would tell him that the wind now blew so fair in England that a disguise was rendered unnecessary.

The approach to Reading reminded him of the first time he'd seen Kate. It was in one of these cottages scattered throughout the English towns where the Word was read and the cottagers risked everything to support the reform movement. It had been hot that day too, but she'd been dressed in a man's heavy cloak and breeches. Yet even then, even thinking she was a man and he being so ill from the ordeal of the fish cellar, he remembered finding her oddly attractive.

They'd laughed about that later, after she'd told him shamefacedly that her brother had abjured and she was determined to take his place smuggling the books. He'd made a joke about it, saying he'd wondered at the time if he was like so many of the monks who sought forbidden alliances to assuage their sexual hunger. Though he hadn't thought that; he'd been too weak to care, and besides he knew his nature. He'd joked about it only to take away the shame she felt for her brother's recanting.

He hoped fervently that he would never bring her such shame. But how did a man know if he had what it took to withstand torture and maintain honor—especially when he had a wife and child to consider? That was the same decision her brother had faced, poor man. John suddenly felt a kindred spirit with him. If his travels led him near Gloucestershire he would call on him to see how he fared.

By the time they reached Reading, the better part of the river was in evening shade. He watched idly as the packet pulled up to the dock to let him disembark. A knot of men were quarreling on the dock.

"I'd stay clear of that lot if I was you," the boatman said.

"I'll heed that advice, my good waterman," John said, picking his way among the hogsheads stacked in the middle of the boat. He reached in the small purse tied at his belt and tipped the man with his last coin.

"I'm not the sort to take a man's last farthing," the boatman said, eyeing his empty purse. "You'll be needing that for your supper, I expect."

"I'll get supper at the abbey. I have friends there," he said, pressing the coin into the boatman's rough hand.

The ruffians on the dock had stopped arguing and started exchanging blows.

"Somebody ought to call the town constable."

"I think somebody already has," John said, nodding at the two men who approached the thugs with drawn short swords.

By the time John strode across the jetty, the drunks were already shackled together with their arms bound behind them. They would probably spend the night locked up in the magistrate's cellar, he thought, for drunken disturbance, no worse for wear in the morning than a bad headache and some angry wives.

"Hey! You there, halt."

John looked around to see who they were talking to. He was alone on the dock. The boatman had already pulled away. Maybe if he pretended not to hear, just kept walking. They probably wanted him for a witness.

"Halt in the name of the law!"

Sighing, John stopped, put down his small valise and turned to look at them. One of the drunken louts was grinning stupidly. Adversity loves company, he thought.

"Did you wish to speak with me? I only just arrived as you did. I assure you I know nothing of this affair."

"You look like a stranger. I don't recollect seeing you in this shire."

"I'm a friend of the abbey."

"Well, pardon me for saying so, but you don't look like a friend of the abbey. The prior's friends are usually more elegantly turned out."

"I've come a long way. I'm a merchant. A Hansa merchant attached to the London Steelyard."

This seemed not to impress his inquisitors. "Here, I have papers to prove it." He pointed to the valise at his feet. "If I may?"

The constable nodded and John reached into the small bag, searching through his soiled linen—he'd brought only the barest essentials so that he could travel easily—even looking inside the pages of his Homer. Nothing. He shook the book of Homer's poems, but the only thing that fell out was one of Kate's hair ribands that he used to mark the page.

Then he remembered.

He'd stuck the forged credentials inside his *Disputation of Purgatory*, thinking he could work on it, then wisely deciding that if he were searched it would be damning evidence. He'd left the credentials behind with the book.

The grinning lout had found his tongue. "If he's a friend of the prior, I'm a fat whore's keeper," he said in a slur of words.

"You are a fat whore's keeper," one of the rogues responded with a snigger. "I've had your wife."

"You whoreson, I'll cut off your cock and feed it to the crows before your very eyes, I'll—"

"You'll shut your filthy mouth before I shut it for good," the constable responded, giving weight to his words with a poke of his sword. Then he nodded at John. "Bring this one in too. The magistrate's already going to be mad at being pulled from his supper. Might as well give him a vagrant to plump his warrants."

"If you'll just send to the abbey—" John said, becoming really alarmed now.

"Do I look like a messenger boy?" the constable grumbled. "Tell it to the magistrate."

"Yesh, tell it to the magishtrate," the drunkest of the rogues mocked.

John hoped the magistrate was more reasonable than the constable. This did not augur a good beginning to his travels, he thought as he trudged up the hill with his stomach growling and not a farthing to his name.

⁓⁂⁓

"No. I think it should be the crimson. Definitely the crimson if I am to become a fallen woman," Anne Boleyn said to the trusted servant who had accompanied her to Windsor. The old woman had been with her since childhood. Anne had left Lady Margaret and the simpering Jane Seymour behind at Hampton Court. This was not a night she wanted either of them around.

She handed the green sleeves back to the maid, along with an underskirt of green satin. "Sleeves of crimson velvet to match the velvet kirtle. And an underskirt of scarlet silk, girdled with a rope of twisted gold and crimson, I think."

I will come to him in shades of red, she thought, *to heat his blood the more.* "And the black heart-shaped coif, studded with rubies. And a single ruby at my throat."

"A very wise choice. The king will be unable to resist you, my lady. The crimson will bring out your eyes. Shall I dress your hair?"

The old woman's smile was conspiratorial, and it warmed Anne's heart on what was to be the most important night of her life. For tonight she was going to be made a peer of the realm, Marquess of Pembroke, with her own lands and rights, not dependent on her father's less than worthy merchant background or her Howard relations. By using the male form of the title, Henry was bestowing on her an honor never before accorded to a woman in her own right. That could only mean one thing. By giving her the title, he was making her worthy to be his queen. The king had made up his mind at last.

And Anne had made up hers. With the power Parliament had given the king, Cranmer now Archbishop of Canterbury, and Cromwell on her side, everything was in place.

Almost.

If Henry wanted one thing more than he wanted her, he wanted an heir. She needed to be pregnant with his child by Christmas.

"No. I will let my hair fall free this one last time, to remind him I am still a maid." *Technically, at least,* she thought. Her maidenhead was still intact, though with Percy she would surely have lost it had not Wolsey interrupted them in the queen's closet.

"Prepare a bath with scented oils from France. There is a blue vial in my garderobe. It is the king's favorite."

Two hours later, when the bathing and dressing was finished and Anne stood in front of her pier glass, she smiled with satisfaction. It was a bold choice. The crimson dress did, indeed, accentuate her eyes, and her hair gleamed darkly against the rich velvet of her sleeves. She might be no blond beauty by court standards, but as she practiced the nuanced glance and flirtatious smile, even beckoning toward the figure in the pier glass as she would later beckon the king to her bed, she felt a sense of power.

"I am ready," she said. "Summon the footman to take this message to the king," she said, careful as she sat down at the writing table not to muss her skirts.

The message simply read, "Your Majesty, I await your pleasure," and was signed "Humbly, Anne."

When the king appeared in person at her chamber door to escort her to the Presence Room, the expression on his face confirmed her choice. But when he leaned forward to kiss the tops of her "little maidens," as he so fondly called them, she gently protested. "Time enough for that, Your Majesty. First we must attend to the business of the evening."

He held her out at arm's length, and looked at her as though he could satisfy his lust with his eyes. "My lady, you are certainly a witch, and you have enchanted a king."

Her laughter echoed down the hall as she walked with him to the Presence Room where she would be announced for the first time as the Marquess of Pembroke. She wondered if any of her enemies would be there to witness her singular honor.

⚜

When Anne led the king to her bedchamber later that night, the room smelled fresh and sweet. The window was open to the warm night air. The only sounds came from the whispered conversation between a passing breeze and the great oaks outside her window. The room glowed with candlelight, and rose petals had been scattered among the rushes and on the counterpane.

Henry smiled when he saw it.

Anne began to undress, removing her coif and tossing her head to better let the candle glow highlight her tresses.

"Shall I summon your maid?" he asked.

"No need, my lord. I'm sure Your Majesty can be relied upon to give any assistance necessary."

She peeled the sleeves away and then, untying her kirtle, stepped out of it. Taking his hand, she directed it to her bodice. His hands moved expertly among the laces until she stood clothed only in the diaphanous silk of her low-cut chemise. This time when he kissed her breast, she made no protest. His tongue was moist and warm against her skin. A fleeting thought of Percy crossed her mind, but she pushed it as quickly away, thinking it treaded on the fringe of treason to think of another man when making love to the king.

"Shall I summon my gentleman of the bedchamber to assist me?" he asked, removing his hat. His voice was husky with desire.

"No need, my lord. I shall undress you."

She lifted the gold chain from around his neck carefully.

With considerably less ceremony he shrugged off his brocade doublet. "There is no reason to hurry, my lord," she said, her voice breathy and low. She untied his breeches and then unfastened his codpiece, letting her fingers linger teasingly.

"Your Majesty is very . . . majestic," she said.

When he was stripped to his braies and garters, she lifted her shift over her head and stood before him clad only in her unbound hair and the ruby necklace. She had a moment of unease. He had never seen her naked before. Indeed, no man had ever seen her naked, not even Percy. Her breasts were too small, she feared, though he had often complained of the queen's.

"Is Your Majesty pleased?" she asked in a very small voice.

The room seemed suddenly very quiet. Even the oaks outside her window paused in their windy chatter.

But she needed no words to tell her His Majesty was pleased.

THIRTY-THREE

*Sing, O Muse, the vengeance deep and deadly; whence
to Greece unnumbered ills arose, which many a soul of
mighty warrior to the viewless shades untimely sent.*
—LINES FROM *THE ILIAD* QUOTED
BY JOHN FRITH WHILE IN READING GAOL

John Frith recognized the smell. He'd been there before. That foul odor of stale sweat and urine was coming from him. Yet it was nothing compared to the fish cellar, he thought ruefully. At least the stocks were in the open air. The rogues arrested with him had been released after being fined ten pence, which no doubt went into the pocket of the magistrate. But John had not the ten pence to pay the fine if it had been offered.

He spent his first night in Reading slumped in the stocks, scheming between intermittent bouts of sleep how best to deal with this circumstance. When the morning fog rolled in so thick it seeped into his skin and clotted in his nostrils, he shivered until his teeth chattered. But by midday the sun had burned off the fog, and he could feel the warmth beating down on his head and the back of his neck.

He kept his eyes closed most of the time, preferring the visions he conjured in his head to looking at his feet and the brown spot of tramped-down earth, the only things within his field of vision. Some tricks he'd learned in the fish cellar were helpful now. He created and then catalogued inside his mind pleasant images of his wife: Strong Kate, waving bravely from the harbor, blinking so he would not see her tears when he kissed her good-bye; Determined Kate, squinting over her needle as she sewed for the new baby, swearing under her breath as she ripped out an untrue stitch; Angry Kate, her eyes flashing with contempt when she talked of the heretic hunters; Sweet Kate, sharpening his quills, reading his copy, rubbing his neck—he imagined he could feel her hands on the aching muscles of his shoulders. He summoned the smell of her hair, the feel of her skin, the taste of her lips, until the constancy of her image became his only reality.

By the afternoon his muscles cramped until his mind tricks no longer worked. He could not stifle his groans, and his stomach burned with hunger. He dreaded the whipping mandated under More's new vagrancy law, but was anxious to get it over. The pain that would come would take precedence over the pain in his legs. Not a relief from pain, but a different agony that might be borne for a time; and if he survived the whipping, he would be free. More might no longer be chancellor, but the law was the law, and what he'd seen of the local law enforcement did not make him think they were inclined to mercy.

His stocks were in the public square, and he considered shouting out his real name to a couple of passers-by, begging them to go to the abbey and tell them of his predicament. Judging from the abuse both real and verbal heaped upon him, however, he doubted the efficacy of such a plan. The fact that his name might fall on hostile ears also gave him pause. After all, he was a known fugitive. A strong man would survive a whipping; a burning he would surely not.

By the third day, he had fallen back on his old fish cellar habit of reciting Homer to occupy his mind, verse after verse in the original Greek. Occasionally a Greek utterance leaked from his mind into his parched throat. Because he kept his eyes closed whenever passers-by approached so as not to invite abuse, he didn't see the women carrying water from the well.

"Poor man, he's gone mad. He's muttering gibberish."

"Give him a drink; he must be starved for water."

Hearing the compassion in their voices, John opened his eyes. He could only see their feet, shod in dusty worn clogs, and a bucket of water one of them set on the ground. He looked at the cool, clear water and thought of Tantalus.

"We can't give him water, Charlotte. It is forbidden."

He groaned.

"'A cup of water in my name,' the Scripture says. It's like giving it to Christ. Would we not give a drink to our Lord?"

They were quoting Scripture. They were Bible readers!

"Please," he tried to say, but his throat was dry, and it came out in a croak.

Gnarled hands dipped hastily into the bucket and held up a double handful of water to his mouth. He lapped it like a dog, until he could feel the roughness of her palm against his tongue. She scooped another handful for him, and he drank, until choking and coughing, he was able to spit out the words, "Please fetch the—p"—no, he could not ask for the priest—"the schoolmaster. Tell him a . . . scholar is . . . wrongly accused."

"He is mad," the other woman said, "or cursed. Let's go before someone sees us comfortin' a vagrant."

"To be punished for giving a drink of water to a thirsty man, it's an abomination, it is." Then patting him on the shoulder, the voice belonging to Charlotte added, "We'll pray for you. They canna punish us for that."

"The schoolmaster," he whispered.

He watched as the feet walked away, then closed his eyes and tried to summon his visions.

❧

"His name is John Frith," Leonard Cox, the schoolmaster, said to the magistrate. "I tell you, the man is a Cambridge scholar. The gibberish your spies heard him spouting was *The Iliad* in the original Greek. You've just about killed him. Let him go."

"Then why wouldn't he give his name?"

"I don't know why. I'm sure he has his reasons. But I'm here to stand for his identity. He is no vagrant. His father is a landowner in Kent. He attended both Cambridge and Oxford and is a man of great reputation and learning, and you have him locked up in the stocks like a common criminal!"

Prudence cautioned him not to add that under the law even a common vagabond should not be left to die of thirst and starvation. Best not to get the magistrate's back up.

But the magistrate must have read his mind. He scratched his head and answered defensively, "We were within the law. How do you know he's who he says he is? That's why we didn't feed him. If a man gets hungry enough, he'll be less stubborn."

Cox tried to control his temper. "I recognized him, that's how I know who he is. Charlotte Bascomb said he asked to see me. I was skeptical, but when he started to talk I remembered his voice. He called me by name—we were at Cambridge together—and when I washed the filth from his face, filth put there by his abusers because you wrongfully put him in the stocks, I knew him immediately."

The magistrate appeared to consider before answering, and then motioned for the constable. "We'll let him go, then, on your surety, but if you talk of this, you be sure and say that he refused to give his name, and he had no papers. We acted within the law."

"Yes, yes, I understand. It'll not be held against you. Now send the constable straightaway before the poor man expires from hunger."

⚜

After a good meal and a bath, John was able, with Leonard Cox's help, to get to the abbey where the prior greeted him warmly, expressing outrage when he heard of his treatment in Reading. The prior had spent a bit of time in the stocks during his year in prison, he said, and knew what that did to a man. He reiterated his support for the movement, but admitted that after the king had released him with a warning to be more orthodox in his teachings, he tried to be more careful.

Yes, he still ran the underground movement, still held the Bible readings, but they were more cautious now about whom they trusted. He happily produced a purse with enough heft to support John as he made the rounds to the merchants and shadow "congregations" as they called themselves. But he gave a warning too.

"Don't be fooled," he said, "by the fact that More has resigned. It is said he's more determined than ever to burn out all vestiges of reform."

"How can a man of learning be so intolerant?" John asked.

"I know. It's hard to believe this is the same man who authored *Utopia*, who once championed humanist causes and new learning. He even agreed with Erasmus that reform was needed."

They were in the chapel abbey, where the prior was taking his tour of duty, the same as the other monks. It was his day to rub the carved wood of the roodscreen with linseed oil and polish the gold and silver of the altar vessels: the elaborate jeweled chalice, the paten, the ciborium.

"Do you not ever wonder," John asked, pointing to the stained glass of the Gothic windows, the gleaming gold of the altar, reflected in the multicolored lights from the sun's rays, "what Jesus would say about all this?"

The prior smiled. "I know what you are thinking, that we should sell the Church's treasure and give the money to the poor, but I would remind you, dear friend, that our Lord said, 'The poor you will have with you always,' when Judas Iscariot objected to an extravagant and expensive form of worship."

"I do not need to be reminded of what the Scripture says, but that was in the context of Jesus' anointment for his crucifixion. We celebrate a living Christ in spirit and truth by emulating His ways, not the ways of the woman who anointed him for burial with expensive perfume—or those of the temple priests."

The prior nodded in what might be construed as agreement. "Consider this too. As long as these altar vessels remain, I can go on with our mission. They give me cover. And they have other, more utilitarian uses. That purse I gave you? It will not be the first time a golden candlestick has been turned into printed Scripture. We have replaced this one with gilded copper. It sheds as good a light upon the host as the gold one and should the archbishop come—" He shrugged. "But they will all be gone soon enough. King Henry will not be able to resist such a treasure. Ironic, isn't it? What was used to celebrate the Prince of Peace will go to fund war with France."

John held up the fake candlestick, hefted it in his hand. "Well, here's one that won't. I thank you. William Tyndale thanks you too."

The prior reached inside his cassock and pulled out a piece of paper, unfurled it on the altar.

"Here is a map with a *c* where you'll find congregations that will lend you support and be glad to hear you preach. Burn it when you have memorized it. Here is a document showing you as a messenger for the priory should you find yourself at odds with the vagrancy law again. You are welcome to rest here as long as needful." He handed John the documents. "I understand you have taken a wife."

"I have. With the assistance of a priest from this very abbey."

"Has that proven to be a happy choice?"

"A very happy choice. We are expecting a child. A Christmas blessing."

The prior smiled wanly. "Then, my friend, you need be especially careful. You do not want your child to be an orphan before it is born. More and Stokesley make quick work of burning these days."

Within two days John felt strong enough to begin his rounds. He left the abbey on foot, not wanting the expense of a horse. The first "congregation" was less than five miles back toward London. The last was near Southend in Essex. He could get a ship there for home and Kate. He would be back in Antwerp before All Saints' Day, God willing.

☙❧

Thomas More looked up from the map he was squinting at, the map of rebel "congregations" that Bishop Stokesley had just delivered to him in his study at Chelsea.

"I knew they were spreading, but I did not know there were so many," Thomas said in disgust.

"That's probably only half. Tyndale's books have done a lot of damage to the Church over these seven years. Would that Cuthbert had taken a firmer hand with him and not let him get away. My predecessor was too disposed toward combating enemies with words."

Thomas shifted the paperweight on his desk to anchor a corner of the map. Upon the completion of Thomas's first anti-Tyndale polemic, Bishop Tunstall had given him the paperweight, a fly suspended in a giant blob of amber. "Don't discount the value of words, Excellency," Thomas said resentfully. He felt a need to remind the bishop of just how much his own words before Parliament had cost him.

The blade of the bishop's jawbone reminded Thomas of a dagger's edge, and he possessed a will just as honed. In spite of his recent silence before Parliament, Stokesley was a formidable ally, stronger than Thomas had had in Bishop Tunstall. But he missed the fellowship of that former alliance.

"Cuthbert meant well," Thomas said. "He just lacked the temperament to follow through. He thought the enemy could be contained with words and argument." He pointed to the mountain of manuscripts anchoring another corner of the map. "But you are right, Excellency, if words alone could do it, Tyndale's vile pen would already have been stopped. I have answered every heretical argument, and yet the books and English Bibles with their profane glosses still seep into England, bringing the stench of an Antwerp shithole with them."

Stokesley pounded the map with his fist. "We must stop them now! Or there will not be enough oaks in England to make the stakes to burn them all. And it's going to be harder since we have lost the cooperation of Parliament."

Thomas couldn't resist one last jab. "God knows I tried. I lost the chancellorship because of it." *While you remained silent.* The unspoken words hung between them.

Stokesley answered quickly, "No man could have done more. You were very eloquent. But you can be sure the heretics know of this development. Their arrogance is stronger than ever. One of them has slipped back in—a bold and arrogant move."

Thomas's ears perked at this. "Is it a name we know? Who is it?"

The bishop smiled, obviously pleased to be imparting this new knowledge his spies had gleaned. "It is said that he is one of William Tyndale's closest friends, though I did not recognize his name. He was arrested for vagrancy in Reading"—he pointed to the map spread out on the desk where Reading Abbey was marked with a larger *X* than the rest—"but unfortunately let go by the local magistrate when the schoolmaster identified him as a former Cambridge scholar."

Thomas's pulse quickened. "Was his name John Frith?"

"I think so. You know of him?"

And so should you, my illiterate friend, More thought. Here was another difference between Stokesley and his predecessor. Tunstall was a scholar and a supporter of the new learning in classical studies. That was one reason Tyndale had approached him about a translation for the English Bible in the first place. This new Bishop of London rightly presented himself as a man of action and not of words. "He is one of the young scholars turned heretic who survived the Oxford fish cellar," Thomas said.

"Ah. I thought I'd heard the name before."

"As well you should. He writes quite prolifically against the doctrine of Purgatory." Thomas was gratified to see the stain of embarrassment on Stokesley's face. He stood up and began to pace the room, his mind whirling. "We must catch him this time. Not only will we stop the profane lies spewing from his pen like venom from the fangs of a viper, but he will lead us straight to Tyndale. We could burn the two of them, back to back. Such a fire would scent the streets of paradise with the burning fat of a bountiful sacrifice."

Stokesley picked up the paperweight and considered it. The fly's wings were outstretched as though it had only meant to alight temporarily upon the sap, to suck its sweetness before being caught for all eternity. He put it down. "What we need is a trap," he said.

"Our traps are already set, Your Excellency." More tapped at the *X*'s on the map. "Here and here and here. All we have to do is bait them. Sooner or later, John Frith will spring one of them."

"And when he does, what then? Under Parliament's new law, he falls under the jurisdiction of the king."

"You need not remind me," Thomas snapped. "It's true, *you* can't arrest him. But even though I've resigned as chancellor, I still have some legal power until a new one is appointed. I can arrest him in the name of the king."

"But how can we catch him, if we don't know what he looks like? Have you ever seen him?"

"We know what he looks like." Thomas fumbled among the papers piled on his desk and pulled out a single sheet. It was an artist's sketch of a handsome young man, with dark wavy hair, a straight nose, and strong winged eyebrows above wide-set eyes that gleamed with intelligence, just as George Constantine had described him to Hans Holbein.

"We will circulate this sketch among all the spies, infiltrating their vile *congregations* in Oxfordshire and Berkshire, and instruct them to draw out each suspect on his opinions concerning Purgatory and the Eucharist. By the time Frith is picked up, we'll have enough evidence that even the king will not hinder his arrest."

Thomas was rolling up the map to return to Stokesley when he was interrupted by a knock. He handed the map to Stokesley and went to answer the door.

"Sir Thomas, there is a Franciscan brother, a man named Richard Risby, to see you."

"Send him away. Tell him I will not meet with him, and he is not to come here again," Thomas said in a low voice.

The bishop looked up from the framed miniature portraits he'd been admiring during the interruption.

"That is your friend Erasmus, is it not?"

"It is. Do you know him?"

"I know of his work," the bishop said, obviously proud to display this one bit of learning. "Who is in the other portrait?"

"Another close friend from Flanders, name of Peter Gillis. He gave me the portraits as a memento of my last visit to Antwerp."

"Holbein?"

The bishop's affectation of knowledge of the fine arts offended Thomas. He despised such posturing.

"No. An Antwerp artist of some renown. His name is Quentin Massys."

"Oh." Obviously the bishop had never heard of him and seemed to quickly lose interest.

"Massys is dead now," Thomas said, trying to draw out the conversation so that Stokesley would not remember the conversation that had interrupted them. Listening at doors was what the nosy bishop did best. "Massys's art will probably go up in value, if his name is not tainted by his sister's heretical association. She has started a Bible-reading society in Leuven."

There, that should divert him. More talk of heresy.

Stokesley put down the miniatures and looked at Thomas, lowering his lids ever so slightly.

"The man at the door—"

"It was only my servant. Luther's influence in the Holy Roman Empire has been more pernicious than—"

"No. The Franciscan named Risby. Isn't that the monk who is associated with the Maid of Kent? The one who has prophesied against the king in the matter of his divorce?"

"It is."

Stokesley picked up the blob of amber, appeared to study it carefully, waiting for Thomas to expand upon his answer, which Thomas declined to do. But the bishop was not a man to leave any scrap of information in the field when he gleaned.

"What do you think of her prophesies?" he asked.

"I think she is a maid who is ill used, more mad than prescient."

"Have you met with her?"

This was the question Thomas dreaded. He hated to give even his friends—today's friends, perhaps tomorrow's enemies—anything to use against him if called before the King's Bench.

"Once. In my capacity as chancellor."

"What did Risby want?"

"He wanted me to meet with her again."

"Will you?"

"I will not. She has prophesied the king's death. That is treason. And treason carries a greater penalty even than speaking against the king's policy in Parliament."

The bishop, who had no rejoinder, hastily gathered up his maps and left with a promise to begin the hunt for John Frith.

THIRTY-FOUR

That same man that runneth away may again fight another day.

—ERASMUS, *APOTHEGMS* (1542)

John Frith looked around the little Lollard congregation in the Essex farm cottage near Chelmsford. He'd walked many miles and had not slept for two days, but the receptiveness to his preaching energized him. Upon his arrival, the congregants had cheered him, waving their English New Testaments in the air.

"I cannot wait to tell the translator about you," he said. "He will be greatly heartened by your faith. I wish that he could be here to see you for himself."

It had been the same everywhere he preached for the last few weeks, from Reading to East Essex. He never gave his real name but called himself Jacob, saying he was a friend of the Bible men from across the sea. He accepted only a warm cloak or a bed for the night, as the October weather had grown chilly even in daytime, and sometimes a little food for the road. But to the many kind souls who offered monetary support, he directed them to deliver what support they could spare to the leaders of their congregations, who would in turn deliver them to the Hanseatic League at the Steelyard, care of Sir Humphrey Monmouth, or if they lived closer to Reading, to the prior at the abbey there.

But he warned them to be cautious. "This arrangement protects both you and me," he said, "as your contributions will be anonymous, and if I should be taken, I will not have your letters of affirmation on me"—and then added soberly, "or know from whom they came."

Now, only miles from the coast, he was feeling better about not being taken, though he knew he could not let his guard down. That's where the danger was strongest. Yet it was hard not to be distracted when he longed to see his Kate and hold her in his arms—if he could still get his arms around her. She was in her seventh month. She would never forgive him—he could never forgive himself—if he were not there for the birth of their first child.

A letter from her had been delivered to him from a messenger at the Steelyard when he'd passed through St. Albans. He'd read and reread it until it was creased and falling apart. He'd managed to send an answer by the same messenger telling her to let Tyndale know that a secret account had been set up at the Antwerp Kontor for them to draw from. If she needed anything, Tyndale would provide it. He'd assured her he would be home shortly, and though he told her how gladly he'd been received everywhere, he did not tell her about the times he'd been followed or his stint in the stocks at Reading.

This Chelmsford congregation had been his largest gathering yet, but he was glad it was drawing to a close. He was weak with exhaustion. Even as the benediction was being said, he was thinking to inquire about a nearby stable where he might stay overnight—he didn't like to endanger the families of the homes where he preached. But the last "amen" had scarcely been offered before a man approached him.

"Father, may I speak with you a moment?"

A man of fairly diminished stature and a sincere demeanor held out his hand.

John grasped the extended hand with what energy he had left. "Please, call me brother or simply J . . . Jacob. As our Lord reminded us, there is only one who is worthy to be called 'Father.' And your name?"

"William. William Holt. I am a tailor from Epping."

"That's where I've seen you before. I thought you looked familiar."

"Yes. I was in Epping. You preached there on the Eucharist, and I was so moved by what you said about the miracle of the heart's transformation being the important thing and not the Real Presence of Christ's body . . . the way you described it, it made perfect sense. I tried to remember to tell it to my friend, but alas, I lack for words."

"Well, it isn't so hard to understand—just say to your friend—"

"Here. Could you write it down? The points of your sermon in Epping?"

From somewhere the tailor produced a bit of paper and a small inkhorn, the kind a traveling scribe might use, and shoved it toward John.

He hesitated for the briefest moment. Tyndale had warned him not to commit anything to writing on the doctrine of the Eucharist. That subject was more certain than any other to incite the wrath of not only the clergy but the king as well.

"I wouldn't ask, but I'm so miserable with words. It makes sense when you say it. When I say it . . . and I couldn't remember your second point."

John grasped the paper and wrote down a simple statement on the doctrine of the Eucharist, listing the three points he'd preached on in Epping, which questioned the very foundation of the mass.

"Thank you, sir. Thank you. Now I can convince my friend of his wrong thinking," he said, glancing at the paper. "Oh. One more thing. Would you sign it?" He smiled apologetically. "So he'll know I didn't just make it up."

Without thinking, John scrawled his name at the bottom of the scrap of paper.

The tailor glanced at it briefly, then smiling, folded it up and put it in his pocket, reached out and once again pumped John's hand.

As he watched William Holt's receding back, John realized that he'd signed his real name. He started to call him back. But what would he say? If he asked for the paper back, he would not only insult the man, but perhaps even call attention to it. Besides, the tailor looked to be an honest man, and even if his enemies did get hold of it, what would it matter? They could just add it the growing pile of heretical sermons preached by John Frith. In two days' time he'd be in Southend. He'd be in Kate's arms, safe at the English House before the next Sabbath, and none of it would matter.

❧

"I am accompanying the king to Calais day after tomorrow," Anne Boleyn announced to her ladies of the queen's privy chamber.

Anne had returned to Hampton Court with a new confidence after her investiture as the Marquess of Pembroke. The king was as devoted to her as a puppy to its master. Verily, she thought, if she held a biscuit in front of him, he would sit up and beg—well, not a biscuit but an incentive of another kind. Of course, she would never do that. It was not prudent to make a king beg.

She had just come from attending mass offered by Thomas Cranmer, the new Archbishop of Canterbury, in the Royal Chapel where she had sat with the king in the royal pew. The trip to Calais had been Cranmer's idea.

"It would be a courtesy to include the plans for your annulment in your talks with the king of France. You might even consider, Your Majesty, taking Lady Anne with you. It would give Francis an opportunity to meet the woman who is to be your new queen."

If Anne had any doubts about this new archbishop, they were laid to rest with that suggestion.

Now she watched with some satisfaction as Lady Margaret Lee tried to choke down her surprise. "Shall we lay out your gowns, my lady?"

"Yes, *s'il vous plaît*. I'd better practice my French. Be sure to include the crimson kirtle. The king has requested it particularly, and the mantle lined with ermine. We are staying at the exchequer's palace, and they say it is drafty. Also my suede sleeves and kirtle. We will probably go hunting with Francis."

She opened her jewel chest and pulled out a few baubles. Her eye lit on a silver tiara. Too presumptuous? No, she decided. It would go with the crimson dress, and Henry might find it amusing. If he did not, she would simply take it off. She tossed it on the pile. She did not miss the look that passed between the two women.

"Be sure and pack in layers with the velvets on top and with bits of lavender in between."

Lady Margaret Lee curtsied her obedience.

"Will we be accompanying you, my lady?" the Seymour woman asked, her pale cheeks almost pink with excitement.

"No, I think not. It will be but a short journey. My personal maid will be sufficient. No need to wrest you from your comforts here."

The Seymour woman looked crestfallen and dropped her perfunctory curtsy.

"Now, if you've enough to keep you occupied, I'm off to the courtyard, where His Majesty has challenged me to a game of lawn bowling." Anne flounced out of the room, trying not to grin at the look of disappointment on Seymour's face. *I wonder if I will be any happier than this when I am queen?* she thought. It was almost a certainty now. She had missed her last period. But even if it had not already happened, it would.

Henry had whispered in her ear that the French ambassador had assured him of adjoining rooms.

~×~

John Frith was thinking only of the narrow strip of sea separating him from safety and the arms of his wife as he approached the docks at Southend. To-night he would sleep in his own bed—if his overworked body could make it that far. The muscles in his legs trembled with fatigue and his stomach growled. Thinking that he must stop to meet at least some of his physical demands, he paused long enough to buy a pint and a pasty from a tavern, but the pint was only half finished when he left the Fox and the Hound, carrying the half-eaten pasty with him.

Had John been less preoccupied, less hurried, he would have noticed the big man sitting alone in the corner, watching him intently, would have been aware as he followed him from the tavern, would have seen the telling nod to a second man in yeoman dress lounging in a doorway across the street. He was also unaware, as he munched happily on his pie, that a third man joined the other two at the juncture where the street opened onto the wharf.

John scanned the ships anchored there. He spotted one with the flag of the Hanseatic League. That would the one he should approach first for passage. A knot of people had gathered and were peering expectantly at a large ship sailing past in the distance. "Look, it's His Majesty's ship," someone shouted. "Carrying more of our money to France, I'll be bound," another said. "Probably got that whore Nan Bullen on board with him."

Shading his eyes with one hand and cramming the last bite of his pie in his mouth with the other, John peered in the distance at the grand ship with the Tudor flags flying. If he could just get on that ship, he could make his plea to the king without having to reveal himself to the layer of courtiers with connections to his enemies. He looked around for a small boat that could give chase. The king might be amused by so bold a move, and if he had Anne Boleyn on board, even predisposed to hearing him out. It was risky. There would be cannon on that ship; the captain might just fire and sink the small boat. But if he succeeded in getting close enough, he was sure he could talk his way aboard.

"Master Frith?"

Startled to hear his real name being hailed in such a crowd, he hesitated just a moment too long before pushing into the crowd to hide.

"John Frith! Stop. We would speak with you."

He darted quickly away from the docks, but he'd only taken a few steps when three burly men surrounded him.

"Unhand me immediately or I shall report you to the dock watch."

He didn't know if there was such a thing as a dock watch, but it was the first thing that came to mind.

"You are to come with us."

John tried to muster what indignation his fatigue would allow. "Under whose order?"

"The Bishop of London."

Suddenly his fatigue was gone as fear pumped new energy into him. His mind cleared. There were some matters about which he did not have to bluff. "The Bishop of London has no authority to make arrests. That authority rests with the king."

"King beint here, Master Frith," one of them said, laughing, and pointed to the ship. "He's too busy to bother with the likes of you."

The men closed in, one wresting John's arm behind his back. The point of a dagger poked through the thick serge of his jerkin.

"The bishop has no right, I tell you. Parliament has passed a law—"

"Tell it to the bishop," one of them growled, pushing John forward.

He was outnumbered. Even if he struggled free, he would not likely get away. He spotted a customs officer, who was taking somewhat of an interest in the whole affair but had obviously decided this was not in his jurisdiction.

"Unlawful abduction," John screamed in the direction of the officer. "Send to Master Cromwell at Whitehall. Tell him John Frith is being unlawfully arrested. I throw myself on the mercy of the king and demand lawful treatment."

He said it more than once, loudly enough so that anybody listening with a sympathetic ear could carry the message, even if the customs officer chose not to. He was still screaming it, when he felt such a jerk on his arm that the pain shot into his wrist. One of the men slapped a hand over his mouth. "Shut your mouth, or I'll have to break your arm."

But as John stumbled forward with his arm throbbing, he was sure that the news would be all over Essex by nightfall—*And to Cromwell's ears, please, God*, he prayed, remembering the fish cellar. He did not think he had the strength to endure that again. This time was different. This time more than his life was at stake. This time there was Kate—and the child they had made together. *Thank God she does not know*, he thought. *Someday, I will tell her. When I have escaped. When all is well.*

THIRTY-FIVE

I come hither, good people, accused and condemned for an heretic, Sir Thomas More being my accuser and my judge. And these be the articles that I die for. First, I say it is lawful for every man and woman to have God's book in their mother tongue. Second, that the Bishop of Rome is Antichrist . . . The Lord forgive Sir Thomas More.

—Statement made by James Bainham
upon his burning, April 1532

Cold crept into the back of the wagon with the evening shadows. John Frith pulled his wool coat tightly about him and tried to think. Most likely, his captors were taking him either to Bishop Stokesley in London or to Thomas More's house where he was certain to suffer the kind of illegal interrogation that More had been conducting for years. His best chance of escape was before they reached their destination.

One of the men had ridden on ahead—no doubt to collect his reward for running his prey to ground—and one of them was driving the team of horses. That increased his odds, but the giant grinning beside him with dagger drawn was big enough to snap him in two. John had initially tried to engage him, hoping to win over his sympathy. Apparently he had none.

"Where are you taking me?"

"You'll know when we get there."

"I don't suppose you would consider tying my hands in front instead of behind? If you are delivering me to the bishop, he might not want damaged goods."

The guard looked suspicious. "What difference does it make where they're tied?"

"My arm has gone numb, and my wrist keeps bumping against the rail."

"It's just an hour back to London."

The wagon bumped and jolted to the rhythmic clip-clopping of the horses and the creaking of the iron wheels. John closed his eyes, pretending to sleep, while his mind darted into blind alleys. If he was going to escape he had to make them stop somehow. Maybe he could fake some kind of seizure to create a diversion. But he would have to be fast, would have to take the guard by surprise. And they would have to be someplace other than this open road so that he could find cover if he made it out of the wagon alive.

As they neared Bishopsgate, he heard hoofbeats approaching. He was reconstructing in his mind the layout of the alleys and lanes around Bishops-gate when the hoofbeats ceased abruptly. The wheels creaked to a halt as the driver reined in.

Now! This was his chance to bolt if he could take the guard by surprise. From his sleeping posture, John opened his eyes halfway to calculate his timing. His eyes popped wide open. Soldiers! The riders wore the king's livery. The guard shifted closer to him.

"We've a prisoner for Bishop Stokesley," the driver said, his voice carrying to the back of the wagon. John opened his mouth to speak. The dagger poked his side, a gentle reminder from the guard.

"Who is he?" One of the soldiers peered into the wagon.

"Frith," John shouted. "John Frith." The dagger dug into his side, but he knew they would not kill him here. This was his only chance.

"I am a scholar from Antwerp, come to see Master Cromwell. These men are holding me against my will. They are thugs and robbers."

John felt the dagger dig deeper, thankful for his heavy mantle and thick serge doublet. "Take me to Master Cromwell—"

"He's a heretic," his guard growled. "The bishop has ordered his arrest."

"I have been wrongfully abducted. Under Parliament's new law, the bishop has no jurisdiction for arrest and detention. If I am to be held on charges, I must be held by the king, not the bishop."

The soldier looked thoughtful.

"Take me to Master Cromwell, if you doubt it. If I am wrong, you can deliver me to the bishop yourself. If I am right, you will have prevented a miscarriage of justice and earned Master Cromwell's favor."

The soldiers conferred briefly, and then to John's great relief, one of them indicated with a jerk of his head that the driver of the wagon should get in the back with the prisoner. He handed the reins of his horse to his companion and took the driver's seat. Within an hour, John was in custody of Constable Kingston of the Tower.

❧⁓

John's first night in the Tower proved not to be as bad as he had feared. The old warder on duty led him to his cell, saying that the constable had already retired to his private quarters and would question the prisoner on the morrow. At least there was a window, high and open to the sky, which would give some light come morning. The starlight filtering through it now revealed the bleakness of the stark little chamber. A mattress with a straw ticking still clean-smelling enough to be preferable to the cold stone floor was the only furnishing.

He was also given a decent meal, though no one had asked him to pay for it, which was good, because he had only one coin for his passage home sewn into the hem of his cloak. He was determined he would not spend that even if he starved.

He was so exhausted he slept well, and to his surprise was given breakfast the next morning, not hearty, just a stale piece of bread and some thin porridge, yet a man could live on it. But how did a man exist without books and writing materials? He couldn't even write to Kate to tell her his arrival was not as imminent as he had thought. If he could just tell her he'd encountered a small delay, not to worry, all would still be well, it would set his mind at ease.

He pondered the thickness of the stone casement and was wondering if anyone had ever escaped from such a fortress when his cell door opened and two men walked in. The tall one with the short sword strapped around his velvet doublet introduced himself as the constable. His companion was also richly dressed but in a velvet cap and robe, obviously a man of some importance, though nothing in his appearance bespoke the noble courtier. Neither did he look like a bishop.

"Master Frith, I will have to admit, I am well pleased to make your acquaintance. I have been curious about you."

"This is Master Cromwell," the constable said. "He takes a special interest in all prisoners who are charged with heresy. You are under his specific jurisdiction, but as I've been told by your arresting officers, you already know that."

John clambered up from the floor, gathering his dignity as best he could, and gave a small bow of recognition to one of the most powerful men at court. "Master Cromwell, all of England has heard of you, but how came you to know of me?"

Cromwell smiled. "I have read your *Disputation of Purgatory.*"

"I am honored," John said, taking full measure of the man, surmising that he was susceptible to flattery. "The more so that the reading of my work defines you as a man of courage since it is banned."

"It is indeed a bold statement. Especially in these times," Cromwell said.

"It is a time for bold statements, don't you agree?"

"If you've a taste for martyrdom. If you do not, I would caution prudence. If you are prudent, you may even turn this circumstance to your advantage. The new queen will have some influence in your behalf."

New queen? Of course. Cromwell was looking ahead. He was known to be a supporter of Anne Boleyn.

"She has taken a special interest in the survivors of the fish cellar. But the Church, the bishops and the archbishop, still pass judgment on matters of heresy through their courts. Even Archbishop Cranmer, who is . . . sympathetic to your cause will be hesitant to overrule a guilty verdict. Bishop Stokesley will be on that court. Thomas More will be his legal advisor. Now is the time for prudence, Master Frith, not boldness. If you are as smart as I think you are, that is all I need to say."

"You are very kind, Master Cromwell. I am honored by your interest and pleased to have your advice. If I may presume to ask one more favor, might I have some writing materials?"

Crowell frowned, narrowing his puffy eyes to slits. "After what I have just said to you, Master Frith, I would not advise—"

"So that I may write to my wife."

"I would not advise that either. Such a letter might lead to your wife or to . . . other friends. Your wife could be used as a lever to gain information or to get you to recant. Your abjuration would be quite a plum."

John suddenly remembered what had happened to James Bainham, how when they could not break him upon the rack, they had thrown his wife in the Fleet. Thank God, More and Stokesley did not know he had a wife or where she lived.

Cromwell placed his hand in a brotherly fashion upon John's shoulder. "Constable Kingston, you need not worry overmuch about the locks. I think our young friend can be given the freedom to visit some of the other prisoners. He is a man of God, a man of compassion." His lips curved into a sliver of a smile. "He may bring comfort to some of them. Also, let him see those visitors who may inquire of him."

The constable nodded.

"And give him whatever he needs in the way of basic necessities. You may charge it to my account."

"I am grateful for your kindness, Master Cromwell," John said, and he was, though there was something about the man he did not quite trust. He was known as a sympathizer of the protestant movement, but he would not be the first man to ride the wave of needed change to power. There was shrewdness in his eyes that bespoke self-interest, and after all, he'd been re-cruited and trained by Wolsey, that paragon of self-interest.

"I will speak to the king when he returns on your behalf. The king, for all his quarrels with the Church, remains devoted to the mass. Remember that in your conversations with residents and visitors to the Tower. More and Stokesley are not above sending in a spy or two."

"And writing materials?" John pressed. "At the risk of abusing your gra-cious generosity. It would be a great boon."

Cromwell nodded. "Your status as a theologian could be very useful to the king, should you find that your conscience allows you to write or speak favorably of his decision to put away the old queen. You are fortunate to be in my hands and not your enemies', Master Frith. But be forewarned, there is only so much I can do."

After he had gone and John's dinner had appeared, with it was a lone candle, some writing materials, a book of Erasmus's sermons—not banned; Erasmus was a master of circumspection, preaching against many abuses of the Church the "heretics" derided but always falling short of heresy, re-maining a friend to More—an example of Cromwell's prudence. But after John had finished his meat pie and weak cider, he did not light the candle or pick up the book or the writing materials. He sat with his back to the wall, staring out at one lone star in the narrow patch of black sky visible to him.

He wondered if Kate was looking at the same star. If somehow she knew he was in peril. A loneliness as black as that patch of sky settled on him.

Captain Lasser was taking on cargo at the Steelyard when he heard the news that John Frith had been arrested. He put down the parcel he was handing off to a crewman. "Does Frith's wife know he's been taken?" he asked Sir Humphrey, who hailed him with the news.

"I doubt it. We've just got word this day. We are trying to get to him to see if there's anything he needs that we can provide. I'm trying to find the words to write to his wife. It's a hard duty. Her brother was a printer and a runner for us before he was caught and his press smashed. She sold me a Bible, a fine old family heirloom, to raise money after her brother's printing business was shut down." He shook his head, and stroked his beard, shaping it to a dagger's point. "How do you tell a woman her husband has been arrested for heresy?"

"As gently as you can," Tom said, thinking how hard it would be to write such a letter—even if it were not to a beautiful young woman and the wife of a man he admired. "I got to know them both when I helped them escape. They were newly married, then. When you sent me to pick him up, you didn't say anything about a wife."

"I didn't know. It was a complication. But thanks to you, it worked out."

"Frith is a good man, and a smart one. He may yet survive. Where is he being held?"

"In the Tower. At least More and Stokesley can't get to him."

"But he'll still have to stand trial?"

"Most likely. Whenever they think they have enough evidence."

"Which they are as busy gathering as a squirrel gathers nuts, I'll wager. When you finish writing that letter, give it to me. I'll take it to her."

"That'll be hard duty too, Captain."

Tom nodded and picked up a crate marked "spices" and put it in a pile for loading. It did not smell of spice, but Tom had learned not to inquire. All he needed to know was that it was marked with a double *X* and would require special handling.

"Hard duty," he agreed. "But she doesn't need to receive such a letter from the hand of a strange messenger."

As his arms were busy loading the crates and fardels marked with a double *X*, he considered his dilemma. He'd always forsworn direct involvement with the reformers—there was no profit and lots of risk. No bishop knew his name and that was a condition most desirable—he'd always been able to sail just beneath their notice—just another smuggler who could bribe his way if caught. But the hard truth was John Frith did not deserve to die at the hands of Thomas More. And the brave young woman he'd first met outside Fleet Prison did not deserve this double portion of pain. If he could promise help, give Kate some hope that her husband could be free, the news would go down less hard with her. But could he really do that? Risk everything to free Frith? Maybe not.

By the time Monmouth returned with his letter and the *Siren's Song* had set sail, Captain Lasser had convinced himself that he should give her a shoulder to cry on when she received the news. She deserved that at least.

·≈×≈·

Kate finished sewing a hem in the lining of her baby's cradle and examined the tiny stitches with satisfaction. Not perfect, she thought, but not too bad either. She spread the soft fabric in the cradle and gave it a little push with her foot.

Resting her hands on her stomach, she spoke softly to the child inside her. "This world is a hard place, but you'll have a soft bed—though it may have a crooked stitch or two in the pillow." The baby kicked as if in response. Kate laughed. "Save it for your father so he can see how strong you are. He'll be here to welcome you into the world as he promised. Maybe sooner."

John had said by Christmas when he'd left, but in his last letter two weeks ago, he'd said he was passing London by and would be home earlier. By All Saints' Day even. "He'll think your mother really is as fat as the baker's wife." She was contemplating that with just a whisper of anxiety running swift-footed through her mind—would he think her misshapen and ugly?—when the maid told her she had a visitor.

"Who is it?"

"I don't know, mistress. I've never seen him before."

"You know we are not to receive strangers here. He could be a spy."

"He says he is with the Hanseatic League, and he showed me a seal to prove it."

"Did he give his name?"

"Captain . . . Lasser, I think."

Kate considered briefly. Tom Lasser always made her uneasy in some vague way. Besides, he was probably here to see John. "Tell him my husband is not here."

The maid bustled off but returned almost immediately. "He says it's you he needs to see, madam. Says he has a letter for you from Humphrey Monmouth."

Humphrey Monmouth. It might be news of John. Please, God, let it not be bad news. I cannot bear it. Not now.

"I will see him in the chapel," Kate said. "We will have privacy there." And in that sacred space, she thought, perhaps a measure of protection against evil news.

≈⋺⋲

When Tom entered the plain little chapel, he did not see her in the dim light. The tiny room was in shadow except for a sunbeam of dust motes from a high-up window that illumined the simple altar with white light. When she stood up and turned to face him, the light gathered her in as well, and it was suddenly hard to breathe in the closeness of that little room.

"You look . . . radiant," he said, his heart sinking at the sight of her heavy with child. As if this task were not hard enough already. "When is the child due?"

"Around Christmas."

She did not smile at him. There was no welcome in her voice. Instinctively he took a step closer.

She stepped back. "You mentioned you had a letter?"

"May we sit here for just a minute?" He gestured toward the bench in front of the altar.

"I do not need to sit. If you do not mind, I am needed in the accounts room."

"Please, sit. I need to talk to you first, before you read the letter."

She went pale. "John? Is it about——"

He put his arm around her waist, guiding her down onto the bench then, feeling her shrink from him, took it away.

"You are shivering," he said.

She sat with her hands folded in her lap. He reached out and touched them. They were cold and pale as though no blood flowed to them. There was only a small brazier in the chapel, and it was not lit. He took off his doublet and placed it around her shoulders.

She seemed to shrink into it. "Tell me what you have come to tell me, Captain." Her voice was small, husky with fear.

"John is fine, and you are not to be overly alarmed if you hear disconcerting news."

"What is *overly* alarmed, Captain?" she asked, her voice rising. "What degree of alarm should I have?"

He was not doing this well. The anxiety he felt coming from her, the fear he felt for her, all was distracting him.

"What disconcerting news?"

"John is going to be . . . delayed."

"Delayed? Is that all? There is more, I can see it in your face. Tell me and get it over with, please, or just give me Sir Humphrey's letter and let me read it for myself."

"John has been arrested," he said, careful to keep his expression benign, his voice level.

Her hands flew first to her face—"Oh God"—and then to her belly as if she could stop the child from hearing. She started to sway back and forth. "Oh please, God, no—"

He tried to put his arms around her to comfort her, but she shrugged him off as though his touch burned. "My husband is in the hands of Sir Thomas More, the man who lives to burn other men, and you are telling me not to be overly alarmed!"

"But he's not. Thomas More doesn't have him." He thrust the letter at her.

She stopped swaying and snatched it from him, devouring it with her eyes as she held it in trembling hands.

"This says that he is in the Tower. That Thomas Cromwell has him and not Thomas More," she said, breathlessly.

"And that's very good news," he said. "Concentrate on that. Do not give up hope. If he is patient, there is a good chance he will be free. He may never have to stand trial."

She stood up then and faced him, her eyes wide with fear and determination. "Take me to him," she said. "I want to see him."

"I do not think that's wise—"

"I don't care what you think."

"You have to think of your child."

"I am thinking of the child. I want him to at least hear his father's voice before—" And then she started to cry. This time when he put his arms around her, she did not pull away but leaned into him momentarily, then her body tensed as it struggled for control.

"Will you take me to him?" she asked, looking up at him. "Please."

"I will do whatever you wish, Kate. But I think—no, just hear me out—if they learn of your existence, they will use you against him. You will become an instrument of . . ." He stopped, searching for a word other than *torture*. "Something they can use to break him down, to make him confess. Now he knows that you and the baby are safe. That gives him something to hold on to. That will keep him strong and give him comfort. I know it would me—if I were in his place."

"But—"

"Let me go in your stead. I will try to get in to see him. I will do everything I can. If all else fails, others have escaped from the Tower—"

She looked up at him then with uncertainty in her eyes. "You would do that? Put yourself in danger for him?"

He just shrugged and said, "He is a good man, and I don't like Thomas More and his band of heretic hunters. A man should have a right to believe what a man wants to believe."

She looked at him as though she were trying to take his measure, asking herself if she could trust him, then she said quietly, "You are a good man too, Captain. I've always known it."

THIRTY-SIX

ate had not felt the baby move inside her for days, not since the
day she got the news that John had been arrested. At first she had talked to
it, reassuring it. Could it be possible the child knew? Did it feel her grief?
Or just the fatigue she felt? Sleep was her lover now, her solace, her dearest
companion, because in sleep she could forget. The honeyed draught mixed
with mead and ground poppy seeds that Mistress Poyntz had given her to
calm her had become a friend whose comfort and blissful oblivion she sought
frequently. Perhaps the baby slept too.

But even when she did not take the draught but lay sleepless and tormented by her fears so that the child could wake, still it did not stir. She
knew then the child was dead. Its heart no longer beat inside her, and her
grief was so profound she prayed to die and instantly repented. *John will need
to know his wife is waiting for him.*

By the time her body expelled the dead child, she had no tears left. Once she called out for John in her pain, and she remembered John was not there, might not ever be there again. When the midwife put her son's still, small body in her arms, she marveled at the perfection of him and wondered if he had blue eyes, but she would never know. The windows to his soul had never opened. She could not have borne to think his soul lingered in limbo as the priests taught. There was comfort knowing that no such place existed in the Scriptures.

After the midwife had washed the perfect little body, and they had wound it in the cloth that was to have lined his cradle—the cloth with the crooked stitches now cradling him in eternity—after William Tyndale had said a prayer and read the Gospel about Jesus calling the little children to him, Kate took Saint Anne's medal from around her neck and, touching it to her lips, placed it in his tiny hand like a rosary. John would not have approved. He put no faith in saint's medals. But John was not here, and William was too kind to scold. She had worn the necklace close to her heart as her son had lain close to her heart. They buried him in the chapel garden. Kate marked his grave with a cairn of stones as round and perfect as his tiny skull. Master Tyndale scratched a deep cross upon the foundation stone and pressed it firmly into the ground. It did not matter that he had not been baptized, William said, his soul was innocent and would return to God.

Kate bled for three weeks, until she thought her blood, like the cistern of her grief, must be endless. Then the bleeding stopped, and she regained enough strength to return to her bookkeeping and editing chores. But the grief stayed. She did not return to the Bible study meetings. She no longer had the heart for it.

They were all kind to her; most of the merchants treated her like the glass their ships brought from Venice, quietly asking news of John, giving falsely cheerful reassurances that she should not give up hope. No one mentioned the child. It was as though he never existed—except to her. Only Master Tyndale spoke to her with understanding.

He knows what they are risking, she thought. He has always known. And yet he goes on as though he's acting on a bargain he's already made. He's counted the cost and calculated the worth, and he is satisfied. But Kate was not so sure she had made such a bargain with God—maybe her ancestors had, but she had not.

She talked with William about that, and he said not all were called to such a bargain.

"Do you think John made such a bargain?"

"I think he has," he said soberly, "and when I think what that might mean for you, I am glad I never found a wife."

"I would not want John to recant for my sake," she said. "I would not want that on my conscience. It must be his decision."

"Then he will not," William said, and the certainty with which he said it sent a chill up her spine. In the presence of such a man, it would be easy to catch faith, as one would catch a fever, Kate thought. Maybe that's what happened to John. She'd had the fever too, once upon a time when the world was fresh with possibility—before she'd lost two babies. Her faith must have been a weaker strain. One did not inherit faith.

"I suppose we must be content with the will of God," Kate said, but she was thinking of her father who had died, her brother who had lived, and how both had suffered, how William had suffered, a hunted animal for a decade. If God wanted His word in English, why didn't God just make it happen without so much suffering? But she couldn't say that to William Tyndale.

By Christmas she had regained enough strength to survive, her days filled with pretense and her nights without the poppy-seed drink. Just after New Year's she had a letter from Captain Lasser. It ran to two pages and she devoured it hungrily. It said that John was being well treated, had not been formally charged with heresy, only suspicion, and was even being given a furlough to visit the palace of his old tutor at Cambridge, Stephen Gardiner, who was now Bishop of Winchester. Since Bishop Gardiner had also been Tom's tutor during his own brief and unremarkable stay at Cambridge, he hoped to be able to sway him to even more sympathy on John's behalf. As Bishop of Winchester he would surely sit on any clerical jury, should John ever have to stand trial, which was doubtful, since there was thought not to be enough evidence to influence the king to hand him over to the "black-robed scavengers."

John is allowed the occasional visitor in the Tower, some of them even known Bible men. I actually got in to see him once. You would have laughed at my sober cleric's garb, as he did when he recognized me. He looked well, only a little pale from being shut inside, but he was in good enough spirits and spoke with great longing of his dear Kate. I assured him that when last I saw you, you were more beautiful than ever and full to the brim, and that you missed him beyond all reason and had to be persuaded not to come to him. He agreed that you should stay where you are. He said to tell you he would have no peace otherwise.

Shortly after, two letters, both dated before the captain's, came from John himself, one for Tyndale and one for her assuring them that he was well and that though he had secretly been given pen and ink and paper, writing was a nerve-racking business, because the minute he heard keys at the door, all had to be spirited away. He closed by begging Kate not to think he had broken faith even if he would not make it home by Christmas to welcome their child.

Her grief came back in a wash of pain. Of course he would not know. How could he know? And then the thought came that if he . . . if the worst happened . . . he might not ever have to know. He would be spared this one grief at least. If he came home, he could better deal with it then. The child had never been as real to him as it was to her. He had not carried it next to his heart.

"Shall I tell him about his son?" she asked William, knowing what he would say.

"You have to tell him the truth. But tell him only that you lost the child, not how long you carried him or the circumstances surrounding his death. John was not here to see how beautiful his son was. He will not feel that loss as keenly as you." She thought she detected a note of wistfulness in his voice. "He will be thinking only of you. Assure him you are well."

William always gave good advice.

❧

John was grateful for his visitors. They were his only break in the dismal monotony of his days. The winter light from the lone window was scant, and the cell was always cold. He'd developed a cough that racked him until his chest was sore. He sat in the dark most of the time, saving the few tallow dips Cromwell allowed him for his intervals of writing. He had almost finished his discourse to John Rastell, Thomas More's brother-in-law and printer. He knew enough of Rastell to know that he was at least listening to the arguments from the other side. If he should be converted, it would be a great thing; not only was he well placed as a licensed printer in England to help the cause, but John liked him.

He worked on his argument to Rastell for hours in his head before lighting his precious candle from the flint Cromwell had sent him. He was still writing in his head when he heard the keys jingle at the door.

His body jerked reflexively, but there was no pen and paper to hide. All the evidence was in his brain. It was too early for supper, so he was to be allowed a visitor then. Perhaps Captain Lasser. He'd promised he'd be back. But when the door opened he knew immediately from the man's stature it was not the captain. John felt a spur of disappointment, for he knew Tom would have news of Kate and home. But he liked the little tailor.

"Master Holt, how good of you to come. It's a long ride from Chelmsford on such a day."

"I came to London to buy cloth. We don't get much fine silk in Chelmsford."

His eyes darted about the cell as he moved in front of the still open door, blocking the view. He said loudly enough for the guard outside to hear, "My wife sent you some of her apple cake. You enjoyed it so last time. I've cleared it with the chamberlain of the Tower."

Then he winked at John and handed him the bundle wrapped in beeswax cloth. The smell of the cinnamon and apples made John's mouth water, but he did not open it. He would wait until his visitor left, and the door was closed, because he knew contained within the core of the cake would be a candle rolled in parchment.

"There's some of that black pudding you're partial to in the bottle."

"I especially love black pudding," John said, thanking the little tailor with a smile and a nod for the ink. "Thank your wife for me. Will you sit with me a while? Tell me what news you hear in your travels around Essex."

Outside the guard shuffled off to join his fellows at the end of the hall. Soon sounds of men swearing as they played dice carried through the open door, masking their own conversation.

The tailor lowered his voice to a near whisper. "Everyone sends you greetings. They worry for your health."

"Tell them to continue in prayer for me, but I am well—" A burst of coughing caused the tailor to raise his eyebrows in alarm. "Well enough under the circumstances."

"We spoke of you at our last Bible reading. The subject was the Lord's Last Supper. I tried to tell them based on the few notes you gave me what you had said, but alas my words lack eloquence."

"That is a subject of much contention even among the brethren. Perhaps it is best that you save—"

"But it was so clear, the way you preached it. I wish they could hear you." And then a light seemed to go on in his head. "If you could write down your sermon—not just the points, but the phrasing in your own words, and I could read it to them, it would be almost as though you were there. They would be much advantaged in their discernment."

When John did not answer immediately, he continued, "Of course, I would not want to do anything to put you in further danger. It's just that we are so hungry for a true understanding of the Word—the Church has turned what should be sacred into some ancient superstitious rite."

How could John deny such a kindred spirit? "How long are you going to be in London?"

"Just through tomorrow."

"I'm not sure I can do it so soon—I have to be so careful lest—"

William Holt shrugged. "If it is too much . . . maybe another time. Either way, I'll call on you again before I leave, if they will let me. There's an inn close by Tower Bridge that makes good meat pies. I'll bring you one."

"Could I prevail on your generosity to bring two? There is a poor man here name of Petite, a grocer who by catching a seeming sweetness in God's Word fell afoul of Thomas More"—he laughed bitterly—"as we all do sooner or later. They searched his home and found nothing and have no witness to testify against him, but More will not see him released even though he is very ill. Sometimes the chamberlain allows me to visit him. A good meat pie might lift his spirits."

"Two pies it shall be then"—and another wink—"and more apple cake to replenish that which you consume tonight. That is little enough pay, for the good work you do. I'll be back tomorrow."

His visitor stepped out into the hall. The guard shuffled down a few minutes later and shut the door. As soon as John heard the key turn in the lock and the footfalls fade, he tore into the apple cake, pulling out the pen and paper. Then dragging the rickety little table that Cromwell had procured for him into the center of the room, he climbed upon it and carefully removed the block that had been cut from the ceiling.

"Psst. Petite," he called in a whisper. "Are you awake?"

He heard a raspy answer. "Come to the hole. I've a treat for you," and he shoved a chunk of the apple cake through.

A hand reached down and grabbed it. "God bless you, John Frith, God bless you."

Then climbing down, John lit his tallow dip, took up the pen and dipping it in the "black pudding" began to write: "The mass is not a sacrifice but a remembrance of the sacrifice and assurance of salvation that God has given us."

The candle flame glowed steadily and brightly as a new flame does. Its steadfastness distracted him momentarily, mesmerizing him. As if in a trance, he placed his ink-stained forefinger in the flame until he felt the burn. Snatching it away with a grimace of pain, he put it to his lips to soothe it. *Thomas Bilney before he was burned used to do this, to condition himself to the pain. Will I have such courage as he showed at the stake?* he wondered. *Many good men have not.*

Yet to do less would disappoint his Lord and bring shame upon himself— and shame to his wife. He would never forget the sorrow in Kate's face when she talked about her brother. Taking his finger from his mouth, he put it in the flame again. Was it his imagination or did he hold it longer that time? This time when he withdrew it, he did not put it to his lips, but ignoring the pain picked up his pen.

THIRTY-SEVEN

Anne Bulleine, Marques of Pembroke, was proclaimed
Queene at Greenych and offred that daie in the Kinges
Chappelle as Queene of Englande.
—THE EVENTS OF APRIL 12, 1533, AS RECORDED
IN *THE CHRONICLES OF ENGLAND DURING*
THE REIGN OF THE TUDORS

John watched from a viewing platform built above Tower Green as the queen's barge came up the Thames. He was more grateful for the sunlight on his face than the opportunity to witness the water parade. Upon the king's orders that certain prisoners were to be let out to witness the new queen's arrival as an act of charity, a celebration of new beginnings, Thomas Cromwell had sent down a list of those prisoners who should review the spectacle. Like his fellows, John had been given a green flag to wave as the queen's barge floated by, and instructed to cheer loudly.

As he watched the sun rippling off the Thames, he considered whether a man could survive such a jump, wondering how many others standing so near the balustrade shared that thought. But for John it was a mere intellectual curiosity. Captain Lasser had spoken to him of an escape plan, but John had a growing certainty that not to attempt to defend his beliefs now that he had been charged with heresy would put a stain upon his honor and hurt the cause—and besides, it would be a fool's jump. The archers on the wall were armed. He'd have an arrow in his back before he broke the surface of the waters.

"That's the queen's boat," the chamberlain who stood with him said, pointing to the biggest barge.

It was marked with the king's arms and followed by lesser barges—as far downriver as John could see—belonging to City of London companies. They made an amazing spectacle, festooned with silk banners of Tudor green and white shot through with silver threads that glinted in the light bouncing off the water. Music drifted up from many of the barges as they passed beneath the platform, interrupted by periodic bursts of cannon in salute.

"What about the old queen?" one of the prisoners murmured.

"There is no old queen. You must be referring to the 'princess dowager,'" he mocked. There was laughter all around.

"Must be good to be a king," one of the guards whispered to another. "I've got myself an old woman I'd like to replace with a sweet young thing."

The lead barge turned and swung around, closer to the Tower.

"Now! Here she comes," the guard yelled. "Shout! Wave your banners."

A chorus of hoots and cheers erupted around him. Caught up in the moment, John shouted, "God save the queen," and waved his banner, more vigorously than he might have except for the sheer joy of the movement of his arms. It wasn't that he begrudged the new queen her triumph. She was after all a reformer and even had sent him her best regards through Master Cromwell, saying she hoped for a day when all such as he would be free in England. Cromwell had suggested that the king knew of John's reputation as a scholar and that if Master Frith would write favorably concerning the marriage John might find himself celebrated rather than incarcerated. But so far John had not been able to do that. A man, even a king, should not easily break a vow made before God. In that and that alone John agreed with Thomas More, who it was said deplored the marriage though it meant risking his own preferment. On much different grounds, John told himself. It was probably not the breaking of a vow that More despised nearly so much as the putting away of a Catholic queen in favor of a protestant one.

The new queen looked up at the prisoners on the platform. John could not see her face well enough to read the expression, but he read pure joy in her movements as she blew kisses and waved her arms high in the air. He wondered what Kate would make of the spectacle. He couldn't say for sure, but he thought she might spare a moment of regret for the abandoned Queen Katherine. Kate was very tenderhearted, and it might just be that she also felt abandoned. She had said as much to him when they first argued over his leaving, before she had agreed to let him go.

Had he not shown his love for his wife in a thousand ways? Yet he had left her behind to serve a cause that if asked he would have to say was greater than one man, one woman—greater even than his love for her. What was that if not abandonment? Captain Lasser had told him about the child. John remembered how it was the last time and grieved that he had not been there to comfort her. He thanked God for Tom Lasser. He was a good friend.

A cloud drifted over the sun, turning the sparkling water gray. The April breeze seemed suddenly sharp. The entourage had moved out of sight.

"Show's over. Time to go in," the guard said.

John fell in line with the others to go back to his bleak cell. Even Petite was gone now, and though he was glad for his comrade's release, there was nobody to whisper to in the black heart of the night. Nobody at all.

☙❧

Anne Boleyn turned in a fury to the king, aware as she did so that he hated her tantrums, but she seemed unable to control her temper since she'd become pregnant. It was almost as though some demon had entered her with Henry's seed. She flung the gold-inlaid walking stick across the privy chamber as she would have liked to fling the giver. The stick had been a New Year's gift to the king from Thomas More when he was chancellor.

"The pious, hypocritical Thomas More disdains to come to my coronation dinner! And you will stand by and let your queen be thus insulted?"

Her trip down the Thames had been exhilarating, people lining the shores in every village, shouting from the quays and jetties, all eyes trained on her even from the wall of Tower Prison as she stood in the bow of the boat, waving, laughing, while the sunlight sparked the jewels at her throat and the pearls sewn in perfect patterns down her sleeves.

But the dinner afterward had not gone well. She had been uneasy, feeling the tension in the room, as the courtiers exchanged furtive looks, bowing to her, sometimes with mockery in their eyes, all the while Henry watching like a hawk, his eyes and ears alert for the obvious slight. Charles Brandon had already been sent home in anger for a reported slight. As Archbishop Cranmer spoke to the assembled nobles and bishops in glowing terms of the new queen's love for the king and her love for England, Anne had taken inventory from her place on the dais. She looked at the board reserved for the king's council. Thomas More was conspicuous in his absence.

Henry carried the tension left over from the dinner too. It was visible in the tightness of his face, the curtness of his tone when he answered her. "Thomas More is of little matter." He picked up the walking stick and examined it thoughtfully, picking at the gold inlay until one piece came loose. He laid it carelessly aside. "He is no longer chancellor."

"Of course it matters! He is still a king's councillor and probably the most respected man in England. You can mark it—his absence will be noted and commented on. It will give heart to Katherine's supporters."

"When Master More thinks on it, his good sense will prevail. He pleaded illness, but he will be at Westminster for your coronation with the rest of the court."

She felt her temper rising with her voice at his easy dismissal of her fears.

"Good sense? When has he shown good sense? Did he show good sense when he spoke against the reform of the clergy in Parliament?" She paced, clenching her fists. "Did he show good sense when he refused to sign the petition to the pope?"

"Would you have him brought in chains to salute you, my lady? The 'most respected man in England'? How think you that would look to Katherine's loyalists?"

Anne heard the steel in his voice and stopped pacing, unclenched her fists. She closed her eyes and breathed deeply, struggling for control. When she answered him, her voice was an octave lower.

"You are right, of course, as you always are. It's just since our wedding was so secret, I would like a public display so that all your subjects can see how happy their king is and know that England will soon have a prince." She reached out and pulled his hand forward so that it touched her belly. "If they treat me with less respect than a queen deserves, they might also fail to respect . . . our son."

His face relaxed into an almost boyish grin. "We will have such a grand ceremony that no one will notice if Thomas More is absent. They will be too blinded by the glory of their queen."

"Tell me," she said, suddenly as greedy as a child, the anger melted away by the prospect of all of London at her feet.

"After Cranmer puts the crown on your head and says the proper prayers, you will progress through the streets of London in an open litter draped in white silk. Standing beneath a silk canopy garlanded with flowers and silver bells, you will wave at the throngs who line the streets to get a glimpse of their beautiful queen. I will ride in front upon my most noble steed to protect you and herald your arrival."

"Yes, yes?" Anne said. "Go on."

He moved closer and kissed her throat, murmuring between the kisses, "Pageants . . . at every stop . . . singing your praises . . . choirs of children . . . trumpets . . ."

And I in my white dress, my dark hair flowing free beneath a jeweled coronet, I shall wave to my adoring subjects. I, a simple knight's daughter, Queen of England at last.

It was a lovely vision that left her breathless.

"Let's to bed, my lord," she said, taking him by the hand.

⚜

The spring day at Chelsea had turned chilly, as chilly as Dame Alice's mood, Sir Thomas thought, as he looked out his study window at the river. His wife was not pleased that they were not going to Westminster.

"You are still the king's councillor. We would have been given a seat of honor from which to watch the coronation."

"You would not have wanted to go without a new gown, and you know we can no longer afford such an extravagance."

"We are not as impoverished as you make us out to be. I still have some income, and you have your estates in Oxfordshire and Kent. Though I would have been content to wear an old gown to ease your mind." But he could see in her eyes that she would not and she knew she would not.

"And our daughters—would they have been content?" he asked.

She sighed heavily. "It is not that we should be denied the spectacle—that's not what concerns me. I am well content to keep me here while the king's mistress is honored." She reached out and touched his sleeve. "But the king will not wink at this slight from such a man as you."

"Such a man as I?" Thomas laughed. "Henry will hardly notice. I am no longer of any importance to him."

But Thomas doubted that was so. His old friend Cuthbert Tunstall had doubted it too, urging him to go, even sending him twenty pounds collected from his friends in the bishopric to purchase a new cloak for the occasion. He had kept the money—the cost of pen and ink had risen—but tried to explain to his cowardly friends that he had gone too far in matters of principle to stoop to curry favor now.

"What have you done to us, Thomas More?" Dame Alice asked quietly.

"I have done only that which my conscience told me, Alice. A man should be expected to do no less."

"You will not reconsider then?"

"I will not reconsider."

"You are not the only one who suffers for your conscience." She went out slamming the door behind her.

Thomas was still standing at the window, pondering what would be the king's next move and how he should counter, marveling how he and "the Defender of the Faith" came to be on opposite sides of the chessboard because of a woman, when he saw a horse and rider approach the house. He recognized the little tailor immediately. His spirits lifted as he went to the door to meet him.

"Master Holt? Come in. Come in. Good news, I hope. Have you brought the evidence?"

The tailor from Chelmsford smiled broadly.

"I have indeed, Sir Thomas. It is not just notes this time, but a sermon, completely disputing the sacred mass in every syllable, just as you asked for."

"Good man. Good man," Thomas said as he grabbed the rolled-up paper. His eyes scanned it with satisfaction. He felt the pull of neglected muscles as the smile spread across his face. "This should do it." He draped his arm around William Holt's shoulders in a moment of rare fellowship. "You will be rewarded in heaven, but you don't have to wait that long," he said, as he rummaged in his desk and produced the twenty pounds Cuthbert Tunstall had sent him to purchase a new cloak.

William Holt looked at the money and shook his head. "No, my lord, I will take no pay. Truth is, it was harder than I thought. I liked the man. He didn't seem like the bad sort I thought. You know he has a wife?"

"I had heard. Do you know where she is?"

"No. He never said."

He did not look at Thomas but out the window. Thomas knew when he was being lied to, but he would let it go for now.

"When will Frith be tried?" Holt asked.

"Not for a few weeks. First, I'll present this evidence to Bishop Stokesley who will show it to the king. Then even the archbishop cannot prevent a trial—and an inevitable conviction. You've done very well."

" 'Tis a pity," the tailor said, shaking his head. "I'll not enjoy seeing him burn."

"Take heart, man. Think of his soul. When faced with the fire, he may even recant. He has that option."

"I don't think so. He doesn't seem like the kind."

"You are probably right," Thomas said, feigning more sympathy than he felt. "Once a fanatical dogma claims a man, it's as though his reason takes a holiday. But you need not be troubled. You have done your Church a great service. Take the twenty pounds. You have earned it."

After William Holt reluctantly put the money in his pocket and left, Thomas read Frith's sermon denying the Real Presence of Christ's body in the Eucharist. With every word, Thomas's excitement grew as he built a prosecutor's case in his head. This should do it. Even the king could not stomach such heresy as this.

⚘

"There is nothing I can do for him. The man is a heretic. He denies the mass. He will have to stand trial," Henry said two weeks later when he broke the news to Anne. He steeled himself for the angry outburst he knew was to follow.

"Most unfortunate," was all she said.

She'd not been herself since the coronation. It's the pregnancy, he told himself. Moods like quicksilver, though she'd always been quick-tempered. Lately he'd even come to wonder if she had the temperament to be queen. Katherine might have been barren but the people loved her, and she was always queenly in her demeanor. Sometimes Anne acted more like a fishwife than a queen. But the last few days, ever since the great tantrum after her coronation, she'd just been . . . distracted, listless. He hoped this strange mood wasn't affecting the child.

In spite of his best efforts, all the expense, the pressure he'd exerted on all the nobles to treat her with deference and respect, the coronation had been a disappointment, and she had blamed him. But he could not make the people love her. Her progress through the streets of London had been met with small enthusiasm and sometimes even insults. Many had refused even to remove their caps in respect, causing the old woman who was always at her side to call out to some in the crowd that their scalps were scurvy, and they were ashamed to uncover them. Some in the crowd had returned the shouted insults, directing them at the new queen. From astride his noble mount, he had pretended not to hear, but caused his horse to prance and toss his golden harness to garner cheers so Anne would hear the cheers and think they were for her. It seemed the best way. If he could not buy their favor with spectacle and free food and drink, he was sure he could not beat it into them.

"I know Frith was a favorite of yours," he said. "Perhaps he'll recant at the last minute."

"Perhaps," she said.

No, not like herself at all.

From the corner of his eye, he watched Jane Seymour as she laid out his wife's nightrobe. When Anne looked at him hard, he turned his gaze away, but his mind lingered, wondering what Jane's cool, fair flesh would feel like, wondering if he could make it blush with passion.

"Leave us," Anne snapped, her dark eyes glittering with resentment. Henry was learning to recognize the beginnings of her temper flares. They always flamed first in her eyes.

The blond-haired beauty dropped her curtsy and backed out of the room, but not before her sympathetic gaze locked with Henry's.

He left shortly after, with Anne's shrewish voice calling after him, demanding he return. He went instead to the jousting field to practice—maybe a few nights alone would improve her temper—and then summoned Archbishop Cranmer to prepare for John Frith's trial.

THIRTY-EIGHT

*. . . [Y]our wife is well content with the will of God
and would not, for her sake, have the glory of God
hindered.*

—EXCERPT FROM TYNDALE'S
LETTER TO JOHN FRITH IN PRISON

ohn was not surprised to see Thomas Cromwell when he came to his
cell a few days after the queen's coronation. He'd noticed a difference in the
way he was treated lately. He'd been allowed no visitors and given no
candles, nor pen nor paper, not even a book to read, except for a copy of
Thomas More's answer to John's sermon on the Eucharist, which just magi-
cally appeared in his cell.

He had torn into that greedily, exultant at the poor argument More made.
Surely, all thinking men would see the faulty logic contained therein. It was
the poorest writing he'd ever seen from More's pen. And then it had occurred to him what the existence of such a document meant. If More was
answering his discourse on the Eucharist, then that meant he had a copy of
John's sermon. He had been betrayed! He should have never trusted the tailor, should have heeded Tyndale's warnings not to write on the subject.
Thomas More had laid yet another trap, and this time John, like a fool, had
stepped right into it. In the last week he'd had plenty of time to think about
what that meant.

"Leave us," Cromwell said to the chamberlain. "Shut the door behind you. I will call when I am ready."

"You are not the bearer of good news, I would guess," John said to his visitor.

A frown wrinkled Cromwell's brow. "A copy of your sermon has come into the hands of the king."

"I wonder how that happened," John said.

"His Majesty may have defied the pope, but he will not stretch to turn his back on the mass. Archbishop Cranmer has set your heresy trial. There is nothing else to be done." There was more accusation in his tone than sympathy. "Now that you have handed your enemies the torch with which to light your fire."

"What about the queen's influence?"

"The queen is distracted by her pregnancy and distressed that she is not embraced by the populace as their rightful queen. Rumor says that she has quarreled with the king. She'll not be inclined to interfere, I think, despite her sympathy. The evidence against you is too strong."

A raven landed on the casement and, jerking its head, pecked at an unfortunate insect. It peered into the room and flew off with a raucous caw and a flap of its wings.

"Will I be tortured first?" John could not look at the secretary. He did not want him to see the fear that must show in his eyes. Was it a sin to be afraid?

Cromwell didn't smile, but for the first time since entering John's cell, his demeanor softened.

"Not with Cranmer in charge and More's influence on the wane. And under the new law, Stokesley can't get to you. The way I see it, you have three choices." He placed his hand on John's shoulder. "You can recant, deny what you have written, promise to embrace the doctrine of the Real Presence in the Eucharist, and throw yourself on the Church's mercy, in which case you'll probably be allowed to go back to your wife in Antwerp after they have made a public spectacle of you." He paused and added bluntly, "Or you can burn."

That was pretty much the conclusion John had come to in this last week. He knew which course, if God granted him courage, he would choose. He'd lacked only one thing, and that had been provided him in the same letter from Tyndale warning him ironically yet again not to write on the Eucharist. In John's letters to and from Kate, they had never broached the subject of his execution, if to speak it was to make it possible. They wrote only of their love and longing for each other. But Tyndale in an early letter had written of a possible outcome, telling him to be of courage. In answer to John's query about how Kate was taking his imprisonment, Tyndale had responded that she had said that she would not have him deny his faith on her account. He was free to make up his own mind. But what freedom really, when he had professed, like the apostle Paul, to be Christ's slave?

The room was very quiet as Cromwell waited for him to consider these two possibilities.

"You said a third. Or did I misunderstand?"

Cromwell shrugged and glanced toward the door. "You can escape."

"Not many men have escaped from the Tower. Not a likely choice." He remembered that Tom Lasser had once tried to convince him of the possibility of concocting an escape scheme. But it would have been at the captain's risk. John had refused to consider it.

Cromwell cocked his head as though listening for some outside noise, then lowered his voice so that John had to strain to hear even in the silence.

"First you are to be examined by the archbishop at his palace in Croydon. You will be in the custody of Cranmer's men. At some point you will be given a chance to escape." Then he added meaningfully, "The guards will not give chase."

Was the secretary saying what he thought he was saying? It was some kind of trap. It had to be a trap.

"I know what you are thinking. But you will not be pursued. Archbishop Cranmer as well as Bishop Gardiner, with whom I think you are well acquainted, will preside at your trial along with Bishop Stokesley. They are functionaries of Church law and will be bound to find you guilty if you appear before them. But both the archbishop and Bishop Gardiner have said they will not pursue you if you try to escape." He shrugged and said as matter-of-factly as if they were discussing the price of grain and not life and death, "Bishop Stokesley, of course, is another matter."

John shook his head. "I'll never make it. Stokesley and Thomas More will have spies all along the route."

"Possibly. But what do you have to lose? If you should make your escape at Brixton Wood, you can go about five miles northeast and arrive at the river close to Greenwich. The guards have been instructed to delay reporting your escape—they will say they were looking for you in the wood, then they will report that you fled west, so you will gain a little time. Follow the river east until you see a certain ship docked. You will recognize the insignia. I believe you and the captain are old friends."

Tom Lasser! Here at last was hope. He trusted Tom Lasser. But here, too, was a new conundrum. It wasn't like the last time the captain and Humphrey Monmouth had arranged his escape. That time he was merely a fugitive from illegal persecution. This time he had been formally charged. Would anything less than affirming his position before the assembled Church body be the same as recanting? Would he be, in effect, like Peter at the devil's campfire, denying the very Christ he'd promised to serve? Even Luther, before seeking sanctuary, had proclaimed his faith to the Church council, declaring, "Here I stand. I can do no other."

Could John Frith do any other?

Cromwell reached into his pocket and brought out a candle and a small roll of paper and pen. "Cranmer is in Canterbury and says he will not be back in Lambeth for a week. I suspect he did that to give you time to think about the proposal and to give your friend time to complete arrangements. I thought you might want to write down some thoughts in case you decide to proceed with the trial. It is sometimes hard for a man to marshal his thoughts—even a man as smart as you—when faced with the threat of damnation."

"How did . . ." Better not to say his name. "How did my friend become involved?"

"Bishop Gardiner was also his former tutor. It seems, like you, he abandoned a promising career in the Church—though for a less holy mission than you and Tyndale. He has convinced the bishop to go along with this. But be forewarned, Master Frith, if this window closes, there will be no other."

Long after John heard the door lock behind his visitor, he sat in the gathering gloom. Twice the raven came back and lit upon the high casement briefly before flying off with raucous cries. If this were a poem, John thought, the great black bird would be a messenger—or a symbolic harbinger of death. But from where he sat, John did not feel like the heroic center of such a poem, and he had not a clue what message the raven might have for him. He just felt like a man, alone and afraid. He longed to see Kate, to ask her advice on what to do. Would she tell him to stand up for his beliefs or would she tell him to escape?

He took out Tyndale's creased letter and read it yet again. "I would not have the glory of God hindered for my sake," quoting her own words. Tyndale was meticulous in such matters. The meaning was clear and yet . . . how could he abandon her?

When darkness came, he lit the candle, but he did not put pen to paper. He could not prepare a defense. What was the use? He had published all his arguments. He could only say with Luther, "Here I stand." But that much he had to do. If he did not, his enemies would brand him as a coward.

He placed his palm over the candle flame and held it there until the pain brought tears to his eyes. Maybe in spite of what Cromwell said, there would be another window for escape, after he had faced down, not just his enemies, but the enemies of the Word. Some way to keep his honor and his life. He closed his eyes and prayed for courage.

✦

Kate saw the *Siren's Song* when it entered the harbor. Every day for weeks she'd gone down to the harbor to watch for it, for news of John. When the familiar rigging came close enough so that shading her eyes from the sun she could make out the name on the side, her heart began to pound. For one brief moment she even dared to think John might be on it. His last letter a month ago had been hopeful of his release after the new queen's coronation. It was a warm June day and the excitement of such a thought made her light-headed as she ran toward the jetty where she thought the boat would dock.

The captain spotted her immediately and waved for her to come aboard, sending a familiar crewman down to help her. She scanned the deck for any profile that might be John's, but when she saw the captain, he was standing alone. One look at his face—even the sardonic smile with which he always greeted her was gone—told her John's homecoming was not imminent.

"When have you seen him?" she asked when they were seated at the captain's table.

Endor put a plate of the sweet buns that Kate had liked so much in front of them. The smell almost made her heave, but it was not from the rocking of the ship in the harbor. Anxiety closed her throat—something in his manner, in the way he would not look at her—made her breath come fast and hard.

"Not for a few weeks. I have been on business for the league, and when I tried to get in to see him last week they said he was being denied visitors."

"But he is still . . . alive?" She could hardly say the words.

He looked away. Dear God . . . why would he not look at her? "He is—"

"Yes. He is still alive." He placed his hand on hers. She looked down at the Venetian lace at his wrist, almost covering her own trembling hand. He withdrew it. "But his prospects are not as favorable as they were."

Her hand went to her chin to stop its quivering. When she spoke it was more statement than question. "They are going to try him for heresy, aren't they?"

"Yes, but don't give up hope, Kate. The archbishop has agreed that if he escapes en route to the trial, he will not be pursued."

"Has Thomas More agreed? Has the Bishop of London agreed?" She tried to stop the quiver in her voice. "How can—"

"We have a plan."

"We?"

"I will help him."

"You would do that for us? You know what you are risking." She studied his face, remembering how he'd laughed with John on their journey to Antwerp, how easy they were together.

"I told you once before, I don't intend to get caught. But there is one thing. He has to agree."

"But why would he not agree? What could—"

But she knew, even before he said it, she knew.

"I think your husband has that something about him that defines honor very narrowly. I fear he is the stuff of which martyrs are made."

She struggled for control. Now was not the time. The time for crying would come later when she was alone, suddenly remembering the despair in Mary's face when her husband was taken, and the way her own mother pined away until she died from grief—Kate had not fully understood that. She had been so naïve, so prideful of her father's memory. But her father had never been given a choice. Was it not just as honorable to choose to live for one's belief as to die for it—especially if one had that choice? Even Jesus had prayed in Gethsemane for the cup to pass.

Kate tried frantically to remember if she had ever said anything to John that might influence him. There had been the time when she told him about the shame she felt after her brother gave in. But surely he would not interpret that . . . but why would he not? Had her own feelings not been ambivalent when her brother gave in under torture? Please, God, let them not torture John. Let him recant before he suffers as her brother had suffered. Let him come back to her as her brother had gone back to Mary and Pip. She had to convince him that he would be worth more to his cause alive than dead.

Endor suddenly appeared beside her and, taking Kate's hand in hers, squeezed it so hard, it almost hurt. She could not speak her sympathy. She did not need to. Kate could read it in her face, in the water welling in her blue eyes. And then she knew. This was what Endor had seen in the water that first time, when she'd run from the cabin upset. That same look of pity and sorrow was on her face today. In Endor's mind John was already a dead man. With this realization, a numbing calm settled over Kate—a sense of detachment as though she were watching herself from a place removed.

"Take me to him," she said. "I have to see him."

"That's too dangerous—for both of you."

"Take me to him," she said. "If you don't, I'll find someone else. I know there are passenger ships that go back and forth regularly. I'll catch one of them."

He didn't say anything, just closed his eyes as if working out some difficult problem. When he opened them he locked his gaze on hers and answered grimly.

"Be watching at the window of the English House at dawn. They'll not let me in. I'll send a crewman to help you with your gear."

THIRTY-NINE

I, Frith, thus do think and as I think, so have I said, written, taught, and affirmed, and in my books have published.
—STATEMENT OF JOHN FRITH SIGNED
BY HIS OWN HAND AT HIS TRIAL ON 20 JUNE 1533

John Frith blinked as he was led out into the sunlight. The bright light hurt, but he didn't want to close his eyes, didn't want to lose the brilliant blues and greens. A ragged little gorse bush struggled to bloom in the courtyard of the Beauchamp Tower. It was a thing of exquisite beauty. He could not resist touching it.

"Do you want him shackled?"

The two men wearing sidearms who had come to claim him exchanged looks.

"I think not," one said in a thick Welsh accent.

"He looks to be a reasonable fellow," the other one, dressed not in livery but in a gentleman's clothes, added.

The deputy shrugged and signaled for the gatekeeper to open the gate that led to the water stairs where a waterman waited to ferry them across the Thames. As they exited the boat, John looked around for the prison cart he expected to be waiting.

"We're on foot from here on," the Welsh porter said, "but don't worry. We've plenty of time. We can rest whenever you want."

"I'm grateful for the chance to walk," John said. "My legs want exercise."

He walked silently between his companions, and since he was the youngest of the three—in spite of his lack of exercise, unless pacing his cell counted—it was easy for him to keep up. His guards ignored him for the most part as they talked of estate matters at Croydon. But they treated him with uncommon courtesy. The Welshman, who John learned was a porter for Archbishop Cranmer, had even brought along a bit of bread and cheese in his pack, which he shared with John. The gentleman declined his offer, but it had been a while since John had tasted fresh bread, and he munched it gratefully.

They'd walked a few miles—maybe as many as five, John guessed; the shadows had already lengthened—when they approached a lonely crossroads. The road to the left was hardly more than a rough path. The porter jerked his head in that direction. The late afternoon shade made the woods look dark and foreboding. This must be Brixton Wood, John thought, just as Cromwell had said. Did they expect him to make a break for it?

The gentleman addressed him directly for the first time. "Here's where we part company, Master Frith. God's speed to you. If you can avoid the wolves, you might make it."

"The fiercest wolves are in London," John said. "One is in the bishop's seat and the other hiding in his den at Chelsea. Compared to them, this wood looks hospitable."

The porter, who had been a jovial enough companion, looked sober. "Well said. We'll give you a couple of hours before we travel on to Croyden. We'll tell them you darted off west, that you'll probably be in Wandsworth by hard nightfall." Then he grinned. "We gave chase, but you were just too fleet of foot."

John felt his eyes start to water. Here was such charity. Such generosity. Their actions were not without risk. "What will the ecclesiastical court say when you come up empty-handed?"

"The archbishop will cover for us. We volunteered for this duty." The porter opened the pack where he'd carried the bread and cheese and produced a small Tyndale New Testament. "Give our thanks to your friend if you make it."

John looked down at the pocket-sized book. A feeling of immense gratification came over him. "I thank you, good sirs," he said. "God knows, I thank you, and may God bless you for your courage and steadfastness." He paused and breathed deeply of the air, reveling in the mossy earthen smell of it after the dank smells of the Tower. "But I'm not going."

"What do you mean, you're not going! Are you crazy?"

"I am an honest man. Why should I not stand and defend that which I believe, that which I have written? If there be justice—"

"Justice! There is no justice to be had in the court you'll be facing." The porter's frustration made his voice rise. "You'll not have the chance of a snowball in hell."

A scuffling on the ground drew John's attention. Both men grasped the hilts of their swords. A disturbed squirrel bolted up the tree.

"You've been gone a while, and maybe you don't know what's been going on here," the gentleman said, his voice quiet, the voice of reason. "Here in England they tie you to a post and set fire to you for saying the things you say."

"I'm prepared for that. I will put myself in God's hands." It occurred to John then that maybe these were the hands that God was using. That maybe these two men had been sent for just such a purpose. But if he let himself believe that, how could he ever know for sure that it was not devil's temptation?

The porter sat down hard on a nearby stump, still shaking his head in disbelief. "Let's sit here a minute, and you think about it."

"I've thought of nothing else for the last week. Believe me. I want nothing so much as to live. I have a wife . . ." No. He could not think about Kate or his courage would melt away.

His guards made no move to resume the journey.

"If you do not wish to accompany me, good sirs, I shall find my own way to Croydon Palace where I will surrender myself to the archbishop."

Only then did the porter get up and stride away. For the last leg of their journey they walked in single file, with John bringing up the rear a few paces behind.

⇥⇤

Kate spent her first night back in London in her little bed above the print shop. *I have completed a circle,* she thought, thinking how the past five years had changed her life and yet how really nothing had changed. She lay awake as before, tossing and turning, filled with fear and dread for a man named John.

The captain had gone in through the same boarded-up window John had pried open and unlatched the door for her. She walked into the little book-shop on Paternoster Row and it was as if she had never left, except for a thick coat of dust that covered everything. A familiar weight of dread and loneli-ness descended on her as though it had hovered there all along, just waiting for her return. She had picked up her broom and started to sweep the cob-webs from the corner, noticing the spotty footprints in the dust below the window where the captain's larger footprints had blurred John's.

"Please, let me"—and the captain reached for the broom—"You just sit. I'll do it," he said.

"When can I see him?" she asked.

"Tomorrow," he said. "I'll take you to see him tomorrow. It is too late tonight. The deputy constable will be on duty. I've learned that Constable Kingston is the one who is reasonable. Especially if one shows him a gold crown in consideration of his reasonableness."

"I cannot ever repay you . . . for any of it. You have been very kind to us."

"I'll think of a way," he said. But the grin that he forced was a poor imi-tation of that mocking smile he usually offered.

After the cobwebs were cleared, he left to go get food. Kate unpacked her small trunk and hung her clothes in the cupboard. When he returned with Endor carrying offerings from her little bake oven, she tried to eat to please him—it seemed important to him and that was the least she could do—but the food had no taste, and it was hard to swallow for the fear lodging in her throat. She was so tired. The smallest movement was an effort. She had not slept at all, since she'd learned of John's impending trial.

Five years. And here she was again alone in her narrow bed above the stairs. She closed her eyes and lay awake listening to the night sounds through her open attic window. *He is so close*, she thought. *Why can I not feel his presence?* And she wondered if he lay awake thinking of her. But still she did not cry. Neither did she sleep.

ᜃ

As Tom Lasser knocked on the door to the bookshop the next morning, some part of him wished he'd never met Kate Frith, wished he could just get on his boat and sail away. And maybe he could one day soon. Put all this behind him. But not today.

Endor opened the door for him. Kate looked up at him with pleading in her eyes, pleading for some kind of good news when he had none to give.

"You can't see him today," he said.

She stood by the window, her body straight and rigid. Her hair was disheveled, a tangled mass hanging down her back and falling in her face; dark circles shadowed her eyes. "Why not?"

How long had she stood watch at that window, waiting for him?

"Because they have moved him. I think we are going to have to get another plan."

"Where has he gone? Are they taking him to trial?"

The breathlessness in her voice made him want to run. There was no point to prolonging the agony. He just needed to tell her.

"Please—"

"They've already tried him, Kate. He . . . he signed a confession of his beliefs."

"No . . . please, God . . . How do you know?"

"I went to the Tower, and they told me he'd been taken to Croydon Palace, so I went there immediately. The trial was over. They'd already moved him."

She leaned against him then to keep from falling. He put his arm around her, feeling her shoulders tremble, and guided her onto the wooden settle under the shop window. The trembling stopped and a fierce rigidity took its place.

"I thought there was a plan for his escape?" Her voice was scarcely above a whisper. "You said—"

"He refused, Kate." He could not look at her. "John has decided to take the martyr's route after all, poor fool. You can't help a man who won't be helped."

Bishop Gardiner had said Archbishop Cranmer had no choice after Frith's statement but to release the prisoner to his ordinary, and since he was arrested at Southend just out of London, Bishop Stokesley was his ordinary. But Tom had to give her some reassurance. Some small hope to hang on to though there was little to none.

"All is not yet lost. He's still alive. I'll find out where they've taken him. They'll give him a couple of weeks. They would rather have his signature on a statement of repentance." Though he doubted that was true. These men were obsessed with burning. "Will you be all right here?"

She nodded mutely. Ever since they'd left Antwerp, she'd had that unnatural, deadly calm that was somehow worse than tears. It was as though her will were a dam behind which the pressure was building. What damage was being done behind that wall he could only guess. He'd seen people driven to madness with less cause. But he did not know how to help her except to return her husband to her.

"It may take me a day or two. Endor's going to stay with you. She'll get you what you need. But stay here, Kate."

When she did not respond, he repeated, "Stay here. It's important. You don't need to fall in the hands of John's enemies. That would not help either of you. Did you hear me?"

She answered dully, "I heard."

She had not promised, but he could hardly lock her up. She would probably be safe enough. After all, More and Stokesley had what they wanted.

⁓ ⁓

When John woke he thought at first he was back in the fish cellar. But Newgate Prison was worse than the fish cellar. In the fish cellar he'd had companionship and freedom of movement and hope. Here he was alone and shackled by his neck to the wall. And he had no hope. How did a man live without hope? *Your hope is in Jesus Christ. Pray to your Father in that name and he will ease your pain or shorten it.* That's what Tyndale had said in his last letter. And that's what John tried to do, though he could not kneel or even bow his head from his fixed position on the wall. Could God hear one man's prayer from this hellish place that birthed so many prayers, so many souls, all crying out to God? Their unspoken prayers, a cacophony of despair, mixed with his pain and swirled inside his head.

They had brought him here after his trial. Stokesley had mocked him for his heresy, dangling rescue before him if he would recant. Thomas More had been there too, laughing, delighting in his resistance. "I understand you've taken a wife, Master Frith, like all the heretics who have deserted the Church. Is she beautiful? Will she be at Smithfield to watch you burn for heresy, or did you leave her behind in Antwerp? Or maybe Holland? Is she with Tyndale, perhaps? Tell us where the heretic Tyndale is, and you can return to her."

But with all their mocking they had only hardened his resolve. And the odd thing was that they took a perverse pleasure in it, as though they really didn't want him to recant. He could see the excitement in their faces, and he almost pitied them their devilish obsession. Their souls were in more peril than his. His body might burn, but their souls were being consumed by the fires of their hatred.

The mind games with which he had freed his spirit from the fish cellar and the Tower no longer worked. He could not recite his Greek poetry; pain had won the battle for his mind, but he prayed for strength and for the wife he was leaving behind. He prayed, too, for some sign that God was pleased with his decision.

But no voice spoke from heaven. The doors of Newgate Prison did not fly open.

After a while he fell into a deep and dreamless sleep. He took that as a sign, for when he woke his mind was more at peace. Kate and Tyndale and even his books seemed far away, almost as though they were part of some other man's life. John Frith no longer had a wife. Or friends. Or a future. He was resigned and his soul was prepared for death. There was only the wrenching, ripping, painful tearing from this world to get through. He prayed it would be over soon.

><

Get up, Kate. It's up to you. You have to find him before it is too late. Kate struggled from her torpor. *Get up and look for John.* But she didn't have the strength. He should be home from Frankfurt soon. He would know what to do. The shelves were almost empty. But of course, the shelves were empty. John had burned all the books. John wasn't in Frankfurt, and she had to find him. What would she tell Mary? But Mary wasn't here. Mary was in Gloucestershire with her parents and John. It was all so confusing and she was so tired. If only she could sleep. She would ask Mistress Poyntz for her sleeping draught. Just this once. What could it hurt? The baby was asleep beneath the stones.

Endor put away the remains of their breakfast. Kate had no memory of having eaten, but only half of a sweet bun remained on her plate. She covered her face with her hands and tried to think. Where should she start? Her mind would not work. The Fleet. She would start with the Fleet. That's where she'd found him last time.

It's not John Gough, you fool. You're not Kate Gough. You're Kate Frith. It's John Frith they have taken. John Frith they're going to torture. John Frith they're going to kill. Your husband. The captain will find him. Sleep, Kate. The captain will find him.

Endor placed a steaming cup in front of her. She grunted and gestured for Kate to take it. When she did not, Endor held the cup to her lips, and Kate sipped the concoction. It was oddly soothing. She sipped again. By the time the cup was emptied, so was her mind. She slumped forward onto the table and slept.

When she woke, the sun was no longer streaming in the east-facing window. Kate got up and washed her face with cool water. She needed to think clearly now. One man in all of England had the power to save her husband and it wasn't Captain Tom Lasser.

"I'm going, out, Endor," she said, scribbling a note on a piece of paper.

Endor shook her head in distress, beseeched Kate with her eyes.

"I have to go. If the captain comes back, give him this. It says I've gone to find John."

FORTY

. . . Christ will kindle a fire of faggots for him and
make him therein sweat the blood out of his body here
and straight from hense send his soul forever into the
fire of hell.

—Sir Thomas More
on the burning of John Frith

y the time Kate walked the two and half miles to Westminster, the ministers were already leaving Parliament House. She approached one of them as he hurried to hail one of the small water ferries that plied the Thames in late afternoon.

"Begging your pardon, please, sir, but where might I find Sir Thomas More?"

He laughed, and something in the tone of that laugh led Kate to believe he was not a friend of Sir Thomas's. "Not here, that's for sure. He will already have gone home by now. If he was ever here. He spends most of his time holed up in his study in Chelsea."

"Chelsea? That's upriver, right?"

"About three miles or so."

She could not walk that far before nightfall. Her disappointment must have shown in her face.

"I'm headed toward Richmond. My waterman will let you off. Of course, you'll have to make your own way back, and it will be dark. You might want to consider waiting until tomorrow."

"I have a friend in service there." How easily the lie came. "I'll not be returning till the morrow. I really would like to be there tonight."

"If you are sure . . ." And he motioned for her to follow.

After a few cursory attempts at conversation as the waterman toiled up-river, the parliamentarian turned his attention to some papers he carried in a bag, leaving Kate to contemplate just exactly what she was going to say to Thomas More. It was going to be hard to throw herself on the mercy of a man she hated as much as she hated him, and then she realized that she didn't even know what he looked like. How could she hate somebody she'd never seen? He was, after all, just a man. Maybe she could stir the compassion his daughter was so sure he possessed.

By the time the boatman pulled up to the little wooden jetty, the lamps had already been lit in the large brick house at the top of a sprawling lawn.

"Thank you, kind sir." She put on her bravest smile.

"Are you sure your friend will be here? A woman alone . . . we're pretty far out."

"She is Sir Thomas's housekeeper. She's expecting me. But thank you for caring and for the boat ride." Before he could change his mind, she stepped out of the boat, and hiking up her skirts to keep them out of the river mud, she ran up the lawn. When she was halfway up, her courage almost failed her. She could run back to the river's edge, hail the boat—the man had seemed a good sort. He'd probably give her some kind of shelter for the night.

Thomas More is the man that tortured your brother and destroyed your liveli-hood, the man who has pursued your husband like a hound from hell and shut him away to await a horrible death. He has taken all you have. What else can he do to you?

She stepped upon the wide veranda and beat upon the door.

～✻～

Sir Thomas poured his visitor a glass of fine French wine. It was an extravagance in which he rarely indulged these days. But at last he had something to celebrate. Bishop Stokesley took the offered glass and sipped it with less appreciation than Thomas would have liked. The man was a philistine. Even Wolsey, that son of a butcher, had had an appreciation for a fine wine.

"There has been no progress then?" Sir Thomas asked.

"No. Bishop Gardiner visited him. In response to his old tutor's appeal, Frith recited the Twenty-third Psalm—in Hebrew, over and over, just staring into space. His mind has slipped into madness."

Thomas had never mastered Hebrew. Why bother? But he harbored a grudging admiration for such an intellect. "A waste of a good mind, but he should have used that fine mind in the service of his Church. There's no point in waiting. How can a madman repent?" He sipped his wine, savoring the taste of it. Being in the king's good graces had carried with it many advantages—some of which he already missed. "I assume we extracted no more information on Tyndale."

"Doesn't matter," Stokesley said. "Henry Phillips has found him in Antwerp as we suspected. Hiding out in the sanctuary of a Hansa house for English merchants. Phillips has been instructed to win his confidence and draw him out. He's a scoundrel, but he could charm the devil if it would put a silver jingle in his pocket." Stokesley closed his eyes, and his thin lips stretched in a skeletal smile. "It is only a matter of time. Patience."

But Thomas was running out of patience. And Phillips was not to be trusted to carry out such an important job. That had been the disadvantage of this pursuit—the low-life miscreants Thomas had to deal with. But it was hard to find a man of honor who made a good spy. Stephen Vaughan was proof of that.

The sound of a commotion in the hall treaded on that thought. A minute later, Barnabas tapped on the study door.

"A young woman, Sir Thomas. She is demanding to see you."

"Send her away. No, wait. Send her to the kitchen. Cook can give her something to eat first. Probably a beggar or some supplicant on a legal matter." Then he turned back to Stokesley. "I have less of that now that I'm no longer a favorite at court. I do not miss it."

Stokesley waited until Barnabas had shut the door. "Frith's execution is set for tomorrow. Smithfield. Will you be there?"

"I think not. My attendance gives the matter too much weight. I suggest you not be present either. We want the people to see him as a common criminal, not some martyr. Unrest already disturbs the population. There have been fourteen suicides in London in the past fortnight and reports of other ill portents, like comets in the sky and a blue cross above the moon, that frighten the peasants."

Stokesley nodded his agreement. "Holt also gave evidence against an apprentice. We'll burn them at the same time. Give the people something real to fear, like the taint of heresy and the Church's just retribution." He drained his glass as though it were some poor ale and rose to leave.

Sir Thomas frowned. "You are welcome to stay the night. Alice will provide a bed for you. I am not so impoverished that I cannot extend hospitality to my bishop."

"It is a warm night and a full moon on the river. I've early business tomorrow, but I thank you. I'll keep you advised of Phillips's progress in regard to Tyndale. Your Church is grateful for your help."

"I am grateful for the opportunity to serve," Thomas said, following his visitor to the door. "It gives me great satisfaction."

He went in to dine with his family for the first time in weeks in a rare spirit of celebration. They were well into the meal when the disturbance happened.

❧❦

"No. I am not leaving. I demand to see—"

The doors to the great hall at Chelsea burst open and Margaret Roper looked up from her place at the table to see a woman, held tenuously in the clutches of Barnabas, hurtle into the room. She was struggling like some wild creature, desperate to break free.

Dame Alice's spoon clattered against her plate. "Holy Virgin protect us," she shrieked. "It's a madwoman."

In spite of the servant's muscular build, he was hard-pressed to restrain the woman, and his voice was breathless with the struggle. "I'm sorry, Sir Thomas. I told her you would not see her."

The woman's hair was unbound and hung down her back in a tangled riot; her skirt was mud spattered and her eyes flared wide with fear or anger. Her glance flicked around the room until her gaze fixed on Margaret's father, who sat at the head of the table as though transfixed. His hand, frozen on the lid of the pewter salver, hovered above the roasted joint.

"Please—Sir Thomas . . . I must speak with Sir Thomas." And with the sound of ripping cloth as part of her sleeve tore away, she broke free and hurled herself at his feet. He drew back from the woman, still holding the pewter lid in his hand, as though it could shield him from some deadly contagion in the interloper's touch.

Meg's sisters screamed as her husband rushed to Barnabas's assistance. There was something familiar about the woman huddled at her father's feet, holding on to the table leg as the men tried to pull her away. She tossed her head and the hair that had obscured her face flew back.

That white smooth skin, that high brow with the faintest blue line pulsing beneath the skin . . .

"Wait. I know this woman," Margaret said. "She is no madwoman. Let her speak her piece. Her name is Gough. Her brother was the printer in Paternoster Row I told you about. Remember, Father? It's been a few years. You released him from prison. Her name is—"

"Kate, my lord. My name is Kate . . ."

The men loosened their hold but stood close to her. William Roper helped her to her feet. She straightened her hair and her spine as she made a visible attempt to regain composure, then gave a small dignified curtsy such as a lady of rank might make to a peer. "Mistress Roper is right, my lord. I met your daughter while my brother was in prison. But my name is not Gough. My name is Frith. Kate Frith, Mistress John Frith, and I . . . have come here to . . . to beg my lord for my husband's life."

There were murmurs around the table as some recognized the name. "Isn't he that translator that . . . he is a scholar, I think . . . in exile for heresy . . ."

Sir Thomas put down the pewter lid and waved his family to silence. He smiled then as if he'd just stumbled upon some wonderful discovery, as if this interruption of his dinner were some kind of gift. Meg exhaled relief. Now this woman would finally see that her father was not the monster she had believed him to be when they first met.

"Mistress Frith. You have my sympathy," Sir Thomas said.

"Thank you, my lord, but it is not your sympathy I am seeking. It is your intervention."

He sighed heavily. The candle nearest him flickered with his exhaled breath.

"Then you've come to the wrong place, I fear. The Church has already condemned your husband." He looked apologetically at those gathered around the table and not at the woman at all as he explained. "I have no jurisdiction in the matter."

"I do not understand matters of legal jurisdiction, sir, but if you say it is so then it must be so, because you are reputed to be an honorable man." She paused as if weighing her words like gold.

Meg thought the quiet pleading in her demeanor quite at odds with the proud creature she'd first encountered in the little print shop.

"But your daughter has told me of your charity and compassion and that you are a man of great influence. All of England knows you to be a man of importance." She looked at Margaret then, as though pleading for some advocacy from that quarter. "I am here to beg for some small measure of that compassion your daughter spoke of, to beg you to use your influence with the bishop."

Her father's answering smile was like a splash of cold water in Margaret's face. Had he always been so . . . cold?

"My daughter, like most devoted daughters, I expect, harbors an exaggerated sense of her father's importance. I'm sure you would speak well of your father, Mistress Frith—though I have heard he died in prison."

The woman flinched visibly, but she remained silent as he continued.

"I can do nothing for you or your husband, and frankly I would not if I could. John Frith is a heretic who has done much damage to Holy Church. As a Christian I can only celebrate his burning. His death will serve as a warning to others."

Meg turned her face away. She could not look at her father, could not bear to see the hatred she saw there. Nor did she look at Kate. She stared at the piece of meat on her plate, congealing in its juices, and wished she had not lived to see this day. Meg glanced up to meet her husband's gaze, and she knew this moment marked the end of all her childhood illusions. There was absolute silence in the room, interrupted by the scraping of Sir Thomas's chair as he stood up.

"But to show you that I am not altogether devoid of that compassion of which my daughter spoke, I will offer you shelter," the great man said. "We will not send you out into the night. There are many wolves that roam the woods between here and London."

The woman seemed to visibly grow taller. She tossed back her head and glared at the man from whom she had just begged mercy. Margaret saw a glimpse of that Kate Gough she'd met in Paternoster Row. "I will take my chances with the wolves, my lord," she said quietly. "For they, being no more than wild beasts, have as much of Christ in them as you. They only kill to survive. You kill for the joy it gives you."

Margaret held her breath, willing the woman to hush.

But Kate did not. "For all your learning, you know less of Christ than the poorest plowman who carries Tyndale's English Bible in his pocket."

Did she not realize—or care—that she was completely in his power? It was madness to say such to a man one thought was devoid of all compassion.

The smell of the roast meat on her plate blending with the fear and tension in the room made the gorge rise in her throat. But when she looked up at her father, she was surprised to see he did not look angry. Kate Frith's words somehow seemed to have pleased him.

"Tyndale! You speak of the translator as though you know him. If you would give him up to . . . the bishops, perhaps I could use my limited influence to see that your husband does not suffer in the flames . . . overlong."

The woman looked at him in disbelief then, spitting upon the floor at his feet, verily hissed at him. "I will not give him up even if you burn me. My husband shall not die for nothing, and when you close your eyes tonight, Sir Thomas More, may the knowledge that you have hounded many good and righteous men to their deaths sear your heart like the white-hot flames they died in."

Beside her, Meg heard Dame Alice gasp. She looked up at Kate then and glittering behind the tears she saw a courage she envied—and something akin to pity. Kate smiled at her, a smile that carried a weary resignation. "I pray, Mistress Roper, that you never know the hurt other wives and daughters have known," she said. "My English Bible teaches me to forgive. I will pray for the strength to forgive your father."

"Take her to the porter's lodge," Sir Thomas said, his tone as sharp as a honed sword.

"Please, Father. She is distraught. You can understand . . . a desperate woman will say anything. Pay her no heed. Let her go with William and me. We will watch her tonight and take her home tomorrow."

His eyes were hard as he answered her. "She will spend tonight in the porter's lodge. If she is of the same stubborn mind tomorrow, Barnabas will take her back to London."

As Barnabas led the woman away, Meg's father lifted the lid on the salver and took out a portion of meat for carving. "Do not look so distressed, daughter. It was a disturbance of no consequence to you. Now, pass your plate if you want more."

~🙣🙡~

Kate spent the night locked in the porter's lodge, unmolested, though the shackles on the wall haunted her with ghostly images. How many tortured souls had groaned against that wall? She saw her brother shackled there, his head slumped forward on his chest. She saw her husband there, his beautiful smile, the most charming smile she'd ever seen, twisted in pain. She saw herself there.

The servant who had restrained her brought her bread and milk, but though her stomach hurt from hunger, she couldn't swallow it. She had been a fool to come here, a fool to think she could save a man who would not save himself, a fool to think she could wring compassion from a stone. She did not sleep, but teetered between a savage anger at a God who did not shelter His servants from peril—from the fury of evil men, from wrath like a dark rain falling from a smoke-filled sky—and desperate prayers to that same God to lighten John's suffering if he could not be saved.

In the morning, the great man himself brought her a bowl of steaming porridge. She turned her face away, unable to abide the smell of it. He shrugged and set the bowl down.

"Now that you've had time to consider your husband's inevitable fate, I thought you might reconsider. I remind you that if you agree to cooperate and draw Master Tyndale out of the English House so that he may be delivered to the proper authorities, I shall use my influence to see that your husband does not suffer a slow and agonizing death. The official who ties him to the stake will strangle him. He will lose consciousness quickly. It will be over in a minute or two."

The nausea that had been threatening her then overwhelmed. As she bent over and splattered the contents of her stomach on the stone floor, he shrank back. Too late. Little specks of vomit covered the hem of his fine linen robe. She had enough strength left to laugh.

"I shall take that as your answer," he snarled, his visage filled with hatred and disgust—the face of the real man behind the mask. Kate wondered if Margaret Roper had ever seen that face.

"Take the creature to Newgate," he said. "She can rot there—until the devil comes to take her down to hell, where she can join her heretic husband."

꘎

Tom Lasser left Croydon without satisfaction. No, the archbishop had done all he could do. He'd given the man a chance to escape and he had refused, and no, he did not know where he was being kept, not even when the execution was set. Once Frith was found guilty, the king's soldiers would carry out the sentence.

Ecclesia non novit sanguinem. The Church does not shed blood.

Nor did the Constable of the Tower have any knowledge of the details of the execution. Sir Humphrey at the Steelyard had no more knowledge of Frith's whereabouts than the captain did. Have you been to the Lollard Tower, he'd asked, his brow wrinkling with worry. But Tom had gone there first.

He could not go back to Kate without some little bit of hope to offer her. He was on his way from the Steelyard to make the rounds of the other prisons when he saw the smoke spiraling up from the river's edge—from the very direction of the wharf where he'd docked the *Siren's Song*.

By the time the captain arrived, the sails were on fire and the mainmast was burning. His men—God bless their black hearts—were still on board, scurrying, carrying buckets, beating at the flames with blankets.

"Fire," he shouted to the dockworkers he passed. "A crown to any man who will fight to save my ship." The most desperate among them, a goodly number, picked up buckets, pails, pans, anything they could carry, and clambered on board. "How did it start?" he shouted to the first mate as side by side they slung bucket after bucket after bucket of seawater on the flames that were by now licking at the deck.

"Most of us were asleep below when it started. Watchman said it was a flaming arrow."

By the time night fell, Tom and his crew collapsed on the deck among the charred embers of the fallen mainmast. The ship was still afloat, but just barely. Her sails were gone, her hull charred in places, even her name obliterated by soot and ash, but she was still a ship. His ship. And she could be restored.

In his exhaustion he thought of Kate Frith and how she was waiting for news. But he had no good news to give her. Bad news could wait until morning. God willing, she was already asleep in her bed above the shop.

He awoke about midnight with Endor bent over him, shaking him awake. She was grunting at him, distraught, trying to tell him something, finally handing him Kate's note. He shook the cobwebs from his brain and leaped to his feet.

FORTY-ONE

*The air longs to blow noxious vapours against the
wicked man. The sea longs to overwhelm him in its
waves, the mountains to fall upon him, the valleys to
rise up to him, the earth to split open beneath him, hell
to swallow him up after his headlong fall, the demons
to plunge him into gulfs of ever-burning flames.*
—Sir Thomas More writing
from Tower Prison on William Tyndale

ill you take a message for me?" Kate beseeched the guard
who brought her the bowl of watery soup from the almshouse. "To a sea cap-
tain named Tom Lasser? His ship is docked at the Steelyard. The *Siren's Song.*"

"Do I look like a messenger?" the guard growled. The soup slopped
from the bowl as he slapped it down.

"Captain Lasser will pay you for the information. He is a very generous
man. Please," she pleaded. "Tell him Kate Frith is locked up in Newgate."

The sight of the soup sickened her. A green skin was already forming on
top of it. She pushed it away so she did not have to look at it. Time might be
when she was glad to see even that. But not yet.

The guard glanced at her, then at the bowl. "I'll leave it, 'case you change
your mind." The ring of keys jingled in his hand, the door slightly ajar.

He is too big. You'll not even make the yard.

"Frith? Popular name," he said. "We had another Frith. He didn't stay long."

Kate's heart missed a beat and then another. "You said 'had'?"

"He left this morning."

Her breath was trapped inside her chest. "Was his name John? A young man? Not yet turned thirty?"

"Hard to tell under all that beard. Don't remember his first name. Strange one." He circled his forefinger beside his temple, a gesture of derision. "Talked to himself. Gibberish mostly."

"He is not strange. He is brilliant. He is a gentle wonderful man whose only crime is providing people with books they can read in their own language."

"A relative of yours?"

If John was here when she was brought in, why had she not sensed his nearness? "He is my husband," she said.

He looked at her sharply, as if she suddenly interested him.

"Do you know where they took him?" she asked.

His expression softened, and he looked away.

Please, God, let that not be pity in his eyes. "Tell me where they took him. I have to know!"

"Smithfield. They took him to Smithfield," he said soberly.

His words rang in her head like the bells of St. Mary le Bow, the floor beneath her undulating with each word. *Smithfield! Smithfield! Smithfield!* The walls swayed to the rhythm of the words in her head. The world was disintegrating around her, all the hope stringing away thread by thread, leaving her mind a tangled mass of raveled wool.

Somewhere a woman was screaming.

～✳✵～

This was no ordinary Friday for Sir Thomas: 4 July 1533. A day of celebration. A day of atonement. The only day more worthy of celebration would be the day the flames consumed William Tyndale, stopping his vile pen forever. He hoped it would be soon. He hoped, too, that he would be alive to see it. Cuthbert had warned him that Cromwell was investigating the Holy Maid of Kent for treason. Thomas had met with Elizabeth Barton on more than one occasion, which fact Cromwell was sure to uncover. Parliament had turned against the Church. Even the bishops had lost their courage— cowards all. It was only a matter of time. He was already preparing his family for the inevitable, even staging a mock rehearsal of his arrest one night as they sat at dinner. It had been instructive to watch their reaction.

But he would not think of that today, he thought, as carrying his flagellum, he entered his private chapel. The sun would be at its zenith now. They would be lighting the fire. He closed his eyes and inhaled as if he could draw into his lungs the smoke from the burning wood and hair and flesh. He lifted his little knotted whip and felt the first sting of pain across his shoulders. Then again. And again, until a shudder of ecstasy passed through his body.

⌁

John Frith felt strangely calm as the soldiers led him and the young apprentice Andrew Hewet, who was to die with him, to the single stake just outside the London Wall. The sun, as if unable to look full upon such an abomination, hid its hot July face behind a smoky haze in a pale sky. John whispered to his companion the words Tyndale had written in his last letter. "If the pain be above your strength, remember, Andrew, 'whatsoever ye shall ask in My Name, I will give you.' Pray to the Father in that Name, and He shall ease our pain."

John had clung to those words these last days as a drowning man clings to a piece of driftwood in an empty sea, praying that his courage would not fail, that his demeanor would give strength and comfort to the other man. The apprentice nodded tight-lipped and closed his eyes as they led him first up the rickety wooden platform and bound him to the stake, his back to the bulk of the crowd.

When it was John's turn, they tied him back to back with Andrew, facing the crowd. As John's bound hands encountered his companion's, he felt the trembling in Andrew's hands. John grasped two of his fingers with two of his own. "Blessed are you when men shall revile you and persecute you for My sake," John whispered. The trembling did not stop.

As they secured his neck and waist to the pole, John looked out at the crowd. Except for the rector who was in charge of the burning, no familiar face looked up at him. That was a good thing. This final loneliness he could not share. If he should be forced to witness the horror on Kate's face, that horror would enter into his own heart, and he could not then endure what he must. He thought of her safe and far away, as though the woman bent over her needlework in the English House in Antwerp was someone he'd loved in another lifetime. Tyndale had promised to look after her. And when Tyndale followed close behind him, Captain Lasser would be there for her.

The rector gave the nod and the two soldiers, one on either side of the stake, stuck their lit torches to the outer brush. The crowd murmured as a single chorus, with one brave voice calling out above the others, "Let them go. They have done nothing wrong."

"Have no more pity for them than you would for dogs," the rector admonished the crowd.

A wind came from out of nowhere and ruffled John's beard, blowing a lock of hair across his face and whipping his loose robe. He was glad he'd inserted the two shillings that were to have been his passage home into the hem of the plain linen garment. It would stay weighted until the brush caught the hem. By the time his robe burned away, the flames would cover his nakedness.

"Blessed are the poor in spirit for theirs is the kingdom of heaven," he shouted as loudly as he could. He would go to his death with the English Scriptures on his lips.

The faces in the crowd looked up at him with wide eyes: some curious, some fearful, some stunned, not wanting to be there but unable to leave. Some gloated. He could see it in the way they licked their lips. Some held tears. Others looked away. He pitied them all, and prayed for grace to forgive the rector and Bishop Stokesley and Thomas More. He could not go to God with hatred in his heart.

"Blessed are they that mourn, for they shall be comforted." Even he was surprised that his voice could ring so clearly with no hint of the trembling he felt inside.

The wood had been stacked high in a pyramid shape and the platform smeared with pitch. He grasped Andrew's hand more tightly as the flames leaped up among the dry tinder with a popping and a shower of sparks.

"Blessed are the merciful, for they shall obtain mercy," Andrew's voice behind John shouted. The flames caught their garments.

"Blessed are the peacemakers, for they shall be called the children of God," John answered. "Blessed are they—" But the heat and smoke stole his breath away and he could answer no more.

He felt Andrew's hand go limp in his and was glad.

"Blessed are they which are persecuted for righteousness' sake; for theirs is the kingdom of heaven," a voice in the crowd shouted.

But John did not hear.

❦

The Steelyard was not much out of his way, the guard thought as he finished his shift and left for home. The woman had said the captain would pay. But even if he didn't, her circumstances had stirred something akin to pity in a heart as callused as his hands. Her keening and hysterical weeping had landed her in the women's ward with the other madwomen who had to be chained. But by the time the matron came, she had let herself be led away like a lamb. He had seen other women who went into the madwomen's ward with that same fixed stare. They only came out in a dirty winding sheet.

When he reached the Steelyard, he scanned the docks for a ship named the *Siren's Song,* but he saw none with that name. Shrugging, he turned back toward home, wondering idly about the burned-out hulk of a ship bobbing like a dead duck in the harbor. Seemed there was enough bad luck to go around these days.

❧

As Tom Lasser read the note Kate left, dread like an anchor weight descended on him. She would be making the rounds of the prisons looking for her husband as she had once looked for her brother. But this time she had not come back. He tried to console himself with the thought that perhaps she had found John and simply refused to leave, maybe even talked some guard into letting her stay with her husband. He would begin by checking the prisons. But he got no farther than Fleet Prison.

No, there was nobody by the name of John Frith there, and no inquiries had been made by a woman or anybody else on his watch. It had been a slow day. Everybody had gone to the execution of those two heretics in Smithfield.

Oh God, he thought. Let her not be there. Let her not have found him only in time to watch him burn.

He smelled the smoke before he got to the city gate, his stomach lurching at the sickening stench of it. The crowd parted as he pushed his way toward the fire, calling out Kate's name. Nobody answered.

By the time he reached the great pyramid of fire, the flames were leaping so high and the heat and stench so fierce that one by one the crowd drifted away. Nothing remained of John Frith that he could recognize. The two charred bodies tied to the stake looked like nothing human. At least Kate was not here to see this, he thought, as turning aside he heaved the contents of his stomach into the ash-strewn dirt. A shower of sparks ate through the cloth of his doublet. Later he would find the small blisters, but he felt nothing but dread as he turned away from the fire to resume his search.

What would he tell Kate when he found her? If he found her.

Kate was in her little room above the shop. "How did I get here?" she asked. But this was not real. Just another of the fever dreams. She would wake with Mad Maud screaming and Sal huddled in the corner of the prison chamber, drooling over her ragged doll.

"Endor found you. She knew where to look." That was the captain's voice, sounding far away. And it wasn't Mad Maud leaning over her. It was Endor. Dear, dear Endor, holding a cup of steaming broth before her. It smelled of stewed chicken. The broth in her dreams had no smell, and she never tasted it.

She did not taste it now, but sank deep into the burning fever.

When she woke later, Endor was still there, but the hand on her forehead belonged to the captain.

"She's cooler now," he said. "Try the broth again."

Kate felt his arm behind her lifting her up. She sipped the broth. It was savory but with the undertaste of Endor's curative. She coughed, sputtering the liquid, and when she gained her breath again asked, "How long have I been here?"

"Two weeks," the captain said.

Two weeks! "John! Did you find John?" She tried to sit up but sank back onto the strong arm that eased her onto the pillow. "Take me to him."

The captain slipped his arm from behind her back and stood up, stooping beneath the slope of the eave. He did not look at her. Just took a deep breath, his gaze settling on an abandoned swallow's nest outside the narrow window. He said nothing. He didn't have to.

"He's dead. John's dead, isn't he?"

"Kate, I—"

"They have killed him."

He kneeled down beside her bed then and took her hand in his, but she snatched it away, as if not accepting his comfort would nullify the certainty. "Was it—" But she could not even frame the words.

"He died easily and with your name on his lips." The words sounded rehearsed. He pleated the coverlet on her bed with his long fingers.

The abandoned nest beneath the eave was suddenly the saddest thing she had ever seen. "You are lying, Tom Lasser," she said quietly. "I know my husband. He died with God's name on his lips if anybody's. He always loved his work more than he loved me."

"Then he was a fool," the captain said with such bitterness that she felt sad for him too.

"No. He was not a fool," she said. "And he loved me. I know he did. He just belonged to God. I only borrowed him for a time."

They sat in silence for a while.

Endor looked at her with wise, knowing eyes. She held the broth to her lips again. But Kate shook her head.

"Was there anything . . . left?" she asked.

He made a helpless gesture with his hands. "A few . . . ashes, some small pieces of bone. Sir Humphrey and I gathered what we could and buried them in the churchyard at St. Dunstan's where Tyndale used to preach."

Tyndale. The last time she had seen her husband, Tyndale had been with her as they waved to him from the harbor. If Tyndale had gone, he would have died and not John. Would he think of that when he heard? "Does Tyndale know?"

"I'm sure he does by now."

Kate nodded, wondering why she had no tears. Her eyes were so dry they hurt.

"I think I want to sleep now," she said, wanting only for them to leave her alone. It wasn't a lie. She wanted to sleep forever.

FORTY-TWO

And though I bestow all my goods to feed the poor,
and though I give my body to be burned and have not
love, it profiteth me nothing.
——FROM ST. PAUL'S LETTER TO THE CORINTHIANS

ate moved through the days and weeks that followed like a woman sleepwalking. She never cried for John. Nor did she go to St. Dunstan's. John did not sleep there any more than his child slept beneath the stone cairn in the Antwerp garden. They were only ashes and dust. Their souls had returned to God. As would hers if she could will it so. But Endor nursed her faithfully, and her body grew stronger with each day.

The captain spent most of his time in Woolwich where his boat was being restored, though he came to see her often, bringing food and money, cautioning her not to reopen the shop lest she call attention to herself. Cromwell had ordered her release, but she shouldn't give Thomas More further cause. He needn't have worried; she had no desire to reopen the shop. On some days she wondered absently about her future, about what would become of her when the captain went away, but it was as though she were watching a character in one of the guild plays. The summer passed without incident—ironic now that she no longer cared. Let Thomas More come looking for her. What more could he do?

Master Tyndale wrote to her. His letter spoke of how John would live on in the great work he did. His words were kind and meant to give her comfort. They did not.

Sir Humphrey came one day to offer her his sympathy and ask if there was anything she needed. She had only to send him word, he said. He returned the Bible she had sold him—it seemed like a lifetime ago—saying he was sure she would want such a family treasure. She thanked him, and when he was gone she wrapped it up and returned it to its hiding place, thinking how the destiny of her family through so many generations, for good and ill, had been bound up with that holy book. But she felt no pride in it as she once had. She felt nothing—until one day she had another visitor.

At first she didn't recognize the young woman who knocked at her door. "The shop is closed," Kate said through the half-open door.

"I saw your light and your silhouette through the window and thought it might be you," the woman said.

"I'm sorry. You must be mistaken—" Something about the woman's demeanor, her sharp little chin, and the little blond girl holding her by the hand sparked her memory. That clear, blue-eyed gaze— "You are Winifred! And is this . . . little Madeline?"

The woman nodded, smiling. "Not a babe anymore." Wrinkles formed around her eyes, and she carried herself with less verve than Kate remembered. There were shadows beneath her eyes and her face looked pale and pinched. The last few years had not been kind to her.

The child, who was the picture of health, looked up at Kate with curiosity. "Are you the book woman who used to live here?"

The laugh felt strange in Kate's throat. "Well, I used to be a book woman. But that was a long time ago." She knelt down and grasped the child's hand. "I see you've been busy in my absence, busy changing from a baby to a beautiful little girl."

Madeline, her eyes wide with pleasure, looked up at her mother. "You were right, Maman"—she nodded as if hers were the last word on any subject—"she is nice."

Kate invited them in and offered them Endor's honeyed biscuits, noticing as the child reached for the sweet what a pretty dress she wore, though the meanness of the fabric belied the elegant stitching. "You are wearing a very pretty bonnet, Madeline," Kate offered with the second biscuit.

Winifred's eyes, a beautiful cornflower blue, a little lighter than her daughter's, crinkled as her smile spread to her eyes. "There are some advantages for a poor child with a mother who is a seamstress," she said.

But Kate noticed how worn-out she looked and how thin her arms were. "Your husband?" Kate asked. "Is he well?"

Winifred looked down at the little girl and said quietly, "My Frenchy was killed in the May Day riots two years ago."

"Oh. I'm sorry," Kate said, remembering that they'd heard about the massacre of the foreign workers even in Antwerp. "We have something in common," she said, after a pause, "I too have lost my husband."

After that, the woman and the child came frequently. Throughout the fall and winter Kate looked forward to their visits, urging Endor to keep a ready supply of the little honeyed biscuits and volunteering to watch the child on the days her mother had to travel some distance. On more than one such occasion, the captain showed up, and seemed to take a liking to the little girl. Kate watched their games and laughed at him, down on the floor in his fine breeches pretending to be a bucking horse whilst Madeline held on to his back, squealing in delight. One day he brought a cat, which Madeline promptly named Ruffles for the white patch of fur at its throat. "Like Captain's," the child said, pointing to the fluff of lace at his throat. The captain responded to Kate's laughter by pantomiming a court dandy.

Kate had noticed he was dressing more elegantly than usual. She surmised that some of those same courtiers that he mocked were helping to finance the rebuilding of his ship with their games of chance. But what could she say, since those same gleanings helped to keep her and Endor in food and candles?

In winter daylight was precious, and since the guild had a strict rule against working by candlelight, Kate offered to watch Madeline every day so that her mother could work uninterrupted. The child was easy to mind, and the bookshop seemed less dreary when she was there. Endor enjoyed her almost as much as Kate. The two of them played with rag dolls, neither speaking a word. Watching their elaborate pantomimes provided Kate with hours of diversion from her grief. She could almost forget about her pain until one day she realized that she had been watching them all afternoon and had not thought of John. Not once. That was when the tears began to flow at last.

She was better after that. Not great. But better. Imagined scenes of John's agony washed across her mind in wrenching waves, but more and more the pain lessened into an aching loss. She even mourned him in her sleep. But the times of forgetfulness grew more frequent, especially when the captain came, bringing delight to Madeline and special treats to all of them.

And soon she had an unease of another kind to distract her as she watched

Winifred grow thinner with each new day. The woman scarcely ate anything at all—not even Endor's yeasty bread.

"Are you well?" Kate asked one day after the little seamstress had a nasty spell of coughing. "Endor has a magic elixir for that."

Winifred drank the aromatic tea and the cough subsided, but Kate thought she saw a speck of blood on the scrap of linen Winifred coughed into before tucking it quickly into her sleeve. Kate did not mention it. She did not want to alarm the child, who was playing with a wooden bumblebee Captain Tom had brought her. It was a clever contraption with brightly painted wings and wooden wheels that whirred when Madeline pulled on its string.

"I will be better in the spring," Winifred said.

"Maybe, but I think you may be working too hard."

Winifred sighed wearily. "It's harder with Frenchy gone." Then she looked up and smiled at her daughter who had paused in her play. "But we're fine, aren't we, Madeline?"

The little girl had been listening beneath the surface of her play. Kate could see it in the scowl between her blue eyes. Kate said as cheerfully as she could, "We'll all feel better when old man sunshine comes back to London, won't we, Madeline?"

Madeline nodded and jerked the bumblebee's string. Its wings whirred and the wheels clattered on the wooden floor, but the child's scowl remained.

❦

By the middle of Advent, it was clear that Winifred was in steep decline. She took to her bed and was so weak she could hardly care for herself, let alone her daughter.

"Let Madeline stay with Endor and me until you recover," Kate said, when after not seeing her friend for several days, she had gone looking for her. She lived in one room behind a tailor's shop, a small room, ill lit for a seamstress, and littered with dress forms and bolts of silk that looked incongruous among the bare, impoverished furnishings. "Endor will come every day to see after you until you're better, and I'll bring Madeline to visit."

She expected a protest, but Winifred looked at her with tears welling in her eyes. "That would be a great relief. Not to have her see me like this and to know that she is cared for," she said before another paroxysm of coughing seized her.

After a week of Endor's curative elixirs for catarrh, none of which seemed to make any difference in Winifred's cough, the captain sent a doctor around to see her, but his report was not good. There was a strong possibility—even probability—that the woman might not recover. Kate could not deny the truth of it when she looked at Winifred, the mere shadow of the spirited young woman who had once run down and cuffed the ears of a pickpocket.

"I know it's a lot to ask. I am already so much in your debt. I can never repay your kindness," Winifred said after Madeline had been with Kate for a fortnight. "But it will only be a few more days. I'm feeling stronger every day."

But Kate suspected from the bright pink of her friend's usual pallid complexion that she was feverish. She would send Endor back with a tea of yarrow, chamomile, and angelica. "I love having Madeline," she said. "She is a joy. Just concentrate on getting better."

"There is one more thing . . ." Winifred lowered her voice so that Madeline, who had fallen asleep in her mother's arms, would not hear her. "Just in case I . . . just in case anything should happen . . . there is a noblewoman by name of Countess Clare that I sew for. She lives in a large house near Bishopsgate, the first lane past Crosby Hall." She looked down at the sleeping child, and stroked her hair gently, obviously trying to collect herself to go on. "When I first began to cough up the blood, I was frightened—my sister did that before she . . . before she . . ."

Kate nodded her understanding, so she would not have to say it.

Winifred continued in a whisper, still stroking the child's pale hair. "The countess agreed to let Madeline go into service as a kitchen maid should anything happen to me. If she could just stay with you and Endor until she gets used to . . . the idea and you could sort of look after her . . . in the beginning. She might be lonely and . . ."

"I will look after her, Winifred. Don't you worry."

Winifred reached out with her other hand, the one not caressing her child, and gripped Kate's. Her skin was alarmingly hot. "You have been so kind to me," she said. "If I could beg one more favor . . . My Frenchy is buried in St. Dunstan's churchyard. I know the priest there. He has agreed . . . all you have to do is ask."

For a moment Kate did not trust herself to speak. St. Dunstan's. *We buried his ashes in St. Dunstan's churchyard.* She tried to swallow her emotions along with the lump in her throat, and prayed the child would not waken. "Of course, it will be done as you wish. But that's just the fever talking. You're going to get better. I'm going to get you something to help bring down your fever. If Madeline wakes up, tell her I'm coming right back."

Winifred closed her eyes and nodded.

Kate returned in less than twenty minutes. The tea was still steaming. The child was still sleeping in her mother's arms. Winifred slept too. But it was a sleep from which she never woke. She died two days later.

～※～

"You must be weary of always coming to my aid," Kate said. It was a gray winter morning and she and Captain Tom stood alone beside Winifred's grave.

The curate of St. Dunstan's had finished reading the psalm and left. Kate could not bear to watch the grave digger heave the dirt on Winifred's frail body. Cold numbed her and loneliness crept up from the grave at her feet. Her legs might have buckled except for the support of the captain's arm behind her back, a support for which she was very glad. She was glad, too, that she'd left Madeline with Endor. The last thing the child would remember about her mother would not be this horrid scene but the comfort of Winifred's beating heart as she fell asleep against her mother's breast.

"I am very grateful, Captain. I do not know how I would have gotten through these weeks and months without you. But I know it cannot go on forever," she said. "This is the last time I will summon you from your friends, I promise. I fear I have become a burden."

"It is a small enough burden, Kate. I think I can bear it."

"Your friend may think it no small burden."

After Winifred died, and not knowing where else to turn, Kate had gone to the lodgings in Cheapside where Tom Lasser stayed when he was not in Woolwich working on his boat. She had prayed he would be there. But when he answered the door the landlord directed her to, she had blurted out her need and immediately wished she had not. From the candlelit interior of the intimate sitting room, a woman's voice had demanded, "Whoever it is, Tom, send them away. I want you all to myself tonight."

"By my friend you must mean Charlotte? She's a widow from Lübeck who just happened to be in London on business. I have known her for a very long time. Her husband was a cloth merchant. Much older than she. He departed this life, leaving her rich and still young enough to enjoy it."

"She is very beautiful," Kate said, remembering the pouting, rouged lips of the blond woman who had peered quizzically at Kate over the captain's shoulder as he shrugged into his doublet.

"Yes, I suppose she is," he said. "She works at it very hard."

By now the grave was half filled and no glimpse of the shroud remained. Kate tried not to think of Winifred's thin bones bearing the weight of so much dirt. But when had she not borne a heavy weight, this woman with her frail body and heart of a lion, her life a struggle from its beginning to its end? So unlike the rich, beautiful widow from Lübeck. Where was the justice in that? Kate turned her gaze away from the grave, unable to bear the sight of it. Had Charlotte been waiting for the captain when he returned last night? Did he tell her how they had taken Winifred to the nuns to be washed and laid out in the chapel? Did he tell her he had paid for the burial service of a poor seamstress? He had given instructions to the nuns as though Winifred had been his own sister. "Tapers at her head and feet all throughout the night," he'd said. He had paid for the grave, too, inside the churchyard, not in the pauper's area. Did the beautiful widow from Lübeck know the heart of Tom Lasser? Kate wondered. Or did she care only about the handsome sea captain with his glib answers and flashing smile?

"I hope you were able to see her again before she left." Kate felt her skin flush at the lie and hoped he did not notice.

"Oh, she hasn't left yet. She'll be here a while. She is making the rounds of the English shops. I'll bring her around for you to meet her if you'd like."

Kate would not like. She felt a sudden and quite unreasonable dislike for the blond widow from Lübeck with her pouting lips. "Don't trouble her. I'm sure she would not be pleased. I recall that she said something about 'having you all to herself.' "

A fine mist had begun to fall, deepening the misery of the day. John slept somewhere in this same churchyard. She had never seen his grave, not wanted to, yet suddenly she did not think she could leave this place without seeing it.

"If you're ready to see it, Kate, I'll show you." As if he'd read her mind. "It's right over there. Next to the wall."

She nodded, ambushed by a sob. He guided her a few feet over from Winifred's grave, just to the edge where a creeping vine clutched at the stone wall. Grassy weeds had grown over the mound. She was surprised at how large it was. "I thought you said—"

"There were a few bones left, scattered among the ashes. We put them in a box."

She pointed to a simple cross, small but carved in stone, at the head. It bore no name. "Did you do that?"

He nodded. "We couldn't put his name on it. It was all Monmouth could do to get him buried in the churchyard."

He walked away a few paces, as she bent to trace the smooth stone with her fingers, feeling suddenly calm and at peace. "I miss you, John," she whispered. "Take care of my friend Winifred. You would have liked her, I know. She was brave. Like you."

Then she stood up and walked away to the place where Captain Lasser waited for her in the shadow of a yew. Neither of them talked as they walked back to Paternoster Row.

❦

"Is Maman still in the ground in the churchyard?" Madeline asked a week after the burial.

"No, she has gone to heaven."

"But I didn't get to tell her good-bye," the child said, pouting.

"You can tell her when you say your prayers. Just give God the message, and he'll see she gets it."

"Will she come back tomorrow?"

"Not tomorrow."

It became a litany between them.

After about a week Madeline looked thoughtful. "Is Maman with Papa?"

"Yes, Madeline. She is with your father," Kate said, relieved that the child finally understood.

"Will Madeline stay with Kate and Endor?" she asked.

"Madeline will stay with Kate and Endor," Kate answered. She could not add *For a while, until you go to live in a great house in Bishopsgate.* The words would not come. Not yet. It was too soon.

"Good. Madeline likes it here."

Madeline's referring to herself in the third person became a pattern that lasted for several weeks, but Kate understood that it gave the child some distance from her loss, and did not correct her. Kate understood all about loss and distance. She was just now beginning to come to grips with the full reality of her widowed circumstances.

The countess had sent a servant by to collect the child three days after the funeral, saying she'd heard of the death of the seamstress and was informed by the curate at St. Dunstan's that the child was with her.

"My lady wishes to know if the child is learning to sew," the footman had said.

"The child does not sew, but she is bright. She is learning to read and write."

"I think my mistress will only be interested in the sewing. The girl will probably start in the kitchens if she cannot sew."

And end there, Kate thought.

She had put the footman off until after the New Year, pleading that the child was still grieving over her mother and was still too young to go into service. *No good can come from putting it off,* she chided herself after he had gone. What was she thinking? Her only support came from a man who would be leaving soon. How was she going to look after herself, let alone a child? Madeline would become just more attached than ever to her new home. When she finally had to leave, the pain would be greater—for both of them.

As the old year passed, Kate dreaded each knock on the door, half expecting the countess's footman to show up to claim Madeline. Even if Kate could figure out a way to keep her, Winifred had said she had an agreement with the woman. Did that mean some legal obligation? What was she going to tell the child, if she had to send her away? But a week into the new year it was not the footman who showed up unwanted.

Kate's first inclination after peering out the window was not to open the door, but before Kate could stop her, Madeline skipped to the door shouting, "It's Captain. Madeline will open the door," and straining on tiptoe, she lifted the bar with both her hands. "Oh," she said in disappointment. "You're not Captain," as Margaret Roper stepped inside.

The child, suddenly shy, ran to Kate and hid behind her skirt.

"I'm so glad you answered the door," Mistress Roper said. "I came right after your husband . . . died . . . and you were not here. I was worried." She stood in the door, the cold air pouring in around her. Kate did not invite her in.

"Your father did not tell you, then?"

"He told me only that you had returned to London."

"I returned to London. The great, charitable Sir Thomas delivered me to Newgate Prison. I was locked up with the criminally insane while my husband was being put to death. I would still be there were it not for the intervention of a good man."

"Oh," the visitor said, her face a mask of discomfort. "I did not know." She held out her hand palm up as if begging Kate for something. "My father . . . if you could have known him before . . . he is not himself. He thinks only of heretics these days. He talks incessantly of Tyndale."

"Then prithee, Mistress Roper, unless your visit is not one of goodwill as you say it is, do not remind him of my existence."

"May I please come in? Just for a moment?" Kate nodded curtly, and Margaret Roper took a couple of steps forward, closing the door behind her. Kate did not invite her to sit. "I have learned a hard lesson about my father. You may be sure I will not mention you to him again. I hope you know that it was not my doing that your brother's press was destroyed. I knew nothing of it. I asked my father to help secure his release. He promised me he would."

"He was released. I am happy to say he lives now in a less hostile clime."

Madeline must have sensed the tension between the women. Usually a happy chatterbox even in the presence of strangers, she clung silently to Kate.

"I did not know you had a daughter," Mistress Roper said. "That makes your husband's loss even greater. I heard he died very bravely. I have prayed for his soul these many months and I wish to tell you I am verily sorry for my family's part in your misfortune."

Kate peeled the child away from her skirt, and lifted her in her arms, feeling suddenly threatened and not just for herself this time.

"And to offer help," Mistress Roper added, glancing meaningfully at the still empty shelves. "I am on my way to the almshouse. My father need not know that his charity extends to his enemies. I can—"

Kate could not believe what she was hearing. "Mistress Roper, I can see by your demeanor and your words that you are truly sorry . . . for . . . the part your father has played in the persecution of my family. But you must know that I would rather take charity from the devil himself than from Thomas More. My daughter and I will be just fine."

My daughter. She had claimed it. Margaret Roper had named it, and Kate had claimed it. Endor, who had been watching the exchange between the women, looked at Kate, and in a gesture Kate remembered, pointed with two fingers of her right hand to her own wide eyes and then to Madeline. *Blue eyes.*

My child will have blue eyes.

My child has blue eyes.

The decision was made. Madeline was indeed her daughter and whatever happened they would be just fine.

"Will there be anything else, Mistress Roper?" Kate asked.

The woman half turned and placed her hand on the latch in response to her dismissal. "Just one more thing, Mistress Frith. Please pray for us. Chelsea is not a happy place these days."

Kate was almost too startled to respond. "I will pray for you, Mistress Roper. I don't think I can pray for your father. I am not a saint."

The woman nodded and shut the door behind her. Months later, when Kate would hear from across the sea about the king's beheading of Sir Thomas More, she would remember the sadness in Margaret Roper's face, and take no joy in it.

꙳

Kate did not welcome the coming of spring. The first daffodils had scarcely lifted their heads in the little flower boxes outside the shop—had they bloomed every year in her absence, bravely waving their yellow banners in defiance and hope?—when the captain began to speak of leaving. His ship was almost finished. Kate began planning how to survive without his support.

Endor sold her honeyed biscuits and sweet buns to the yeomen workers and watermen on their way to the docks each morning, bartering sweet goods for flour from the miller's wife and milk from the dairyman. Kate did scrivener's work for the unlettered among them and copied broadsheets of love poems and songs to sell, rolling them into bordered scrolls and tying them with bits of lace and ribbon from Winifred's stores. What swain could resist picking a love poem for his sweetheart from Madeline's basket as she skipped among the market stalls? Even Ruffles the cat worked. At long last they were free of the rats that would have wreaked havoc on their baked goods. They would survive without the captain.

Yet she dreaded the thought of his leaving. Madeline would especially miss him. And Endor—Endor might even decide to go with him.

Kate would miss him too; she could not deny it. She had been content as long as he was nearby in Woolwich, and she could look forward to his visits—for Madeline's sake, she'd told herself. Surely, what she felt for the captain was no more than the affection a helpless woman owed her benefactor. But it was not his kindness that invaded her dreams. She woke more than once laden with guilt as she tried to conjure John's face. What kind of woman dreamed of another man with her husband in his grave a scant few months? Could a woman love two men at once? she wondered. But it didn't matter. Tom Lasser would be gone soon and Kate would have endless years of loneliness to repent those dreams.

FORTY-THREE

Gray-eyed Athena sent them a favorable breeze,
A fresh west wind, singing over the wine-dark sea.
—FROM HOMER'S *ODYSSEY*, BOOK I

On the first day of May, when all of London was celebrating and every churchyard and square was festive with Maypoles and morris dancers, Captain Tom Lasser did not join the raucous festivities. Instead he donned his best finery and headed for the dim cave of his favorite fleecing tavern. It was in Southwark near the bear-baiting pit and cockfight arena so that when the gamblers wearied of the cheers and jeers of blood sports, they could retire to the Fighting Cock Tavern to quench their thirst and find a more patrician game. With blood heated by violence and wanton death, they were always reckless in their wagering.

Tom squinted as he entered the room lit only by one glazed window, and when his eyes adjusted, he surveyed the pickings. He did not want to go else-where. He also had good luck at the Boar's Head, but time was short. The crowds would grow rowdy, even riotous, late in the day and he'd promised to walk Charlotte home from the dressmaker. At a trestle table beneath the win-dow, a couple of courtiers played at hazard, but dice games were not for Tom. The only way a man could win at dice was with the help of Dame Chance—or by cheating. Tom never cheated and seldom bet on chance. A man who could read faces didn't have to do either in a game where he could bluff.

In the shadow of the dead chimney, a table of three sat hunched over a deck of cards. Two looked to be of the merchant class and one was a dandified cleric whom he recognized with some surprise. The prospect of playing against Henry Phillips—again—was not altogether a pleasant one. Tom had flattened the upstart's purse the last time they'd played at cards, only to learn later that the money the youth had lost had been his father's. The high sheriff had foolishly entrusted his savings to his Oxford-educated son to "invest." An unfortunate decision. Tom had later heard that Phillips's father had disowned him, and he felt a little guilty about that. But if Phillips hadn't lost to him, he'd told himself, then somebody else. He was a ripe plum for the picking. Tom just happened to be standing under the tree. And it had after all been for a very good cause. The sheriff's money had gone to buy new rigging for Tom's ship.

At the sound of the latch falling back into place, Henry Phillips looked toward the door, and his gaze locked on Tom's. His eyes glinted hard as steel before he flashed a hearty smile and waved. "Captain, come and join us. The game is better with a fourth."

Tom hated to pluck the same pigeon twice, but Phillips was an easy mark and such an eager one. And he did not want to keep Charlotte waiting, so he sauntered over and asked, "Primero?"

Phillips motioned for him to sit down. "If I remember correctly, Captain, that's your game."

"Italian rules or English?" Tom asked, settling into the fourth chair.

"English," one of the merchants said. "We don't declare hands. Stake is two crowns. Rest is four."

"Here, you do the honors, Captain, just to show I've no hard feelings," Phillips said as he handed the deck to Tom to "lift." The merchant to Tom's left drew the lowest card and dealt.

"I'm surprised to see you, Master Phillips," Tom said, frowning deliberately at his hand. It was a decent hand: one court card from each suit worth forty points. But the value of the hand didn't really matter. He would lose the first two hands deliberately to draw the merchants in. "I heard you were living on the Continent," Tom said as he made a show of discarding all four cards and drawing four more.

"I am. I've just returned to London to draw payment on a new business venture."

And you can hardly wait to lose it, Tom thought. "Congratulations," he said, glancing at the piles of coins in front of Phillips. "It seems you have found a wealthy patron."

"A very influential patron," Phillips said, drawing in the pot he'd just won with a simple primero valuing only about twenty points. The merchants must be novices for Phillips to win with such a low hand.

"The Bishop of London has employed me to represent some Church matters on the Continent," Phillips said with bravado. "I've also made some valuable connections in Flanders."

"Good for you," Tom said, wondering to what purpose the Bishop of London could possibly put such a poseur. But then it was Church business. And Phillips was charming enough to ingratiate himself almost anywhere. He could be a perfect spy. He had one of those boyish faces a man or a woman would be eager to trust—if you didn't look too closely at the eyes that lied.

The attention returned to the game, with the betting and the passing and the folding. They swigged on the fourth hand, with everybody folding, the money staying in the pot. On the fifth hand, Tom picked up his cards to find a low hand. Unfortunately the cards had run against him since the first hand, but the afternoon was getting on. Charlotte would be waiting for him. Now was the time. He discarded none of the cards and forced a pleased expression.

Two more rounds of vying and the merchant beside Phillips vied two more crowns. Phillips's eyes clouded, but he saw that bet, discarded one card, and revied. Tom calculated the heap of money in the center of the table. It was just about enough to pay his ship out of hock.

"I vie the rest," Tom said, putting four crowns in the center with a confident flick of his lace cuffs. The two merchants folded. Henry Phillips fingered his cards nervously and after an interminable silence and a slight twitching of his left eye—a distress signal that Tom recognized—threw his cards facedown with a grunt of disgust. Henry Phillips was nothing if not a coward, and a coward could always be bluffed.

Tom feigned a look of surprise and pulled in the pot, shrugging. "Well, gentlemen, looks like Dame Fortune smiled on me this time."

Henry Phillips retrieved his cards and turned them up. Supremus: a six, seven, and ace of hearts with a point value of fifty-five.

"Show your hand, sir, if you please," Phillips said, his smile tight.

"If you insist," Tom said with a laugh. "But I don't think you'll like what you see." He turned over his cards: a jack of spades and a two of spades with a worthless heart and a club. The hand was worth only twenty-two points, the lowest hand on the board.

Phillips stood up, staggered back against his chair. It clattered to the floor. The tavernkeeper slapped a tankard of beer onto the table opposite them and shouted, "I'll have no rowdiness." The hazard players ceased their game and looked in their direction. Tom kept his seat, neatly counting his money into stacks.

Phillips's arm darted out, sweeping the cards from the table, then he pounded the table with his fist. "God's Blood, I declare you are a lying whoreson," he shouted.

Tom had Phillips figured for a hothead but a cowardly one. Still, he was thinking about the dagger in his boot when the merchant stayed Phillips's hand. "He beat you square. Let it go."

In the pause that followed, Tom stood up, picking up his money with deliberation, then bowed. "I thank you for the game, gentlemen, and I would stay to let you win some of your money back, which you verily would, but, alas, it seems our young friend is too choleric to continue. It's probably prudent if we let it end here." Then, with a mock salute to the simmering Henry Phillips, "Better luck next time, Master Phillips."

"There won't be a next time, you bloody bastard."

As Tom hurried back to Cheapside to meet the lovely widow of Lübeck, he laughed aloud. He was almost sure the flaming arrow that burned his ship was sent from Bishop Stokesley—or from Thomas More. Now in some roundabout way the bishop's money was making the last payment on his ship's repairs. There was a pleasing justice in that and he wished they could know it.

❧

By Saint Gregory's Day on May 9—Kate always remembered because Gough's print shop had once printed his beautiful fourth-century poems about the Holy Trinity—the captain showed up early at Kate's door. His ship was ready for inspection, and they should be the ones to pronounce it seaworthy. Her heart sank like a stone, but she put on a smile and bundled Madeline into her prettiest bonnet.

The sun was at its apex and dancing on the water by the time their hired trap and horse clopped onto the cobblestone of the Woolwich wharf. The air smelled of the green spring and the sea and the almond scent from the marzipan ship Madeline clutched in her sticky fingers.

"You spoil her," Kate had said when he presented it to her.

"It's a special occasion," he said. "The marzipan will help her remember it."

She had rarely seen him so excited. *He can't wait to go back to sea,* she thought. *He'll not give us a second thought.*

There were several boats in the harbor, some still festooned with May Day banners and from one or two she even heard pipers playing music— only one caravel, though, of the right tonnage and with a square-rigged mainmast, but it looked different.

"There she is," the captain announced proudly.

"Where?" Kate asked. "I don't see—"

"There." He pointed to the caravel and laughed. "Same ship. New name."

Kate shielded her eyes to try to make out the fancy lettering on the side of the ship. The sun obscured it. "You loved that name. The sea was the one siren you couldn't resist."

"Maybe I have found another," he said, winking at Madeline as he helped her down from the trap, then assisting Endor and finally Kate. The touch of his hand was reassuring. She felt safe in his presence. *You're a fool, Kate. He is a dangerous man—more likely than not to end his days swinging from a gallows. Why should you feel safe with him?* She removed her hand as soon as she gained her footing on the cobblestone, but a little shiver went up her spine when he placed his hand on her waist to guide her onto the gangplank. After she and Endor had walked across and stood safely on the new deck that smelled of pitch and fresh-cut lumber, he picked up the giggling Madeline and joined them.

Glowing with pride, he showed them the refurbishments. "A bigger, safer space for Endor with a new bake oven."

Endor's visage glowed. But Kate did not share her enthusiasm as it became plain that the captain planned for Endor to go with him, after all. And with such an enticement, how could she resist? Her little cabin even had its own porthole, but more important, Endor worshipped the ground beneath Tom Lasser's boots. She would not refuse him.

"Let me show you the new captain's quarters."

Kate approached the door beneath the poop deck, noticing that this cabin, too, had been enlarged. She opened the door with a little sinking feeling in the pit of her stomach, remembering John, what an intimate little nest they'd found there, how they'd slept together in the narrow bunk like two nestled spoons. It seemed like yesterday and yet so long ago it might have been a dream.

The room was much nicer and larger: same table cluttered with charts and sexton and astrolabe, same blue map on the wall—the color of Madeline's eyes—same keg of water mounted to the wall, everything the same but with a larger bed. The other bed that was no more than a bench was still there, and a dresser with a mirror above it had been added. A silver-backed comb and brush glimmered on a fringed shawl covering the dresser. Kate felt herself blush. Of course. The beautiful widow. Had she picked out the shawl? Did the silver-backed comb belong to her?

From above deck came the sound of shouting voices and ropes being dragged, the creaking of wheels.

"Endor, will you take Magpie up on deck?" He winked at Madeline. That was his pet name for her. "She might want to watch the men rig the mainmast."

Endor nodded and reached for Madeline's hand, apparently oblivious to the sticky marzipan. The two went off happily together.

The captain turned to Kate, who suddenly felt embarrassed to be alone with him in this intimate space. She moved to follow Madeline and Endor. He reached out his hand and lightly touched her arm. "Well, what do you think?"

"I think it much improved. Certainly more spacious and quite well appointed."

"I'm glad you approve. Charlotte did it."

"I thought that might be the case," Kate said. "Your widow has excellent taste."

He cocked an eyebrow and smiled that little crooked smile that she'd first seen outside the Fleet. "*My* widow? Well . . . yes, I suppose she does. But that's not what makes her such an extraordinary woman."

Kate's face grew hot as she mumbled, "I'm sure she's quite extraordinary in many respects."

"What do you think of the new name?" he asked, suddenly serious.

"I couldn't really see it for the sun—"

He pointed to a miniature plaque above the door. *The Phoenix*.

"Ah," she said. "Out of the ashes. The new from the old. John would have approved," she said. "He never met a classical allusion he didn't love."

"I was thinking of him when I named it. That's why there are Bibles being loaded into the hold. There will always be Bibles in the hold. I am no martyr, but I can at least do that. But I was thinking of something else. I was thinking of us as well."

"Us?"

"You and me and Endor and Madeline." He paused as if waiting for her response. When she made none, he continued. "The four of us. We could be a family. Formed out of all the ashes of our burned-out lives."

The cocked eyebrow was gone, the smile as well. What was he talking about? Was he mocking her? But she read no mockery in his eyes. He took her hands in his and raised them to his lips, kissing first one and then the other in a gesture so gallant it stole her breath away.

"But . . . your widow . . . from Lübeck. I thought—"

His lips curved into that half-smile again, which she never quite knew how to read.

"*My widow,* as you so quaintly put it, lives above a little bookshop in Paternoster Row. Charlotte chose the shawl, the combs, the brushes—the polished pewter in the cupboard—for you, Kate. At my request. We are, as I told you, only old friends."

Kate recalled the quizzical look on the woman's face and doubted if Charlotte would have characterized it just that way. She had the look of a woman sizing up her competition.

"I am asking you to marry me, Kate Frith. I am asking you to go with me on some wonderful sea quest. You have the same yearning for adventure in you that I have. I know it. I think I have loved you since the first time I saw you bargaining with your pennies outside the Fleet for your brother's life. My God, you were a sight to behold. When I rescued the two of you out of Bristol—that seems a lifetime ago—I used to watch you leaning out over the ship's rail, like fair Helen, your face raised to the spray, your hair blowing in the wind . . . how I envied John. It was hard to hide that envy."

Kate sat down hard on the smaller bed, the bed on which she'd once lain with her husband while the captain stood above them on the deck. What would John think if he could hear this? He'd written from prison how Captain Lasser had befriended him. Had he guessed? Or would he feel betrayed to hear him confess it now?

Her skin felt hot with excitement. She had to admit she'd felt some fascination, even attraction, for the handsome, reckless sea captain who mocked the world and its most venerable institutions. But she knew, underneath that sardonic shell, Tom Lasser was a good man. And even if she convinced herself that it was not a betrayal of John's memory, she could not bear to lose another good man to the king's justice. She did not know how to explain this to him.

"You are foolish in your choice, Captain. I have no dowry," she said more coldly than she meant to. "Even the roof over my head belongs to my brother."

If he noticed her coldness, his expression gave no hint. "All the better. We will not have to worry about selling it. Just board it up as we found it and leave it until your brother reclaims it." He sat down beside her, still holding her hands. The lace of his cuff tickled her wrists. "*The Phoenix* will carry us far away, somewhere away from kings and power-hungry clerics with their fierce religiosity. Someplace men decide for themselves what they will read and write and think—even believe."

She gave a bitter little laugh. "The world does not have such a place," she said, "outside of men's dreams."

He shook his head, squeezing her hand more tightly. "But there could be such a place. There are lands beyond the western sea—"

The skeptical Captain Tom Lasser, a dreamer after all. Who would have guessed it? She laughed out loud. "The western sea! I get seasick just in the Channel."

"All of Endor's supplies have already been loaded. Including a goodly supply of ginger."

It was a fantasy to acknowledge such a possibility, a silly game, but she would play it a little longer. "There are rats in the hold." She shuddered. "I don't think I could abide the rats for the many weeks we would have to spend at sea."

"If the Magpie can be believed, Ruffles is a very good mouser." His smile was wicked in its confidence—wicked and irresistible—his teeth white against his curving lips. What would those lips feel like against her skin?

Suddenly it was a game no more. Time for the fantasy to end. She could not look at him but looked down at the white oak flooring rubbed hard and smooth, like her heart. He would sail on the next tide. By Michaelmas her face would fade from his memory as John's was beginning to fade from hers.

"I have been widowed less than a year," she said. "I cannot dishonor the memory of my husband by taking another to my bed so soon after. It is the last thing I can do for him."

He put his hand on her chin and gently lifted her face. Her gaze met his and she saw no mockery, no scorn in his dark eyes. "John is gone, Kate. We are still here. We do the best we can. Today. Sacrificing your happiness or mine will not bring him back. You are like me. We are not the stuff of martyrs. We don't die for what we believe—if we have a choice. We live out our beliefs. I am no saint like John. I am just a man. But saints don't make good husbands."

"John was a wonderful husband." She bristled.

"And now he is gone, and you are sad. But consider, Kate, if he was truly a good husband as you say, he would want you to be happy, not to live out the rest of your life grieving for him, alone, like some nun who has shut herself up in a convent. I came to know him well. He loved life, and he loved you. But you said it. He just loved God more. If you are happy, then he has not abandoned you. His life is fulfilled and so is yours."

Kate suddenly saw John's earnest face, like a gift, as she had seen it so many times, deep in concentration, bent over his books, absorbed completely and joyfully in his task, her mind conjuring his image clearly for the first time in weeks. She looked up at the man who had just proposed marriage to her, his face also earnest in a way she had rarely seen, only once really, when he was guiding his ship into safe harbor.

Could a woman hold the memory of such a love as she'd had with John in her heart and that memory not be diminished by her love for another?

"Quest," she said almost in a whisper.

"I'm sorry—"

"You said we would go on a sea quest. What are we questing for?"

"Why, fair winds, my pretty Kate, fair winds and wine-dark seas."

She recognized the reference from Homer, from the book she'd bought from the Antwerp dealer so long ago. No wonder John had got on so well with the captain. In so many ways they had been kindred spirits. "I will not play Penelope to your Ulysses," she said. "I will never be left behind again."

He threw back his head and laughed. He touched her cheek. "We'll be questing for truth, Kate, the kind John died for. And love. The kind of love that you and John had. Love is the only ship that floats in rough seas. I can't promise you we won't have rough seas, but I can promise you love."

Then, "Captain Lasser," she heard herself say, disbelieving. "It seems you have taken away my objections, and I have no other. What do I have to lose?" she said through her tears. "Except another good man?"

He pulled her to him and kissed her. When he released her, he held her out at arm's length and gave her that same mocking grin she'd first seen through an iron grille in Fleet Prison. "Believe me, Kate, I will take every precaution to see that doesn't happen. For both our sakes."

"When are you leaving?" she said, not yet used to the idea.

"We, my pretty Kate, we leave tomorrow. I have a couple of Baltic runs for the Hanseatic League. I know a reformist preacher who will marry us in Lübeck."

"But tomorrow. So soon. There's no time——"

He strode to the chest and opened it. The sight took her breath away. It was filled with clothes. "Charlotte?"

"With Endor's help."

"You were pretty sure of yourself, Captain," she said.

"You said it yourself. What do you have to lose?" And he kissed her again.

The next day when the tanbark sails of *The Phoenix* filled and she sailed out of the harbor, Kate Gough Frith, soon to be Lasser, sailed with it, accompanied by her daughter Madeline, a cat named Ruffles, her friend Endor, and an heirloom illuminated Bible. She lifted her face to the morning sun, putting her faith in God, her hope in Tom Lasser, and her trust in Endor's ginger tea.

HISTORICAL NOTE

he historical record deals with John Frith less fully than with his friend William Tyndale, whose sixteenth-century translation of the Bible into the English language helped provoke the Protestant Reformation in England and later formed the foundational document for the King James Bible. History records the martyrdom of this exceptional young scholar before he reached his thirtieth birthday and the circumstances surrounding his career and execution for heresy. The historical mention that he had a wife, about whom nothing beyond the fact of her existence is known, is the basis for the fictional character of Kate Frith. History also records that a bookseller and printer named John Gough was caught in the sweep that began the most intense persecution of Protestants in England outside the reign of Mary Tudor.

Sir Thomas More's role in all stages of that persecution is part of the historical record, and the story of his struggle with Henry VIII concerning the king's marriage to Anne Boleyn and subsequent break with Rome is also well documented. On July 6, 1535, two years and two days after John Frith went to the stake, More was executed for treason. He was charged with denying the validity of the Act of Succession because it denied the authority of the pope in matters relating to religion in England. Margaret Roper is said to have bribed the constable of the Tower to remove the boiled head of her father from its exhibition pole on Tower Bridge, and to have hidden it so that his memory could not be further dishonored. More's last days in the Tower were made more bearable with the knowledge that his nemesis William Tyndale, who had been betrayed by Henry Phillips and arrested in May of that same year, also languished in prison in a castle in Vilvoorde, eighteen miles from Antwerp. William Tyndale was executed by strangulation and burning in October 1536.

Queen Anne Boleyn was beheaded on Tower Green, May 19, 1536, after she failed to produce a male heir. She was charged with committing incest with her brother George, adultery (treason) with a music master, and even practicing witchcraft to bewitch the king. Shortly after Anne's execution, Jane Seymour became the third wife of Henry VIII.

Thomas Cromwell, who succeeded Thomas More as chancellor, is best known in history for carrying out the king's orders for the dismantling and pillaging of the monasteries in England. Within a year of Tyndale's death, Cromwell had convinced the king to approve distribution of the English Bible. (It was Tyndale's Bible, but it did not bear his name.) Cromwell was beheaded for treason in 1540. Thomas Cranmer, Archbishop of Canterbury and the author of the Book of Common Prayer, was burned at Smithfield as a heretic in 1556 under the rule of Queen Mary, Henry's daughter by Katherine of Aragon, also known as Bloody Mary.

In 1543 Catherine Massys (sometimes spelled Matsys), sister of the painter Quentin Massys, was burned at the stake in Leuven for reading the Bible.

Martin Luther died of illness in 1546. His wife Katharina von Bora survived him by many years, living and raising her children in poverty.